NORTH AYRSHIRE

10019362 5

CANCELLED

One Perfect Witness

by

Pat Young

D1628288

Copyright © 2018 Pat Young

The right of Pat Young to be identified as the Author of the Work has been asserted by her in accordance Copyright, Designs and Patents Act 1988.

First published in 2018 by Bloodhound Books

Apart from any use permitted under UK copyright law, this publication may only be reproduced, stored, or transmitted, in any form, or by any means, with prior permission in writing of the publisher or, in the case of reprographic production, in accordance with the terms of licences issued by the Copyright Licensing Agency.

All characters in this publication are fictitious and any resemblance to real persons, living or dead, is purely coincidental.

www.bloodhoundbooks.com

Print ISBN 978-1-912604-84-5

North Ayrshire Libraries	
10019362 5	
Askews & Holts	13-Dec-2018
AF	£8.99
	I

CANCELLED

Also By Pat Young

Till The Dust Settles

I Know Where You Live

Praise For Pat Young

"An accomplished plot, plenty of twists and turns and excellent characterisation made this book a real page turner." **Kate Moloney – Bibliophile Book Club**

"Till the Dust Settles is an intriguing read and one I actually flew through in one sitting." **Joanne Robertson – My Chestnut Reading Tree**

"Loved it from start to finish." **Jo – Goodreads Reviewer**

"This is a you gotta read book, a brilliant debut. Really excited about this lady's writing. Superb!" **Susan Hampson – Books From Dusk Till Dawn**

"'Till The Dust Settles' is an intense, powerful and heart-wrenching read about love, loss and ultimate devastation." **Kaisha Holloway – The Writing Garnet**

"What a clever book, I couldn't put it down." **Cariad – Goodreads Reviewer**

"It was suspenseful, thrilling, addictive, captivating and left me guessing the whole way through." **Dash Fan Book Reviews**

"A gripping read to keep you on the edge of your seat." **Misfits farm – Goodreads Reviewer**

"…it has the author's excellent attention to detail and great writing style and I loved the lot." **Donna Maguire – Donnas Book Blog**

"Another stunning thriller from Pat Young ..." **Livia Sbarbaro – Goodreads Reviewer**

"OMG! I have just devoured this book in almost one sitting apart from time to get some shut-eye!" **Sharon Bairden – Chapter In My Life**

"Pat Young's 'I know where you live' is a thrilling read and makes the reader do abit of soul searching along the way." **Susie – Goodreads Reviewer**

Dedicated to the memory of
Marg and Mal Brierley
who left us far too soon.

CHAPTER 1

Brackenbrae Holiday Park, Ayrshire, Scotland
Sunday 27 May

Today was the worst ever.
They stopped talking when I walked into the kitchen. That's always bad.

Mum's face was pink, as if she'd put on too much of her blusher stuff. 'Have you washed your hands?' she said, in her snippy voice. I tried a smile. At school they tell us a smile's infectious. Mum didn't catch mine.

Dad was at the table, pouring wine. 'Hello, Charlie. Had a good day?'

'He was swimming,' Mum said, as if I'd done something wrong.

Dad smiled. 'Ah, you've been swimming?' He sounded like a kids television presenter I used to love. When I was five. I wish he'd stop speaking to me like that.

'Ask him if the pool was busy,' said Mum, and I understood.

I held up one hand and one finger. Actually, there was only me and an old man but I know it's never good to hold up two fingers.

Dad frowned but still managed to sound like Jolly Joe. 'It's early in the season,' he said, with a kind of chuckle.

Mum turned from the oven and gave him a look. 'It's a bank holiday weekend, Richard, and we had five people in the swimming pool?'

'Six, if you count Charlie.'

'Charlie doesn't count!'

Dad carried on as if she hadn't said anything wrong. 'It'll get busier once the weather warms up. Don't fret.'

The casserole banged onto the table and the dishtowel flew at Dad's face.

'Don't fret?' Mum said, through her teeth, kind of low and threatening. 'Christ! You're like a bloody ostrich.'

She doesn't usually swear when she knows I'm listening, but she didn't say, 'Sorry, Charlie.' In fact, she didn't even seem to remember I was there.

Dad said nothing. He does that a lot, instead of arguing.

'How long are you going to carry on with this charade, Richard? Pretending everything's just fine. Barging on with your obsession?'

Ostrich, charade, obsession? I didn't get it. Still don't. I reached for some bread and sank down into my chair to munch it. Dad took a chunk too but he didn't eat his. Just picked out the soft, white centre and rolled it between his finger and thumb till it turned into a grey bullet. 'This is neither the time nor the place,' he said quietly.

It was like they were speaking in a secret code.

Mum passed me my plate and snapped at me, 'Sit up properly.'

'Viv, please. Don't take it out on the boy. It's got nothing to do with him.'

I watched the steam rising from the stew. I was starving, and I love beef stew. Even though it burned my tongue, I shovelled it in, so I could get away.

'Don't gobble your food, Charlie. Have you forgotten all your manners?'

'Come on, Vivienne. That's not fair. Let's have a nice family dinner and we'll talk about this later.' He reached for Mum's hand but she snatched it off the table. He gave a little cough and moved his fork instead. Then, in his Jolly Joe voice, he said, 'The summer staff arrive tomorrow. That'll be fun.'

I smiled, to please him, and took another piece of bread to dip into the gravy.

Dad's good at choosing nice summer staff. 'Natalie's coming back to run the Kidz Klub. Charlie, you remember Natalie?'

How could I forget Natalie?

Mum said, 'The pretty one who plans to be a schoolteacher?'

My cheeks started to go all warm.

'I think our Charlie might be a little bit in love with Natalie,' said Mum. 'Look, he's blushing.'

I didn't mind being embarrassed, if it made them happy. It was good to hear them laughing for once. Trying to look cool, I jabbed a piece of meat on my fork and stuck it in my mouth, like a cowboy at a campfire.

Mum stopped eating. 'Hang on. *One* leader for the kids?'

The bad atmosphere sneaked back into the room, sly as a cat.

'We need to save money, Richard, but that's a risky way to go about it.'

'I'm not trying to save money and you're right, she can't run Kidz Klub on her own. The boy from Paris will help.'

'What boy from Paris?' Mum was all snappy again.

'I found us a champion swimmer.' Dad looked pleased with himself. 'Ideal for pool duty *and* he sounds like an excellent Kidz Klub leader.'

'Sounds like? When did you meet him?'

Dad doesn't look so confident now. 'I didn't, actually.'

'How come? You told me you'd sorted the summer staff months ago.'

'I did, but then the guy I'd taken on for the pool phoned. He's got a permanent job in his local Asda. Good for him but it left me in a bit of a pickle, time-wise. I'd kept Sebastien's application letter, he was my second choice, remember? So I offered him the job.'

'Without an interview? Are you off your head? He could be a total psycho.'

'I'm sure he's not. Anyway, how can you interview someone who's in Paris?'

'Skype? FaceTime?' Mum's lips went all screwed up. Like she was eating an apple before it was ripe. 'You've never set eyes on this guy and you're taking him on for the whole summer. This is going to cause trouble,' she said. 'I can sense it.'

'It'll be fine.' Dad took a sip of his wine.

Mum made her tutting noise. 'For God's sake! As if we don't have enough to worry about, you're taking on randoms to look after the kids.'

'Give me *some* credit, please, Viv. He's on a two-week trial and it's not as if he's some guy who just walked in the gate. All the appropriate checks and paperwork have been completed. We agreed, didn't we, that it makes sense to have workers who speak different languages if we're aiming at a European clientele?'

She chewed and swallowed for about a minute. 'You're going to have to abandon Phase Five.'

'Absolutely not.'

And off they went again, arguing, as if they were the only ones with stuff to worry about. I wish they knew. Wish I could tell them.

I left the table, missing pudding, and it was apple crumble, my favourite. They were so busy arguing they didn't even try to stop me. No one noticed me slipping out the door. That's when I decided I had to do something.

Now it's bedtime and I've got Dad's gun hidden under the mattress.

Tomorrow they'll notice me.

***

CHAPTER 2

Ayr, Scotland
Monday 28 May

Seb stirs, glad to escape his troubled dreams. He cautiously raises one heavy eyelid. Light, sharp as a laser, hits the back of his eye and sparks a headache. It can't be time to get up and yet the room is filled with light.

He remembers his landlady's advice about closing the blind *and* the curtains if he didn't want to be awake at 5am.

A pressing need to go the toilet and a simultaneous desperate longing for a glass of water force him to open his eyes. The effort of sitting up makes his head pound. He presses the heels of his hands deep into his eye sockets, setting off a starburst. Head spinning, he stumbles to the tiny en suite and empties his bladder.

He turns to the basin, scooping water greedily into his mouth before he even thinks of washing his hands. Hearing Mother's reprimand in his head, 'Sebastien, please, a glass!' he removes a plastic beaker from a metal hoop above the basin. It smells of dried toothpaste and something even less savoury, but Seb doesn't care. The water's cold and refreshing. He refills the little tumbler twice and glugs it down, thankful.

His stomach seems less grateful for the sudden icy downpour. It heaves threateningly and Seb moves towards the toilet bowl, wondering if it's time to get on his knees and prepare for the worst. His mouth fills with hot saliva. He swallows and waits.

When he's sure it's safe to leave the toilet, he fills the beaker a fourth time and takes it into the bedroom, being careful to place it on a little mat on the highly polished bedside cabinet. 'See, Mother,' he thinks, 'I'm not a complete slob.'

Seb locates his rucksack at the foot of the bed and rummages in a pocket till he finds a foil of paracetamol. He presses two capsules into his hand and throws them down his throat before grabbing the plastic tumbler and washing them down. He flops back onto the bed, hoping to sleep while the painkillers take effect. Maybe the nausea will have worn off by then too, if he's lucky. Too late, he remembers the curtains and lies awake, wondering what the hell he's doing here, all alone in a country whose people and customs seem strange. A sudden pang of homesickness makes him long for Paris. Home seems very far away and his parents even more distant.

He counts the days in his head. Can it really be three weeks since Father dropped him at the airport, still offering to pay for first class to Glasgow and a taxi to Ayr? Seb had been grateful but determined to do it his own way. A cheap flight to Manchester then north under his own steam, seeing the Lake District en route, walking or hitching rides from anyone prepared to pick him up. Sleeping in his little one-man tent wherever he could find a place to pitch it, or in hostels and cheap B&Bs when he found himself near a town. His only problem had been that bull near Dumfries who taught him to never assume a field is empty.

Everything has gone according to plan, even his arrival in Ayr, timed to perfection. So why the hell did he have to go and get drunk on his last night on the road?

He remembers scoffing a 'fish supper', straight out of a yellow polystyrene container, thinking Mother would have a fit if she knew. Defiantly, he'd licked the salt off his greasy hands, disappointed to finish the last chip and crumb of batter. The smell of vinegar stuck to his fingers for hours.

He found himself on a long promenade and took a stroll along the beach, feeling like a holidaymaker. The tide was out, and the shoreline seemed endless, curving off around the bay towards a castle on a cliff-top. He sat on the sand as the sun dipped behind an island, and watched the embers of the dying day turn the sky to burnt sienna. What a pity he couldn't take a photo to send home.

When the sun finally slipped from view he got up and kept walking, loath to return to his B&B. A stone pier jutted into the water and Seb couldn't resist its draw. He couldn't wait to wake up each morning and look out over the sea. Half a dozen fishermen stood silhouetted against the umber sky, their rods tracing fine arcs. Seb stood and listened to the sound of the waves gently breaking.

One of the fishermen looked up from his line and nodded. 'Right, mate?'

Seb thought for a moment then said, 'Fine, thank you.'

'Fish are no biting. I'm packing it in. Anybody fancy a pint?'

'Of beer?' said Seb, before he realised the invitation had not been meant for him.

The man laughed. 'Vodka, if you like. All the same to me, mates.' The fisherman packed away his rod then turned to Seb. 'Looks like it's just you and me, pal. You comin or no?'

'Yes, please. I'd like to.'

The man looked Seb up and down. 'You foreign?'

'French,' said Seb.

'Great football players, the French.'

Seb nodded. 'Your rugby team is very good, I believe.'

'Rugby's for posh boys. Nae offence. What's yer name?'

'Seb.' The man didn't offer his name and Seb thought it best not to ask.

They followed the river, passing modern flats and a leisure centre. A faint whiff of chlorine stirred years of memories.

'See that there?' The man was pointing at a high crumbling wall. 'Ever heard of Oliver Cromwell?'

Seb nodded.

'He built that. A fort. Hard to believe, eh?'

As they walked, the man told Seb about Cromwell building a citadel in Ayr.

'Sixteen hundred and something. Never paid much attention at school, me.'

'I thought Oliver Cromwell was English,' said Seb, keen to show interest.

'He wis. Sent here to keep us under control. Same old, same old.' The man shook his head as he walked and said no more until they reached a flat-fronted building painted white and blue. 'This is us,' he said, pushing open the door.

The room was small and filled with men, all of whom stood watching a TV screen above the bar. Round the edges of the room, elderly customers sat at copper-topped tables. Against one wall a slot machine flashed garishly, its jangly music competing with the television and a guy tuning a guitar in the corner. A shout went up from four men playing darts, 'Ya jammy bastard!'

Seb felt a tug on his sleeve.

'Here, mate. Yer pint. Cheers.'

Seb took the large glass, trying not to spill the dark liquid over the brim. 'Cheers,' he said, 'and thank you.' He raised the beer to his companion, then to his lips and drank. It was cool and slightly bitter. Very different from the blonde lager that was popular in France. Not that he was a connoisseur. A couple of bottles at his friend's was about his limit.

Seb swallowed till his thirst was quenched. As he lowered the near-empty glass, a loud burp escaped his lips.

'Better oot than in, pal!'

Seb looked round at the man on a stool beside him. He could have been any age from thirty to sixty. His face looked not so much lived-in as wrecked by squatters, and his bleary eyes may once have been blue. Now they were red and rheumy, but they had a sparkle that told Seb he was being made fun of.

He smiled, conscious that others were listening. 'Pardon me.'

'Ye're pardoned. Could ye go a wee half?'

The men laughed while Seb tried to work out the joke.

The barmaid glanced over. She was wearing an outfit she must have borrowed from her granddaughter. Her face, plastered with garish make-up, was a kind face.

'Josie,' she said, 'that's no fair.'

'Jist trying tae buy the bloke a drink.'

'Ah, another drink?' said Seb, understanding at last.

'Aye.' He touched the rim of Seb's glass and tapped it twice with a grubby nail, making it ring. 'But not a pint this time. A wee goldie.' He enunciated each syllable as if speaking to a rather dim-witted child. 'No comprende, amigo?'

The barmaid crossed her arms and leaned on the bar. Seb tried to keep his eyes off the massive breasts that poured towards him like pink lava. 'Josie's asking if ye'd like a whisky.'

Seb considered for a moment. Would it be rude to refuse a drink? 'Thank you. I mean, please. Yes.'

As it turned out, he had to refuse several drinks. After far too many pints and 'wee goldies' he made a promise to come back soon and began saying his farewells.

He staggered home to his 'digs' with a good feeling about this Scottish adventure. So good he even considered calling his mother, till he remembered he'd no phone.

That was last night.

This morning's a different story. Seb groans and buries his face in the pillow. Of all the days to be hungover, when he was so keen to make a good impression.

If only he could sleep for a while. If only the damned seagulls would stop their screeching and screaming. Seb imagines them perched on every rooftop like a scene from an old movie he once saw. How can anyone sleep through that racket?

He should get up and go. So what if he leaves the guesthouse early? The full Scottish breakfast, as described by his landlady when he checked in, holds no appeal this morning. Dressed in his last clean t-shirt, Seb packs up his gear, lets himself out of the guesthouse and heads to the seafront.

Much though it hurts his head, the quality of the light is special, even though there's no sign of the sun yet. The Island of Arran sits out in the bay, hazy and indistinct compared to last night's glory. The water is millpond calm, lapping onto the sand in tiny wavelets.

His new best friends in the pub claimed it's an easy walk to the Heads of Ayr and their directions turn out to be straightforward. A pleasant stroll along the shore ends at a metal bridge over a narrow river estuary that's swarming with swans and ducks. The Doon, he presumes. Keeping all houses on his left and his eyes on a ruined castle perched impossibly close to the edge of a cliff, he follows a quiet path that brings him out, as promised, at a road with a pavement along one side.

He wonders what Brackenbrae will be like. None of the drinkers seemed to know much about the place, apart from one man. 'Oor Joyce works up there. See the guy that owns it? A nutter.'

'Thought yer wife liked working for him?' said Josie.

'Aye, she does, but he's still a nutjob. Wait till you see it, Seb. An old farm, just ruins when they bought it. They've spent thousands doing it up and now oor Joyce says they're trying to sell glamping holidays.'

'Glampin? Whit the hell's glampin?'

'Camping, for folk that have mair money than sense,' the barmaid replied, her smile replaced by a sour look that made it clear what she thought of glamping.

Seb's stomach gives a sudden churn and he can't decide if the roiling is due to nerves or last night's excesses. Hoping the nausea will pass soon, he stops and eases his rucksack from his back. He rubs his shoulders where the straps have been chafing through his t-shirt. He discarded his top layer earlier, the minute the early morning sun peeped over the eastern horizon to his left. But standing exposed on the road he feels a cool edge to the breeze and thinks about putting his fleece back on. Bizarrely, the breeze brings with it a heady scent of coconut from the yellow flowers of prickly bushes that start on the other side of the hedge and cover most of the hillside.

He can't be far away now. Follow the A719 heading for Dunure, he was told. Stay on this road till you pass a big holiday park on the right-hand side. Some of the guys in the pub called it Butlins but the barmaid put them right.

'Last time it was called Butlins, my Jason was a wee boy. It's Craig Tara now and it's beautiful. Ah widnae mind a holiday there. In fact, ah widnae mind a holiday anywhere.'

'Aye, well, it will always be Butlins tae me,' said Josie. He then went into a description of a place where hundreds of people came from the city to live in rows of wooden buildings and eat together in huge dining halls.

'Like a prisoner of war camp?' Sebastien asked, causing another wave of laughter.

'See you, son? You're a pure tonic, so ye are,' said Josie, and although Seb didn't understand the words, he could tell it was a compliment.

Smiling at the memory, Seb hoists his backpack onto his shoulders, wondering if he'll ever make sense of the way Scottish people talk. Or the mess he's left behind in Paris.

***

CHAPTER 3

Brackenbrae Holiday Park, Ayrshire
Monday 28 May

My room's still dark but I can tell it's morning. Mum bought me a special blind last week to stop me waking up too early. A slice of light pushes in at one side, just enough for me to see Spiderman on the wall.

Maybe I fell asleep for a wee while, but it seems like it hardly got dark through the night. Miss Lawson once told us about the lands of the midnight sun. Alaska, Norway, Finland and one more that I'm too tired to remember. It never gets dark there in the summer and people go bonkers. If every night was like last night, I'd go bonkers too.

The Thomas the Tank Engine clock beside my bed says it's half past five. I want a new clock, with a proper alarm that will get me up when I start high school, but Thomas was a present from Gran and Pops, and they're dead now. Mum thinks I want to keep it forever but seeing it makes me feel like a little kid.

I'm going to put on the same clothes I wore yesterday. Supposed to put dirty clothes in the basket and Mum sorts out clean ones, but today I'm up too early.

I lift a corner of the mattress. It's heavy to hold up and the gun seems much bigger than when I hid it. As if it's been growing like Jack's beanstalk while everyone was asleep. Everyone except me.

Mum lost her temper last night. Big time. I could hear them from the top of the stairs.

It was way past my bedtime. But I needed to know what the fight was about, the one that started at dinner. I always sit near the top of the stairs, so they don't know I'm listening. It wasn't hard to work out they were still fighting, even though I could tell they were trying to keep their voices low.

'Richard, we're up to our necks in debt.'

'But if we want to compete with that place along the road, we have to invest in Phase Five.'

Mum made a kind of snorting noise.

'Vivienne, what's happened? You used to share all my dreams.'

'Your crazy dreams.'

'Maybe so, but you always believed in them.' Dad sounded like he was nearly crying. 'You've planned and schemed with me, laboured till your hands bled, even gone without new clothes, all to turn our dreams into reality.'

I couldn't hear if Mum said anything.

'What's changed, Vivienne? Have you fallen out of love with Brackenbrae?'

'Of course not. But I'm tired of seeing you work yourself into the ground, year in, year out. I'm bone-weary, Richard, and the summer season hasn't even started. I look ahead and all I see is long days where everyone can enjoy Brackenbrae, except us. I see weeks on end where you've no time for your son, far less for me.'

'That's not true.'

'Yes, it is. But what I'm really sick of is worrying about money. We can't keep on spending funds we don't have.'

'Don't worry about it.'

'Don't worry about it? Is that all you can say every time I mention money? I *do* worry. It's my *job* to worry. One of us has to. Have you any idea how much we owe? How big our debts are? Go on, take a wild guess.'

Dad didn't know the answer.

'It's not only the vast amount of debt that worries me, Richard, although that's terrifying enough to keep me awake at night. It's the fact we've sunk everything my mum and dad left me into the business, and your inheritance too. Lifetimes of savings, all gone. If we lose Brackenbrae, there will be nothing left to show for their hard work, not to mention our own.'

'Now you're being silly.'

I hoped he was out of punching distance.

'Don't you dare call me silly.'

Knew that was a dangerous thing to say.

'I don't mean you're silly, I meant that's silly talk. How can we lose Brackenbrae? It's ours.'

'It's *not* ours, Richard. The debts are ours, and if the lenders demand their money back, or the business fails, we'll be left with nothing.'

'Oh, surely not nothing? You're overreacting.'

I couldn't believe it. Would he never learn? Even I know you don't say that to Mum. She must have given him one of her scary looks because the Jolly Joe voice had gone when he spoke again.

'Anyway, why would the business fail? It's a great business. That's why they gave us a loan in the first place.'

'*Loans*, Richard, loans. Plural. What you don't seem to understand is how much things have changed since we first started out. Haven't you heard? We're in a recession.'

'Yes, I'm aware of that, Vivienne. My head is not completely buried in the sand. I know these are difficult economic times, but don't you see? That's good news for us.'

Mum interrupted. She tells me off for that, but I could tell she was losing her patience. Her voice was getting all high and shouty. 'What the hell are you talking about? How can a recession be good news?'

'When people have less disposable income, they choose cheaper holidays, don't they?'

'For God's sake, Richard! Be realistic. When people have no disposable income, they don't *take* holidays, they stay at home. There couldn't be a worse time to be in the tourist trade.'

Silence from Dad. He was learning.

But Mum wasn't finished. 'If they're looking for cheap holidays they go to places like the one along the road. Where they get a huge pool with six flumes and amusement arcades with a thousand fruit machines and cheap booze and bingo and a choice of bars and umpteen restaurants where they can stuff their faces with burgers and chips and guzzle cola all day long. They don't go glamping, paying over the odds to stay in a yurt or a glorified garden shed.'

Oh dear, that was rude.

'They're log cabins, Vivienne, blockhouses, actually. Also, when the tower is refurbished, we'll be able to offer visitors a unique experience, the chance to sleep in a sixteenth-century tower.'

'That's if we're not bankrupt or divorced by then.'

Divorced? Like Oliver's mum and dad? There was a long pause. Was Dad as shocked as me? His voice sounded so sad and tired when he spoke, I hardly recognised it. 'What should we do then? Give up on our dream? Sell Brackenbrae and walk away?'

'That may be the first sensible thing you've said for years. Yes, maybe it's time we considered selling up and moving on.'

'Sorry, Vivienne, I can't do that.'

'Well, I'm not sure I can do *this* any more.'

Dad said something I didn't hear and she shouted at him, well, screamed more like, 'You're obsessed with this place. You've no time for me, no time for Charlie, no time for anything but bloody Brackenbrae.'

There was a horrible silence. It seemed to last forever. I sat there wishing one of them would speak.

Mum did, finally, but in a wavery little voice, so soft I could hardly hear her. 'Will you do one thing for me? Can you please, please forget about Phase Five?'

After a long time, Dad said, 'No, Viv. I can't do that.'

'Well, I'm not prepared to go on like this.'

It all went quiet. Then the EastEnders music started. I crossed my fingers. Really hoped they were having a cuddle on the sofa. I uncrossed them again when I heard one of them slam the back door. I rushed to my room and peeped out. It was Dad, and he was heading for the bar.

That meant I had plenty of time to take his keys and get into the gun cupboard.

***

CHAPTER 4

Ayrshire, Scotland
Monday 28 May

Seb has been getting used to the vagaries of Scottish weather, but he still can't believe how quickly it can change. The sky over Arran has altered in the few minutes he's taken to get his breath back. White fluffy cumulus clouds that looked charming against the blue sky when he left Ayr have turned grey and unpleasant. Like his face, if his mother is to be believed. That's what she said about a month ago. It was probably a joke but you never knew with Mother.

'Sebastien, you should see your face. It's as dark and surly as a thundercloud. Come on, son, give me a little smile.'

Seb wanted to oblige but she was really getting on his nerves.

'Mother! You can't keep me wrapped in cotton wool forever.' He folded his arms and slouched against the kitchen worktop.

She tipped her head, as if trying to look puzzled. 'I'm sorry, Sebastien, I just don't understand. You don't need a holiday job. We give you a generous allowance, don't we?'

'Yip, guess you do. But that's not the point. I'd like to earn some money of my own.'

'Tell you what. Father will be home in an hour. Why don't you speak to him over dinner about one or two days a week with the firm? You can learn the ropes and earn a few euros at the same time.'

She patted his arm as if the matter was settled and began to pull at a loose thread on his cuff. Seb moved away, beyond her reach.

'I want to go to Scotland. My English teacher says it's a brilliant thing to do before we start uni. He spent the summer in Edinburgh before he did his degree. Really helped his English, he says.'

'Edinburgh? I'm not even sure they speak English in Edinburgh. Besides, your English is already excellent. As it should be with the small fortune we've spent on summer courses.'

'I know that and I'm grateful, but a fortnight with a family in Essex isn't the same. Mr Lagrasse says we need to immerse ourselves in the language and culture. You know I've always wanted to go to Scotland.'

'But it's so cold and always raining.'

'I don't care about that. Anyway, I'll be going in summer, to the south-west coast where palm trees grow, like on the Côte d'Azur.'

'When you say, "I'll be going", you make it sound like a foregone conclusion.'

'It sort of is. I've found a job on a campsite.'

'They won't pay you properly. Everyone knows the Scots are mean.'

'They've got to pay a minimum amount by law. They call it the living wage.'

'Tell me, Sebastien, what would this job involve? Do you have any idea? Bearing in mind that none of us has ever set foot on a campsite, far less holidayed on one.'

'Don't turn up your nose like that.'

'Well, really, son, who can blame me? Call me a snob if you will, but I can hardly think of a worse place to spend one's summer. Can you imagine, all those creepy crawlies in your tent, having to share showers, not to mention toilets, with other people. No, thank you, not if it were the last holiday in the world.'

'No one's asking you to go, Mother.'

'Please tell me you won't be cleaning toilets?' She grimaced.

'It's not cleaning toilets, it's organising the Kids Club, except they spell it with two Ks and a Z, apparently.'

'What does organising a kids club with a badly spelled name, involve?'

'Please, can you forget about spelling and grammar for once and listen?'

Mother pretended to zip her lips closed. That annoyed him too, but he carried on, trying to explain.

'It's basically about providing activities for children, a couple of hours a day. There will be two club leaders, me and a girl. I'll get full board and lodging, one day off every week, loads of free time, and money. It sounds great.' He didn't mention the fact that he was also expected to be the lifeguard for the pool. The less she had to complain about the better.

'I'm sure it sounds wonderful, Sebastien. But I've made my position perfectly clear. I don't want you to go.'

'Sorry, but I've already accepted the job. I've got a two-week trial, starting on the twenty-eighth of May. I leave on Friday.'

'Which Friday?'

He flicked his hair out of his eyes but didn't have the courage to look at her. His answer came out more like a question, as if he was still looking for her permission. Which, in a way, he was. 'Err, next Friday?'

'But that's weeks before the job starts.'

'I know. I plan to go walking, see a bit of the country first.'

Mother didn't make any response. In fact, she didn't say another word, not even goodbye on the day Father took him to the airport.

Now here he is, within touching distance of Brackenbrae, but not feeling as good as he'd expected.

The clouds over Arran are gathering, dark and menacing, and all the warmth has gone out of the air. The sea, a dark bluey green earlier, has turned slate grey, to match the sky. It's as if someone has adjusted the colour setting, fading the picture to monochrome.

Seb takes his fleece from around his waist and pulls it over his head, glad of the extra layer. He doesn't understand how a day that starts warm and sunny in the early morning can turn this cold. Maybe it will be different in high summer.

A car pulls up alongside him and the passenger window rolls down. An elderly man leans across an equally elderly woman and says something entirely unintelligible. Seb says the first thing that comes into his mind. 'No, thank you.'

'Suit yersel,' says the driver. 'Ye'll be soaked in five meenits.' The car disappears in a cloud of blue fumes that leave Seb coughing. When the first cool raindrop hits his face, he understands that he has just refused the offer of a lift. The rain starts in earnest and Seb looks at the darkening sky, hoping his mother's dire predictions about weather, and everything else, will prove wrong.

***

CHAPTER 5

us slithers his way across the steep slope of the field, swearing first at the rain, then at his smart leather shoes. Even his rugby boots would have trouble gripping this wet, slippery grass. He struggles to stay on his feet and swears again, this time at Kirsty. She was adamant that crossing the Carrick Hills would be a shortcut – faster and safer than the road.

His thin T-shirt is no match for rain and soon it's sticking to his chest like a cold second skin. Last night, when he caught the bus that runs along the coast to Dunure, the last thing he expected was to be invited to a 'sleepover'. All he had in mind was a decent meal and a few pints in the little pub, recommended online for its good food, warm, welcoming atmosphere and beautiful harbour-side setting. His steak was juicy, charred from the grill, and the chips were chunky, the way he likes them, but he'd felt uncomfortable eating alone in a restaurant full of couples. He'd refused dessert and settled the bill, keen to escape to the bar.

The place was buzzing, full of young, farmery types, male and female. All downing pints like there was a world shortage of beer.

If girls back in South Africa think they can keep up with the boys, they need to come here and see Scottish lassies in action. That Kirsty chick was matching the guys, pint for pint. Maybe that was why she was all over him? Gus prefers to think it was his accent, which he was exaggerating for her benefit. Hey, whatever turns them on! Usually it's his physique that gives them the hots. He remembers pushing his sleeve up to show off his guns and ending up in competition with a local farmer dude that everyone in the pub seemed to know. Ian, or Ewan or maybe it was McEwan, Gus couldn't recall, but Farmer Boy was doing his best to impress Kirsty – the two of them had history, no doubt about that. When the biceps were held side by side, fully pumped, the dude's pale freckly skin was no match for Gus's tanned, tattooed hide. An arm-wrestling contest was suggested, and Gus was happy to oblige. Not only that, he was so certain he'd win, he took Ewan McEwan's bet and put every last penny on himself. Lost the lot. The regulars roared their delight, especially when McEwan picked up Gus's money, held it in the air and said, 'The Milky Bars are on me, boys!'

Gus, raging at his own stupidity, turned his anger on Farmer Boy and charged him as if they were on a rugby field. It was an uneven contest, with the locals bailing in to protect their own.

The barman saved Gus's hide by stepping in and calming his regulars. Gus could tell whose side he was on. He grabbed Gus by the arm and said, 'This is a restaurant bar not a pub. Now please leave, while you still can.'

Gus shook him off and stood his ground. 'Okay, okay. I'll go. Once I've finished my beer.' He raised the almost full glass to his lips and downed the lot. McEwan, fight forgotten it seemed, slapped him on the back and said, 'No hard feelings, mate. Let me buy you another pint.'

'He's just leaving, Ewan,' said the barman.

'Okay, John.' Farmer Boy touched a hand to his temple in a mock salute. He turned to Gus and raised his eyebrows. 'See you again, mate.'

Gus was happy to go. He didn't like to lose, ever, and he wasn't going to stick around and be patronised by some country bumpkin. Beating him should have been easy. Throwing a rugby ball and tackling a hundred kilos of winger makes you fit. But it seems heaving straw bales and shoving cows around seven days a week does too.

How long since he last did any serious training? Not since Toulouse, when he was playing full-time. Pity he blew that one. Nice set-up. Free accommodation. Not the fanciest but he had his own room to bring girls back to. French lessons thrown in, so players from abroad, like him, could integrate. He liked it down there. Nice weather, like South Africa, and cheap red wine. Too much cheap red wine, as it turned out. Still, it was good while it lasted, and he was lucky the team kept him on for the full term of his contract. Then let him go with a recommendation. One that left out any mention of his 'roid rage', as far as he knows. It's no big deal anyway. Everybody takes steroids these days, if they're serious. Although, it was kind of suspicious that Glasgow Warriors weren't even prepared to give him a pre-season try-out. Bet the bastards discussed him on the phone. Why didn't that occur to him before now? What if the Warriors guy has been in touch with the team in Ayr? Telling them, 'Don't touch the big South African. He's mental.' Charming turn of phrase the Scots have got.

Ayr are a good rugby team, by all accounts, but way below his league. What is it they say about beggars and choosers? Plus, it's nice round here. He didn't fancy Glasgow, to be honest. Not a good place for a guy on a short fuse, from what he's heard.

Some of the drinkers last night were rugby followers. Seemed to think he'd have a good chance with Ayr next season. According to them, the team's been lacking someone with speed and Gus's build.

What if Ayr don't take him on? What if they've heard about his reputation for losing control, when the 'red mist' comes down? He might be back in the pub, looking for Ewan to see if he needs some extra brawn over the summer. Now he's lost all his money, he'll need to find work of some kind. Even if his mother could afford to pay for his ticket back to South Africa, she wouldn't.

Right now, his priority is finding his way back to his 'hotel' in Ayr in time for breakfast. He needs to get some food inside him and plenty of it. It might be a while till he can afford another meal. A few hours' sleep would be good too. Kirsty used up all his energy last night. He couldn't believe his luck when she followed him out of the pub.

He'd heard someone shouting, 'Hey, wait for me,' but didn't think the shout was for him.

'Hey, Big Guy! Wait.'

He stopped, half way up the steep narrow road, and looked back as if he was admiring the pretty little harbour and hadn't noticed her.

She half walked, half ran to catch up with him, saying, 'Hang on a minute.' He smiled, enjoying her wobbling towards him in strappy stilettos and skin-tight leggings.

'Who, me?' he said. 'I'm not wanted around here.'

'Don't know who gave you that idea,' she said, taking his arm. 'Come on, I've got some beers in the fridge.'

Pity she had to throw him out before five. Not even a goodbye kiss, far less a coffee. Claimed he had to leave before her husband got back in off the nightshift! Gus wasn't convinced about the husband, but he jumped into his Calvins double-quick and got going. No point in sticking around to find out the hard way.

When he asked her to lend him his bus fare, she said, 'A bus? At this time of the morning? No chance. You'll be quicker walking.' She led him to the door and pointed towards a yellow hillside. 'Up across the fields and over the Carrick Hills, then left along the road towards Culroy.' As if she'd just had a brainwave, she added, 'You'll come in past Ayr Rugby Club at Millbrae. Ideal. You can check it out.' With a tight smile and a terse, 'Right, on ye go!' she shoved him over the threshold and slammed the door. In the distance the skies are clearing and, like a phantom, a huge island appears on the horizon. It's like a volcano sitting out there waiting to erupt. He can't believe he didn't notice it last night. Still, the weather looks like brightening up a bit and the rain's not as heavy. Just as well because this so-called shortcut is turning into a cross-country challenge. She surely didn't mean for him to drag his sorry ass through these thick gorse bushes. Yellow flowers and a nice smell that reminds him of the beaches at home. Pity about the thorns that are doing their best to tear his skin off. Gus advances, warily as a boxer, his fists protecting his face.

***

CHAPTER 6

After the huge holiday park that Josie called Butlins, the directions, or perhaps Seb's recollection of them, are increasingly vague. 'Up on your left,' said one guy, leaving a lot of options open. 'On the side of the Carrick Hills,' added his pal.

Seb, hoping he's got it right, decides he'll take the first road on his left. A sign for the Carrick Hills convinces him he's on the right track and even better, the rain slackens off. That's bound to be a good omen.

It feels good to be close to his goal at last. Surely his parents will be proud when they hear he made it all this way. Even Mother, however grudgingly, will have to admit it's an achievement. Maybe she'll be so glad to hear he's safe, she'll forgive him for going against her wishes.

Poor Father. Bet his life's been hell since Seb left. Dinner on his last night was excruciating. Mother hadn't spoken to him for days.

Seb watched her take a tiny sip of wine, then touch her lips to a pristine white napkin, leaving the faintest kiss of red lipstick on the linen. She'd barely touched her soup, but she rose and cleared Seb's and Father's plate without a word.

He exchanged a look with Father, thinking they must look identical, mouths turned down in a clown's parody of sadness. A sudden lifting of Father's left eyebrow broke the tension and they burst out laughing, only to stop with a synchronicity so perfect, they sniggered like naughty schoolboys.

At the end of the narrow path through the bracken I get to the thick gorse. I wish the sun would come out. That's one of the things I remember from that day, the last time I was in here. How dark it seemed in amongst the bushes and how lonely. With no one to help me.

Five years ago, almost. I was nearly seven. Robbie was twelve. I push the memory away. Today will be different. I've got a gun and if anyone tries to hurt me or make me do stuff, I'll shoot him.

Like the scythe, the gun looks light when Dad's got it. But it's heavy and I'm tired. No sleep. No breakfast either. I've got plenty of reasons to turn back if I want to.

Up ahead, the little path splits in two. Both ways look the same. Not sure which way to go, I put the gun down till I decide and swing my arms back and forward, giving them a rest. A crowd of birds fly out, making me jump. They sound annoyed at me for interrupting them.

A tiny shiver tickles the back of my neck, like something bad is going to happen. Need to stop being a coward. 'Don't be such a scaredy-cat, Charlie.' Mum's always telling me that. Maybe she's right.

Maybe there's nothing for me to be afraid of. Not now. The memory starts to slide out of its black corner again, like slime. I shove it back into the darkness and look up at the sky, hoping for sunlight.

Right or left? Left, I think, because it's aiming towards the top of the hill. Through the glen. Up close, the gorse smells like Mum's expensive suntan lotion. Now I know why I've never liked that smell. It reminds me. But the wee flowers are lovely. So tiny. Bright enough to turn the whole hill yellow.

The path's full of hollows and dips. It's easy to walk on the downhill bits, but the uphill bits are hard with this big gun to carry. I need to watch out for roots and boggy bits too.

The bushes are getting taller now and the branches are thicker. It's much cooler too. Wish I'd put a jumper on. I need long sleeves. Gorse might look pretty, but if you get too close it'll rip your skin off. Like the feral cat that used to slink about our yard.

Something moves near my feet. Gone before I can spot it. My heart's banging. What if it's a snake? What if it's an adder? They can kill you. Jonathon Brown in Primary Six saw one once. Lying on a stone beside the path. But that was on Arran. Not here. Don't think we get snakes here.

I try to get away, just in case, out of these bushes. I swipe at a branch, but it whips back and hits me in the face. Scratching me with its thorny claws.

I blow out a huge breath and try to calm down.

Got no idea where I am. Can see sunshine further up the hill, but down here it still feels a bit rainy, like there's mist in the hollows. Or ghosts, waiting for me.

I'm usually too scared to come this far, even with the boys from school. They came round one day last summer holidays, for my birthday, and we played commandos. They wanted to go up into the woods, but I shook my head and wouldn't go. We were running all over the place, with no teachers or parents to spoil the fun. Before it was time for everyone to go home, we had dinner in the café. Big Mark gave us all the toppings we wanted on our pizzas and we got endless refills of fizzy drinks because Mum wasn't about. The boys said it was supercool but I kept wondering why Mum wasn't there. Then she came in with a new frock on and Dad was behind her with a big cake and eleven candles burning. Big Mark brought the fire extinguisher through from the kitchen. Said I was getting so old the cake was a fire hazard. Everybody laughed and then sang: 'Happy birthday, dear Charlie,' and I blew them all out. In one breath.

I like it when the boys in my class come up here. Doesn't happen very often. Mum says we live too far away and it's not handy.

A long shadow falls on my path and I nearly drop the gun. I look up, expecting a giant. It's only a tree with dark liquid oozing out of the bark, like blood on a skinned knee. I touch the trunk and the stuff sticks to my fingers. Smells like the cleaning spray Joyce uses on the toilets.

My stomach's so empty it's grumbling at me. Skipping breakfast isn't good for you, Mum says, so that's probably why I feel a bit sick. Or maybe it's that stinky pine stuff on my fingers. I wipe them on my shorts, rubbing my hand up and down. Trying to get rid of the smell and the stickiness. Stupid to wear shorts today. Just because it was sunny and warm yesterday. Dad says we can get all four seasons in one day here. 'If you don't like the weather,' he says, 'hang on half an hour. It'll change.' He's right. The rain's gone off and I can see a wee bit of blue sky up through the branches.

There's a commotion and I think it's me, disturbing the birds again. One bird, much smaller than the rest, is fluttering from branch to branch, surrounded by big, black crows. Each time the little guy settles, a crow dive-bombs it. I'm going to fire the gun and scare them off. I unwrap the red fleece and put my hand in my pocket for a shell. Then I hear the bushes moving. Someone's coming.

***

CHAPTER 8

Iwriggle under the thickest gorse I can find, ignoring the spikes, and flatten myself to the ground. If I keep my head down long enough, the person will walk straight past and never see me. I'm good at hiding.

I hold my breath.

The noise gets closer and closer. Louder and louder. Then quieter again. Think he's walking away.

I count elephants, in my head. It's a good trick for counting seconds. I usually imagine a chain of them traipsing past me, like the parade in The Jungle Book film. When I get to sixty, that's a minute.

I don't even get to ten. Can't concentrate. I lift my head. One centimetre at a time, trying not to make a single sound.

Someone's standing on the path, watching me.

I curl into a ball. In case he's got a dog. Saw a hedgehog do that once, when it was frightened. It worked. The dog lost interest and walked away.

I stop breathing. Keep my eyes shut tight. Try not to twitch the tiniest muscle. Pray he hasn't seen me.

Dead bracken whispers near my ear. My nose is so near the ground I can smell the earth. Think I might sneeze. I let out my breath a tiny little bit at a time but it still sounds loud as thunder.

Another few minutes pass, or maybe it's just moments.

'Hey, kid. You okay?'

When I don't answer he says, 'What you doing out here on your own at this time of the morning? You should be tucked up in bed.'

My legs are trembling, my hands too. I curl up tighter. Squeeze my knees to my chest so hard I can hardly breathe.

'Come on. Up you get.'

I don't move.

'Hey, listen. You need to get up. You can't lie there.'

I slowly raise my head. I see a face with wide, hairy nostrils and eyes that bulge as he leans towards me. His breath reminds me of the old dog Pops had when I was small.

The man touches my elbow and I flinch away from his hand. The bad memory's so strong my stomach feels like I'm falling down a flume.

'Easy, buddy, easy.' He takes a step away from me. Holds his hands up like he's under arrest.

I have to stand up and show him I'm not afraid. I crawl out and get to my feet, trying to hide the gun behind me.

'Playing cowboys?'

He waits, as if he expects me to say something.

'All by yourself?'

My legs are shaking. Wish I had long trousers on to hide them.

'You lost or something?'

I shake my head.

'Come on over here. Don't be scared. I won't hurt you.'

That's what Robbie said.

Inside my head, something snaps. I feel full of courage. I look the stranger right in the eye and bring the gun from behind my back.

'Going to give me a look at your gun? Cool.' He holds out his hand. 'Hand it over, then.'

I don't hand it over. I snap it shut, like I've seen Dad do. I smell metal and oil as the mechanism locks into place.

'Shit! That doesn't sound like a toy. Is it some kind of replica?' He holds out his arms this time. 'Can I see it, please?' He smiles as if he expects me to just do as he says.

Without taking my eyes off him, I slowly raise the gun. Till it's pointing at his chest. The smile slides from his face like slime off a stick. He moves away from me. A branch catches the back of his leg and he stumbles. I raise the rifle a little more. Settle it against my shoulder. Copying Dad. It feels so heavy I think my legs might buckle, but I don't feel a bit afraid. I feel powerful.

I rest my cheek on the gun. Make a show of placing my finger on the trigger.

He starts to scramble through the gorse, backwards. His eyes never leaving my face. The thorns snag his shirt but he doesn't seem to notice. Suddenly he stops and stands with his hands in the air.

'Take it easy, kid. Watch what you're doing with that thing.' His voice sounds kind of wavery. 'Put it down now, please. The joke's over. You've had your fun.'

I want him to keep going. Run. Get away from me.

He doesn't move. Well, just his arm. He stretches it out towards me, in slow motion. 'Come on,' he says, very quietly, coaxing. 'Just do what I tell you and you won't get hurt.'

Like the last time.

I stare at him. Right down the barrel. Slowly, very slowly, I shake my head. Then I pull the trigger.

***

CHAPTER 9

Ayrshire, Scotland
Monday 28 May

Seb slows to a stop, disheartened. Why didn't he pay more attention to where he was going? Or stay in bed for a few more hours then take a taxi? He's hungover, hasn't slept and could really use a shower. This is not the kind of first impression he'd hoped to make on his employer. As Father likes to remind him, you never get a second chance to make a first impression.

This job is too important to lose. He couldn't bear to have to return home a failure after all the fuss and upset he's caused by coming here.

A watery sun is drifting free of the horizon and starting its climb. The rain seems to have cleared and the sky's a slightly paler grey than before. It might turn out to be a decent day yet.

He takes off his fleece, rolls it up tightly and squeezes it into one of the side pockets of his rucksack. He runs his fingers through his hair and smooths it back off his brow. Mother's always stroking his hair, going on about the colour, claiming she sees highlights of pure gold in the copper. Says it's exactly like she remembers her father's hair when she was a child. He smiles, remembering how he always responds to this soppy nonsense. 'World's maddest mother!' he says and they both laugh. Or at least, they used to.

He should have had a haircut before he left. A long, floppy fringe falling into his eyes all the time might not impress a new boss. Normally he'd have asked Mother what she thought, or she'd have given her opinion without being consulted. But not this time. Same with his packing. No help or advice whatsoever. He did all his own washing and ironing and had to make up his own mind about what clothes to bring. Father's no use at that kind of stuff. Mother usually packs for all three of them. Already he's had to buy more socks and he could use another T-shirt or two. He'll get some in Ayr, on his first day off. Once he's been paid.

It's so quiet up here. A million miles from the city bustle he's used to. If it's true that some cities never sleep, Paris is one of them.

In the bright yellow bushes, little birds are singing their hearts out, and some crows in the taller trees shout at each other with their throaty, raspy call. Perhaps they're singing too, in the only voice they've got. A big pine cone drops, tumbling from branch to branch, like a bauble in a Christmas tree. A busy workforce of insects hums in the hedgerow, and down on the main road a motorbike engine roars, screaming for a gear change.

Seb steps off the road and walks on the grass. After weeks of pounding the tarmac, it feels soft as a silk rug, springy as a trampoline. The bounce comes back to his step and he lengthens his stride.

Apart from a blister on his heel he's had since the outskirts of Manchester, he's in fine shape, probably the fittest of his life. As long as a raging hangover, a headache and a growing thirst don't count. If he hadn't been stupid enough to get lost, he'd be there by now, enjoying a glass of cold water. He thinks longingly of the bottle of Evian that Mother always keeps cooling in the fridge. He imagines the blast of cold air in his face as he opens the door. He feels the touch of the bottle under his fingers, can almost taste those first mouthfuls, shockingly cold and thirst-quenching.

Cans of Fanta, Cola and 7up float before his eyes, their sides running with cool beads of moisture. His childhood favourite, Orangina, in its funny, fat bottle and that diluted fruit syrup his grandmother always made. With ice cubes clinking against the glass. This must be what it feels like to see a mirage in the desert.

They were talking about it last night in the pub, debating the best quencher for a hangover thirst. One man claimed nothing could beat milk and set off a chorus of gagging sounds. Someone said, 'A pint. Hair of the dog.' At the thought of beer, Seb wants to throw up in the hedge. The majority vote went to something Seb had never heard of. It sounded like Eye Urn Brew.

'B, R, U,' said Josie. Spelling out the word did not make its meaning any clearer to Seb, but he remembers Josie's description of the drink and how it looked when the barmaid sat a glass of it on the counter. 'On ye go, son. Taste that!' Seb had been reluctant at first but it became obvious that it would be an insult to refuse. 'Scotland's other national drink, that is, pal,' said one hard-looking drinker, who did not sound like he wanted to be Seb's pal. The bright, almost fluorescent colour made him expect an orange flavour, but his taste buds found nothing they could recognise. He smiled and emptied the glass, listening to a heated debate on whether the drink had to come in a glass bottle to be an effective hangover remedy. 'Cans are a pure waste o time.'

'An see they plastic bottles, well, they just kill the flavour.'

'Kill the flavour?' said Hyphen Man. 'It's no Gewürz-fucking-traminer! He'll drink it through a shitty nappy if his hangover's bad enough.'

Seb doubted that but, man, he'd kill for a glass of Irn Bru right now. He repeats the name over and over, taking pleasure in rolling the r in that particularly Scottish way. It makes him smile, wondering what Mr Lagrasse will make of his English accent after three months of this.

He's a few metres past the sign before it registers with his brain. Brackenbrae. He says it out loud, enjoying the double r sound, walking on.

Wait a minute. A sign to Brackenbrae. He turns back. There it is. Brown letters burned onto a flat wooden sign, and an arrow, pointing across the hillside. A little wooden stile's been built into a rickety fence that's keeping a few indolent-looking sheep off the road.

Despite the weight of his rucksack, Seb's over the stile like a gazelle. He hesitates, wondering if this could be another mistake. The pathway isn't clear, just a vague track through the grass. It could have been made by a couple of wandering sheep. It looks like it heads into thick gorse and a few wind-wasted trees. Maybe not such a smart idea with a big pack on your back, on your way to a new job. But then, someone has gone to the trouble of making and erecting a signpost. He looks back up the road. It's clearly leading to the summit. He can see masts at the top, another landmark mentioned by his drinking companions.

Seb looks out towards the bay, drawing the sea air deep into his lungs, smelling it, almost tasting the salt on his tongue. This is a different seascape from any he's ever seen. The Mediterranean is azure blue and filled with boats. Everything from luxury yachts lying in the bay off Monte Carlo, to huge container ships heading out from Barcelona. Here only one boat crosses the water, its solitary wake a churning white against the graphite sea. Seb watches its red funnel and decides to make a trip across that sea a priority this summer.

To his right, in the distance, white windmills march over a hillside, just like in France. The sight makes him feel a little homesick, not for Paris so much as for the village in Aude where Mamie lives. It reminds him that she deserves a phone call, so he can thank her for the book she sent for his birthday and the spending money she tucked inside the cover as a surprise.

Seb ups his pace. The sooner he gets there, the sooner he can get settled in, borrow a phone and make his calls home. Mamie will say, as she always does, 'How is my favourite grandson?' What Mother will say is anyone's guess. If she says anything at all.

***

CHAPTER 10

Don't know what will happen when I lower the gun, but it won't be nice. The way the guy jumped when I pulled the trigger. The look on his face. Don't know what came over me. I knew the gun wasn't loaded, but he didn't. I'm a bit ashamed, to be honest. I'd like to say sorry.

I expect him to come at me like a bull that I've poked with a pitchfork. But he starts laughing. You'd think I'd just told the funniest joke ever. As if he's crying, he wipes his eyes, one after the other. Then he looks straight at me. Oh dear. Now I'm for it.

'Well done, kid. You almost had me there. Of course, I never thought for a moment that gun was loaded, but hey, great joke.'

With a sudden lunge he reaches for the gun and grabs hold of it. I refuse to let it go and we do a little tug of war. Then he starts to prise my fingers off the barrel. They look like matchsticks, easy to break. I let go and he takes the gun out of my hands.

'Where the hell did you get a gun like this?' He examines it, stroking the wooden butt. 'Do your folks know?'

My guilty face tells him the answer.

'Oh dear. They don't, do they?'

I shake my head, my eyes on his.

'Your dad's not going to like this one little bit, is he? Here you are, out in the woods, all by yourself, with his gun, and he doesn't know a thing about it.' He sucks in a long breath of air through his teeth.

I start crying. Can't help it.

'Come on now, kid. Don't be a cry baby.' He pokes at me with the gun barrel but he's smiling, as if he wants to make me laugh. 'Quit the sniffling. Big boys don't cry.' He starts to walk around in front of me, waving the gun about as if it weighs no more than a water pistol. 'I tell you what, it's your lucky day. I ought to give you a good hiding for pulling that stunt, but I'm in a really good mood this morning, thanks to that little blonde chick I met in the pub.' He scratches at his groin.

I step back. Two or three steps.

He puts the gun down and unzips his jeans. I start to run, stumbling and falling into the gorse. Its branches grab at me, scratching and trapping me in that same sickly-sweet smell.

I hear a hissing sound and the smell changes. I turn round and see him peeing into the bushes.

I crawl towards the gun but he's too fast for me. 'Oh no, you don't,' he says, in a sing-song voice, as if he's teasing. He holds the gun out of my reach with one hand, while he closes his zip with the other. 'Why don't we have some fun, you and me? Just us two men, out in the woods together, eh?'

I shake my head. No, no, no. It can't be going to happen again. I reverse, pushing against the gorse. Its thorns feel like a thousand tiny daggers in my back.

'Come on. Give me some ammunition, partner,' he says, pointing at my pocket. He sounds ridiculous, putting on a cowboy voice, as if he's trying to make me smile. 'We're gonna do ourselves some shootin', boy. Hand me the goddamned ammo.'

I've already made one big mistake this morning. Got a terrible feeling I'm about to make another one, but I don't think I've got much choice.

He fiddles around until he manages to load the gun. He closes it, tucks it under his arm, cowboy-style, and swaggers off into the woods. Half of me hopes he's forgotten I'm there. Might be able to escape, fetch Dad.

'Come on, partner,' he calls to me over his shoulder. 'I've done me some gun-shootin' back home. I'm an ace shot.'

That's a lie. People who are used to handling guns treat them with total respect. Dad has told me often enough.

'Come on, kid. Don't chicken out now.' He disappears into the woods.

I look around, hopeless. I've got such a bad feeling about all this. Just want to run for home but I can't let a total stranger wander off with Dad's best gun. I've got to follow him. I trudge along through the gorse, trying to keep him in my sight.

This is so bad. Dad's told me thousands of times. 'What's the Golden Rule of hunting, Charlie? Never, ever walk around with a loaded gun.'

***

CHAPTER 11

Seb can't take his mind off the thirst. He's had hangovers before. Not a lot, to be honest. Just after one or two parties. But never anything like this.

Usually, it's a case of staying in bed till it wears off. With Mother bringing him painkillers for his headache and chilled drinks of Evian. Last time she even put a cool washcloth on his brow. Now, that was nice. When he'd told his mates, they'd been incredulous and insulting, and Seb suspected a little bit jealous. What he'd give right now to be back in his own bed with his mother fussing over him. He wouldn't snap at her to keep the shutters closed. Or demand that she keep the noise down. He'd say, 'Thanks,' and give her a hug, if he could get his head off the pillow.

Pillow. What a thought. Crawling into bed, pulling the duvet up to his ears and sleeping. Till he doesn't want to sleep any longer. Seb tries to remember when he last had a lie-in. Not since he landed in the UK, that's for sure. Even before that, he'd been so wired about coming away, he was waking at dawn, making lists in his head and, at times, fretting about the fight with his mother – wondering if he could put it right before he left.

Maybe he can have an early night tonight. Explain that he wants to recharge his batteries for work tomorrow. Work is worrying him. All the bravado he showed to his parents wore off long ago and now he's panicking. What if he can't handle the kids? What if they don't like him? Or worse, what if his boss or his colleagues don't like him?

The thirst is back. Forgotten for a few moments but no less demanding. He's never been this thirsty in his life. His throat feels like it's closing down from lack of moisture and his tongue feels twice its normal size. It's like he's used up all his saliva. The taste in his mouth is rancid, as if someone has over-garlicked the food and yet he's not eaten garlic for weeks. His breath must smell like a dead dog. Imagine breathing that at his new boss. At least the Scots don't go in for kissing. One small mercy.

He was asked about that in the pub last night. 'Haw, French Boy. Is it true the men aw kiss wan anither in Paris?'

Seb had shrugged. Someone pointed. 'See that? It's cried a garlic shrug.'

'It's a Gallic shrug, ya eejit,' said Josie.

'Gallic, garlic, whit's the difference? Dae it again, pal.'

Seb had shrugged again, raising his shoulders in a way he'd been doing his whole life, without a thought.

The men had laughed.

'Ah'm no keen on garlic,' said Josie.

'Garlic? Ah love it. See that garlic bread? Ah could eat ma body weight.'

'Whit? Two ton?'

More laughter. It seemed this was how Scottish men had a conversation. One guy made an observation, someone else made a joke about it and everybody laughed. Banter, they called it, a new word to Seb. Only when the conversation turned to football did the tone become serious.

Seb heard little discussion of politics. Not a fraction of what he might expect in a bar in Paris. The name of the Prime Minister had been mentioned at one point, followed by a chorus of expletives. 'As bad for Scotland as Margaret-fucking-Thatcher,' was Hyphen Man's opinion.

Seb plans to wander in to the pub another night and see if he can engage one or two of the same guys in a more philosophical discussion. Without so much 'banter'. He enjoys a good debate, has been missing the ones he has with Father. It will be good to hear what those men really think about big issues like Scottish independence. He was too timid to ask last night. It will be fun finding out how they think. Once he gets used to the accent.

'Who wants kris?' Josie asked at one point. 'Ye like kris, son?'

Seb shook his head. 'Sorry, I don't know him.'

Josie pointed at the stacks of coloured boxes under the gantry. 'Tattie kris! What kind dae ye like? Tamata? Salt n vinegar? Plain?'

Seb shrugged, causing another bellow.

'Take tamata, Seb! That's wan a yer five a day.'

He ended up sampling all the flavours. He can't even remember what half of them were. Prawn something or other that had no taste of prawns, just sugar, chemicals and salt. They all tasted salty. Hence the thirst that's driving him mad this morning. It's not hard to imagine going insane in the desert.

But he's not in the desert. He's in Scotland. The wettest wee country in the world, according to his new pals. There must be something he can drink, even a puddle from the recent rain. The path begins to fall away under his feet and at the bottom of the incline, a stream burbles over stones.

Seb starts to run, lop-sided, downhill and upstream at the same time. The ground is uneven and tufted and the bank is steeper than it looks. As he veers down the slope, his backpack swings sideward and he overbalances, grabbing for handholds that don't exist. Building up speed, he runs stumbling into the shallow water. His feet splash and slide as he tries to slow down and right himself. His toe catches on a stone and he lurches out of control towards the opposite bank. He lands hard, on his knees, the full weight of his pack forcing him face first, into the gorse.

He lies there, giving himself time to recover his senses. The backpack shifts and he moves with it, a stab of pain flashing. At first he can't work out where it's coming from. His ankle, he thinks, twisted in the fall. Or his left arm, jammed at an unnatural angle beneath his body. His face, savaged by thorns? When the world turns red he has his answer. Blood runs into his eyes, blinding him. He shoves at the ground with his free hand till he rolls over onto his back. His spine bends to the shape of his rucksack and he feels like a tortoise marooned on its back.

He touches his forehead then peers though bloody eyelids at his hand. Everything is red, the brightest, most vivid red he's ever seen. It streams past his nose and he smells the old iron tools in Mamie's garden shed. It runs into his mouth and he tastes again the coin that almost choked him when he was little. Mother cried when he spat the centime into her hand and hugged him as if he'd done something clever.

He wipes his mouth, his nose, his eyelids, but his hand only slides in blood, smearing not cleaning. He raises his arm and wipes the side of his face on the sleeve of his T-shirt then pulls at the neck, stretching the material to clean his lips.

He must get onto his feet and look for help. He clenches his stomach muscles and raises himself into a sitting position. The blood immediately runs into his eyes. He gathers the front of his T-shirt in his fist and lowers his face till the material touches his brow. He holds it there, ignoring the pain as he presses hard, hoping to stem the flow. When he takes the cloth away it is soaked and bloodied. What the hell has he done? He increases the pressure, wincing. Still the blood flows through the thin cotton till his fingers are wet with it.

Seb closes his eyes and sits, dizzy, waiting for a wave of nausea to pass. With his middle finger he tentatively explores his forehead, trying to work out where all the blood is coming from. His fingertip finds a hollow, almost a hole and he wishes for a mirror or his phone so he could see the damage. Now his finger has found the wound, it seems unwilling to stop probing, drawn like a tongue to a tooth cavity.

He needs medical attention, maybe stitches. If only he'd paid more attention in biology lessons, he'd know how much blood the body can afford to lose. His shirt is sodden, maybe he's already lost too much. He can feel panic rising inside his stomach and going all the way to his fingertips, making them tremble. His whole body begins to shake. Is it cold or shock or loss of blood? He tells himself to stay calm. Getting hysterical won't help. That's one of Father's lines. It drives Mother mad, like 'You're overreacting,

Catherine.' That one winds her up too. The thought of his parents brings tears to his eyes and seems to bring him to his senses.

'Come on, Seb. Get a grip, man,' he says, hoping the sound of his voice will help him focus on what he needs to do. Sitting here crying like a little kid is not the answer. He has to get on his feet and find someone who can call an ambulance. He hauls himself semi-upright and searches the steep bank till he spots the culprit. Not what he expected to find, but a bright tag of blood proves its guilt. The gorse bush. One branch, broken by who knows what, its white pointed end sharp as a scimitar. He pulls at a piece of loose bark, exposing more of the creamy white stalk and touches the jagged point, like a chef testing the edge of a blade.

He drops onto his bottom and leans back on his rucksack, eyes closed in despair. It would be easy to go to sleep. It's quiet and peaceful and he's so terribly tired. *Don't go to sleep.* He doesn't know why that's vital, but he knows it to be true. He's got to remain conscious. He rolls onto his side and crawls towards the stream. He needs water. To wash his face, to rinse his eyes, to get rid of the blood. As he kneels there, making a cup with his hands and splashing water on his face, he tastes it and registers its temperature, its earthy taste, and he drinks and drinks. His thirst quenched, he watches his blood drip red into the water, disperse like a smoke ring and flow away.

***

CHAPTER 12

Wish I'd gone home when I had the chance. Now it's too late.

The gorse is getting thicker and the path is narrow, hardly a path at all. Like a sheep made it, or rabbits, not a person.

Don't have a clue where we are. Been concentrating on following the stranger and I've lost my way. No idea how far I am from home but I'm pretty sure Dad will be up by the time I get back. If he sees me he'll want to know where I've been. Can't tell him but he'll know something's wrong. Maybe if I run home now, all the way, I can sneak back up to bed and no one will ever know anything about my plan.

But which way to go? Miss Lawson always says, 'Think, Charlie, think.'

If I keep going, I should come to Brown Carrick. Then I can turn around and follow the path back to Brackenbrae. But what about Dad's gun? If I go home without it, Dad might get into trouble the next time Johnny Hastings comes to do his inspection.

I start to run, hoping I'm going in the right direction for home. Just want to get out of here. When I get back I'll take Dad to the gun cabinet and try my very hardest to tell him I'm sorry. Nothing is working out the way I wanted, but at least I'll get Dad's attention.

It's hard running on the hillside and I think I might have gone the wrong way. When the guy suddenly appears, I know I have. He swings the gun over his shoulder, far too casual. Making me nervous.

I know the rules about guns. Dad taught me when I was about ten. First the Golden Rule, of course and then, 'A gun should always be broken when not in use.' That used to confuse me. No matter how often Dad explained that broken means open in the middle and bent over your arm, I still think it's a silly word. There's nothing funny about it this morning. I catch the stranger's arm and point to the gun.

'What is it? You want the gun?'

I nod my head.

'Sorry. It's my turn to play with it.'

He still thinks it's a toy? Surely he can tell it's real? Why can't he understand that he needs to be careful?

I don't think he's very intelligent and he knows nothing about guns. But he seems determined to shoot something, stalking through the gorse like a guerrilla soldier. He keeps swinging the gun from side to side, as if he's sweeping the area for enemy activity.

I bet the only shooting he's ever done is on video games. We step out of the gorse and a flock of birds rises from a tree. He swings the gun to follow them but he's not quick enough.

'Damn! Too slow on the trigger.'

I stand and wait while he plays Action Man. I kick at the grass with the toe of my trainer and concentrate on making a hole in the earth. He'll get bored soon.

'Pssssst!'

I look up. He's aiming in my direction. Getting his own back. Playing the same trick on me. Except this time, the gun's loaded.

I shut my eyes so tightly I see sparkles of colour.

I'm going to die.

A shot.

Then, nothing.

No birds, no wind, nothing but a deep noisy silence and a pain in my ears. Would it hurt this much if I'm dead?

I open my eyes. He's saying something, maybe screaming it, but I don't hear.

I'm not dead. I'm deaf.

He seems to be yelling at me, but he looks pleased about something. I shrug to show him I can't hear what he's saying, use my hands to cover my ears. It's too late to protect them but it feels right. My head's got the school bell ringing inside it.

He tugs at my arm. Points behind me. I turn but there's nothing to see.

His mouth makes an 'okay' as he nods and holds up one thumb.

I'm not okay. My ears hurt but he keeps talking as if I can hear him. I shake my head and try hard to listen. His mouth keeps moving. Eventually I catch a few words or maybe I read his lips, I'm not sure.

'Got something... big... sound of it. Might... deer... think...?' The words are faint, but I think I can hear them.

'Come... it fell... down... the dip.'

He gallops off and disappears down into a hollow. I don't move.

'... Christ.'

I heard that.

'Fuck.'

His voice is still faint, as if I need to turn up my volume, but I know something's wrong. He keeps saying the same swear words over and over again. Can't hear well enough to be sure but it sounds like he's scared.

Bet he's wounded something, a stag, maybe. I've heard what an injured stag can do. One nearly killed a woman in the highlands one time.

I'm staying back. It's not my problem.

I hear noises, so muffled it's hard for me to tell what kind. It sounds like panting or snuffling. Poor thing must be in agony. I should run and get Dad, but that will take ages and I'll get into deep, deep trouble. The guy will too. He should never have fired that gun. He's got no permit. Dad will get into trouble too.

I bite at the skin on the side of my thumb. My hand's shaking so much my nail taps against my teeth. Maybe I should go down and shoot the deer properly, to put it out of its misery. Cowboys kill their horses because that's the right thing to do when a creature is suffering.

Or I could run up the road and get the farmer. He could come and finish the deer off. Take it away in his truck. Only thing is, Dad knows everyone round here so he'll find out, sooner or later. Anyway, how can I explain that I need help? This is a total disaster and I'm to blame. I stole a gun and handed it over to a stranger. Then gave him ammunition. Dad's going to kill me.

I need to get that gun back.

I stop and listen, from a safe distance. All I hear is a curlew's sad song away up the hillside. No more swear words. No more sounds of the deer dying.

I take a few baby steps closer to the edge of the banking. It's steep with a wee burn at the bottom. He's just standing there. Staring at something on the ground. The gun's lying behind him as if he dropped it. If I'm quick I could get it and run.

I step over the edge and the soil falls away under my feet. I start to slide downhill in a mini-avalanche of earth and stones. Don't want to fall into the burn and I don't want him to see me taking the gun.

All of a sudden, he drops to his knees. His shoulders are moving up and down. The strange awful noises are coming from him. He's crying, but not like me, or Mum. Like Dad when Pops died.

Why is he so upset? Is it the sight of a dead animal? I don't want to see it either, but I take a deep breath and step forward and lean over his shoulder. I see a trainer, a sock, jeans, a T-shirt covered in blood. This doesn't make sense. Why is this person lying by the burn? Why is he covered in blood?

The stranger jumps to his feet and grabs me by the arms.

'I didn't see him. I didn't see him.' He shakes me with each word, as if he's desperate to make me understand. My head wobbles but he doesn't seem to notice. 'I just saw his hair, just that fuckin' red hair. You understand?'

I don't.

'I heard heavy breathing, kind of panting? You understand what I'm saying?'

Don't know what he's talking about but I know I've got to nod.

'He was coming up out of the dip, yeah? I thought it was a deer or something.'

I keep nodding.

He stops shaking me.

'Shit, I don't know what I thought.' His voice fades out. He lets me go and I stumble. He catches me and kind of puts me on my feet. Then he drops to his knees, snivelling like a toddler.

'Listen to me. I didn't know it was a guy. I swear, I didn't know.'

He looks up into my eyes. His hands are clasped as if he's praying. 'Please, please believe me,' he says. 'I didn't mean to kill him.'

***

CHAPTER 13

As if he's looking down from a helicopter, Gus sees himself. Kneeling there, begging a kid to forgive him. How must this look?

He stands and draws himself up to his full height, blocking the boy's view. He takes him by the shoulders and shakes him, just once, to get his attention.

'Look at me, kid.'

He leans down so their eyes are level.

Different emotions flicker across the boy's face. He looks bewildered and terrified. His eyes are huge as if he can't believe what he's seen. He glances towards the body like it might have disappeared or something. Gus shakes him again.

'Don't look at that. Look at me, buddy.'

The boy meets his eyes, for only a second, then looks away again. He leans to the side to see past Gus. It's as if he can't stop looking at the body. As if he hopes it might have gone the next time he looks.

Gus gives him another shake and turns him away so he can't see the guy. 'Are you listening to me?'

No reaction. It's like the kid's in a trance.

'Hey! Are you listening?'

The kid nods. At last.

'What's your name?'

No answer.

'Can you tell me your name?'

The boy shakes his head. Can't tell? Won't tell? No point in forcing it.

'What happened here, it was an accident. A terrible accident. But an accident. Do you understand?'

The boy nods.

'Good. How was I to know he would appear like that. I thought it was a deer. You get what I'm saying?'

The boy nods again. This time he keeps nodding, although Gus isn't asking him anything. Then he starts to cry, in this quiet, sobbing kind of way. His head still nodding. Gus feels sorry for the kid, for that's what he is. A child.

'How old are you, buddy?'

No answer, but the nodding stops.

'Ten? Eleven? Twelve?'

He nods. Twelve years old. Small for his age. But still a kid. Poor little bugger. He puts his arm round the child's shoulder, intending to comfort him, but the kid squirms away. With an accusing look on his face. As if Gus might hurt him next.

Who can blame him? Seeing it from the kid's point of view. He's out in the woods, minding his own business. Although what business he had being out here with a gun, Gus can't imagine. Anyway, the kid runs into this total stranger and the next thing he knows, there's a dead body.

Dead. That word. Gus's stomach turns at the thought.

'Wait,' he says. 'Wait there. I need to check something.'

Maybe the guy's not dead. It's impossible to tell. He's lying face down as if he slithered back into the little gully. Gus puts his fingers on the guy's neck and feels for a pulse. Nothing. He moves his fingers to another spot, holds his breath while he waits. His fingers come away bloodied.

'Oh no, please, no.'

Fighting the weight of a huge rucksack, Gus rolls him, just far enough to see his face. Except he can't. His face is still there, not blown off by the gun, thank God, but bathed in blood. Gus looks for a wound. There it is, a hole in his forehead. Shocked, he lets the body go and it rolls over again, face down.

'Jesus,' he whispers. 'What are the chances? I've never fired a gun in my life. Then I hit a guy smack in the middle of the head? Like I'm some damn sniper or something. Fuck, man!'

The kid turns but says nothing. Just stands with his hands over his ears, staring at the dead guy lying there with his backpack still strapped on. He looks as if he's tripped and face-planted. Like he'll get up any minute now, laughing.

Except he won't – this isn't a cartoon and he's a corpse. Gus can't take it in. He gets that weird feeling again that he's hovering above the ground. Looking down at himself. Watching a scene from a horror movie.

A sour taste fills his throat, making him retch. He leans over but nothing comes up. His hands are shaking and there's a sweat on his face that feels icy cold.

'Shit.' He's just killed a guy. He appeals to the kid, 'Shit! What the fuck am I gonna do?' and suddenly sees how this must look and how it will look to other people.

He needs to think fast. If he reports this, with no witnesses except a child, he's done for. He's a foreigner who just shot a Scotsman. He'll get no mercy. They'll lock him up and lose the key. In a flash, Gus sees his whole life disappear. No rugby career. No triumphant return to South Africa to prove them all wrong. No college, no girls, no beer, no life. No life. Jeez, what if they've got the death penalty here? He'll get the electric chair. No, that's America. Here, they hang people. Oh fuck, he could die, all because this asshole comes charging out of the gully at him. It's so unfair. Anyone would have fired. It was automatic, a kind of survival instinct. What the fuck was he supposed to do, with a gun in his hand?

He strides back and forth, his head in his hands, fingers clutching at his hair. Pacing across the little stream, he barely notices the cold water rippling over his trainers, soaking his feet. The main thing is to stay calm and think. There must be a way out of this mess. There has to be. Every problem has a solution. All he has to do is find it.

The kid. The witness. The only witness. Gus checks to make sure he's still there. He hasn't moved an inch. It's like he's standing guard over the body.

Gus runs up the banking, his feet sliding and skittering on the loose soil. He looks around in all directions. Nothing but those yellow bushes and a barren hillside. No houses to be seen, no sounds to be heard. Just the bleating of sheep and, in the distance, a lone seagull.

There has to be a way out. His life can't end like this. Before it's even started. It's not fair. He's got plans. An idea starts to form then fizzes into life like a match struck in a dark room.

If he can cover this up, no one will be any the wiser. There are only three people involved in this cock-up. One's dead and one's a scared little kid.

If he can deal with the body, the boy should be easy.

'Hey, kid, come away from there. There's nothing you can do for him. You can see the blood for yourself. He's been shot in the head, it's obvious.' He pauses for a moment; not sure the kid has heard him.

'Did you hear me? I said he's been shot. And you're to blame.'

The boy's head snaps round. He looks up at Gus, disbelief all over his face.

'That's right, you heard me. An innocent guy's been shot in the head. Because of you.'

He stops to let the words sink in, then repeats them, in case the kid's too stupid to understand. 'You shouldn't have been out here with that gun, should you?'

The boy slowly shakes his head, agreeing. Maybe he was thinking the same thing himself.

'No gun. No dead guy. See? It's all your fault.'

The boy's face turns crimson. He shakes his head, furious as a terrier with its teeth in a rat. Gus makes his way down the bank, keeping his voice low and trying to goad the kid into a reaction. 'Hell, you know you shouldn't be carrying a gun. It's illegal. You're far too young.'

The boy launches himself at Gus. Soft fists batter his chest. Small feet thrash against his shins and bony knees bang into his thighs. One kick catches him in the crotch, but he twists to the side and suffers only a weak jab of pain. He grabs the skinny arms and puts a stop to the pummelling, but the legs still thump away. He can tell the boy is doing his very best to hurt him. He tightens his grip on the youngster's arms and uses them to lift him up till their faces are nearly level. Anger and fear battle in the boy's eyes. When fear appears to be winning, Gus knows he has the upper hand. All the fight oozes out of the child, and he goes floppy as a rag doll.

Gus lowers him to the ground and lets go of his arms. The boy stands there in front of him with his head down, weeping in silence.

Gus tries to make his voice a little kinder. 'You worried about what your dad's going to say?'

The boy looks straight into his eyes. The tears are streaming down his face.

'Bet you're scared you'll get into a whole lot of trouble, aren't you?'

The kid nods solemnly and Gus knows he's hit the right spot. He tries to sound casual, although he can feel his heart racing. His pulse rate must be sky-high. 'I think you're right to be scared. I would be.'

He lets that sink in, all the time nodding his head as if he's weighing up a problem.

'Hang on a minute. What age did you say you are? Twelve? Yeah, I'm pretty sure that makes you a minor. You should be alright.' He laughs. 'You've nothing to worry about.'

The child looks up at him with hope in his eyes.

'Relax. I can't speak for Scotland but in South Africa you can get away with anything till you're fourteen.' He laughs again. 'No one's gonna prosecute a twelve-year-old for something like this. Phew! Bet that's a relief, eh, buddy?'

The kid smiles, nodding. It's clear he wants to believe what he's hearing, and Gus feels like a real bastard. But this has to be done.

'Your dad? Well, that's a different matter.' He watches the smile slide off the boy's face and wonders if he's being unnecessarily cruel. No, this is no time for compassion.

'Your dad lets you wander about with a gun and some poor hiker gets shot? You can't be held to blame for that, but your dad?'

He sucks air in through his teeth, making as much noise as he can for as long as he can, leaving it to the kid's imagination. Till the look on his face tells Gus all he needs to know.

'Pay attention to me, kid. You can still get out of this mess. I'll help you. I'm not gonna say a word about this to your dad, or anyone else. Okay?'

The boy nods his head, looking ridiculously trusting. Gus feels like the biggest shit on the planet. If he had a choice he wouldn't do this to anyone, far less a child.

'This will be our secret, yours and mine. What do you say?'

More nodding.

'Wish you'd tell me your name. Can you do that?'

The kid shakes his head. He seems determined to give nothing away. Probably been warned within an inch of his life not to talk to strangers. Under any circumstances. Gus smiles at the bizarreness of the situation and the child smiles back at him. Eager to please by the looks of him.

'Fair enough. Is it okay if I give you a name?'

Nod.

'Good. I'm gonna call you Noddy. Do you like magic, Noddy?'

Another nod.

'Good. Well, Noddy, you and I are going to do some magic. We're going to make this guy here do a vanishing act. We'll make him disappear.' Gus is almost beginning to enjoy this when he glances at the body and a sickening heave of his stomach brings him back to stark reality. But this is no time for hesitation. He has to push on.

'No one will ever know you took the gun and caused this accident. In fact, no one except you and me will even know there *was* an accident. Look around. No witnesses. You can get away with this.'

The boy doesn't look convinced.

'Hey, don't look at me like that. It's a great plan. Guaranteed to keep your dad out of prison. You up for it?'

The slightest of nods tells Gus he can go on.

'Here's what we'll do. We'll dig a hole and bury him. We'll make a secret pact to never talk about it to anyone, ever. Then you'll go your way and I'll go mine. Good plan?'

The kid shakes his head.

'Well, smartass, can you come up with a better one? Like I call the police right now?' He takes his phone out of his pocket and pretends to dial. 'Hi, is that the police?'

The kid dives at the phone, trying to grab it out of his hand, but Gus is too fast.

'No?' He makes a show of switching off his phone and returning it to his pocket. 'Okay, good decision. Your dad would find it tricky telling the police how a kid like you got his hands on a lethal weapon. He'd have a hard time explaining how a twelve-year-old ended up wandering the woods with a gun. Using happy hikers for target practice.' He points to the dead body and sees the kid shudder.

'Right then. We've got to make sure we do a good job of burying him. Otherwise the first wild animal that comes along will dig him up and eat him.' The boy flinches at the gruesome suggestion and Gus can see he's made his point. The kid swipes his forearm across his face, all the way from his elbow to his fingertips. A trail of snot smears across his tear-stained cheek. He grinds the heel of his hand into one eye socket and then the other. When he goes for a deep breath it turns into a wracking hiccup. Gus tries not to feel sorry for him.

'Let's get started. I think he's too heavy for us to move very far, so let's see if we can leave him down in the gully.' As Gus makes his way down the incline, the ground slides from under him. Digging a grave here will be a challenge, especially without a spade, but looking for any sort of tool is too risky.

He walks up the tiny valley, cut through the hillside by the stream as it makes its way down towards the sea. Where the little river has altered its course, the bank is undercut. Not far from the body he finds a spot where there might be enough room for what they need. He hunkers down and begins to scrape away at the soil.

It comes away easily. Far more easily than he expected. Shouldn't be too hard to dig if they both work at it. 'Thank Christ for that, at least,' he mutters to himself.

'Right then, Noddy, come on over here and we'll get started. Need to get this done as quick as we can, eh?'

As expected, the boy says nothing. He seems to hesitate for a few moments and then comes over, jumping the stream. He kneels down, his head hanging low. A dribble of spit dangles from his chin, like cheese from a pizza, but he starts to dig his fingers into the soil and scrape it back.

'That's it, buddy. We'll get this sorted, you and me. No worries.'

Once they'd loosened the first layer, the soil wasn't so obliging. It would take a long time to make a big enough space to hide a body.

'This is no good. We need something to dig with. You stay here. I'll be back as fast as I can.'

From the top of the bank he stops to look back. It's a tragic scene. A dead man and a sad little figure, digging like a toddler in a sandpit. At least they're well hidden in that hollow. But if it hadn't been for the hollow, the accident would never have happened. If he'd had a chance to catch sight of the hiker coming up out of the dip, he'd never have made that awful mistake. But only the top of his head appeared. That ginger-coloured hair looked so like a fuckin' deer ... Gus, well, he just reacted. Hell, anyone would've made the same mistake, wouldn't they?

***

CHAPTER 14

I know why this is happening. It's the curse. I should have stayed away from these woods. I come back one time and someone else dies. What happened the last time, with Robbie, wasn't my fault; he made me do those things.

I keep my head down and try to dig but the soil's too hard. Think I hear a noise, coming from the dead guy. Maybe he's still alive. I rush over to his side and touch his arm.

He stays still and silent. I want him to wake up so I shake him, gently. He doesn't react. I shake him harder. I try to turn him over so I can give his face a slap, like they do on the telly. Or maybe even mouth to mouth. Anything to save his life. I push and heave at his rucksack. I get him turned nearly half way and I see his face, all bloody, with a hole above his eye. It's horrible, like the 18 film my friend's big brother showed us one time that gave me nightmares.

The hole isn't bleeding, just kind of trickling, as if the tap's been turned off. But it's gross. I tell myself not to be such a baby. I try again, rolling him this time, but with the big rucksack and all, he's too heavy for me. He flops back like a giant doll. I touch his neck. Think maybe I feel something. Not sure. I'm trembling so much my teeth keep banging against each other. Now my hand's all bloody. I wipe it on my shorts but the redness won't come off.

A girl in my class got hit by a car and went into a coma. Mum said people in a coma look dead but it's really a long, deep sleep. We all had to say a prayer, every day, and it worked. Molly woke up and now she's okay. She can dance and everything. I wish this guy would wake up and be fine too.

He doesn't look like a hiker or a hillwalker. They've all got the same kind of anoraks and boots and hats with bobbles. A bunch of them come into our café on a Saturday morning.

He's wearing trainers and he's got no anorak, unless it's in his backpack. Maybe he's got a phone in there? We could get an ambulance to take him to the big hospital. Bet they fix comas and stuff.

The stranger comes back. Carrying two sticks. 'Come on,' he says, 'these'll make the job a lot easier.'

I don't move. We can't bury this man. He might just be having a coma. I put my fingers on his neck.

'I already did that. He's dead, kid, and we need to get a move on. Before somebody comes along and finds us. Way up Shit Creek.'

Don't know what that means, but his face tells me it's not a joke. He grabs a handful of my T-shirt and pulls me along. He's too rough. I try to get him off me and he slaps the back of my head. Hard. You should never hit someone on the head. It can give people brain damage. He shoves me in the back and I stumble into the burn. My feet get soaked and I skin my knee on a stone, but he doesn't care.

'Get digging,' he growls, kind of quiet, but scary. He hands me a stick. Not sure what I'm supposed to do with it.

'Like this, look.' I watch him scraping away at the soil of the banking, making a flat bit. Like a mini cave.

'You want another slap, kid?'

Stupid question.

'Well, you better get to work.'

I dig and dig as hard as I can, moving a little bit of dirt at a time and pushing it away to the side. The stick hurts my fingers and I keep changing hands. Eventually he tells me to stop. He throws down his stick and goes over to the guy. Starts to haul his backpack off. Watch out, I want to shout. You'll hurt his shoulders.

He throws the rucksack to the side like it weighs nothing.

Next, he pulls his T-shirt over his head. His body is all muscled, like a bodybuilder's. He rubs the gun with his T-shirt. Rubs really hard, all over, as if he's polishing the gun, then hands it to me.

His voice kind of nice again, he says, 'Can you check that for me, please, buddy? Make sure it's not loaded?'

Bit late for that but I do what he says. Exactly like I've seen Dad do it. I leave the gun broken.

'No, shut it, like it was before.'

The gun clicks shut and the stranger shudders.

'Now give it to me.' He holds out his hand with the T-shirt on it and catches the gun at the very end of the barrel. Like he doesn't want to touch it again. As if he's scared of it or something.

'Let it go. I've got it.'

He takes it from me, holding it in the shirt, and walks carefully to the top of the river bank. He stops, checking no one's coming, I think. I run up to see what he's doing. I'm not sure about this.

'Okay. You want to take it? Give it back to your old man? Explain to him what happened when the gun was fired? Good luck with that one.' He shrugs his shoulders, as if he doesn't care what I do. Giving me time to think, maybe. Doesn't take me long. I shake my head.

'Right decision. Now, get out of the way. Stand back.'

He throws the gun, really hard and really high. It spins and tumbles in the air then disappears into the thick bracken. I can't even see where it landed. It's a good hiding place.

'No one's ever gonna find that,' he says, picking up his T-shirt.

He gives out a big, long sigh and goes to look at the body. 'Come on now, bud,' he says. 'Let's get him hidden too.'

No way. We can't bury him. It's not right. I'll get another curse on me.

'You take his feet.'

I don't.

'Get his feet. Lift his legs.'

I shake my head. He can't make me do this.

He punches me in the belly. Like a boxer. I bend over and some sick comes out my mouth. It lands on my trainers.

He holds up his two fists and says, 'Want some more?'

I shake my head. A string of sicky spit swings back and forward. I wipe it away.

He puts his shirt back on and reaches for the dead guy's hands. Grasps them tight and pulls. Huge muscles bulge on his arms and shoulders, even his legs. The body starts to move. The poor guy's face is scraping along the ground.

'Help me out here, buddy.' He tugs again and the body moves a bit further. Slowly and not far enough. He looks at me. 'Please.'

I could leave him here and run for it. He's a stranger. He doesn't know where I live. He'd never find me. Anyway, it's got nothing to do with me. He's the one with a dead body in his hands and a gun hidden in the bracken.

Dad's gun. The one I stole from his locked cupboard.

I know this is all wrong, but I need to help. For Dad's sake. I take hold of one ankle with both hands. Try to lift. No wonder the stranger can't manage on his own. I never imagined a thin person could feel so heavy.

'Try again, when I count to three. One. Two.'

On three, I lift with all my might and the body moves a bit further. It takes us ages but finally we get him to the place where we made the hole.

'This will be the hardest part,' says the stranger, 'but we'll manage. On my count, ready?'

We heave on three. Heave again, then push. We're both on our knees, shoving the guy way into his hole in the river bank. Like he's a mole or a rabbit.

I hear a noise. He's heard it too. He looks at me and I lip-read, 'Shit.'

***

CHAPTER 15

A black face stares curiously from the top of the banking. 'Hell's teeth!' The stranger gives a funny kind of laugh. He picks up a stone and throws it. The sheep bleats as if it's annoyed and hurries away.

The stranger blows out a big deep breath and says, 'That was scary.'

How can a big man like him be scared of a black-faced ewe?

'Jeez, Noddy, I thought we'd been rumbled. We'd better get our skates on or the next face looking at us might not be so friendly. Come on, give me a hand to start covering him up.'

We dig with our hands, putting back as much of the dirt as we can, but it doesn't cover the guy.

'This is no good. We can't leave him like this. The first dog or fox that comes by will have him for breakfast.'

I screw up my face.

'Sorry, Noddy, but it's the truth.' While he's talking to me, he sits back on his hunkers and looks at the banking. As if a light bulb comes on in his head, he says, 'Hang on a minute, I've got an idea.'

He pushes past me and climbs up the banking till he's standing where the sheep was. 'Get out of the way, kid,' he says, in a kind of quiet shout. He flicks his hand at me, making sure I get it.

I move down to the side of the burn and watch. Like Andy Murray waiting for a serve, he opens his legs wide. He gets his balance, then springs up in the air. When he lands, a whole lot of soil and gravelly stuff slides down the banking on top of the dead guy.

When he jumps again, an avalanche of dirt rolls towards me. He gets ready again and this time the whole banking gives way and a huge slab of grass slides, with him falling behind it. He rolls out of the way and the landslide comes to a halt. I watch a few wee stones that seem determined to keep rolling all the way into the burn.

I look for the body, but it's disappeared. Sealed into its own wee cave. Completely buried under the river bank.

The stranger walks towards me, dusting his hands off one another. His T-shirt is filthy and his jeans have got blood on the legs. His face is dirty too and his hair is full of soil and grass.

He claps his hands one last time and says, 'Job done. Nobody's ever going to find him in there with two tons of soil on top of him.'

He holds out his hand to me, smiling. 'Good work, buddy,' he says. Think I'm meant to shake hands, but I'm not touching him. I hide my hand behind my back.

'Be like that then.' He gives me a push and I stumble into the water. He drags me out of the burn and shoves me again. 'Move,' he says. Don't like the way his voice sounds, so I move.

When we get to some bigger stones, he leans on my shoulder till I sit down on one.

'Look at me, kid.'

The sun is higher now, kind of blinding me. Wonder if he's doing it deliberately. He waits till I'm looking at him. I put my hand up like a sunshade.

'Listen carefully. You and I are never going to set eyes on one another after today. Soon you'll forget you ever met me. Right?'

I look away, from the sun and him.

'Right, buddy?' he says again. He's waiting for an answer. So I nod.

'Good. You're going to head back to wherever you came from and forget any of this ever happened.'

Not possible. Still can't forget what happened the last time and that was five years ago.

'Right?'

No, not right. How am I supposed to forget that a young guy just got shot and I helped bury him?

'I said, "Right?" Did you hear me?'

Nod. Only meant I heard him. Not that I'll forget, but he doesn't seem to notice.

'However. There's one thing I don't want you to forget. Okay?'

Wish he'd make up his mind. Forget. Don't forget.

'Okay?'

Nod.

'Christ. Why don't you just answer me?'

Shrug my shoulders.

'Never mind. Pay attention. That guy up there?' He points upstream as if he thinks I might have forgotten already. 'Don't ever forget that you're to blame for him dying. It's your fault. You brought the gun. Didn't you?'

Nod.

'It's got your fingerprints on it. Only your fingerprints. You know what that means, don't you?'

He doesn't wait for me to nod this time.

'It means that if he's ever found, even if he's just a skeleton – you know what a skeleton is?'

Of course I know what a skeleton is. He must think I'm stupid.

'Even if he's nothing but a pile of bones, and they don't know who he is, they'll know he was shot and they'll know who shot him. People don't last forever but fingerprints do. They'll hunt you down. They're very good at that, the police.'

He stops talking. To make sure I've got time to think about what he just said. Don't need a lot of time.

'You understand what I'm saying?'

Nod.

'So you'll do your best to forget everything? Forget you ever saw me. But never forget you're a killer.'

I want to ask him how he thinks I can ever forget killing people. Today makes four of them.

'One last thing, before we say goodbye forever. You're going to promise me you'll never tell a soul, not a single person, ever, what happened this morning. Right?'

Nod, over and over and over.

'No, Noddy, that won't do. I've had enough of your nodding. I'm gonna have to hear you promise me.'

Shake my head.

'What is it you kids say? Cross my heart and hope to die? That's it.'

Please, God. Not that.

'Say it, Noddy. Cross my heart and hope to die. So I know you'll keep your promise.'

This can't be happening. Not again.

'I need you to say it. I promise I will never mention this to anyone. Ever. Cross my heart and hope to die.'

If only he knew what happened the last time. He wouldn't want me to say it.

I draw a quick cross on my chest, feel my nails scratching.

He grabs my shirt, pulls me to my feet. Then off my feet. Right up close to his face. 'That's not enough. Say it!' His spittle hits me on the cheek. I want to wipe it away. His eyes are screwed up, mean, and his face is turning red. But I can't say those words. Ever again. No matter what he does to me.

My shirt's going to cut my arms off. Or strangle me. A button pops off and I drop a wee bit. He lets me go. I land on my skinned knee and fall over. He kicks me, in my ribs. I curl up into a ball again. Cover my head. More kicks – my back, my bottom, my legs. Anywhere. Everywhere. Till I don't know where.

***

CHAPTER 16

Think I've been lying here for hours. Don't know when the kicking stopped. Just glad it did. I'm scared to open my eyes. Scared to move. Scared to breathe. Because it hurts. But I can't lie here all day. Mum and Dad will be worried. They'll come and find me, or call the police.

'Get up.'

Oh no, he's still here. Thought he'd gone. Thought that was why the kicking stopped.

'Get up. Now!'

I lift my head, just enough to see where he is.

'Don't worry. I'm not going to hurt you any more. For now. That was a taster of what will happen if you ever talk about this to anyone. Understand?'

Nod, very slightly.

'Understand?'

Push myself up so I can get onto my knees. Wrap my arms round my body, like bandages. He grabs my shirt again and hauls me to my feet. Can't straighten up. Stay doubled over, looking at his shoes. Brown leather, all scuffed and dirty now. Kind of pointy toes. Town shoes.

I nod a few times, so he knows I understand. I really, really do understand. Don't ever want to get hurt like that again. In my whole life.

'Right, Noddy. I'm going to help you up the bank and show you the way back to the path. Then I'm going to wait here and give you a ten-minute start. You don't have to worry. I won't be watching to see where you go. I'm not going to follow you. I'll be going in the other direction.'

He takes my arm and pulls me up the slope. It hurts but I try not to show it. I'm not going to cry in front of him. At the top he shows me a little sheep track through the gorse.

'That's the way we came. It should take you back to the footpath. Where you go from there, I've no idea. Couldn't care less. Now, beat it.'

I walk away a few steps, going as fast as I can with all my sore bits.

'Hey, kid?'

Don't want to look at him.

'Kid?'

What does he want now? Why can't he just let me go? I look round.

'See you later?'

He starts laughing and I know it's because of the look on my face.

'Just jokin, buddy. You'll never see me again. As long as you keep our secret.'

I run and stumble till I'm in the gorse. Its smell makes me feel sick. Don't remember coming this way earlier. But then, I wasn't watching.

I reach a clearing and face the sea while I get my breath back. Rub my eyes, hard, and try to stop the tears. The sea and the sky look just the same as they did earlier, but I know everything has changed. I want my mum so much I start to run again, but my skinned knee makes me limp and my ribs hurt when I breath hard.

What about the gun? Can't go back for it, in case he's still there. I'll come and look for it tomorrow after school. Or at the weekend. If I'm lucky Dad might not find out it's missing for ages. He doesn't shoot it very often. Getting rid of 'pests' himself is just another way to save money.

Nearly there. Can see my tower in the distance. Wish I could lock myself in and not see anybody ever again. That's what I should have done, instead of taking the gun. That would have got their attention. If I'd refused to come down for days. Not even for food or anything. No one would have got hurt. Bit late now for good ideas.

The damage is done. To that poor guy in the grave and to me too. It's not just the pain of the sore bits I mean. It's all the other stuff I was doing my best to forget. The guilt, the sick feeling, the horrible black slime that I've tried so hard to keep in its corner.

What about the curse? I didn't say the words this time, but I thought them. I wanted to say them. To shout them in his face the way I shouted them at Robbie. Does thinking something bad make it real or do you have to say it out loud?

Wonder what the time is? The sun has moved a lot since I got up but that doesn't tell me anything. Don't hear much sound coming from Brackenbrae, but it's always quiet here. The main gate's open. That means Dad's up. Opening the gate is his first job of the day. Eight am sharp. Joyce usually gets here about half-past. I always hear her singing before I go to school. If she starts in the house she usually gives me money for sweeties. She always whispers, 'Shh, it's our wee secret, eh?'

I've made up my mind. No more secrets. I'm going to walk straight into the kitchen and let Mum and Dad see the state of me. Mum will cuddle me and cry. She'll see all my sore bits and they'll ask me what happened. I'll take them along the path to the burn and tell them. I will.

If I'd told them what happened the last time I was in the woods, everything would be different. But I didn't get the chance and then I couldn't. But this time I will, definitely.

Nobody's about. No campers, no workers. The back door's open but the kitchen door's closed. I hear Joyce talking so it must be coffee time. Don't want Joyce there but I've got no choice. I take a deep breath, touch the door handle and stop. Someone else is speaking and I know her voice. Natalie.

She says, 'Should we be doing this?'

'Och, aye. The boss would never grudge us a wee coffee. Last thing he said, before they went off, was, "Keep an eye open for Natalie. Make sure she gets settled in alright." So that's what I'm doing.'

Natalie's here. But Dad's not and Mum's not.

'Anyway, how's your love life?'

'No time for romance, Joyce. I had no idea teachers worked so hard.'

'Away! Nine till, what? Three? Monday till Friday? See the holidays they get? Weeks and weeks. Never at their work and then they've the cheek to say, "Keep yer weans at hame. We're having an inset day." An inset day? An excuse for a skive, if you ask me.'

'Stop it, Joyce. I know when you're winding me up. Tell me more about Brackenbrae. You really think the business is struggling?'

'Work it out for yourself. It's a holiday weekend and I've got one wigwam to clean, and one cabin.'

Natalie bursts out laughing. 'Not a wigwam, Joyce. A *yurt*.'

'A *yurt*. In Ayrshire?'

'Glamping is very trendy. I think they could be on to something. I've got friends that tried it for a hen weekend in the Borders. I understand it's all the rage amongst the West End set.'

'Well, until they all start flocking down here for their glamping holidays, this is still a campsite.'

There's a pause then Joyce says, 'You'll never guess what her ladyship did on Friday? She only stuck a sign at the main gate saying, "No campers." No campers? It's a bliddy campsite!'

Sounds like Natalie's choking on her coffee. 'What did she mean?'

'She meant, "No riff-raff." She doesn't want ordinary folk with their tents. In case they lower the tone.'

'But that's madness. Brackenbrae should be grabbing all the campers we can get and what about hikers? Isn't there a new coastal path or something? I heard some guys talking about it in the Union one night. I'm sure one of them had a book. They were planning to walk it this summer.'

'Aye, well, they better keep walking cos they'll no be pitching their tent here. Unless it's a *yurt*, of course.'

'Oh, Joyce, you're priceless. I've missed you. Listen, how's your husband?'

'Oor Alec? Och, he's alright. Too fond of the drink, but he's a good enough man.'

'Well, to answer your question about my love life, I'm still kissing frogs.'

Joyce laughs, then coughs. 'Waiting for Prince Charming? Well, watch you don't wait too long.' She starts to sing, 'One day my prince will come. One day I'll find my love.'

The sound of her voice makes me cry.

'Shh! You'll wake Charlie!'

They think I'm upstairs asleep.

'How's he doing?'

'His mum says he's "not himself", whatever that means. That's why we've to let him sleep. She says he's awful tired. But that's about as much as they ever tell me. Ask the boss and he'll just say, "I'm sure he's fine." Wait, I've just remembered something. This morning the boss said something like, "I've no idea how he is." Or what was it? "I don't know the answer to that question, to be honest." That's it. He honestly doesn't know how his wee boy is. That's just sad, so it is.'

'The whole thing's sad. All that trauma of his friend dying in the fire.'

She's wrong. You're wrong, Natalie. Robbie wasn't my friend. His mum and my mum were friends. That's not the same and anyway, my mum wasn't really his mum's friend. She was just a woman Mum met at the SWRI one winter when she went to learn how to make scones and knit jumpers and stuff.

'Terrible thing to happen. The wee soul was over here playing with Charlie the day before.'

Not because he was my friend. Only because Mum felt sorry for his mum. I heard her telling Dad. 'She's not really my type, but she kind of invited herself and I didn't like to say no. Poor thing, stuck out there on her own with two kids. In that horrible wee cottage.'

'The next thing we know, there's been a fire. Cottage burnt down and the whole family wiped out in their sleep. The mum and two wee boys, one just a toddler.'

'And Charlie never saw his friend again?' says Natalie. 'How awful for him.'

'Nothing but a blackened shell now, that wee house. On the road to Dunure.'

'Do you pass it on the way to Fisherton?'

'Aye, on the left-hand side.'

'So Charlie sees it when he goes to school?'

'Every day.'

Another pause. A long one this time.

'Oh, Natalie. We'll need to keep an eye on wee Charlie, so we will. See if we can help him.'

***

CHAPTER 17

When he's sure the kid's gone, Gus half-sits, half-collapses onto the grass. Since the moment that gun fired, he's been running on pure adrenaline. Now it seems to have evaporated and he feels sick to his stomach. He puts his head between his knees and waits. The nausea passes but it doesn't take the guilt and fear with it.

What the hell's he going to do now? He's a foreigner, on a limited visa, with no job, practically no money and now he's committed a murder. Whatever spin he likes to put on it, a murderer's what he is. If he gets caught, well, that doesn't bear thinking about.

He'd like to run for home. Trouble is, he's got no money and right now, no way of getting it. Even if he did know someone who could get their hands on the cash, he doesn't want to admit he's a loser. He left South Africa to be a big-time rugby star in Europe. How is he going to tell everyone back home that it didn't work out in France, it didn't work out in Glasgow and now he's blown it in Ayr? This time nothing to do with his rugby or his temper.

The same temper could have killed that kid if he hadn't got it under control in time. Maybe there's something in this 'roid rage' thing. Bad enough on the rugby pitch but kicking the hell out of a child? Man, that's so out of order. Poor little guy seemed genuinely petrified. Still, harsh though it was, it means there's no danger of him telling anyone. Let's hope he's got the sense to lie to his folks if they see the bruises. Say he got into a fight at school or something. Cos, boy, he's gonna have some bruises tomorrow.

Gus gets to his feet. It's time to get out of here. He needs to head back to Ayr to that grotty bed and breakfast joint. It's little better than a doss-house, once you get past the lacy curtains. He'd decided to move out today, find somewhere better, but now he's lost all his money, he's got no option but to sleep there. *If* he decides to stick around for his try-out with Ayr Rugby Club tomorrow.

Realistically, it's likely to take a few days, maybe even longer, before someone reports the hiker missing. How will anyone know where he was when he disappeared? No one starts a manhunt by digging up remote hillsides.

Gus walks to the makeshift burial ground for one last check. You'd never guess a thing. The mini-landslide he created has completely engulfed and hidden the body. The grave looks natural, like any other part of the landscape. Once a few sheep have wandered back and forward to the stream, the bank will look as if it's always been like that. He checks for footprints and scuffs a bit of dirt here and there to cover any tracks he or the kid might have left. The job's a good one. Gruesome, but sorted.

As he retraces his steps to the path, he remembers the guy's rucksack. He can't leave that lying out here for someone to come across. If he takes it back with him to Ayr he's bound to find somewhere to get rid of it. He hoists it onto his shoulder and sets off, trying to remember where he was going before this nightmare kicked off.

What the fuck was he thinking about, getting involved with that kid in the first place? He should have left him there, lying curled up in a ball. Look where being kind has got him. He should have walked on by. Kid wants to wander around the woods at stupid o'clock in the morning, that's not Gus's problem. Then, when he's trying to be nice, making sure the kid's okay, he turns the gun on Gus. Shit, what was that all about? Talk about adrenaline rush. He almost shit his boxers. He thought his time had come.

The boy must be some kind of retard. He was acting strange from the get go. Flinching every time Gus went near him and what about that refusing to speak carry-on? Kid had no idea how to interact with a stranger. It was like that movie where the two hunters wander into backcountry where all the locals are inbred.

Who's gonna believe a kid like that if he does decide to say something? But he won't tell. He understands enough to realise there's big trouble ahead if the guy and the gun ever get found.

Gus pushes on, keen to get off the hillside before anyone sees him. The road over the hill is not as steep as it looked from the coast, and he's soon on the other side and following the directions the blonde doll gave him early this morning, which seems like a long lifetime ago. When his only care in the world was whether he'd get a job throwing a ball about.

There have been surprisingly few cars on the road till now, but when he reaches a narrow stone bridge, he sees a queue forming. His first reaction is to try and hide the dead guy's rucksack from the drivers. But no one knows it's not his own and secondly, nobody seems to give a shit about him. They're all too busy with their own lives. He needs to remember that.

The big hotel on the other side of the bridge rings a bell from Kirsty's instructions. Ayr Rugby Club must be close by, but he can't see any sign of a stadium or pitches. They're a good club, he'd expected a ground big enough to see from the road. He decides this is not the time to go exploring and keeps walking, past a ruined church and further along, a low house with a thatched roof. A cluster of tourists pose for a selfie under the sign that says Burns Cottage. Means nothing to him, but it must be famous.

After a mile or so he stops a woman with one of those doodle dogs. The stupid mutt keeps jumping up on him while its owner pleads with it, 'Noodle, stop. Be a good boy.' She apologises to Gus, 'I take him to obedience classes, you'd never guess. Noodle, leave the nice man alone.'

The nice man would like to kick Noodle in the nuts, an obedience lesson with instant results, but laughs instead and asks her how to get to the seafront.

Ten minutes later, he opens the door to Avonlea Guest House and a bell jangles above his head. Before its echo dies, the same torn-faced woman he met last night appears. She eyes his rucksack suspiciously and for a moment Gus thinks she must know it's not his.

'Checking out early, are we?'

'Got a couple of things to sort in my room. I just popped out for some breakfast.'

'I'm surprised you got served dressed like that.' She points at his T-shirt, her nose screwed up as if she can smell the blood that's smeared down the front.

Why didn't he notice it before? He attempts, too late, to cover it with his hands.

'You look like you've been in the wars.'

'Yeah, I got into a bit of a rumble with some locals last night.'

'Glasgow, probably. Not Ayr boys, I'm perfectly sure. Anyway, you didn't have to go out. We offer breakfast as an option. Full Scottish with tattie scones and everything. I told you that when you checked in.' She made it sound like an accusation.

Gus has no idea what a tattie scone is, but it doesn't sound tempting. Especially if the kitchen operates to the same level of hygiene as the shared bathroom.

'How did you get in last night? The main door gets locked at eleven.'

Jeez, this is worse than living with his mother. Gus wants to tell the old bat to fuck off and mind her own business but decides charm might be a better bet.

Laughing quietly, he lowers his head and smiles, as if he's a bit embarrassed. 'You've caught me. Didn't actually make it back last night. Sorry.'

The woman sniffs and pats at her hair. 'Makes no difference to me where you slept, as long as you're having a pleasant stay at Avonlea.'

'I might be moving on today. Slight change of plan. I was wondering, could you possibly give me a refund if I check out?' That would be one way to get at least a few quid in his pocket.

'Too short notice.' She points to a sign on the wall behind her. A quick glance reveals a list of rules, printed in bold red italics. No drinks allowed. No eating in the bedrooms. No refunds.

'No worries,' says Gus, hoping she doesn't think he's taking the piss.

'Check out's at half-ten, mind.'

'What, even if I've paid for tonight?' Gus had thought he might grab an hour's sleep. Clear his head. Help him to plan his next move.

The woman tips her head towards another sign. This one is in handwritten block capitals. 'Half-past ten. No exceptions,' she says in a voice you wouldn't want to argue with. She hands him his key and says, 'You've got twenty minutes.'

Gus heads for the stairs.

No bed had ever looked so tempting as the meagre single in the corner. What he'd give to slide under the faded nylon bedspread right now and switch off for a few hours. Forget the pile of shit his life has become.

He lowers the hiker's backpack to the floor and sits on the edge of the bed. The sight of the rucksack sends a gush of something vile to the back of his throat. He lies down till it passes. What harm would it do if he fell asleep? Is she really going to come banging on his door in twenty minutes? So what if she does? He can tell her to fuck off. He's paid for the night. Surely the bed is his for twenty-four hours?

Determined to grab some sleep while he can, he strips off the dirty T-shirt and shuts his eyes.

The hiker appears and Gus shoots. He opens his eyes and blinks. What *was* that? He clears his mind, tries to think of something nice. Last night's blonde obliges. His sleepy eyelids droop.

Bang! The hiker dies. Again. This time Gus sees his face. Covered in blood. Gus rubs his hands on his thighs. As if his subconscious believes his palms are covered in the hiker's blood. Gus closes his eyes a third time, scared of what he'll see. He's in the woods. He forces his eyes wide open. Gets off the bed. Rushes to the sink in the corner and splashes cold water on his face. Takes the tiny bar of soap and rips the paper off, desperate to wash his hands. Despite the lack of warm water they're soon clean, but he rubs and scrubs till the sliver of soap becomes a wafer and disappears completely. He rips a towel from its hook and hides his face in the threadbare cloth. There's no comfort in the harsh fabric and the hiker's face appears again. He opens his eyes to banish the image and concentrates on the shape of the sun-filled window.

Gus checks the time. He's got ten minutes till checking out time.

The hiker's rucksack sits in the middle of the floor. Accusing him.

Should he leave it here? Walk out the door and make it his landlady's problem? She doesn't strike him as the type to hand it in to the police. But still. No point in asking for trouble.

He needs to take it with him and dump it at the bus depot. Or the train station. Walk away and leave it. Yeah, and spark a major security alert. He'd heard the announcements at the airport and at Glasgow Central station. Every five minutes a recorded voice made threats about what would happen to your luggage if you left it alone. The Scots seem to be obsessed with unattended luggage and all these places have CCTV cameras everywhere. He'll be seen and recorded.

A dumpster behind a hotel or supermarket might be his best bet. But before he can abandon the bag, he has to make it anonymous. He can't risk leaving any trace of the hiker that could spark off a search. He starts to undo the straps on the hiker's backpack, noticing that it's quality gear. High-end stuff and at least ten times the price of his own grotty old kitbag.

He could keep this bag and bin his own? The idea's a good one, worth thinking about and probably safer than dumping it. Gus upends the rucksack and empties the main compartment onto the bed. The hiker's clothes are crumpled as if he's been on the road some time. They're also top quality. Boxers that boast designer names on their waistband. The kind Gus would wear all the time if he could afford them. Socks with subtle logos and T-shirts with big shout-out brands across the chest. A sweater so soft Gus can't resist touching it with his cheek. Feels like the real deal, some kind of posh, luxury wool? The label confirms – one hundred per cent cashmere.

The outside pockets contain walking gear. A fleece jammed into one. Waterproofs into another. All good quality. Gus recognises the logo but can't place it. He's never owned anything that expensive in his life.

The dude had excellent taste and clearly, plenty of cash.

Gus stops and rubs his hand over his jaw and then his scalp. Feels the stubble but doesn't register the need for a shave. He's going through a dead guy's gear. Checking out the quality and the style, as if this was no more than a clearance sale.

He comes across a bag full of toiletries. Body wash. Deodorant spray. A razor. He sees the hiker's face. Clean-shaven? Hard to tell. Too much blood.

Gus swallows, forcing bitter liquid back down his throat.

Where do you stop with this kind of invasion? You handle a guy's boxers, does that make it okay to look in his toiletry bag? Open his wallet? Go through his personal belongings? You can't get much more personal than a dude's boxers.

Gus fingers the zip on the last pocket. The one where he would keep the important stuff if it was his bag.

He slides the zip. It runs easily, quietly, but Gus cringes at the sound. As if it might wake the whole house and tell everyone he's about to take a dead guy's money. For that's what this is about. Has been all along. He wants to know if there's enough cash to pay for his escape.

The pocket opens. Gus hesitates for a moment. He's not a thief, never has been. But then, he's never been penniless either. Or homeless. Steal or go hungry? It's a no brainer.

He pushes his hand into the pocket and his fingers touch soft leather – a wallet. It doesn't feel very fat. What harm will it do to look inside? His heart sinks. Two tenners and a fiver, all from different Scottish banks. One English ten pound note, with its big picture of the Queen. That makes thirty-five quid. Not even half of what he lost in the stupid arm-wrestling bet last night. Tucked into a separate compartment, he finds a bunch of euros, familiar from his time in France. Gus looks for the orange and blue notes, fifties and twenties. There aren't any.

He counts the cash and counts it again. It's not going to get him on a flight to South Africa, but there's enough to solve his immediate cash-flow problems. He might have to sleep in a shop doorway tomorrow night but at least he's got enough cash for food. He raises the money to his lips and kisses it, then folds up all the notes and sticks them in his hip pocket. He can sort them out later. Change the euros if he needs to. He's got about five minutes left to get the hiker's stuff sorted and his own bag ready to go.

***

CHAPTER 18

They've got it so wrong. Natalie and Joyce. I want to burst in and tell them. Robbie *wasn't* my friend.

Instead I sneak up the stairs to my room. It's still dark, apart from a slice of light at the side of the blind. The bundle I made in the bed hours ago looks just like a boy sleeping.

I run across and climb in, shoving the pillow boy out of the way. Pull the covers up over my head and remember the red throw, out there by the path where somebody will find it.

That's too bad. I can't go back into those woods. Ever. What if the guy's still there, waiting to give me another kicking?

Footsteps on the stairs. Not Mum, she always runs up. Dad takes stairs two at a time, but this person is coming up slowly, as if he shouldn't be in my house. Or doesn't know where he's going.

I pull the duvet up over my face and hold my breath.

The door handle turns, clicking gently like it does when Mum comes in to say goodnight. She thinks she's being silent but I know all the sounds in this house. The handle always does a wee click at the last minute. Then a tiny squeak as the door opens. I wait for the creaky floorboard at the end of my bed.

No creak. Must be the stranger. Looking for me. I should have waited to make sure he didn't follow me home.

Need to breathe but I'm scared he hears me, or sees the covers moving up and down. Why doesn't he just get on with it? Come in and shut the door. Kill me, or whatever it is he's here for. Can't hold my breath any longer. Big breath in.

'Charlie? Are ye sleepin, wee man?'

It's Joyce. I'm safe. I want to sit up and howl, but I don't move.

'Charlie,' she whispers again. 'You okay?'

Eventually the door shuts and her footsteps tell me she's gone downstairs. When she gets to the bottom she says, 'He's still sleeping, Natalie. Is that right, do ye think?'

The kitchen door closes before I can hear what Natalie thinks.

Where are Mum and Dad? This is just like the last time. I want to tell them what's happened but they're not here. They're never here when I need them. They're rubbish. I hate them. Wish I had normal parents and a normal house. In the town. Miles away from woods and the terrible things that happen in there.

The back door bangs shut, the way it always does when Joyce goes in or out. I run to my window and pull the blind away. The sun hits me in the eyes and makes me blink and squint. Joyce and Natalie are crossing the courtyard. Joyce shouts something that makes Natalie laugh. Then Joyce waves bye and goes into the toilets to start cleaning them. Wonder what Natalie would say if she knew about the dead guy. I watch her drag a big suitcase towards the barn where the summer workers live.

It makes me think about the guy's rucksack, lying out there on the hill, waiting for someone to find it. I might as well phone the police right now. Tell them there's a dead man buried on Brown Carrick.

**

CHAPTER 19

It's time he was gone, but Landlady of the Year hasn't come a-knocking yet and there are still a couple of things in the rucksack he wants to check. A travel wallet and a skinny book with a photo on the front. *Ayrshire Coastal Path: The Official Guide Book*. Gus allows a few pages to flicker past his thumb then turns back to something that caught his eye on the first page. It's a message, written in French, but short and easy for Gus to read.

Dear Sebastien,
Here's to a wonderful summer in Scotland. I'm sure you will have fun with the contents of this book!
Sending you all my love, always, Mamie.

Sebastien. He's called Sebastien. Gus says the name out loud, no idea why. Before he knows what he's doing, he finds himself talking to the guy, as if he were here in the room.

'I'm sorry, Sebastien. I really didn't mean to hurt you. But why the fuck did you have to choose that moment to walk into the path of a gun and get yourself killed. It's not just your own life you've screwed up, you stupid bastard. It's mine too.'

Who's this Mamie who's sending him all her love? What if she's his girlfriend? Someone who will come looking for him when she doesn't hear from him in a day or two. Maybe a hiking geek, same as him. 'Here's to a wonderful summer in Scotland.' Shit, that sounds like this Mamie is here too, hiking. Maybe she's on the hill right now, looking for Sebastien, wondering why he hasn't waited for her. Maybe they'd planned to meet up in the pub in Dunure. Shit, shit, shit. It never crossed his mind that the hiker would have company.

Gus tries to picture this Mamie person. Young, like Sebastien, but dressed in hiking clothes that a grandmother could wear. That's it, of course, Mamie's not a name, it's French for Granny. One of the props in Toulouse, a slab of a man, used to talk about his mamie all the time and the other guys ripped it out of him.

Relief makes Gus laugh out loud at his mistake. He shuts up fast in case the landlady hears and remembers he's supposed to have left.

So, this Granny's sure Sebastien will have fun with the contents of a hiking handbook?

'You need to get a life, mate,' Gus says, without thinking. Guilt hits him like a high tackle. He throws the book in an arc towards the pink plastic waste bin under the wash basin. It misses. Topples the cheap flimsy bin and lies there accusing him.

He starts to transfer his own clothes into the rucksack. They only half fill the space, so he pushes the hiker's waterproof and fleece back in. They're too good to dump anyway, Gus might be glad to wear them, if the weather turns bad. If they don't fit, well, he can always sell them. No point in trashing something that might come in handy later.

Taking a deep breath, he opens the travel wallet, hoping for more money, travellers' cheques, anything. He finds a European passport, French, and casts it aside. That explains the euros and the French grandmother. Some insurance-type stuff, some pages that look legal and complicated and a letter, well, an e-mail that's been printed off.

The bottom left-hand corner has a green and blue logo. Meant to be hills and sea by the looks of it, and, in a fancy font, 'Brackenbrae – so much more than a campsite.'

Dear Sebastien,

We're delighted you decided to accept a vacation job here at Brackenbrae. Thank you for sending paperwork – I'm pleased to report that everything seems to be in order and you are authorised to take up your duties here. They will be, as agreed, to organise our club for children and to supervise the swimming pool – not at the same time, don't worry! Your hours and remuneration will be as outlined in our previous correspondence. We may ask you to help us out of a tight spot if we're very busy, but you'll have plenty of free time to explore the local area and of course you won't be the only student working at Brackenbrae, so you can expect some fun with the other guys.

We look forward to meeting you at some point on Monday 28 May. Any taxi from town will bring you out here, but I've heard some refuse to come up the drive. Too many pot-holes, they say. What a joke. Every road in Ayrshire's like the surface of the moon. Anyway, it's a short walk if your taxi drops you at the road-end or you decide to take the bus. Don't make the mistake of getting off too early – at the place along the road. We're a much smaller affair, and much classier. You'll find Brackenbrae's more a 'glampsite' than a campsite.

Regards,

Richard

Firstly, what the hell is a 'glampsite'? Secondly, Sebastien is not going to turn up for work. Today or any other day.

What if this Richard, the owner probably, calls the cops when his babysitter slash pool-boy doesn't report for duty? He might get in touch with Sebastien's folks and check where he's got to. They might start an international search for him.

He folds up the email, his hand shaking in a way he's never noticed before. But then, he's never killed anyone before – no wonder he's scared. Nothing in his life will ever be the same again. Especially when Sebastien is reported missing. Won't take long for that kid to talk and the police will start looking for Gus.

But maybe the campsite owner won't care where Sebastien's got to, as long as he has all the workers he needs to run his place. Maybe Gus is worrying too much. Mr Glampsite will soon find some other sucker to do his child-minding and pool supervising. What a job. Imagine doing that all summer. Mind you, it would be a piece of piss. Any brain-dead fool could do it.

Why would Sebastien's parents assume the worst had happened? Kids go off travelling all the time, don't they? Change their plans without telling their folks. Hell, when did *he* last call his mother? The time at home is a couple of hours ahead so she'll not even be awake yet. Still sleeping off last night's bottle, unless things have changed. When she finally wakes up, Gus won't even cross her mind. He ignores the tiny jab of pain that stings each time he remembers how little his mother cares. Maybe Sebastien's folks will be the same. Getting on with their lives and letting their kid get on with his.

Gus needs money to get home. To make money, he needs a job. There's a job going at this Brackenbrae place. Maybe he could give it a day or two then swing by and ask if there's any chance of some seasonal work. That's not unreasonable, at this time of the year. There must be loads of students in Scotland looking for summer jobs.

Wait a minute, he's due to try out with Ayr Rugby Club. He could hold this job in reserve, in case Ayr don't take him on. He wouldn't be surprised if Glasgow have tipped them off. What if they've said don't touch the South African, he has anger issues? Gus isn't sure he could take another rejection. With all that's happened this morning, will he be able to play his best game and showcase his talent? Being rejected for his temper is one thing. Being told he's not good enough would be much worse. Ayr can stick it up their ass. He can play rugby when he gets home. That's his priority now. Getting home as soon as he can.

He picks up the hiker's passport and opens it again. This time he takes a good look at the photo, expecting to see the red hair that he can't get out of his mind. The definition is so poor the hair looks brown. Did he just imagine that sudden flame of copper in the shaft of sunlight? The dude in the picture could be anyone. Well, maybe not anyone, of course, but any unsmiling white guy with no facial hair, scars or disfigurement.

He looks the age you'd expect a student to be, but hey, what age is a student these days? Gus has played rugby with some guys who seemed to be hell-bent on studying till they're thirty. Or till their rich folks stop paying the bills.

Gus tucks the passport and email into the travel wallet, pushes it into the secure pocket of the rucksack. As he zips it shut, he remembers the book, lying by the bin. Not clever. He kicks the plastic bin out of the way and picks up the book.

He stows the hiker's clothes into the old threadbare holdall he's had since he was a teenager. He sets both bags by the door and scans the room, to make sure he's forgotten nothing. The bed beckons from its murky corner under the eaves. The bed he's paid for.

He adjusts the position of the bags so they're blocking the door and turns the button on the lock so it can't be opened from the outside. As he flops onto the bed, the divan screeches in complaint. Sounds exactly like his landlady, he thinks, as he closes his eyes, hoping for sleep.

***

CHAPTER 20

I get out of bed and run to the bathroom. Skid on my knees to the toilet, just in time to be sick. Even when nothing comes out, my stomach keeps trying. Heaving like it wants to come up my throat and splatter into the toilet too.

I want my mum. She usually comes when I'm sick. She's like a heat-seeking missile. Something tells her I need her and she just appears. Mother's instinct, she calls it.

If she was here she would grab a wet flannel and kneel beside me on the floor. She'd gently wipe my mouth. She'd stroke my hair off my face. She'd hug me and tell me I'll be alright.

But she's not here. I don't know where she is.

I stand up and grab some toilet paper to wipe my own face. Throw it in the bowl with the sick. Press the button and watch it flush away. Try to look in the mirror. My eyes are crying from being sick so everything looks blurry. I can see my face is dirty, all streaky with trails under my eyes. I lift the tail of my shirt to wipe my face. My bare belly looks like I've been paint-balled. Red marks everywhere he kicked me.

I wash my face and dry it on a white towel. Except it's not white now, it's mucky. My shirt's all messy with blood and my shorts too. I take them off and throw them in the dirty-washing basket. Five seconds later I take them out again. Mum will go crazy if she finds them. Can't leave them in there.

I take small, careful steps back to my room and sit on the bed. Everything looks the same as it did this morning. It looks like a wee boy's bedroom. A happy boy with nothing to worry about. Not a boy with kicked-in ribs and another terrible secret to keep.

I shove my clothes under the bed. Where the gun used to be. Grab clean clothes from my drawer. A sweatshirt and jeans. Got to cover my arms and legs.

I go down the stairs, very carefully, listening. Every step hurts, but the house sounds empty.

I open the kitchen door. See my bowl and mug on the table and a glass of orange juice. Why is Mum not here to give me my breakfast?

I take a sip of juice but even though I'm thirsty, it doesn't taste right. Not cold enough, as if it's been out of the fridge for ages.

I open the Coco Pops packet and stick my hand in the bag. Mum hates me doing that but she's not here so I shove a handful in my mouth. They taste bad too. I spit them into the bin and a bit of sick comes up. Spit it out too.

Mum's left me a note in my cereal bowl.

Morning Charlie,

Hope you had a good sleep. Didn't want to wake you.

Dad and I decided late last night that we had to go to a meeting this morning. Boring business stuff.

Have your breakfast. Joyce will be around if you need anything while we're out.

We'll be back in the afternoon. Definitely before teatime. Big Mark will make your lunch.

Remember now, no matter what he says, you are only allowed ONE glass of coke.

Love you. Stay out of trouble.

'Stay out of trouble.'

If only she knew. I'm going back to bed.

I wake up feeling like I'm swimming towards the light from the bottom of a deep pool. The closer I get to the surface, the sadder I feel. Want to sink again, back down to where nothing bad happens, but I'm rising. Can't fight it. I break the surface and burst back into the real world, remembering. Like gasping for air, like a fish that's just been caught. Can't stop thinking about the hiker and the stranger. Wish I could go back to sleep.

The new blind is still closed. With an orangey pink line round the edge. The sky's turning red. That means the sun's setting. I've been sleeping for ages.

I hear voices downstairs. Mum and Dad are back, at last. Don't remember Mum coming into my room. My throat is jaggy, like that time I had an infection, and there's a nasty taste on my tongue. Want to spit but my mouth is too dry. Need a drink of water. I roll over, to knock on the floor, but my ribs hurt too much. I flop onto my back and wait.

At last I hear Mum's footsteps running on the stairs. I pull the covers up to my chin and wait for the door to open.

She tiptoes in. When she sees I'm awake, she says, 'Aw, Charlie. Are you feeling poorly?' Her voice is kind. It makes me want to cry, but I try not to.

She comes and sits on the edge of my bed. 'Poor wee you,' she says, gathering me into her arms. I have to try really hard not to groan with the pain. 'Joyce says she thinks you were sick in the toilet. Is that right?'

Now I'm going to get into trouble for leaving the toilet all covered in sick.

She cradles my head against her chest, like when I was small. Feels good to be cuddled, but she's squeezing too tight. It makes the bruises hurt.

'Sorry,' she says, letting me go. 'I forget you're a big boy now. You don't want your mum's hugs any more.'

She's wrong. Hearing her say that makes me so sad I start to cry.

'Oh pet,' she says, wiping my eyes with a soft tissue. 'Now I feel terrible about going off without you. We didn't think you'd want to come. It was meant to be a quick business meeting.' She makes a kind of 'humph' noise. I can tell she's cross with somebody. Dad likely.

'We're discovering nothing's ever quick in this business. Especially making money.' She's talking as if I'm not even here. Has she forgotten me already?

'You were sound asleep when I looked in on you this morning, curled up like a bundle of bedclothes. I didn't want to disturb you. Have you been in bed all day?'

Nod. Wonder if a lie counts as a lie if you don't say it out loud.

'Maybe I should call Doctor Kennedy to come and have a look at you?'

No way. I love Doctor Kennedy with her funky hair and her crazy glasses. She's funny and she's very, very kind. But she's too good. She'll work out what's happened to me. She always knows what's wrong with people. Then she fixes them. Not even Dr Kennedy can fix this mess. I wish she could, but no one can.

I shake my head and try to stop the tears. The stranger told me to act normal when I got home. Don't do anything to cause suspicion, he said. Wish he'd thought of that before he battered me. If anybody sees my bruises, there'll be trouble. Maybe that's what I should do, let Mum see the damage. She'll call the police. They'll find him and he'll have to confess and then they'll dig up the body. Yes, that's what I'll do. I'll show her how he hurt me. I catch the edge of my duvet and push it down to my waist.

'No,' says Mum. 'You stay there and have another little rest.' She tucks the duvet under my chin, tight and snug round my shoulders. I always feel safe when she does that. 'Mum will fetch you a nice cool drink and we'll see how you feel in an hour or so. Okay, my beloved boy?'

Nod and close my eyes. Mum sits by my side for a while. I feel the mattress move slightly, as if a gentle wave has caught me floating. She gets up and tiptoes out. The usual floorboard squeaks and the door closes with its soft click.

What would happen if I went downstairs now, took Dad by the hand and led him out to the grave? I know what – he wouldn't go. They'd pack me off back to bed. Even if I could make Dad come with me, what then? My fingerprints are on the gun and the gun belongs to Dad. We'll both get sent to jail and the stranger will get off. They won't even look for him.

Mum comes tiptoeing back, then Dad, and I pretend to be asleep. Don't want to see their worried eyes. They leave my bedroom door open. Can hear them whispering on the landing. Dad says they should call the doctor.

Mum says wait till morning, see how I am then. She says I'm like her. Always bounce back after a good night's sleep. 'Just you wait,' she says, 'he'll wake up full of beans.' Not sure about that, Mum.

What if the hiker's got a mum and dad? He'll never see them again.

I imagine him in his lonely grave on the hillside. I'd hate to be out there when it gets dark. Somewhere near my window an owl calls and I shiver, as if I'm watching that horror movie again. Soon all the night creatures will be roaming the hill. Feral cats. Foxes. Sniffing the cool air. Smelling the stranger.

***

CHAPTER 21

Paris, France
Monday 28 May

The sun has spent its day running golden fingers over the city. Evening rays reach across the pale carpet towards Catherine's feet. The pool of light is as red as a bloodstain, and she moves her foot away.

The only sound in the apartment is the impatient tapping of her fingernail on the hall table. She studies her reflection in the mirror. Her face looks older, drawn and nervous. What if Sebastien doesn't want to speak to her? What if he is still cross with her?

She takes a step back from the table, avoiding her reflection and moving away from the tall vase of lilies that always sits there. Normally she loves the way their scent permeates the whole house, but tonight, standing this close to the huge, waxy heads, she feels nauseated. A tiny click on the line confirms that, after endless weeks, a connection is finally being made. 'At last,' she sighs. Her time in the wilderness is almost over. In a few seconds, she'll hear his voice again, that infectious laugh, his gentle teasing. She takes one deep breath and blows it out again, preparing herself. She has already decided how she'll start the conversation, but she hopes their chat will be natural and easy, the way it's always been.

'It has not been possible to connect your call.' The line goes dead.

She mutters a quiet and most unladylike swear word and dials again, glancing at her watch then scolding herself for her impatience. The same dispassionate voice informs her that her call cannot be connected. She knows Sebastien's number off by heart. Still, she tells herself, she must have misdialled. Glad to have an explanation for his failure to pick up, she puts the phone down. Then, consulting a little notebook, she checks the number and redials.

Maybe she ought to have called earlier, but she wanted to wait until Eric came home so they could enjoy the call together. Also, if she were to be frank with herself, she would have to admit how much she needs Eric's moral support at the moment.

Even though it's only seconds, the longer it takes to get through, the more her anxiety grows. Surely her precious boy will not ignore her call? That has never been Sebastien's way. The line sounds different this time; the call's going to be answered. She holds her breath. When the robot speaks again, she slams the phone down. Her shoulders sag under the weight of anticlimax and disappointment.

'I can't get through, Eric. Or he's not answering. It looks as though he doesn't want to speak to us, or perhaps I should say, to me.' Her voice catches. As she hangs up, the last rosy ray of light disappears, leaving the hall gloomy and lifeless.

Eric comes and puts his arms around her. She leans against him and wilts into his embrace. He feels solid and he smells good, a mixture of woollen sweater and musky aftershave.

'Catherine, there are a hundred reasons why he might not answer his phone. This is his first day so he's probably still at work. Remember they're an hour behind in the UK. Or he's already settled in and too busy having a good time with his new friends, or his battery is run down, or he's broken his phone, or he's run out of money to pay the bill. We don't even know what his network coverage is like. There may be no signal. It's Scotland, remember. Fairly primitive place from what I can make out.'

She says nothing.

'Would you like me to try on my mobile?'

'Not sure it will make any difference.'

'Let me get my phone and we'll give it a shot. What is there to lose?'

'No, not tonight. I feel wrung out. We'll try again tomorrow.'

'Do you think perhaps his employer may have confiscated his phone?' He holds her away from him and beams at her. 'Anything to stop that infernal ringtone of his.'

Mostly to please him, Catherine smiles, thinking of the ridiculous cartoon tune Sebastien downloaded a few months ago. She tries to keep the smile intact as she looks up into Eric's face. 'I just feel so disappointed. It feels as if he's been gone forever and I was really looking forward to speaking to him. All day I've been waiting to make that call. I expected to hear his voice tonight and now I can't. Oh, Eric, I miss him so much. How could I have been such a fool, letting him go like that?'

'I know you miss him, darling. I understand exactly how you're feeling. I was really rather keen to chat with him tonight myself.' He lets go of her, giving her upper arms a little squeeze of reassurance. 'Why don't you go and mix us a G & T while I fetch my briefcase? Use that new botanical gin Danielle and Vincent brought and remember, cucumber slices, not lemon.'

Catherine busies herself with preparing the drinks. As the ice cubes tumble musically into the crystal glasses, she examines her feelings. Nervousness she can understand. Sebastien's never been away from home before. It really is a 'big deal' as he put it. She slices cucumber into wisps then decides chunky might be better for a cocktail. Her guilt she can understand too. She behaved abominably. Like a spoiled child. It's only right she should feel remorse. She lifts the heavy gin bottle and unscrews the cap, raising the bottle to her nose and inhaling the fragrant spirit. She pours a generous amount into Eric's glass and a careful measure into her own.

What she can't understand is this constant anxiety. No matter how hard she tries to distract herself or tell herself she's being silly, she cannot get rid of this awful feeling that something has happened to her son. A fresh wave of panic washes over her and she tilts the bottle again, sloshing more gin into her glass. This is not the time to be frugal or calorie-conscious. The tonic water, fresh from the fridge, opens with a whisper and the liquid sparkles as she pours, just a splash for Eric and a flood for her. The cucumber drops in and a glass swizzle stick sends the cocktail swirling as she carries the tray onto the balcony.

She and Eric fell in love with this apartment and paid a premium for its view of the Paris skyline. No matter how often she stands on this balcony, she never tires of looking out over the city where she and her son were born. The evening sun has cast the Eiffel Tower in solid gold and painted the white stone of Sacré-Coeur a deep coral pink. She puts down the tray and leans on the balcony rail for a few minutes before she smooths her skirt and sits down at the table.

When Eric appears, phone in hand, she sets his glass in front of him and raises hers, waiting.

'Sorry it took me so long. This looks delicious,' he says, touching his glass to hers. The crystal sings like a tuning fork. 'Cheers, darling. Here's to Sebastien.'

'Sebastien,' she says, her voice catching. She smiles, stretching her lips tight and her eyes wide, to keep tears at bay.

'Now, let's get a hold of the little bugger.' He grins, knowing she'll react. Ever since Sebastien was tiny, his father has affectionately called him 'you little bugger'. When he wouldn't sleep. When he dirtied a freshly changed nappy.

'Remember when he found the box from La Maison du Chocolat you'd hidden for my birthday?' She smiles, picturing Sebastien as a four-year-old covered in luxury chocolate. 'He didn't even like them.'

'No, but the little bugger had to try every single one in the box to work that out, didn't he?' They laugh together, the first time for a while.

It goes quiet as they each take a sip of their drink. On the street far below a wailing siren races to a distant emergency, and a cavalcade of cars, horns blaring, announce a wedding party en route to their celebrations.

Catherine takes another mouthful, much larger this time, enjoying the sensation of ice, the sharp taste of the gin and the effervescence of the tonic. She waits for Eric to speak.

'Scotland and England are the same, aren't they?'

'Well, I'm not sure everyone would agree. Don't the Scots want independence, like the Basques and the Catalans?'

Eric laughs. 'I don't mean politically. I know they're very different culturally. Scotsmen wear skirts, for God's sake. The English are more like Parisians.'

'Are they?' Catherine raises her eyebrows. 'I wouldn't have thought so.'

'Anyway, I meant the dialling code. Is it zero, zero, forty-four for Scotland as well as England?'

Catherine puts down her glass and slaps her forehead dramatically. 'Oh, Eric, I'm so stupid!'

'I'll give it a go.'

She adjusts the front of her hair, laughing with embarrassment. 'I forgot to add the international dialling code. No wonder I couldn't get through.'

'Shh. It's ringing.' He holds his phone out, offering it to her. She shakes her head. She's lost her nerve. Anyway, it's probably better if Eric speaks. She watches his face, trying to read his expression. A tiny reaction tells her the phone's been answered. Eric clears his throat.

'Hello, Sebastien.'

Catherine feels sick with relief. All that stupid fear for nothing.

'How are you doing?'

Catherine moves to her husband's side and puts her head close to his, so she can hear her son's voice, planning to listen for a bit before she speaks to him. At last.

Eric turns to look at her and shakes his head.

'Well, son, we just wanted to say hello and hear how things are going. We understand how busy you must be. It's great that you're having a good time. Give us a quick call when you pick this up, will you? We're both dying to talk to you.'

Eric offers her the phone again, nodding his encouragement for her to say something, add to the message, talk to the voicemail.

She can't.

***

CHAPTER 22

Brackenbrae
Tuesday 29 May

Thomas blows his whistle and the Fat Controller says, 'Come on, Thomas. Time to go.'

I bang The Fat Controller on the head to shut him up. Stupid alarm clock. Wish I'd lost that in the bracken instead of the gun. Didn't need an alarm to wake me. I've hardly been asleep. Couldn't get comfy all night. I'm hurting too much, all over.

Need to get up before Mum comes. She'll make me take a shower and I can't let her see me. She's not supposed to come into my room or the bathroom without knocking. But she still does, sometimes.

I've got to pretend everything's fine. Or she'll send for Doctor Kennedy.

Can hear Mum's voice snipping at Dad before I even open the kitchen door. Think they've forgotten how to be nice to each other.

Cough to clear my throat. To let them know I'm coming.

'Hello, wee man,' says Joyce.

I smile because I like Joyce, but why is she even here?

'Aw, look,' she says, 'he's feeling better. That's magic, so it is.'

Mum comes and hugs me. It hurts so I squirm, and she says, 'Oh dear, my boy's getting too big for cuddles.'

'Ach, they never get too big for a hug from their mammy. Charlie's just embarrassed cos I'm here. Well, I need to get on with my work. Now, Boss, you're sure it's okay if I slip away early? Only appointment I could get. A cancellation. It was either that or three weeks' time. It's terrible so it is, the time ye've to wait to see a doctor.'

'Shortage of GPs, Joyce,' says Dad. 'Stressful job these days. Nobody wants it.'

'For the money they get, I'd take their job, stress or no stress.'

'Ah, that's the trouble, Joyce. We couldn't do their job. Anyway, looks like our boy here won't be needing the doctor after all.' He ruffles my hair and turns to Mum. 'See? Told you he'd be back to his old self after a good sleep.'

'He still looks a bit peaky to me. What do you think, Joyce?'

I want to shout, 'Hello-oh! I'm right here.' Hate it when they talk about me as if I'm not even there.

I sit down and lift the packet of Coco Pops. Undo the plastic clip we put on bags. 'Cos Mum goes mental if we forget. The smell of chocolate makes me gag. Too much like yesterday. I shut the clip again.

Mum's watching me. I know that look. Suspicious. Open the clip and pour some Pops. Drown them in milk and start supping. Mum says, 'How many times, Charlie? Take your cap off at the table. Remember your manners.'

'Right, thanks for the coffee,' says Joyce, standing. 'Where do you want me to start? In the house?'

'Perfect, thank you, Joyce,' says Mum. 'Oh, and please remember to do under the beds, will you?'

I shove my chair back and run for the stairs. Three at a time. Crawl under my bed to get the dirty clothes. Can't reach the shorts, they've landed right at the back against the wall. I crawl in, army-style, hoping Joyce won't appear with the hoover.

I grab the shorts and run for the bathroom. Pass Joyce at the top of the stairs and slam the bathroom door shut before she can stop me. I turn the lock and lean against the door for a minute while I try to decide what to do. I could throw them out the window and hope they land on the roof. But what if the wind blew them down into the yard? Maybe I could wash them myself. But then how would I get them dry? Or even clean? Could I flush them down the toilet, maybe? Imagine if they got stuck. I could rip them or cut them up and flush them away, a wee bit at a time. I'm opening the cabinet to look for scissors when Joyce calls out, 'You okay, wee man?' She bangs on the door. 'Charlie, are you all right? Wait there and I'll get your mum.'

I put my hand over my mouth and blow hard. It makes a big, loud farting noise like James McTaggart showed me.

'Oh, sorry, son. I'll go and leave you in peace.' A moment later the hoover starts to wail. I wait till it moves away from the door then I strip off my clothes and put yesterday's on. Even touching them makes me want to be sick, never mind putting them on next to my skin. I put my clean clothes on top of the dirty ones and flush the toilet, twice.

I open the door and peep out. They're at the bottom of the stairs. Looking up.

'Okay, mate?' says Dad.

Nod. Smile, as if I'm embarrassed, then hurry downstairs. Trying not to show how much my bruises hurt when I walk, I head for the back door.

'Wait, Charlie. You've not finished your cereal.'

Dad says, 'He'll come back when he's hungry. Don't worry.'

'Charlie!'

When Mum sounds like that everyone does what she says, even Dad. My hand's already on the door knob. I could ignore her and go. But I don't. She's walking towards me. She's noticed something.

She plonks my baseball cap on my head and pulls down the skip. 'Don't forget your cap,' she says, 'and come in for some Factor 50 if it gets sunny, will you?'

I nod and try to make a run for it but the jeans on top of the shorts are too tight. I kind of waddle out the door.

'Don't bang the door,' she says, as I close it behind me. Quietly, for once, to keep her off my case. Round the side of the house and across the courtyard, pass the old stables, where the Kidz Klub meets. Not going to it this summer. I've decided. Even if Mum wants me to. I know she only liked me to go cos it kept me 'out of her hair'. Stupid thing to say. As if I'd want to be in her hair.

The tower looks strong and safe. That's why it was built. For the family who lived here to hide from bad stuff and to keep watch. Just like me.

Mum doesn't like me coming in here. Dad knows that but he doesn't tell on me. He even helped me with the ladder, so I can get up to the flat bit. You could go even higher in the olden days, Dad says. It's not safe now. I'm not allowed to go up there. Nobody is. So it's a perfect place to hide things. Like clothes covered in dirt and blood.

Get them off as quick as I can. Once the door's barred. I bundle them into a tight ball and throw. They go up in the air. Then separate and float back down. The shirt swoops and lands on my face. Yuk! Snatch it off. Quick! Roll them into a tight sausage and throw harder. This time they fly up and kind of wait there, hanging in mid-air. Get ready to catch them and keep them off my face. The shorts land on the ledge and disappear, but the shirt opens like a bird spreading its wings and hangs in the air for a second. Then it drifts down again. Need to weigh it with something. That's why the shorts were easier. They've still got some ammunition in the pocket. Shouldn't have been throwing that stuff about. Forgot. Anyway, they've gone. I don't need to worry about them any more.

I pick a stone out of the wall by the door where it's crumbling a bit. Wrap it in the shirt and throw. Up it goes. Then the stone comes out and keeps flying. Hear it landing on the ledge with a clatter. The shirt's going to come down again. It snags on the edge. Flaps a bit in the draught. I wait, with my hands ready to catch it. It's stuck. Not up, not down, just hanging there, red and brown with the dead guy's blood.

Maybe I could climb up and get it. If I wasn't sore everywhere and scared of falling.

I climb the ladder and lean out towards the shirt. No way. Can't reach it. Need a long stick or a brush maybe, one of Joyce's.

I go back down the ladder. On the first level there's a kind of platform thing that I can walk on. That's where I have my den. Mum says it's too dangerous, but Dad says grown men have walked on that ledge for centuries and it hasn't collapsed yet. He says if I'm careful, it's okay. Just don't tell Mum. As if.

There are four windows. Well, not windows. Glass wasn't invented in those days. Holes in the wall. Spyholes. For seeing out. To watch for enemies.

***

CHAPTER 23

Paris

Catherine's mobile rings as she's going down the escalator into the Métro. She slips the silky rope handles of her carrier bags onto her right arm and unzips her handbag. Since the day she had her wallet stolen she keeps her bag zipped closed at all times. Even here, on a moving escalator, she's not comfortable with her bag open. Any one of the passengers streaming past on her left could rob her and be gone down the tunnel before she could react. She puts her fingers into the little pocket where she keeps her phone and takes it out, clutching her unzipped bag close to her body. Sebastien's name is on her screen. Sebastien's calling! Fumbling like an idiot she slides her fingertip across the screen to accept the call and raises the phone to her ear.

It stops ringing.

'Damn. Damn. Damn.' The woman in front of her turns round and gives her a curious look, which Catherine ignores. 'Damn,' she says again, defiantly.

Was she too slow to answer? Or did the signal die as the moving staircase takes her way below street level? She checks the icon. No signal.

Catherine takes a step to her left and runs down the remaining stairs, not caring who she bumps or jostles as she passes. When the last metal stair flattens and disappears underground, she steps off and hurries over to the up escalator. Cursing her high heels, she runs past her fellow passengers until a group of tourists block her path, standing two abreast and laughing noisily.

Catherine mutters an apology and squeezes past.

'I told you, John. Parisians are the rudest people on the planet,' says a voice that sounds uncannily like the Queen.

The tourists laugh but Catherine doesn't care. She's got to get this call. 'Come on, come on,' she mutters as someone else steps into her path. Have these people no idea of etiquette?

She sees a patch of sky and pale grey buildings with their little wrought-iron balconies. Cars and taxis honk at each other and at pedestrians foolish enough to jaywalk on the Champs-Elysées. At last she's free to cross the broad pavement and find a space against a wall where she can stand, out of the crowds. She selects 'Recents' and taps Sebastien's name. Praying he'll answer, she clasps the phone to her ear and raises her eyes in supplication. On the top of the Arc de Triomphe tiny people stand looking down, as if they're watching her. The phone rings and rings. Suddenly, 'Hello?'

Catherine checks her screen. It says Sebastien. No mistake.

'Hello?' A woman's voice.

'Hello? Sebastien?' Stupid thing to say but she can't help herself.

'No, sorry. You don't know me. My name's Jen Wilson.' The woman is speaking English, but her accent is not one that Catherine has ever heard before.

There's a pause and she has no idea what to say to fill it.

'Hello? Hello? Is there anybody there?'

'Yes,' says Catherine, hesitantly. 'I'm here. I'm Sebastien's mother. May I speak to him please?'

'Sorry. He's no here. Jist me. I've got his phone.'

Clearly. But why?

'It wis lyin in oor field.'

'Pardon me?'

'The phone. In oor field. I found it when I went oot to bring the kye in for milkin. I'm surprised it's even workin. But I sat it on the Aga for a while to dry it oot, right enough.'

Catherine has no idea what on earth the woman is talking about. 'I see,' she says, although she doesn't.

'The battery wis flat. We had to go into Dumfries yesterday to buy a charger an that. It's been plugged in for hours and see? Now it's sorted. I was going to hand it in to the polis, but my man says they'll jist keep it. A nice phone like that.'

'Is Sebastien there, please?'

'Nup. He's away. As far as I ken, anyway.'

'He's away? Far?' It was all she could make out.

'Aye. I mean, yes. Where are you?'

'Paris. I'm in Paris.'

'Paris, you say. Very nice. Never been tae Paris. Well, that's tricky.'

'Sorry?'

'For getting the phone to your son.'

'My son's not here.'

'Oh, right. Is he still away hiking?'

Catherine doesn't know what to say. Sebastien should have started his holiday job by now, but she has no idea where that is. 'Yes,' she says. 'Hiking. Why was he in your field, if you don't mind me asking?'

'He was camping. Gave us a right laugh, I can tell ye. We watched him climbing the gate.' The woman laughs, as if she can't resist. '*We* ken that's Bob the Bull's field, but your boy didnae.' She laughs again. 'Oh Jeez, you should have seen him. Running for his life, like one of yon Olympic sprinters. Auld Bob would never hurt a soul, big docile lump that he is. But your boy jumped that five-bar gate like the hounds of hell were on his heels. We were having a cuppa in a wee patch of sunshine at the front of the farmhouse. Oh, the laugh we had.'

Catherine can picture the scene and she smiles, despite herself. The woman's laughter is infectious. 'Was he okay?'

'He was fine. His pride was wounded, maybe, but he could see the funny side. We don't usually encourage folk wandering into our fields. We had a crowd of hippies one year, in the field beside the burn, and we could not get rid of them. But your boy, Seb, you could tell he was different. My man went out and showed him where he could pitch his tent, near the house, and I handed him out a wee bit of dinner and a mug of milk once he got himself organised. He's a lovely young man. A real credit to you.'

Catherine finds she's getting used to the accent, enough to understand that these good people have been kind to her son and are now being kind to her. 'Thank you very much, Mrs Wilson.'

'No bother. We fair took to him, my man and me.'

Not a clue what that means but it sounds warm and complimentary, so Catherine thanks the woman again.

'Och, my goodness, what's a shower and a wee bite of breakfast to us? We've eggs galore. We were sorry to see him go.'

Not as sorry as I was, Catherine thinks.

'Anyway,' says the woman, suddenly business-like, 'how are we going to get Seb's phone back to him?'

Seb. It's years now since he asked to be called Seb. She refused, insisting on using his given name, even when he went to high school and everyone called him Seb. Same with her refusal to eat informally some nights at the breakfast bar in the kitchen or on the balcony. No, no, it had to be the dining room table in the evenings. Why was she always so determined to do things her way?

'Hello? Are you still there?'

'Sorry, yes,' says Catherine. 'I was thinking. Would you mind sending it here? We'll pay for the postage, of course.'

'Not a bit of it. You give me your address and I'll get the phone away to you, first class. I'll put the charger thing in too. It's no use to us.'

'That's very generous of you, Mrs Wilson.'

'Aye, well, don't believe everything you hear about the Scots.'

Catherine gives the woman her address and offers once more to cover her expenses.

'Indeed you will not. I'll be offended. Hang on a wee minute, my husband wants to say something.'

Catherine hears a deep, gruff voice in the background, his accent even thicker than his wife's.

'Aye, Wullie here says, will ye do us a favour?'

'Certainly. Anything.'

'Tell that boy he's never to pass our door without lookin in.'

***

CHAPTER 24

Ayrshire, Scotland

Arran's so clear today, I can see the houses from here. The ferry's half-way across, leaving a trail of white water. Wish I was on the boat to Arran or anywhere.

It's very quiet. Tranquil, that's what Dad always calls it. Unless Joyce is singing. She's not in a singing mood today. Maybe because she's got to go to the doctors. Hope she's okay. Don't want any more people dying.

Back to school tomorrow. This is a teacher training day. One time, on a training day, they had a meeting about me. I heard Miss Lawson whispering it to Mrs Hall when she came in to borrow some felt tips.

I was sure I'd be sorted for going back to school tomorrow. Now I'm not sure I will. My plan backfired on me and I've got an even worse secret to keep.

I hear Dad's voice down below in the courtyard. Can see him from Spyhole Number 4. He's on his mobile. He looks up from his phone and smiles. Not at me. He doesn't know I'm up here. That's what's so good about this place. I see and hear loads of stuff and no one ever knows I'm watching.

Dad walks forward, his arms open, as if he's going to give someone a hug. 'Natalie! Great to see you again. Welcome back.'

Natalie steps into Dad's hug. She looks different from last summer. Something's changed, maybe the colour of her hair. She looks even more beautiful. Same smile that lights up her whole face. Thought nothing could make me feel happy again, but Natalie's smile helps.

'Let's get everyone rounded up,' says Dad, his Jolly Joe voice booming up to me. 'Once we make sure no one's missing, we'll give them the tour. You know the place as well as I do, Natalie. Maybe you should be the one showing the new staff round.'

Natalie giggles, like a wee girl. Miss Lawson says laughter's like a bug, you get it from other people. For a second, I catch the giggles from Natalie. Then she stops and I remember I've got nothing to laugh about.

I need to catch Dad on his own. Maybe get him to come in here. But that shirt's still dangling there. If I waste any more time trying to hide it, I'll miss Dad. Got to go. Can sort it later.

I reverse carefully down the ladder and take one last look back up. It's flapping there, like a blood-stained flag after a battle. Kind of taunting me.

I take the wood bar off the door and open it just wide enough to peep out. Don't like anybody to see me coming in or out. Coast's almost clear. I wait till Dad disappears back into the house and step out, closing the door behind me.

'Charlie!'

I feel my face going pink.

'Do you still do hugs?'

Nod.

'Not too grown up?'

I smile and Natalie hugs me. Too tight for my sore ribs. I make a kind of groaning noise. Natalie holds my shoulders and leans down a bit. She takes my cap off and looks into my eyes. Her face is all hopeful. I look away.

'It's great to see you again, Charlie,' she says, handing me my cap. 'I've been looking forward to spending some time with you this summer. Look at you, you've got so tall.'

Why do adults say that kind of stuff? Kids don't go around telling them they've got so fat. Or so old. It's a stupid thing to say.

At least Natalie doesn't do that thing to my hair. That head-rubbing, hair ruffling thing a lot of them do. I stick my cap back on in case she's thinking about it and nod, cos it's rude not to answer.

Even though it wasn't a question. Anyway, I'm only about two inches taller than last year. Mum measures me all the time, like she's worried I'm going to be a dwarf or something. So it's a really stupid thing for Natalie to say. I just stand there with my arms by my sides.

'Listen, Charlie, we'll have a chat soon.'

Did she really say that? Natalie of all people?

'Once I've got settled in, eh? Speaking of which, I'd better go. Your dad wants us all in the café for a welcome meeting. Then he's going to do the tour. You coming to Kidz Klub this year?'

Wasn't planning to. But she's so full of fun, she makes me want to go along. I do a kind of shrug thing with my shoulders.

'Excellent. You're such a good help to me. Don't know what I'd have done without you last year. After Joe left.'

I liked Joe. Not sure why he left before the end of the summer. But Natalie made me her second-in-command for the last week and we had loads of fun.

'Listen, I've got to run. Here's the boss. Will you pop into the playbarn later and help me remember where everything is?'

Of course I will. I'd do anything for her.

Dad's heading for the café. Doing that striding thing. Taking huge giant steps. I run to catch up but I've got to kind of jog alongside, he's going so fast. I catch his arm. Make him slow down. He frowns at me. 'What is it, Charlie?'

I tug on his arm till he stops. Got to tell him.

Dad pulls his arm away from me and sorts the papers he's carrying. 'What's up?' He can't be bothered with me.

How do you tell your dad there's a dead boy buried on the hillside?

I tug on his sleeve, pulling his arm. He drops his papers. He sighs, really loud, and bends to pick them up. I try to help and he says, 'Don't mix them up. You've caused enough trouble.'

He shuffles his papers, putting them back in order. Without looking at me he says, 'Sorry, Charlie, didn't mean to snap at you. It's just, can't this wait? See, I've got to go and brief the summer staff and I'm already running late.'

He looks at my face for an answer. I pull on his arm again.

'Son, I'm really busy right now. Can't this wait?'

Before I can stop it, a great big tear runs down my face, but Dad doesn't even notice.

'Come on,' he says, shifting his papers so he can put his arm round my shoulders. I want to cuddle into his side, but he starts walking. Taking me with him. 'Let's go meet the new staff. You'll see Natalie.'

I pull my cap down a bit. Don't want Natalie to see me crying or wiping my eyes every time a tear pops out. Can hear people in the café. Laughing. Natalie's giggle and a deeper laugh that I don't recognise.

Dad pushes the door open and walks in ahead of me. Three people are sitting at a table, their backs to us. Natalie and the two new guys I've never met before.

'Hello, everyone,' says Dad, in his boss voice. I stay behind him and sit on a chair at a different table, keeping my head down so Natalie won't see my face, all blotchy from crying. She'll think I'm a baby.

'Welcome to Brackenbrae,' says Dad. 'This won't be formal, don't worry. Just a chance to get to know each other and the campsite.' I've heard all this before; so many times I could do the welcome talk myself. Unique setting, blah blah. Offering something different, blah blah. Austerity, blah. Staycation, blah. Glamping, yurts, eco-camping, biomass energy blah-de-blah-de-blah. Usually I switch off, think about football or something. Interesting stuff. Not today. Today I'm concentrating on every word he's saying. To keep my mind off the guy in the grave. I'm going to tell Dad, the first chance I get.

'Right, Natalie, you're an old hand so you can go first. Tell these new guys a bit about yourself, and bring me and Charlie here up to date at the same time. If you want to mention what a great place this is to work and what a good boss you've got, that will be fine by me.'

They all laugh when Natalie says, 'Nothing like fishing for compliments, Boss.'

Dad gives a kind of cough. Like he's pretending to be embarrassed.

'You're right, though,' says Natalie. 'Brackenbrae is a lovely place to work. I mean, look at that view.'

I know without looking she'll be pointing to the window that Mum and Dad argued over for weeks the winter before last. Dad wanted to put new glass in the old frame. 'Keeping the character' he always calls it. Mum was determined they needed to 'capitalise on our best assets'. She won. Weeks later, a gigantic lorry arrived, with a crane and everything, and a huge pane of glass was set into the old stone. Turned the whole wall into a window, but it closed the café for half the summer.

Natalie and Dad sound like they're giving a geography lesson. Talking about Arran and Ailsa Craig. The bird colony. The curling stones. Although it's not his turn to speak, one of the new guys interrupts. Miss Lawson tells us off for that. He tells us his name is Pim. Keeps asking questions. Showing off, Miss Lawson calls it.

'What species of birds, please, and is it true that Ailsa Craig granite makes the best curling stones in the world?' What a geek. The other one doesn't speak. Think I'll like him better.

I stare out at the scenery while Natalie tells us about herself. Arran's gone all misty like it's ready to disappear. I've heard Natalie's story before but it's not hard to listen again. She's got a nice voice. She tells us she's wanted to be a teacher since she was five years old. That she used to line up her dollies and teddies and teach them.

'It's my passion,' she says. I can tell she means it. 'I can't wait to qualify and get started.'

Want to peep round Dad and watch her. But I don't. In case she says, 'Oh, Charlie. What's the matter?'

'I love being here, organising Kidz Klub. Best job in the world. Thanks for having me back, Boss.' She stops talking and the café goes quiet. Except for Big Mark banging saucepans through the back.

'I should like to go next, please,' says Pim.

He would.

He tells us he's from the Netherlands, but we can say Holland if we find it easier to remember. Tells us a load of stuff about himself. Bor-ing. I stop listening for a while. But then I start to worry and feel sick again, so I tune back in to take my mind off it. He's still showing off. Claiming he speaks fifty languages. Or maybe it was fifteen. Still don't believe him. When he says he's here to work on reception and in the bar, so he can improve his English, Natalie groans loudly.

'Come off it, Pim,' she says. 'I was born here and your English is already better than mine.'

'Yes, but that is understandable. You are Scottish. The language here is not the same as the proper Oxford English which I have studied.'

Can't resist a quick look at Natalie.

She spreads her hands and raises her eyebrows but she's looking at the other new guy.

Dad says, 'Thanks, Pim. Well, that just leaves you, Sebastien.'

***

CHAPTER 25

He clears his throat, ready to say something, though he's not sure what, when the boss says, 'Sorry, hang on a minute. I forgot someone.' He leans back in his chair so they can all see the kid sitting behind him. A boy, small and slight, who looks about ten. No one's ever gonna make a rugby player out of this kid, that's for sure. His head is down as if he's sulking about something and his face is hidden under the skip of a baseball cap that looks far too big for him. The boy doesn't want to be here and he's making it obvious. He lifts a hand to swipe at his eyes. Poor little sod. Young enough to cry but old enough to feel embarrassed about it – a shit stage, but every boy has to go through it.

'Everyone, please meet Charlie.'

The boy sits staring at his feet, as if he's just discovered them at the end of his legs. He does not respond or react in any way to his father's words.

In a patronising voice that would annoy any self-respecting kid, the boss says, 'Charlie's my son and my right-hand man.' The boy doesn't look up, even when his father says, 'Smile, Charlie.'

'Actually, Boss, he's *my* right-hand man,' says Natalie, as if she's trying to lighten things up. 'My second-in-command, aren't you, Charlie?'

Charlie's ears flush crimson and it's hard not to feel even more sympathy for him. He's clearly got a crush on Natalie.

She says, 'Charlie's a great help in the summer holidays. Wait till you guys see.'

There's still no reaction from the boy other than his chin turning a deep pink that matches his ears.

Everyone seems to wait a moment to let the child say hi or something but he's either in a really bad mood or tongue-tied with embarrassment. Maybe both.

The boss gives them all a wave and announces, 'Charlie says hi. You guys will get to know him later. He's a great kid.'

No wonder he's got issues if they treat him like a moron all the time. The atmosphere is awkward and it's hard to know what to do next.

'Hello, Charlie,' says Pim. 'I am very pleased to meet you and looking forward to becoming your friend.'

The kid doesn't look up. Probably avoiding eye contact, thinking the last thing he wants to be is Pim's pal. Who can blame him?

Natalie comes to the rescue.

'Charlie's great fun once you get to know him, just a bit shy. But hey, I'm dying to hear about Seb.'

'You're right, Natalie. Time we heard what the swimming champ has to say for himself.'

'Euh, ok,' he says quietly, hoping he sounds at least a little bit French. 'Hi, everybody.' He raises his hand in a mock salute and reminds himself to smile. *Make them like you so they don't hate you.* His motto in life. Handed down by his father. The only advice he ever got from the man. He speaks slowly and carefully. Partly so he can concentrate on what he says and how he says it, partly to fill the time and to hide the fact that he's got nothing to say about 'himself'.

'I'm Sebastien, pronounced say-bass-tee-ang, but please call me Seb, it's much easier.' They laugh. He turns to Natalie, exaggerating the French intonation. 'I thought we could be Seb and Nat? Better for the children? But then I say to myself, Natalie's such a pretty name, you may not want to shorten it. It's French, oui?' Might as well find out what he's up against here.

'Aye, I mean, oui, it's French, but not because of any family tie or cultural connection, sorry.' Natalie wrinkles her nose. 'Apparently, it was the name of a character in a book my mum was reading when she was in labour.'

'You do not speak French then?' he asks, his fingers crossed, trying his hardest to sound credibly French himself.

Natalie looks at him as if he's the most stupid person she's ever met. 'Of course I do.'

He holds his breath, sure he's going to be tested and found wanting, again.

'Hors d'oeuvres, crème caramel, joie de vivre, déjà vu, aperitif.' She stops for a moment, obviously thinking, then starts again, 'Bon appétit, eau de cologne, boutique, croissant, baguette, souvenir, bon voyage.'

'Enough,' says the boss, with a groan. 'We get it.'

They all laugh, apart from the boy, of course, and Pim. 'What about you, Pim?' asks Gus. 'Is French not one of your languages?'

'At school, I tended in my studies to focus on English and German. Now, at university, I am learning Spanish and Mandarin Chinese – these are the most widely spoken languages in the world. Much more useful than French. No disrespect intended.'

'None taken, my friend,' he says, sending Nat a sly smile. 'Well, I'm French, but my accent isn't too strong because my father worked all over the world and I tend to pick up whatever I hear around me.'

'Well, in that case, it'll no be long till you pick up a great glottal stop, pal,' says Nat, her Scottish accent suddenly so much broader than before.

'I have no idea what a "glottal stop" is.'

'The glottal stop is a consonant formed by the audible release of the airstream after complete closure of the glottis,' says Pim.

'Are you for real?' says Natalie, shaking her head.

'Yes, of course. I am merely sharing with you the definition we were taught in phonetics. The glottal stop is a plosive created by complete closure and then opening of the glottis, which is part of the larynx. The symbol for this sound is a sort of question mark.'

'Thanks, Pim,' says the boss, 'very interesting, but I think we should move on and hear a bit more about Seb here.'

Damn, it was handy letting Pim fill the time with his drivel.

'I thought you sounded a bit South African,' says Natalie. 'When I first met you, that is, but now I can hear the French coming through. Much nicer accent.'

'Well spotted, Nat. Yes, I lived in South Africa for a number of years.'

'Ah, do you speak Afrikaans?' says Pim.

Afrikaans. Dutch. Not much difference, some would say. This could be tricky. 'Nah, not really.' He does but the more general he can keep all this stuff, the easier it will be. 'A few phrases, here and there. Do you, Pim?'

'No, but since it is largely based on Flemish, Dutch and German, I imagine I could learn it very quickly.'

'No need for that. We're both here to improve our English, no?' He turns to the girl. 'Anyway, Nat, you're right. I'm French by birth. I've been living in France for some time – the south, Toulouse, and then Paris.'

'I am not fond of the French,' says Pim. 'Especially Parisians. They are very rude people, in my experience.'

The Dutchman's starting to get on his nerves; plus no self-respecting Frenchman would let anyone get away with that remark. He can't let it go and seem credible.

'Hey, who asked you, buddy?' It comes out harsher than he intended and in his own normal voice.

Chair legs scrape on the floor with a screech that makes Nat cover her ears. The kid's on his feet.

Gus sees the boy's face. Sees the boy staring at him, recognising him.

He waits for the kid to point an accusing finger and say, 'That's him, Dad. That's the guy I was telling you about. The one who shot the hiker then made me bury the body.'

Gus's head is filled with a noise that no one else in the room seems to hear. He thinks back to the beating he gave this kid, who suddenly looks much smaller and more vulnerable than before. Gus wonders, for the first time, how badly he hurt the little boy and prays it was enough to make him say nothing.

Gus contemplates getting to his feet, making some excuse to leave, when suddenly, like a startled animal, the kid turns and runs. Out the café door and gone.

'Well, I wonder what that's all about?' says the boss, shrugging his shoulders.

'Hormones, probably,' says Nat.

'Already? He's not even twelve.'

'That's about right. Primary Seven it usually kicks in. Sometimes sooner.'

'My god, I thought we'd years to go before we hit all that stuff.'

'Children grow up very fast these days,' says Pim.

'I suppose they do. Even Charlie,' the boss says, with something like regret. 'Actually, it's just as well he's gone.' He nods at Natalie. 'It will give us a chance to explain about his condition.'

Gus hopes the 'condition' is not one that will be made worse by a kicking or he could be in even more trouble than he ever thought possible. He wonders if he can get to his room and grab his stuff without bumping into the kid. He needs to get away from here and head for London or Birmingham, Glasgow even, any big city where he can disappear. But he has to be fast. Before the kid tells his dad and the cops arrive, looking for him. And a dead guy.

***

CHAPTER 26

'Right,' says the boss, looking at his watch. 'Time's marching on.' He gathers his papers and says, 'Let's show you around Brackenbrae. We can talk about Charlie as we go.'

'Prepare to fall in love, boys,' says Natalie. 'This has got to be one of the ten most beautiful places in the world.'

'I think, Natalie, you must be hyperbolising. What about Petra and New Zealand and Victoria Falls and–'

'Och, shut up, Pim,' says Natalie, with a smile that guarantees she'll be forgiven. Gus and the boss exchange a look. It's clear that Natalie has voiced what they were all thinking.

As they walk across the 'original cobblestones' of the courtyard, the boss recites figures and facts about Brackenbrae. The old stone buildings are thought to have been erected as early as the late-thirteenth century by the Kennedys of Carrick, a powerful family who ruled over much of Southwest Scotland. The Ayrshire coastline is dotted with castles, most now, like Brackenbrae's tower, fallen into a state of disrepair.

Gus's brain can't focus on historical stuff, even on a normal day, and he zones out. All he can think about is how quickly he can get to the dorm, grab his stuff and get out of here. It was crazy to think he could pull off a stunt like this. He should have stuck to his original plan and dumped the dead guy's bag – by this time tomorrow it would have been in landfill somewhere. Gone forever. Like its owner.

Gus should have disappeared, got far away from here while he had the chance. While he was just a random, passing stranger that no one could possibly identify. Least of all a traumatised kid.

He could be in England by now. Heading for a city full of immigrants, with lots of little businesses happy to take on a guy with his build. No questions asked, no papers needed.

Or he could have sent out an emergency message on Facebook. A call for help. Maybe he could still ask everyone he knows to send him some money so he can buy the cheapest ticket home. Or anywhere. He could even go back to France. As long as he gets out of the UK.

The boss doesn't give Gus much chance to consider his options in peace. It's obvious he expects a reaction to every little detail he tells them about his business. He seems to be waiting for Gus to say something. He smiles, nods, and tries to pay attention. No point in causing suspicion.

They hear how the boss spotted the tower from the main road one day and came to investigate. How he bought the whole place for next to nothing because no one else could see the value in a derelict tower with a few humble barns and dwellings around it. His eyes burn with commitment as he shares his dream: that one day Brackenbrae will be in all the good travel guides as an upmarket holiday destination on the beautiful Ayrshire coast.

'It is already very highly rated on Trip Planner,' says Pim. 'Every comment is a positive one. I took the liberty of checking before I took this job.'

Natalie nudges Gus in the ribs. When he looks at her she rolls her eyes.

'Unfortunately, there are only a few comments. Is that because you are not generating enough business?'

'Does this guy not know when to stop?' whispers Natalie.

The boss coughs and shuffles his feet a little. 'You've hit the nail on the head there, Pim. We're up against it with that huge place along the road.'

'Two, in fact. I could not help noticing a second place for large caravans. Both with access to the beach.'

'Seriously, Pim?' says Natalie. 'Can I get you a shovel? Help you with that hole you're digging?'

Like a flashback in a movie, complete with an explosion effect, the dead guy looms in front of Gus for a nanosecond then disappears. Gus feels for the barn wall to steady himself, then leans against it. Natalie notices and touches his arm.

'You okay, Seb?' she asks gently.

He pushes away from the wall, fighting the adrenaline-like after-effects of whatever just hit him. 'Yeah, it's cool. Didn't sleep too well last night. That's all.'

'If you're nervous about working here, there's no need. Trust me. You'll love it.'

The boss is explaining his business plan, telling them how he plans to erect tipis and build safari houses. Expand the place by developing Phase Five and adding value to the property.

'Don't forget the posh pods,' says Natalie. 'I think they sound brilliant. En suites and everything. Now that's what I call glamping. It's going to go astral, this business. You'll see. Keep the faith, Boss.'

The boss rubs at his cheek, the skin moving under his hand. 'Thanks,' he says. 'Wish the locals were as enthusiastic as you. The application for the tipis has been blocked by the council. "There'll be nae wigwams here," was the comment from one councillor apparently. "Whit dae they think they're playin at? Cowboys and Indians?" That's the mentality we're dealing with.'

This is a man under pressure. A man with more worries than he can count. He's not going to be looking for anything else to add to his stress. What if the kid hasn't told him yet about what happened on the hill?

Maybe if Gus sticks around and does a good job for a while, keeping an eye on the kid, he can get away with this.

He's busy telling himself not to be crazy, the only solution is to run for it, asap, when he hears Natalie say, 'Don't you think you should tell the guys about Charlie, Boss? Before we bump into him and there's a misunderstanding?'

'You're right, Natalie. Thanks.'

The boss gives a throat-clearing cough and Gus wonders what's coming.

'Charlie doesn't speak. At all. That's it in a nutshell.'

Pim strokes his thin, patchy beard. 'He is muted?'

Natalie laughs. 'Mute, Pim. We say, "mute" not "muted" – that's only for televisions, not people.'

Pim looks puzzled.

Gus is desperate to know more but is scared to ask. He waits.

'Well, he's not mute, Natalie,' says the boss. 'Not really. Is he?' It's surprising how vulnerable the man sounds and how he seems to be deferring to Natalie.

Natalie shakes her head. 'By the way, mute is a term best avoided, Pim. It can cause offence.'

The boss inhales noisily, as if it will be an effort to explain. 'Charlie has what they call traumatic mutism. As far as we know.'

Natalie seems keen to help him explain. 'See, he used to speak, quite normally, and then he stopped. All of a sudden, when he was about six or seven.' She looks at their boss. 'That's right, isn't it?'

The boss nods. 'Yeah, just before he turned seven.'

'What happened?' asks Pim. Gus is grateful for the Dutchman's lack of tact.

'We don't know, Pim. Not exactly.'

It's obvious from the man's tone and his body language that he doesn't want to talk about it. This is the best news Gus has ever had in his life, but he needs more details.

He hopes Pim will be too thick or insensitive to read the signs. Sure enough.

'Will he speak again?'

'We prefer to believe it's temporary, Pim. In Charlie's case,' says the boss, his voice upbeat. 'So we treat him as normal and we ask that you do the same. Be kind to him, be patient with him and, above all, don't get angry with him, please.'

'Well, of course not,' says Pim. 'I imagine that would be back-setting for the boy.'

The boss, to his credit, laughs and gives Pim a friendly clap on the shoulder. 'You're right. That would set him back.' He turns to look at Gus, then Pim. 'So, guys, even if you find his lack of communication irritating, please don't show Charlie you're annoyed or impatient with him.'

Annoyed or impatient, thinks Gus. Bit late for that. He just gave this kid a front row demonstration of full-on 'roid rage'. That should be enough to set him back alright.

'Apart from that,' says the boss, 'the main thing is, don't expect a response from him. Apart from nodding.'

Gus remembers the boy nodding. Desperately. Poor little sod. Terrified and not able to say a word to stop the beating. Still, all to the good, by the sound of things. Gus can hardly believe his luck.

He's still sick about what happened. As in sick, ready to vomit. Even more so since he recognised the kid. But it's happened. There's nothing he can do to change that fact.

Sure, he might have done things differently, if he'd had more time to think. If he'd been on his own. But having that kid there made things a thousand times worse. If the fuckin' kid hadn't been wandering around with a gun, none of this would have happened in the first place.

So why should Gus run away?

In any case, running now would look very suspicious. It might spark a manhunt for Sebastien Lamar. That's the last thing Gus wants.

'Feel free to have a lie-in tomorrow morning,' says the boss. 'It may be your last for some time. I'm a real slave-driver.'

Natalie nudges Gus. 'Don't listen to him. The man's a pussy cat.'

This is a luckier break than he deserves. Gus decides to stay.

***

CHAPTER 27

Wednesday 30 May

Glad it's a school day today. Don't want to bump into that Sebastien guy. Stayed inside the house this morning till Mum started the engine. Then ran out and jumped in. Like a bank robber in his getaway car.

Mum seemed surprised. Usually she has to keep shouting my name. She hasn't worked out yet that I wait till she shouts, 'Charlie. Come ON. We're late.' Same pattern every morning. We're never late.

It's not that I don't like going to school. School's fine. Just prefer to get there when the bell's ringing. Enough time to get out the car and run for th e line. Not keen on hanging about.

When I start the Academy, I'm planning on being late every morning. Not very late, just a minute or two. To avoid the bullies in their hunting ground.

Easy for me to go in late. Nobody ever expects an explanation. Pretty sure it will be the same at the Academy. The teachers have all been told already that I'm coming in August. I'll be on a list with the kids that can't read yet, like Jayden Jeffries, and the ones with allergies, like Simon, who nearly died in Primary Two because nobody knew he was allergic to nuts and the teacher gave out mini-Snickers to everybody who got full marks. Now we don't get prizes, just stupid stickers and certificates. The teachers all know we'd rather have sweeties, but it's not allowed. Can't have peanut butter sandwiches in our lunch boxes either, in case we breathe on Simon and he dies.

That makes me think of the dead guy again, for about the millionth time. Kept waking up last night, remembering. Mum came into my room, to tuck me in and say goodnight. I so wanted to tell her, but the words wouldn't come. Now I'm worried I'll never be able to talk again. All the experts have said I *can* talk, it's just that I choose not to, at the moment. I've been believing that. Up till now.

Robbie's house goes past on the left-hand side. I try not to look, but it's there. Always. Bits of wall, black and sooty. Bits of roof, like skinny skeleton bones, black too. Wish I could go back in time. Not to see gladiators or dinosaurs or any of that stuff. So I could stop what happened to Robbie and his mum and the wee baby.

'Right, Charlie, jump out. Mind your lunch box and eat every scrap, please.'

Get out slowly, trying not to hurt my sore bits. They're worse today. Mum doesn't seem to notice.

'Bye-ee,' she shouts as the car door shuts and she drives off. Bet she's already thinking about something more important than me. I watch and wave, although she's not looking. The car turns right. She didn't tell me she was going into town. Again.

First part of the day is assembly. Everyone, except me, sings a song and then the head teacher gives out 'important information'. It's usually boring stuff about remembering to bring back permission slips with a signature from whoever looks after us. One time, Jonny McCreadie had no permission slip and we all went to the pantomime without him. He had to stay behind with the crabbiest teacher. The one that doesn't like pantos, or children.

This morning it's a little talk, with a PowerPoint about being kind to other people and not hurting anyone. I think they mean me. Wonder what would happen if I stood up right now. Everybody would look at me. Imagine if my voice came back with the whole school listening. Imagine if I said, 'I can talk and I know where there's a dead body buried.' They'd all think I'm bonkers.

After assembly we go to our classroom and work in groups. It's language time. My group has to write a story about something interesting that happened at the weekend. Miss Lawson says a story is called an essay in the big school but we're not to worry, it's just a story with a fancy name.

Copy the title from the Smart Board. The Long Weekend. Take a ruler and draw a neat line under the title. Put the ruler back in my pencil case.

This is my chance. Could write it all down and then it won't be my problem any more.

Imagine Miss Lawson showing my story to the head teacher. The head teacher phoning Dad. 'We're a bit concerned about something Charlie's written in a story. Can you please come in for a meeting?'

***

CHAPTER 28

What a crap night's sleep. Gus feels exhausted by everything that's happened and wishes he could stay in bed. Even though the boss offered them all a bit of a lie-in, Gus doesn't want to take the piss. He needs this job.

He dreaded getting into bed last night. Was worried about lying there for hours, terrified to close his eyes in case the dead guy appeared. But all he remembers is hearing Pim fart, wondering if there was any chance of getting a room to himself and then nothing. Sweet merciful oblivion. Till two twenty-seven when he woke abruptly, had a second or two of not knowing where he was, then whammo! The face was back. The coppery hair, the blood.

Gus got up, feeling like he might be sick, and went outside to use the campsite toilet block. The sky was clear and filled with stars. He stopped in the courtyard and gazed up at them. He'd never believed in heaven, but suddenly he was filled with a hope that the guy he'd shot might be up there, having a great time. Poor bastard deserved better than lying out there on that hillside. Gus shivered. There was a pale icing of frost on the roof slates. Or was it a trick of the moonlight?

In the fresh, cool air his nausea passed, and he hurried back to bed, keen to grab a few more hours' sleep. But his feet were cold and he couldn't get comfortable in the narrow bed.

Pim was snoring. An owl was hooting in the distance. Then, as he got drowsy and closed his eyes, whammo! Wide awake again. He tried desperately to think of something else. Anything but the dead guy. The one who should be lying in this bed right now.

The rest of the night he'd done his best to stay awake. He was as tired as he'd be after a mega training session, but he daren't let his eyes close. He imagined the dead guy hovering beside his bed. Watching his eyelids, waiting for them to drop, so he could rear up and make Gus shoot him again and again.

At one point he'd heard a baby crying, somewhere, plaintive, distraught. He couldn't understand how any mother, or father, could sleep through that. Then the sound changed, and he remembered some talk of feral cats that came round in the night.

Now it's morning and he needs to make a move. He pushes up on one elbow and looks across at the other bed. It's empty, made up perfect as a barrack bunk, as if no one's ever slept in it. Pim must be up already and have gone to work.

He swings his legs over the side of the bed and sits there with his head in his hands till he hears the door open.

'Good morning, Seb. I have brought you coffee.'

Seb. That means him.

'Hey, thanks, Pim. You don't have to do that.'

'You're right. I don't have to do this, but Nat suggested it. How could I say no?'

Gus takes the cup. 'Well, thanks anyway, mate. Appreciate it. You been up long?'

Pim consults a large watch. 'One hour and thirty-seven, no, thirty-eight minutes.'

Gus sighs. This guy could be hard work for a whole summer. Especially sharing a room. 'Yeah, I was kinda looking more for a rough guess as an answer, you know?'

'I prefer to be precise when at all possible. It is my way.'

'Great.' Gus raises the mug in a toast. He slurps at the coffee. It's hot and strong. 'Thanks, buddy,' he says. 'Hey, was I asleep when you got up?'

'Well, of course, I did not look closely to check, but yes, I think so. Before my ablutions, I did seven sun salutations. It is my morning routine.'

'Great,' Gus mutters again. Well, either the guy was very quiet, or Gus has been in a deep sleep. That's good. At four o'clock this morning he feared he might never sleep again.

'I must go back to work now. Please return the mug to the café.'

'Sure thing. If you see Nat, will you tell her I'm on my way?'

He finds Nat in the playbarn, rubber-gloved and surrounded by a dust cloud.

Gus coughs and waves a hand in front of his face. 'Isn't there some health and safety law against this?'

'Och, shut up. I get enough of that shit on teaching practice. Grab a duster and get going. Didn't expect to see you this early. Our esteemed employer said we could have a lie-in this morning.'

'I prefer to be early.'

'Well, don't go making a habit of it. You'll only make the rest of us look bad.'

'Excuse me, but where does it say in my contract that you're my supervisor?' Gus frowns and tilts his face so she'll know he's kidding.

'It doesn't, but I've worked with guys before and in my experience, they require strong leadership.'

'Hey, hang on. That's a bit sexist.'

Nat grins at him. 'Prove me wrong.' She throws him a duster, which he catches at the top of its arc. 'Fast reactions,' she says, nodding.

'Not always a good thing,' says Gus, thinking of that trigger he pulled yesterday.

'Hey, smile! I'm impressed. Now let's see if your dusting's as good as your catching.' She dangles a pair of pink rubber gloves in front of his face. 'Marigolds? I've got a spare pair.'

'Not my colour. Yellow, maybe. But pink? Not so much.'

They work in silence for a while, Gus following Nat's occasional instructions. He clears each shelf so she can dust and wipe it down. Then he replaces the piles of paper, boxes of paints, cartons of felt tips and they move on to the next.

Half-way through a row of old cupboards, he decides it will be okay to ask the question. 'What's the deal with Charlie?'

Nat stops dusting and looks at him. 'Why do you ask?'

'I want to get it right. Poor little sod.'

Nat smiles and he relaxes a bit.

She reaches for her phone and checks it. 'Yeah, near enough,' she says. 'Come on, I could use a break from all this dust. Let's go over and see if Mark will make us a coffee.'

The coffee's rich and bitter, and Mark has a good line in banter, but Gus is glad when a buzzer goes off in the kitchen and the big chef disappears through the swing door.

'So,' says Nat, leaning forward to lean on the little table, her chin resting in her hand. 'Charlie.'

'Yeah, I've heard about kids like him. Never met one though. I'd hate to get it wrong and make things worse.'

Nat shakes her head. 'I don't think there's a chance you'll make things worse, Seb.'

The name jars but he knows he's going to have to get used to it. Fast.

'You think so?'

'I'm pretty sure. The fact that you're taking the time to ask advice shows you're a caring person. You wouldn't hurt a kid if your life depended on it. I can tell.'

Gus smiles, feeling like the world's biggest hypocrite. 'Yeah, yeah, yeah. I'm a regular superhero. Now we've got that out of the way, are you gonna tell me about Charlie before this coffee break's over? You sound as if you know a bit about the condition?'

'I've been studying it for an optional project. I've got a five-thousand-word paper to write for the start of term. It's fascinating. Some kids just stop talking.'

'What did you call it? Something mutism?'

'Traumatic mutism. That's the official term. Something horrendous happens and the child closes in on himself. Or herself. Can't speak about it and won't speak about anything else. That's very simplified, of course.'

'Fine by me. I'm a pretty simple guy. Does anyone know what caused Charlie to clam up?'

Nat grimaces at his choice of words. 'His parents think it's related to the death of a school friend. One day the boy was here playing with Charlie, the next, sadly, he was dead. His mother and baby brother too.'

'How?' asks Gus, hoping there was no gun involved.

'A fire. Dodgy electricals, they think. All three died of smoke inhalation, apparently. Ghastly business.'

'Charlie stopped speaking?'

'Yes, unfortunately.'

'Double tragedy,' says Gus, thinking the very opposite. 'Will he ever be able to talk, do you think?'

'He could talk right now, Seb,' says Nat. 'If he wanted. There's no physiological reason that he can't.'

Her face is very serious. 'I saw a wee girl with it last year. Similar situation. Her grandfather was driving her and her wee sister to school when he suffered a fatal heart attack at the wheel. Ploughed into a bus queue. It was carnage at the scene, I was told.'

'Christ! What a thing to witness.'

'Can you imagine anything so awful? For everyone concerned. It doesn't bear thinking about.'

'And the girl won't ever speak again?'

'No. I'm afraid she won't.'

Gus thinks he sees tears in Natalie's eyes. 'What? Never? How can they tell?'

'She died, Seb. She took her own life. Suicide at eleven.'

There's no doubt now about those tears. Gus touches her shoulder.

Nat sniffs loudly. 'Sorry, I can't get my head round it. That's why I'm determined to help Charlie.'

'What can you do?'

'The best thing we can all do is talk to him, as much as we can. Especially if he seems comfortable with you.'

'What do you mean by comfortable?'

'Charlie seems to take to some folk and not others.'

'Not sure he'll take to me.' The words are out of his mouth before he can stop them.

'Oh, he will, Seb. He might not get Pim, but I'm certain you'll be a hit. He just seems to like some people more than others. For example, he adores Joyce.'

'He adores you even more, I imagine.'

Nat smiles, as if she doesn't want to take any credit for being adorable. Gus doesn't doubt for one minute that Charlie loves her. Charlie and all the other kids she meets.

'What do I do if Charlie doesn't like me?'

'Just carry on as normal. Talk to him as often as you can. He might act a bit weird, like he did yesterday, running off for no reason. But he'll come around.'

'Okay,' says Gus, trying to sound sincere, 'I'll give it my best shot.'

'You know what? I've got a feeling that, between the two of us, we'll have Charlie speaking before the summer's over.'

***

CHAPTER 29

France
Monday 4 June

'I'm sorry, Mrs Lamar. No sign of the post yet.'

Catherine tries not to look devastated. The sad frown on the face of the young concierge tells her she's failed.

'I'll bring your package right up the moment it's delivered. Promise.'

'Sorry, Adrien. I don't mean to be a pest. Thank you for your help.'

'Not at all. With pleasure.'

Catherine says goodbye and turns to wait for the lift. She looks at her watch. It's only 10am. How will she get through another day if the parcel doesn't arrive? Afraid she won't, she decides to make a call to Scotland.

Mrs Wilson answers with a cheery, 'Hello, Dumfries 252971?'

'Good morning, Mrs Wilson. It's Catherine Lamar, Sebastien's mother. I'm wondering if you were able to post the phone?'

'Indeed I did, first class, the morning after we spoke. I even paid for one of their fancy padded envelopes, and insurance, in case it went missing. See, that's what happens when you sell off the Post Office. What can you expect?'

'Do items often go missing in the post in Scotland?'

'Well, not usually, but it happens.' The woman chuckles. 'Wait till I tell you: my neighbour, a flighty thing, once sent for some fancy underwear. To spice things up, in the bedroom department, as she put it.'

'What, it never arrived?'

'So she says, but there was talk her man had intercepted the postie and taken delivery himself. We've no idea where the "long-cherie" went, but there was a wicked rumour going round here for a while.'

Mrs Wilson laughs again and Catherine can't help smiling. She'd like to meet this woman, she thinks. Have an espresso or a glass of wine with her.

'But usually parcels get to the right place, you'd say?'

'Oh aye, normally. To be fair, they said between three and five days for France. Let me ken if you don't get it by the end of the week and I'll kick up a stink. Have you heard from that lovely boy of yours, by the way?'

Catherine's heart beats heavily. 'No, not yet, I'm afraid.'

'Whit are you afraid of, dearie?'

Catherine uses the expression as a turn of phrase, nothing more, but it sounds as if the kind-hearted woman has taken it literally.

'I'm afraid something's happened to him, Mrs Wilson. I just have this dark foreboding. I can't shake it off, no matter how much I try to distract myself.'

'Och, don't be silly, lassie! He's just a daft boy, like the rest at that age. Lost his phone and would never think to use a phone box. See this technology. The young yins can hardly function without it. You'd wonder how we ever managed, wouldn't you?'

Mrs Wilson's upbeat reaction saves Catherine from unburdening herself to this generous-hearted woman who has no need to hear a guilty diatribe. Catherine makes a promise to ring Mrs Wilson when the phone arrives and to be sure to drop by Learigs Farm if they're ever in Dumfries and Galloway.

The house is silent. She's often spent the day alone, when Sebastien was at school and Eric at work, but she's never found the quietness unnerving before. She switches on the radio, listens for a moment before searching impatiently for a more pleasing sound. Eventually, when she can find nothing to engage her, neither music nor chat, she switches off and looks around her tidy, spotless kitchen. There's not a trace of Sebastien.

She takes a towel and wipes an already-gleaming draining board, wishing with all her heart he was here to leave annoying circles of brown liquid from his half-rinsed coffee mugs. How many times did she ask him to put them straight into the dishwasher?

He just laughed, sometimes ruffling her hair, affectionately, messing up her sleek style, knowing that annoyed her too. When she objected, he'd say, 'Just getting my own back, Mother. You've been doing that to my hair for years.'

He was right. She couldn't stop herself touching his hair. Especially when it darkened from baby blond to the gorgeous reddish gold it now was. How she longed to stroke his hair off his forehead, even if he did pull away, saying, 'Mother. Will you quit that, please?'

Towel in hand, she wanders through the hallway and into Sebastien's bedroom. Like the kitchen, it's far too tidy. She regrets changing his bedlinen and lifts his pillow to her face, hoping to catch a scent of him, but all she smells is the fragrance of fabric conditioner, as if Sebastien's head has never lain there. She puts the pillow back and smooths its cover. What wouldn't she swap, right now, to turn back the clock to the days when he was little? When he loved nothing more than having the covers tucked tightly round his neck as she said sternly, 'Hey, you bedbugs! I'm warning you. No biting tonight.' He'd smile sleepily as she kissed his forehead and whispered, 'Night, night, sweetie pie. See you in the morning.'

All these nights his bed has been empty. All those mornings since she last saw him. How many more till this torture ends? Catherine dabs at her eyes with a pretty white handkerchief, embroidered by her mother-in-law, and sticks it back in the pocket of her cardigan.

With another empty day stretching ahead of her, she's awash with regret. If she could turn back time, she would handle it all differently. She would swallow her pride and say, 'You know, I've been thinking about it, Sebastien, and you're right, a holiday job will be fun. You'll come back speaking fluent English, but with a funny accent.' He'd have laughed at that.

They could have shared the excitement of planning his adventure. She could have shopped for clothes with him, advised him on what to pack, got to know his plans. When she first discussed it with her mother-in-law, Mamie had cautioned her. 'I don't think you should try to block Sebastien on this, Catherine. I've rarely heard him so excited and I think it will be the making of him. What are you worrying about? I know all grannies would say the same thing, but really, Sebastien is a wonderful boy. He's kind and caring, full of life and very intelligent. He might get into a few scrapes when he's away but he's not going to do anything stupid, is he?' Her mother-in-law had touched her arm, trying to reassure her. 'You've done a good job, dear, brought him up well, taught him good values and sound judgement. He'll be grand. He'll have an unforgettable summer and he'll thank you for it. I urge you to let him go with good grace, Catherine. Otherwise…' Leaving the sentence unfinished, Mamie raised her eyebrows and Catherine understood. He'll go anyway, Mamie was going to say and she was right, that's exactly what he did.

'If you love someone you have to set them free. Believe me, I know what I'm talking about.' Her mother-in-law's words come back to her as she empties the coffee grains into the bin. 'A mother's job is to give her child wings to fly and a nest to come back to.' The words of a wise woman. Someone who's been there. Someone who lost a child.

The doorbell interrupts her reverie. Catherine rushes to the door and almost snatches the package from the concierge's hands. Fortunately, good manners prevail, and she remembers to thank the man and give him a tip.

She stands in the hall and turns the parcel over and over. Now that it's finally here, she's reluctant to open it. As if she's worried the contents will be a disappointment.

She fetches some scissors from a drawer in the kitchen and carefully cuts off the end of the tan-coloured bag. Some dusty paper stuffing escapes from the padding and flutters to the floor. She doesn't bother picking it up.

The phone itself has been sealed in bubble wrap and Catherine feels grateful to Mrs Wilson for making sure it got here safely. She struggles for a moment with the Sellotape that forms an outer skin, before using the scissors to slit open the wrapping.

Sebastien's sleek phone slides onto her hand, cold. Catherine pictures it lying in the Scottish field where he dropped it. She raises it to her lips, savouring the connection to her son.

True to her word, Mrs Wilson has included the charger she bought specially. The phone is showing fifty per cent charge. When it prompts Catherine for Sebastien's passcode, she taps in the four digits that represent his date of birth and hopes for the best. When that fails, she tries Eric's birthdate. Without much hope, she keys in her own and feels ridiculously pleased to see the phone unlock.

The background wallpaper is obscured by rows of apps, but Catherine can make out her own face and Eric's in a photo taken last year in the Seychelles. She didn't know Sebastien had that photo. It's touching to know he wants to see them every time he uses his phone. Perhaps he's been missing them more than she thought.

Catherine taps the email icon and scrolls through Sebastien's inbox till she finds what she's looking for.

Dear Sebastien,
Again, we're delighted you've agreed to come and spend the summer here with us at Brackenbrae. We feel sure you'll be an asset to our small but enthusiastic team. I've attached our new brochure to give you a flavour of the place. We look forward to seeing you here on Monday 28 May, any time that suits you. Let me know if you need a lift from the station or the airport.

It was signed with best wishes from Richard. The owner, presumably.

Catherine scrolls down and taps the screen to download a pdf file. She taps again and waits. When the document opens, the seascape on the front cover is breathtakingly beautiful. 'Brackenbrae,' says a font as understated as a whisper. 'So much more than a campsite.' Catherine flips quickly through the virtual brochure, noting how professionally it has been put together. She can understand why Sebastien felt drawn to this place, and would like to see more, but for the moment she is interested in only one thing – contact details. She finds a website, a phone and fax number, and a postal address on the last page. Dunure Rd, Ayr.

Catherine flops onto a kitchen chair. She's found him. At last.

She reaches for her handbag, finds her diary and notes the Brackenbrae details, then dials the phone number, remembering to add the UK code this time. She nibbles on a fingertip while she waits. Nothing happens. She checks the phone screen. Dead. How frustrating, the battery was showing a charge when she unwrapped it. Is this another reason why Sebastien didn't call them at the start of his trip?

She retrieves her own phone from her handbag and dials the campsite number again. It rings only once.

'Brackenbrae Holiday Park. Pim speaking. Good morning. How may I help you, please?'

Catherine realises too late that she ought to have taken a moment to prepare an English version of what she wanted to say. 'Euh, hello. Euh, can you tell me if my son is there, please?'

'I will certainly do my very best, Madam. Your son, is he in a yurt?'

'I'm sorry. I do not understand.'

'What type of accommodation does he have, your son?'

'I'm afraid I don't know.'

'I see. Then can you perhaps tell me your son's name?'

'Sorry, of course. How stupid of me. His name is Sebastien Lamar. He's French.'

'Ah, you mean Seb, I think.'

This is no time to argue about names. 'Seb, yes. From Paris. Is he with you?'

'No, Madam. I'm sorry.'

Catherine's joy vanishes.

'He is not with me. I believe he is in the playbarn, working.'

Like a phoenix, her poor burnt heart soars again. 'Oh, thank god,' she says, quietly.

'Sorry?'

'No, it's okay. Do you think you could possibly go and get him?' Catherine tries to ignore the butterflies that are fluttering in her stomach.

'I regret to say that I am not authorised to leave the office at this time.'

Catherine sighs with relief at the reprieve, then gets angry at herself for feeling that way.

'But when I see Sebastien, I shall certainly tell him that you called, Mrs Lamar.'

'Yes, please. Do that.' The moment the words leave her mouth she regrets them. 'Sorry, no. I'd rather you didn't mention this call to Sebastien.'

'It is no trouble, I can assure you.'

'No, please. That's kind of you to offer, but I'd prefer it if you didn't. He's a big boy now and he wouldn't like his mummy checking up on him.'

The receptionist laughs. 'I see what you mean. I would feel annoyed too, were my mother to call for this purpose.'

'I thought so. You won't tell Sebastien I rang?'

'Your secret is safe. I swear it on my very life.'

Catherine can't help smiling at the language. 'Your English is quite exceptional.'

'Thank you very much indeed. I am doing my utmost to achieve a high standard.'

As she says goodbye and disconnects, Catherine wonders how Sebastien, no, Seb, will get on with this colleague. She looks forward to finding out.

She leans back in her chair and closes her eyes, enjoying the warm contentment that comes with knowing her son is safe.

She dials Eric's mobile. He answers on the second ring. 'Have you heard from Sebastien?' he says, his voice so full of hope she can picture his face, all lit up.

'Sorry, my love, not yet. But I've got Sebastien's phone. It got here safely and so did he. Well not here. *He* got *there* safely, is what I'm trying to say. To the place he's working. In Scotland. Brackenbrae.'

'Slow down, darling. You're babbling.'

'Sorry, Eric. I'm excited, relieved, thankful, delighted. Oops, and babbling.'

'That's okay. Did you speak to Sebastien?'

'No. He's working. But I don't mind. As long as I know he's there.'

'That's wonderful. Well, I'm afraid I'm working too. I'll see you later.'

'Just one thing?'

Too late, he's gone. She wanted to ask him if she should order up a new phone for Sebastien. She knows he'll say yes. 'Can't have the boy that far away from home without a reliable phone.' That's what he'll say.

All the nightmare scenarios she's been imagining since Sebastien left have served no purpose, other than to drive her mad. Now that she's seen where he's living, she can close her eyes and imagine that beautiful view of the sea with the island in the distance.

Her next call is to Mamie.

The phone rings and rings. Catherine pictures it on the little table in the dark hallway of the house where Eric grew up. She can almost hear the metronomic tick-tock of the pendulum in the antique grandfather clock. She can see Mamie opening the panel on its well-polished front, a little Sebastien standing patiently at her side. Mamie reaching inside to catch the chain. Placing it in Sebastien's small hands and watching as he pulls and pulls till the heavy weight on its end rises and the clock's set to keep time for another week. Seems so long ago and yet so recent it could be yesterday.

'Hello?' Mamie's voice sounds frail, her breathing laboured.

'It's Catherine, Mamie. How are you?'

'Fine, dear.' The woman's a saint. Catherine has never known her to complain.

'You seem a little breathless? Are you using that inhaler the doctor gave you?'

'I keep forgetting. I'm turning into a silly old woman.' Mamie laughs, as if failing health and memory is all a huge joke. Maybe it is.

'Mamie? Are you sure you're quite well? You sound a little wheezy.'

'Of course, I'm well. Never you mind about me. Have you heard from our lovely boy yet?'

'Yes. Well, no. I mean, not directly, but I know why he hasn't been in touch.' Catherine relates the story of the lost phone, making Mamie laugh at Mrs Wilson's account of Sebastien being chased by the bull. When Mamie's laughter ends in a bout of harsh coughing, Catherine frowns. 'Should we pop down to see you this weekend?'

'Certainly not. I'll be grand. There's a bug going around. In a couple of days, I shall be as good as new.'

'Good. I hope so. Eric thinks we should go to Scotland once Sebastien's settled in and pay him a surprise visit, but I'm not sure.'

Mamie asks, 'Now, why wouldn't you go, for goodness' sake?'

'Because I don't think he'd want us to. Also, because I am so ashamed at how I sulked and grumbled before he left. Mamie, I didn't even kiss him goodbye.'

'That's terribly sad, Catherine. You and Sebastien have always been so close.'

'We were, until I ruined it all.'

'You haven't ruined anything. He's just trying to prove to you he can stand on his own two feet.'

'I just have this terrible feeling,' she says, then stops, not wanting to put her fears into words.

'Oh, that's normal when they leave home. He'll be fine. But why put yourself through this? Eric's right, you should go and see him, even if it's only for an hour or so. It's a long way to go, I know, but you can make a little holiday of it, once you've seen with your own eyes that he's fine. Catherine, I believe very strongly that when there's disharmony in a family, it's the mother who should always be the one to make the first move. To stretch out a loving hand and smooth the wrinkles on life's bedspread. I don't think you should let this go on any longer.'

'Perhaps you're right.'

'I am right. I lost one of my boys, I expect you know that, although I never talk about it. But I can tell you this, if I had my time again, I would do things differently. Forgive and forget. Sadly, I could never forget, and Henri could never forgive. Then it was too late. Please don't make the same mistake I did. Go and see that precious boy of yours, while you can.'

'You're right, Mamie. I'm being ridiculous. I'll give Eric a call later. Ask him to get our flights booked. Pronto.'

'Good girl. Now, stop worrying. Knowing our Sebastien, I'm sure he's having a whale of a time.'

Mamie laughs and again it turns into a coughing fit.

'Are you sure it's okay for us to go to Scotland? Shouldn't we wait a week or two, till you get over this cough?'

'Don't you dare,' says Mamie, when she gets her breath back. 'Go. Be sure to give Sebastien a big kiss from his granny and tell him I want to know if he's walked that coastal path yet.'

***

CHAPTER 30

Ayrshire

C an't wait to get home, but Mum's late. Everybody else is away, but I'm not allowed to leave the playground till Mum gets here. What if something bad's happened to *her* now?

There's a corner where I can see all the roads, if I stand on the wall and hold onto the railings. The main road that goes to Ayr, the one down into Dunure, called Station Road. Silly name. Dunure hasn't even got a station. The one that leads up the hill towards Brackenbrae.

I spot Mum's car, parked in the layby. Why doesn't she come and get me if she's here?

I go back inside to look. Maybe she's been here all along. In a meeting with the head teacher, maybe.

About me, likely, and what a freak I'll be at the Academy.

The staffroom door opens. 'Hello, Charlie? You still here?'

Nod.

'Mum not here yet?' Miss Lawson looks worried.

I point to the next door with its shiny gold sign. Head Teacher: Mrs A Walker. Beside it, there's a sticker with a big smiley face and underneath a poster that says, 'Welcome to our school. Glad you're here!' Mrs Walker is trying to make visitors think she's friendly, and most of the time she's nice, but she can be really scary too. Hope Mum's not scared.

'Did you want to see Mrs Walker? She's not here, Charlie. She had to go to a meeting at County Buildings this afternoon. Did you want to see her about something very important?'

Shake head.

'Can I help?' Her arms are full of sheets of paper.

Another shake.

'Well, I'm sorry. Everyone else has gone, I think. Do you need me to call Mum for you?'

Smile and shake head. Point to the door.

'You can wait with me till Mum comes, if you like. Help me to put away all this photocopying?'

I like helping Miss Lawson, but I shake my head. Mum will be here soon.

'Okay, you pop out and wait for her. I'll be leaving in ten minutes. If she hasn't turned up by then, we'll phone and see what's happening. All right?'

Nod and smile. She's lovely. We'll all miss her when we go to the Academy. Wish I could tell her that.

'See you in a bit.'

Wish I could tell her that Mum's car's in the layby. But even if I could, don't think I would. Because I've got a bad feeling about why Mum's late.

Run to the corner and stand up on the wall. A black Mercedes, sleek as a panther, slides into the layby behind Mum's car. Can't see who's driving. After a moment, Mum gets out, closes the door and bends down to wave her fingers.

I hunker down behind the wall and watch the black car glide down and stop at the main road. The driver has black hair, a neat, kind of fancy beard and a very white shirt. That's all I've got time to see before the car turns right and accelerates off with a whooshing noise that sounds very powerful, like the Batmobile. He's heading for Ayr, whoever he is. What were you doing with my mum? I want to shout after him. But he's gone.

Run to the steps and sit down, so Mum won't know I've been spying on her.

'Sorry, Charlie,' she says, all rushed. She's dressed up fancy. With her high heels on and those shiny tights she wears that make her legs look like a supermodel's, Dad says.

I scowl at her.

'Please don't look so cross.' Her voice is tinkly, like she knows a funny joke. 'I'm not usually late, am I?'

That's true.

'Dad had some paperwork he wanted me to look at.'

That's not true.

'Didn't notice the time till he said, "Shouldn't you be picking up Charlie?" Sorry, wee pal.'

That's not true either. Why is she lying to me? Why not the usual 'boring business stuff'? That's what they always say when there's something they don't want to tell me.

She reaches down for my school bag and lunch box and says, 'Come on then, kiddo. Let's get you home.'

As we walk towards the gate, she says, 'Where are the teachers? You shouldn't be sitting out here all alone.' This sounds more like Mum. Always ready for a moan these days. 'Any weirdo could be passing.'

I point to the school.

'Did someone ask if you were okay?'

Nod. A lot. Don't want her kicking up a fuss, getting Miss Lawson into trouble.

'That's good.'

Her happy mood seems to be back. She sings on the way home. 'All the single ladies. All the single ladies.' She doesn't even like Beyoncé. Should have heard her when one of the boys in my class told her his new baby sister was called Beyoncé. She went on about it all the way home in the car then told Dad and laughed. 'What are these people like,' she said, in her snooty voice.

That was when she started going 'private'.

'He's not going to a private school, Viv.'

'Give me one good reason why not.'

'We can't afford it. Is that a good enough reason?'

Haven't heard it mentioned for a while. Thank goodness. It's hard enough for me without a school where I'll not know anybody. That was another good reason Dad gave her, and they'd have to drive me every day and the uniform costs a fortune. Dad had loads of good reasons not to send me. I was glad.

Wonder what she'll tell Dad about where she's been? I'll have to listen tonight.

'Right. Straight upstairs and out of your school clothes please. Have you got homework to do?'

Make a sad face. Doesn't usually work but today Mum laughs and goes, 'Okay. It can wait till after tea.' She never lets me off with homework. Definitely something fishy going on. Get upstairs fast.

'Charlie!'

Oh no, she's changed her mind.

'Charlie?' Her voice is sing-songy.

Thump my foot on the floor, to let her know I'm coming. Once I get my school stuff off.

'Can you run quickly and find Dad for me, please?'

Halfway down the stairs, I mime, 'Where?'

'No idea, but he can't be far away. Fast as you can, please, Charlie.'

Jump down the last two stairs and sprint out the door and across the courtyard.

Suits me to find Dad. Because I've decided I'm definitely going to tell him. Today. The minute I find him. I'm going to tell him about the dead person. He'll know what to do.

Turn the corner, fast, skidding, and barrel right into someone. Someone big. I bounce right off him, like in a cartoon. Land on the ground, on my bum. Look up with a grin, because it's funny. Expecting to see Mark or maybe even Dad, smiling back at me.

But it's that Seb guy. He's *not* smiling.

He towers over me, muttering swear words, grabbing at my T-shirt. He drags me to my feet and up onto the tips of my toes. 'Well, well, well. Look who it is. Not seen you for a few days, buddy. Been keeping out of my way?'

I stare at him. Never been so afraid of anyone in my life.

'You need to watch where you're going, dumb-ass. Now, are you gonna say sorry or what?'

Shake my head, desperate to get away.

'Is that no, you won't apologise?'

Shake my head. In case that's the wrong answer, I nod, then change my mind and shake. His crazy eyes look into mine. He must know I can't speak. Dad will have told him by now. Or Natalie. Or Joyce.

He drops me, as if he's touched something disgusting. I stumble back and stand there, with my head down. Hoping I'm off the hook, like a wee fish that gets away, cos it's not worth bothering with.

He steps towards me. Starts jabbing his finger into my chest. Then he leans in close, and whispers, 'Say sorry.'

Don't want to look at his face. I stand there as if I'm made of stone and concentrate on my shoes. His big hand comes up again. Prods at me twice more, even harder this time. Two jabs, sharp as a knife. How can one finger hurt so much?

'Come on, asshole,' he says, quietly. 'Look at me when I'm talking to you.' He waits and waits. I've got no choice but to look up at him.

'You listening to me?' He's whispering again. Much scarier than shouting. 'This can't speak stuff? Pile of horseshit! Everyone knows you can speak. Seems to me you're nothing but an attention-seeking mummy's boy.' His mouth is so close to my ear his stubble scratches my cheek. As he draws away he stares into my eyes, like he wants to hypnotise me. 'Come on. Talk. All you need to say is, "Sorry." One word. Apologise. Before my patience runs out.'

When I say nothing, he glances around the corner like he wants to make sure no one's coming. He pounds one meaty fist into his other palm. It makes a punching noise, scary as claps of thunder.

'See this?' he says, holding his fist in front of my face. 'Well, say, "Sorry, Seb," before I smash it into your skinny gut.'

I'm going to tell Dad anyway, the minute I can, so I might as well talk now.

I put my teeth together and make the Hissing Sid noise I learned when I was wee.

'Ssssss.'

Nothing else comes out.

Try to add the o sound, but nothing happens.

'Ssssss. Sssssss.' Why can't I make the word?

He laughs like a movie villain. 'Look at you. You sad little pisser.'

I check my shorts, in case I've wet myself without realising.

He laughs again and watches the corner. I wish Dad would come. Or Mark, Mum, Natalie. Anybody.

He folds his arms. Like he's got all day.

I try again. Feels like my stomach's going to come out my mouth, but only the tiniest hissing sound escapes.

He cups a hand behind his ear. Like a bad actor pretending to listen.

'What did you say? Doesn't sound like, "Sorry". How do I know you're not saying, "Piss off"? That pathetic hiss could be anything. How do I know you're not calling me an asshole?'

He grabs my hair. Yanks me up till my eyes are level with his.

'Last chance, buddy. Say. Sorry. Seb.' He hisses every s sound, as if he's trying to wind me up as much as he can. The long gap he leaves between the words are scarier than anything.

I can't make the words. No matter how hard I try. Can't get past the s. This isn't fair. I was the one who decided to stop talking. Surely I get to decide when to start again.

Seb laughs quietly and shakes his head. 'Okay, bud. I guess it's true. You don't talk after all.' His voice is kind again, like it was when I first met him and he thought I was lost. Sounds as if he feels sorry for me.

I squeeze my eyes tight shut to stop any tears from getting out.

'Yeah, it's a pity you can't talk. I was kinda hoping you could tell me about that fire.'

The fire. How can he know about the fire?

'You know, the one your friend died in?'

I open my eyes but I won't look at him.

'With his mum and his poor little baby brother.' He looks as if he's being really clever.

'Did you have something to do with that fire, Charlie?'

Try to look away, at something in the distance.

'I think you did. That's why you won't talk. In case you have to tell somebody what really happened, eh?'

My eyes look at him before I can stop them.

'Thought so.'

Something in his voice makes me keep staring at him, as if I'm hypnotised.

'Is that why you won't talk. In case the truth comes out?'

I make myself look away again. Pretend he's not there.

'Eh?' Such a tiny word, but scary the way he says it. He starts prodding me again till I look at him.

His raised eyebrows tell me he wants an answer, so I nod.

'Now you've got two things you won't want to talk about, and another dead body. Let me see, now, that makes one...'

He's counting on his fingers.

Shut my eyes.

'Two, three, *four* people dead? Wow, no wonder you don't want to tell anyone. You got some kind of hex on you, kid? I think I'll keep well out of your way from now on.'

Keep my eyes screwed up tight.

When I open them, he's gone.

***

CHAPTER 31

France
Tuesday 19 June

Catherine looks around Sebastien's room, checking she's not missed anything.

This is the first time she's been able to spend time in his bedroom without bursting into tears. Amazing what having a sense of purpose will do.

She has already been through his wardrobe, twice, and his chest of drawers but found nothing worthwhile, apart from the pale-blue sweater that she can't stop raising to her cheek. Does it really still smell of Sebastien, or is she imagining it? Why didn't he take it with him? It's merino wool, softer than any sheep's wool you can find in France. Perfect for the chilly Scottish climate. Eric brought it back from a business trip to New Zealand. He'd wanted her to go with him, make a holiday of it, but she'd been unwilling to leave Sebastien, claiming he wouldn't study for his exams if she didn't keep on his case. She knew at the time that wasn't true, and knows it still, for Sebastien has always been motivated to work hard in school. Would it have made any difference if she'd gone with her husband, pleased him by saying yes?

Maybe she'll go next time, if another opportunity arises. By all accounts, New Zealand justifies the long flights. It seems to be a beautiful country, very like Scotland in fact. Well, she's never been to Scotland either, but that's about to change.

She holds the jumper at arm's length and examines it properly. This will never fit Sebastien now. His swimmer's shoulders would surely burst the seams and it will be far too short. Her boy has turned into a young man.

Eric chastised her last night for thinking of Sebastien as a boy. 'You need to remember *that* when you see him. No treating him like a child, especially if his workmates are within earshot.'

'Okay, okay, I get it,' she said, laughing.

Eric grabbed her in a hug and kissed her ear, making her wriggle out of his arms. 'It's so good to hear you laugh again, I can't tell you.'

Catherine folds the jumper and places it back in the drawer. It might be too small, but she's not ready to throw it out yet.

She turns to Sebastien's birthday gifts, piled in the corner. Far too many to take with them.

'Now, don't go packing too much stuff,' said Eric as he left for work this morning. 'Remember, everything we take, Sebastien will have to bring home and he's only got a rucksack.'

Catherine lifts one carefully wrapped package after another and weighs each in her hand, all the time thinking how sad it is that Sebastien wasn't here to open them on his birthday.

Come on, Catherine, she reminds herself, no negative thoughts. A week ago, she was worried she might never see Sebastien again and now here she is, packing to go and visit him in Scotland. She selects the two gifts she knows Sebastien will enjoy – a ludicrously expensive box of his favourites from La Maison du Chocolat and a bestseller he's been talking about reading. She carefully places the presents on top of her suitcase, trying not to spoil the bows she spent ages tying. As an afterthought, she grabs a soft, flat package – a technical base-layer that was meant for skiing but might be handy if he's finding Scotland too cold. She squashes it into the zipper compartment on the lid of the suitcase and closes it.

She is just getting into the shower when she thinks she hears the phone ringing in the hall. She turns off the water and listens. Yes, the house phone's ringing. Her first instinct is to run in case it's Sebastien, then she decides to let it go to the answering machine. When she hears Eric's voice, she smiles and grabs her towel. He'd better not be ringing to say he's running late. She has no intention of missing the flight. Even if she has to travel alone.

'Catherine, if you're there, can you pick up please?'

She can tell from his voice. Something bad has happened. She grabs the phone. 'Eric?'

***

CHAPTER 32

Scotland
Wednesday 20 June

'Morning, Seb. I've just been hearing you were on a pub crawl the night before you got here?' says the boss as they cross the courtyard.

A few pints in that place in Dunure where he made an arse of himself? 'A pub crawl?' he says, playing for time.

'Pubs on the riverside, along from the harbour?'

Gus doesn't remember any riverside. 'Oh yeah,' he says, hoping his employer will elaborate. 'I've been in a few bars in my time.'

'Joyce was saying her husband saw you in his local. Having a right old laugh by the sounds of things.'

Shit, this could be tricky. In more ways than one. Probably best to say as little as possible. 'You know me, Boss. Always up for a laugh.'

'Apparently, you couldn't understand the natives?'

Time to think quick. 'Sorry, what did you say?'

'I said–' The boss stops, realising. 'Oh, I see what you did there. Very good.'

Change the subject. Fast. 'I was hoping to get the chance to speak to you alone, Boss.'

'Why's that?'

'Just to let you know that I'll be happy to work extra hours, any time you like, say, if Joyce is not available to help with this wedding idea.'

'Okay, thanks. I'll bear that in mind.'

Gus looks up at the tower. 'No windows. When did you say this was built?'

'Nope, no windows. That'll be the first job, making it wind and watertight. Most of the castles you see dotted along the Ayrshire coast date from the sixteenth century. We think there's been a tower here from about the same time. Whether it's this same tower, we can't know for sure.'

'What's the reason for it? Defence?'

'We think so. There have been some pretty bloody scenes around here, you know.'

Gus immediately thinks of the corpse on the hillside on this man's own land. 'Really?' is all he can manage to say.

'Oh yes, you wouldn't think so, would you? But this coast was a great place for smugglers at the time of Robert Burns. You've heard of Robert Burns, haven't you?'

'Of course.' He hadn't, apart from what Nat had told him yesterday. 'Wrote "Auld Lang Syne" I believe.'

'Probably the most sung song in the world.'

'From Times Square to Tokyo,' says Gus, hoping he won't be asked to sing.

'Well, here we are,' says the boss, reaching the door of the tower. He puts his shoulder to the old door, which looks flimsy enough to push open with one finger. Gus wonders if he should offer to help.

The boss coughs as if he's embarrassed at his lack of strength, then barges the door like a TV cop. He rubs the top of his arm and laughs, shaking his head.

'Should I have a go, Boss?'

'It's okay. I've worked out why the door won't open. It's Charlie. He must be inside with the door barred. Don't know why. He should be getting ready for school.'

Great, the kid again. He's gonna turn up everywhere from now on. Gus was a real shit, asking him about the fire, provoking him, but the kid's reaction was unbelievable. You'd think he'd caused the fire himself. All Gus was trying to do was make sure Charlie really *couldn't* talk, but he may have hit gold with this fire business. It might be the extra bit of pressure he needs to keep the boy terrified.

Gus meant it when he said he'd be trying to avoid the kid as much as possible. Now he's gonna come face to face with him. While his father watches.

'Charlie!' The boss makes a megaphone with his hands. 'Open up.'

'Maybe I should go back and help Nat?' says Gus, hoping to get away. He was far crueller to the kid than was necessary. A mistake, perhaps, but he needs to keep the boy silent.

'No, no, it's okay. She'll manage for ten minutes. Probably still gassing with Joyce. Charlie? You need to open the door now. I have to come inside. You need to grab your stuff for school and get going. Mum's waiting.'

There's a grating sound of one piece of wood dragging across another.

'This door will need to be replaced, as a priority,' says the boss. The door opens a few inches. The boss gives it a little push. 'Come on, son. I need to have a look at the tower. Let me in.'

The door swings open and the boss steps inside. Gus hangs back.

'Come on in, Seb. Charlie's made the tower into a kind of den, haven't you, Charlie?'

There's no sign of the kid. The boss points to a makeshift ladder that leads up to a stone ledge running around the inside of the four walls.

'He'll be up there. He'll come down in a minute.' He lowers his voice. 'Not quite himself at the minute. Not sure what's got into him.' Then he speaks up, in a loud, jovial way, 'Well, what do you think of the place, Seb?'

'It looks amazing. How old did you say? Four hundred years?'

'Not quite. Three hundred and something, we reckon.'

'Are the walls intact?'

'Yes, and the roof.' The boss points up. 'Although it's not all original wood.'

As Gus looks towards the rafters, something catches his eye. A rag of some kind snagged on the stonework several metres above their heads. Dirty, and stained with what looks like blood. Hard to tell from this distance but it looks like a kid's shirt.

A kid's shirt? He glances at the boss to see if he's noticed it. He seems to be focused on the first level. 'Charlie, can you come down, please?'

Gus raises his shoulders, as if to say, kids.

'You're going to be late, Charlie,' says the boss, 'and you're being very rude.'

'It's okay, doesn't matter,' says Gus, delighted that the kid's avoiding him. 'How do you see the place when it's finished?'

The boss rolls his eyes. 'How do *I* see the place?' He gives a little laugh. 'I see it as a money pit, to be honest.' The boss has dropped his voice again. 'But Vivienne has her heart set on this wedding scheme and *she* sees the tower as our "unique selling point". Every successful business has a USP. Did you know that?'

'She might be right. Although I'd think the views might be enough of a USP.'

'Oh, I get that. Which is why the top floor here is to be the "room with a view", three hundred and sixty degrees. Glassed in, of course.'

'Of course.'

'So the bridal couple can sit up there sipping champagne and wishing on a star.'

'With a perfectly good bed waiting?'

'That's what I said, Seb. What self-respecting man is going to ponce about star-gazing on his wedding night?' The boss starts a dirty laugh then clamps a hand over his mouth and points to where his kid is hiding. 'Oops,' he whispers. 'Hope he didn't hear that. Maybe he has his headphones on?' He crosses his fingers and makes a face that shows he cares what the kid thinks. 'Right, Charlie, if you won't come down, I'm coming up.' He starts to climb the homemade ladder. It doesn't look strong enough to support a man's weight and the boss only ventures a few steps.

'Do me a favour, Seb? Don't tell my wife about this ladder or, God forbid, that you saw me climbing it. She hates the idea of Charlie playing in here, far less scrambling up to the first level. But hey, every boy needs a den, don't you think?'

'If you say so, Boss. My lips are sealed.' Shit. Why did he have to say that? 'Tell you what, I'll make myself scarce. Work to do.'

***

CHAPTER 33

When I know he's gone I stick my head out over the ledge and look down at Dad.

'Charlie,' he says, 'why didn't you come down when I called you? Bit rude.'

Shrug, as if I don't care. Although I know that's cheeky. Dad doesn't say anything.

Want to talk to him. Right now. Want to say, 'Dad'. Just one word.

I'm sure I can, if I try. Not scared of Dad. I put my teeth together. Tongue behind them. Try to make a sound. All that comes out is air, through my teeth, and a bit of spittle.

'Are you okay, son?'

Nod. Try again. Make a choking sound.

'You going to be sick, Charlie?'

Shake my head, although I do feel sick. Very, very sick. Always thought I could choose when to start speaking again. But it looks as if my voice is lost. Maybe forever. When I could talk, I didn't want to. Now I want to, I can't. It's not fair.

'Come on, son, down you come.' Dad's kind voice makes me want to cry. I'm nearly twelve. Can't keep blubbing like a baby all the time.

'What are you doing out here anyway? It's time for school. Mum will be going mental.'

Know I'm supposed to laugh when he says that. Try to smile, but it's hard with tears pushing to come out of my eyes.

Dad reaches up and helps me down the ladder. At the bottom, he gives me a hug. 'Are you sure you're okay to go to school?' He takes hold of my shoulders and kind of crouches down so his eyes are level with mine. 'I'm sure Mum won't mind if we tell her you're not feeling well and need the day off?'

He doesn't know I'm trying to be late. Deliberately. To avoid 'bump-up day'. A minibus is taking us to the big school. All the kids who are coming up from Primary Seven will be there. Miss Lawson calls it induction. It's to get us used to the new school so we know what to expect and then we don't have to worry about it over the summer holidays. As if that will help.

'Go on then. Mum will be waiting, and you don't want to make her mad.'

I don't move. If I miss the minibus, I won't have to go and be inducted.

'Go, Charlie. Run and get your stuff. I'll head Mum off at the pass.' He makes a gun of his fingers and goes, 'Pow, pow!' I jump as if he's fired a real gun and he laughs. He thinks I'm kidding and I think I'm going crazy.

Mum isn't going crazy. In fact, she isn't even waiting for me. She's fiddling with her phone in the kitchen. I grab my bag and my lunch box and stand at the door. We're not supposed to take a packed lunch today. We're supposed to go the dining hall in the Academy. But Mum doesn't know that. Cos I didn't give her the note.

Mum looks up, surprised to see me. She glances at the kitchen clock. 'Oh, sugar,' she says, 'we're late. Let's go.' She lifts her bag and the car keys and runs out. I trail after her, slow as a snail, and get in the car.

Mum used to chat to me all the time. I didn't need to speak. She told me everything and she was always asking me questions. I think she believed I would answer one day. Forgot that I couldn't talk.

There's an ad on the telly. A kid and his mum, or dad, can't remember, in a car and the wee boy is chatting away. It says, 'Talk to him now and he'll talk to you when he's older.' Or something like that. I think it's so the teenagers watching will tell their mum or dad that they're thinking of taking drugs. Then their mum or dad, both likely, will say, 'Listen, son. That's a really bad idea.' I'm scared I'll never be able to talk to my mum and dad about all that stuff.

I'm too frightened to tell them about the dead guy, but even before that happened, I wanted to tell them I'm scared of getting bullied at the Academy. Now I've got my very own super-bully living right here at Brackenbrae and I can't say a word.

Mum's not talking at all this morning. She's not interested in me. She seems to be in a world of her own. As if I'm not even in the car. Wonder if she's going to meet that guy again? She's dressed up kind of fancy.

She stops at the school and leans over. 'Kiss?' she says. She smells lovely. I kiss her cheek and get out of the car.

'See you later. Have a good day.' And she's gone.

Miss Lawson comes running up to me. 'Oh, Charlie. Thank goodness you're here. I thought you were going to miss bump-up day. Quick, jump on the minibus.'

When Mum picks me up at home time she sees me getting off the minibus. But she doesn't ask where I've been. Usually she would guess where I might have been, but not today. She seems all excited about something but she doesn't tell me what it is. Just waits for me to get in and says, 'Hi, Charlie.'

All the other kids will be telling their mums about bump-up day. How big everything is at the Academy, especially the pupils. Some of them are huge. I saw a great big boy in the corridor and almost had a heart attack. I thought it was Robbie.

It's funny I've been thinking about him today because when we pass the place where his house used to be, Mum says, 'Look, Charlie. Somebody's knocking down the cottage. I hear they're building a brand-new house.'

She looks at me in her wee mirror. I nod and smile to show her I've heard. I'm happy the ruins won't be there any more.

'Half an hour till teatime. You got homework?'

Shake my head.

'No? Sure?'

Nod.

'Suppose it's nearly the summer holidays. Okay then, scoot and get changed out of your school clothes.'

I make sure my bedroom door is closed before I take off my school polo shirt. Every day I inspect my bruises. Most have gone, though I can still see some of them, but they're turning a kind of pale yellow. Almost brown. Wonder why people say 'black and blue'? I was red and purple and now yellow. I'm a world expert on bruises.

***

CHAPTER 34

France
Sunday 24 June

Catherine looks at Sebastien's birthday gifts, piled on his bed. They should be in her suitcase heading to Scotland. She sighs and closes his bedroom door, feeling guilty for being so selfish when Mamie is ill.

Where on earth is Eric? He said he had a few things to attend to, in case they'd be gone a few days, but she thought he'd be home hours ago. If he doesn't get here soon they'll get caught up in rush-hour traffic and who knows when they'll make it to Mamie's.

Eric was adamant she shouldn't call Sebastien, but Catherine disagrees. All day she has been pacing the hall. Looking at the phone. Checking her mobile for messages, then reminding herself that Seb doesn't have his phone. The old one's being recycled by the manufacturers and the new one is sitting there in his bedroom, with his presents, waiting to go to Scotland. No point in posting it, she thought, when they can deliver it in person. Maybe she should take it with her and post it from Mamie's. Sebastien must be going crazy without it. These young people depend on their phones.

Damn Eric and his opinion. She's going to call that Brackenbrae place and tell Sebastien about his grandmother. He has a right to know what's happening.

'Brackenbrae Holiday Park. Pim speaking. Good afternoon. How may I help you, please?'

Oh no, not this guy again. 'Hello, my name is Catherine Lamar. I'm calling from Paris. I'm Sebastien's mother.'

'Ah, hello, Mrs Lamar, I'm remembering now. Do you wish to speak to your son?'

Catherine can hardly believe her luck. Sebastien must be right there, near the phone.

'Yes, please. Put him on.'

'I am very sorry, Madam, but Seb is not here at the moment.'

Catherine feels her disappointment like a sharp kick. 'It's really important I speak to him.'

'I understand, Madam, but he is not here.'

'Where is he?'

'I imagine he is working. Or it is possible he has finished for the day.'

'Do you think you could find him and ask him to come to the phone? Listen, I know you probably don't want to hear this, but we seem to have lost all contact with Sebastien and it really is causing me some distress. Now his grandmother is in hospital and we're very worried about her.' To her shame, Catherine starts to cry. Not silent, dignified tears, but great heaving sobs.

'I am most terribly sorry but as I explained before, I am not authorised to leave my post in reception.'

Catherine dries her eyes and tries to bring her breathing under control. She heaves a huge sigh. Heavy enough for him to hear. She hopes it might melt his heart. It seems to work. He says, 'Ah, perhaps the situation is not irretrievable. Is it convenient for you to hold on?'

'Of course,' says Catherine, thinking she'd hold on for the rest of her life if it meant she could hear her son's voice again.

'One moment, please.'

Catherine hears the phone being put down and wonders if he has deserted his post. Then a shout of, 'Charlie, can you come here, please, and do a very large favour for me?' There is no audible reply, but then Catherine hears the receptionist asking someone if he would be so kind as to go and fetch Seb and bring him to reception immediately. 'It is imperative that he takes this phone call.' Again, there is no reply that she can hear, but the receptionist comes back on the line and says, 'I have taken the matter in hand, Mrs Lamar. If you will bear with me, I am sure Seb will be with you shortly.'

Catherine waits, rehearsing what she will say to Sebastien, rephrasing several times in her head, until she gets the wording perfect – non-alarmist, non-accusatory, loving and caring, conscious of how fond her son is of his grandmother. No pressure to come home and see Mamie. No moral blackmail. No questions about why he hasn't been in touch.

She checks her watch. Five minutes at least must have passed since she said she'd hang on. She imagines Sebastien refusing to come and speak to her. She tries to picture the scene. A workmate, a friend perhaps sent to fetch him to the phone. Sebastien asking who it is. Shaking his head when he hears the word 'mother'.

She hangs up.

***

CHAPTER 35

Scotland

S ometimes it's good that I don't talk. Like when Pim grabbed me before teatime and asked why I hadn't fetched Seb.

When we sat down to eat, Mum seemed excited, but I still don't know why.

They talked about her meeting. It went well.

They talked about Dad's day. It went well too.

They asked about mine. Did it go well? That's all. None of the questions they always used to ask me. Did I get full marks in my maths test? Did Miss Lawson like my project? Did Mackenzie McMullen get into trouble for dyeing her hair blue? They didn't ask about bump-up day.

What will we 'talk' about when I go to the Academy? Mum won't be dropping me off at school any more so she won't see anyone going in the school gates. She won't know what colour Mackenzie's hair is. She won't see the other mums and hear the gossip. How will she ask me about people in my class? She won't know their names or anything about them. I won't come home with stickers or certificates to advertise my good scores in tests. If I can't speak, will we sit here and not communicate at all?

They send me outside for a bit after tea, but it's no fun any more doing the things I used to do. I'm too scared of turning a corner and running into Seb. He knows about my tower and now I don't even feel safe there. Why did Dad have to show him?

Wonder if Natalie's in the playbarn? I hardly ever see her now, because she works with Seb. Wish I could ask her about him. Pim seemed quite upset earlier when he asked me to fetch Seb to the phone. He was whispering something about Seb's mother being on the phone because his granny's ill. She was crying, Pim said. Worried that she's lost all contact with her son. Imagine anyone being sad that they can't see Seb! Yet he was kind to me at the start, that day. Before the shooting. That must be why he's not phoned his mum. Because he can't talk about it. Just like me when that thing happened with Robbie and I couldn't tell my mum.

Maybe I *should* have tried to find Seb. It's not his mum's fault that I'm scared of him. I could have caught hold of his arm, pointed to reception, mimed a phone call, pulled his sleeve to get him to go and speak to his mum. Yeah, right. Imagine me pulling Seb. He'd have swatted me away like a midgie.

I try the door of the playbarn. It's not locked. Open it and peep in. Seb and Nat are both there. Standing very close together. Far too close. Get away from her, I want to shout. Don't you touch her!

Natalie's giggling. I used to make her giggle all the time.

She looks up into his face and goes onto her tiptoes.

I get a funny feeling, way down deep in my body.

It looks like he's going to kiss her. Or she's going to kiss him. I don't know anything about kissing, I've never tried it. But I know I shouldn't be watching.

I let the door go and run. It shuts with a bang.

Can't get to sleep.

Mum and Dad are talking. Not fighting, using their quiet voices.

I move down a step. Hear Mum say, 'She loved it. Says it's perfect. Or it will be. She loves the barn. We wouldn't have to do a thing to it. Just clear out all the Kidz Klub stuff and make sure it's spotlessly clean.'

'What about flowers, lights, all that stuff?'

'Brides like to do all that styling stuff by themselves these days. There are magazines, websites, Pinterest pages galore, telling girls how to do it. Boys too, of course.'

'Boys?'

'Yes, boys. The gay wedding market is a big one and Sheona says our place will appeal, up here on the hill.'

'Gay weddings. Hadn't thought about that. What did she say about the tower?'

'She *especially* loved the tower. Says nowhere in Scotland is offering a bridal suite like that. With views to die for, like ours.'

Mum sounds really excited, but Dad's calmer. 'Where are we supposed to get the money to refurbish?'

'That, my darling, is what we have to find out, but I suspect it could be money well spent. Sheona's talking ten thousand pounds per wedding, for exclusive use, plus extra income from the yurts and cabins.'

'Ten grand? Are you kidding?'

'Now, that's worth doing up an old tower for, don't you think?' Mum sounds happier than I've heard her for ages.

'What about Charlie?' says Dad.

I move down a stair. Can't miss this.

'Pardon?'

'I said what about Charlie? He loves that tower.'

'He is not even supposed to go *in* that tower, Richard. I thought we agreed. It's far too dangerous.'

'But he likes it in there. It's his place. His space.'

'Rubbish. I don't want him anywhere near there. Hear me?' Her snippy voice is back. No wonder Dad's saying nothing.

Eventually he gives a cough and says, 'I'm pretty sure Charlie tried to speak today.'

'Oh my God. Why didn't you tell me this before? What did he say?'

'That's the point. Nothing. But I'm sure he tried very hard. Do you think something's bothering him?'

'What makes you say that?'

'Well, after all these years, he tries to tell me something. Which made me think, he's not been his usual self, has he?'

At last. They've noticed me.

'He'll be thinking about going to the Academy. Every kid worries about that. Didn't you?'

'I couldn't wait to go. Do you think that's all it is? Natalie mentioned hormones.'

'Oh, for God's sake! He's eleven.'

'He'll be twelve soon.'

'He's a baby.'

Why don't you stick up for me, Dad? Tell her I'm not a baby any more.

'I've been wondering. Do you think it's time to reconsider the notes thing? Before he goes to the Academy. We could get him an iPad to write on. That would be cool.'

Mum sighs so loudly I can hear it from almost the top of the stairs. 'He will *not* be writing notes. You think it will make any difference where he writes them? Do you want him branded a weirdo who can't speak and walks about with a tablet? Imagine the fun the bullies will have with that.'

Yeah, just imagine.

'Vivienne. Face facts. Charlie can't speak. He just proved that.'

'He can! How many experts told us that? He can!' She's shouting now.

Dad goes, 'Shh. He'll hear you.'

'He's in bed, he won't hear, and you won't listen to me. Maybe one day, when he's ready, he might speak again. But not if we let him write notes.'

It all goes quiet. Discussion over.

***

CHAPTER 36

France

Catherine stares through the windscreen, trying to ignore a child in the car in front. The boy, about six years old, is sticking his tongue out so far it's a wonder he doesn't choke. 'I knew we'd get caught on the Périphérique.'

Eric fiddles with the radio, probably looking for a traffic update. 'We've barely covered a kilometre.'

'This isn't normal traffic. We're still ahead of rush hour.'

'Why didn't you come home sooner?'

'I told you, Catherine. I had loose ends to tie up. We may not be back for several days.'

'Is it that serious?'

'I don't know. My brother was a bit sketchy with the details. Broken hip, I know that much, and her breathing's giving them cause for concern. It does not sound good.'

'Tell me again what happened.'

'Apparently she fell and lay all night on the kitchen floor.'

'Oh, poor Mamie. On those hard tiles. She must have been so cold and in terrible pain.'

'She seems to have been knocked out, or asleep, they're not sure. She hasn't been able to tell them much.'

'How did she manage to call an ambulance?'

'She didn't. You know how those old dears gather at the bread shop for a gossip every morning?'

Catherine does. She likes to fetch the bread when they visit Mamie, enjoys listening to the old folk chatting in their Occitan dialect, although she doesn't always understand everything they say.

'One of her neighbours noticed Mamie hadn't appeared. You know Josiane?'

'The tiny lady who looks like a sweet little mouse?'

Eric laughed. It was good to hear. 'Yes, that's her. Well, she went round to check and, of course, the shutters were all closed.'

'Unheard of.'

'Correct. Josiane rang the doorbell and called the police when there was no answer. They broke the door down and found her on the kitchen floor.'

'Any idea what caused her fall? Did she blackout? I told you she didn't sound good the last time I phoned. Very breathless and forgetting to use that inhaler thing she got.'

'There was a stool overturned and a pot of jam smashed on the tiles.'

'Oh dear. Sounds as though she was setting the table for morning.'

'Yes, and climbed up on a bloody stool. How often have we told her?' Eric bangs the steering wheel with the flat of his hands. She knows his anger comes from love of his mother, but he points at the cheeky kid in front who has moved on to sticking one finger in their direction. 'Why isn't that bloody kid strapped into a car seat? Don't his parents care what happens to him if they have an accident?'

Her thoughts go immediately to Sebastien. What if he's had an accident and that's why he didn't call back. She reminds herself again that he's got no phone.

'Do you think Sebastien might be at the hospital when we get there?'

Eric looks round at her. 'What makes you think that?'

Too late she realises her mistake.

'Did you tell him to come?'

'No, I didn't.' It's not a lie.

Eric stares at her. Just as well the traffic has ground to a halt again. 'You phoned, didn't you?'

Catherine nods. 'But I didn't get to speak to him.'

'Well, how could he possibly know to come?'

She says nothing.

'Catherine, that's not fair. We don't even know how serious Mamie is yet. There was no need to alarm Sebastien. You know he adores his grandmother.'

'That's why I felt he had a right to know she's in hospital.'

'I think you're being selfish.'

'Excuse me. In what way am I being selfish?'

'We can't go to Scotland, so you're manipulating Sebastien into coming home.'

His words sting, but she tells herself it's worry talking. 'That's not true. I'm hoping he gets the chance to see Mamie, before…'

'Before what? Before she dies? Moral blackmail, Catherine – it's your specialty.'

'That's a terrible thing to say.'

'Well, look me in the eyes and tell me you're not hoping he'll turn up at the hospital and then come home to Paris with us?'

***

CHAPTER 37

Scotland

Usually I can't wait for the summer holidays. But not this year.

Nothing to look forward to. Mum and Dad are too busy. Nat's not interested in me.

Seb seems to be everywhere. I can't get away from him. At least on a school day I'm safe for seven hours.

Mum and Dad think he's wonderful. Heard them talking about him last night. What an asset he is. So good with kids. Such a hard worker. Nothing's too much trouble. 'Very charming,' said Mum.

Even Joyce likes him, and she doesn't like everybody. 'Ah'm no very good at sufferin fools,' is what she always says. She hates Pim. 'There's a fool, if ever ah saw one. One of these days he'll choke on his fancy words.'

It seems Joyce and Natalie are always giggling when Seb's there. Or talking about him when he's not. If it's a nice day, they bring their coffee outside and I can hear them from the tower. Seb said this. Seb did that. How Natalie thinks he's so funny and Joyce thinks he's so handsome. Although not a bit like how she pictured him, whatever that means, rom what her Alex said the night he met Seb in the pub.

Seb. Seb. Seb. I'm sick of the sound of him. I wish he'd just–

Have to stop myself. Must not finish that thought. Know what happened the last time I made *that* wish.

Instead I wish he'd just go away. Home to France. Or wherever it is he came from.

Mum asked him to speak to me in French. She told me and Dad one teatime. Thought it might be good for me.

One day I was getting into the car with Mum, and Seb walked by. 'Morning, Boss Lady,' he said, with a big, beaming smile that showed his sparkling white teeth. Yeah, very charming. Mum laughed her silly, tinkly laugh. The one that annoys me.

'Hi, Charlie!' he said to me, putting his hand up for a high five.

'Surely you mean, "Bonjour, Charlie"?' said Mum.

He gave a kind of bow and said, 'Bonjour, Charlie.' They both laughed, as if he was the funniest guy in the world. I didn't give him a high five.

It's my birthday soon. Not even looking forward to that. Mum says I can ask some of the boys if they want to come. Not sure I want to.

It was cool last year with the pizzas and fizzy drinks and everything, but I was only eleven on that birthday.

Some of the boys have been twelve for months already. Don't think they'd want to come here and play. That's for wee kids, they'd say. Martin's party was a movie night. We went round to his house and watched three films and one of them was a 12A. Mum doesn't let me see those at home. For Justin's birthday we got dropped off on the high street and all went to Burger King for lunch. His mum wasn't even there or anything.

Mum says I'm lucky to be having a party at all because I don't deserve one. She's mad at me for being in the tower. Says it's far too dangerous. At first, she said I wasn't 'ever to set foot in there again'. But Dad said, 'That's not fair, Viv. At least let Charlie get his stuff out.'

'He shouldn't be in there with "stuff".' She made those little comma things in the air and her voice was nippy. But at least she agreed I could go in one last time and clear out my things.

So I'm going. Right now. In case she changes her mind. The moment I open the door to the tower I can smell body spray.

He steps out from behind the door. My heart starts to batter.

'Hello there, Charlie,' he says, as if it's normal to hide behind doors and frighten the life out of people.

He's so casual, you'd think he has a right to be there. 'Listen, Charlie, there's no need to be afraid of me.'

Oh yeah? That'll be right. The rainbow bruise on my arm still hasn't faded away.

'As long as we keep our secret, we'll both be safe. Won't we?'

Nod.

What's he doing in here? That's all I want to know.

'Bet you're wondering what I'm doing in here?'

How does he do that? It's like he's got a superpower.

'Don't worry. I'm here to help you.' He points up to my shirt. It's fluttering gently. Hanging there like a blood-soaked pennant from an ancient battle. 'It wouldn't be good if the workers found that and handed it over to your mum, would it?'

Shake my head. It would not.

'Gimme a hand here then. You keep an eye on the door. I nearly shat myself when you came in. We don't want anybody wondering why you and I are in here together, do we?'

The back of my neck feels kind of weird and I stroke it with my hand.

'Right, you stand guard and I'll get this sorted.'

He's got a bit of rope with a hook attached to the end. He throws it up and it comes straight back down and hits him in the face. 'Fuck.'

I try not to laugh. He looks down at me, as if to check. Glad I'm not smiling.

'Thought this would be a piece of cake.' He coils up the rope, like a cowboy. Throws again. This time the hook goes higher. It touches the shirt and drops again. Seb's ready. He catches it.

Third time lucky, I think.

'Third time lucky,' he says, throwing again. Up it flies. Down it comes and as it falls, it snags the shirt. It drops at my feet. I pick it up and run.

***

CHAPTER 38

France

By the time they reach the A61 to Carcassonne, it's late and getting dark.

'What do you think, Catherine? Should we go straight to the hospital or leave it till morning?'

'I don't know, darling. I'm not sure we'll be able to see Mamie this late.'

'I suppose that depends on how ill she is. Earlier, when I spoke to Paul, he said they were all sitting with her. I don't know if they've gone home.'

'I think we should at least go and ask how she is. It will put your mind at rest and, who knows, they may let us see her.'

As they approach the first junction for Carcassonne, Catherine says, 'Please can you take the next exit so I can see the city? I love it at night when it's all lit up.'

'You never tire of that view, do you?'

'No wonder. It must be one of the most beautiful in all of France. You take it for granted because you grew up here.'

They speed along the motorway that sweeps around the town and Catherine gasps in wonder when the city comes into view, as always. The fifty-odd turrets of the medieval city glow, floodlit against a navy-blue sky. 'Gets me every time,' she says.

'Want to stop at the viewpoint? I know you love it.'

'No, thanks. Not this time.' She strains to watch the turrets disappear into the distance then lifts her handbag as they leave the motorway and join the ring road.

'Not time to get out yet,' says Eric, laughing.

'I know. I just thought I'd give Sebastien another ring.'

'It's nearly 11pm, Catherine. You can't call a campsite at this time of night. They'll be closed. Leave it till tomorrow.'

'You sure? What if–'

'Never mind what if. There'll be plenty of time to call tomorrow. Speaking of which, did you remember to bring his new phone so we can post it from my mother's?'

'It's gone. I popped out and sent it while I was waiting for you to come home.'

'Good. How long did they say it would take to get there?'

'A few days. She refused to be any more specific.'

'Bloody nonsense, in this day and age. There's probably another strike planned that they haven't announced yet.'

'I should have ordered it online and had it sent directly to Scotland.'

'Bit late now.'

Eric is silent till they reach the big new hospital on the outskirts of town. Mamie, when they finally find her, is asleep alone; Paul and his family having been sent home for the night. A nurse assures Eric that his mother is 'comfortable', with her pain under control now. She points to a thin tube taped to the back of Mamie's hand. The area around the needle blooms dark with bruising. Catherine touches it gently with her fingertip. Mamie's skin feels smooth as the finest writing paper.

'I'm sorry about that,' says the nurse. 'Elderly patients like Mrs Lamar tend to bruise easily. Their skin is so very thin. It looks more painful than it is, I promise.'

'I certainly hope so,' says Eric, sounding unimpressed.

'Our priority when she came in was to make her as comfortable as possible. She was very agitated and disorientated and seemed to remember very little about what happened. She passed out on the floor, possibly from the pain.'

'Can pain make you lose consciousness?' asks Catherine.

'Oh yes, if it's severe enough. It's the body's way of protecting itself.'

'Did she have a CT scan to check for head injury?'

'Yes, it was clear.'

'Do you think she just overbalanced and fell? Apparently she was up on a stool, reaching into a cupboard.'

The nurse shakes her head. 'The number of times that happens, you wouldn't believe. She may have lost her balance, or it may have been a drop in blood pressure that made her dizzy.'

'Will she need surgery?' asks Eric.

'Almost certainly. An orthopaedic surgeon will see your mother first thing in the morning. We'll have more information for you then.'

'Should we stay with her, do you think?'

'To watch her sleep?' The nurse smiles, kindly. 'My advice is to go home and get a good night's sleep yourselves. There's nothing you can do tonight.'

'We've driven from Paris.'

'You must be shattered then,' says the nurse, putting her hand on the small of Catherine's back. 'I suggest you give us a call in the morning. The night staff will take very good care of her, don't worry.'

'There's one thing I need to ask you,' says Catherine. 'Our son is away working in Scotland. Should we send for him? He's very close to his grandmother.'

'Is he due to come home?'

'No, he's only been away a few weeks. He was intending to be gone for the summer,' says Eric, 'but my wife thinks we should bring him home. To tell you the truth, she's missing him.'

'Oh, I get that. When my son went off to university I missed him terribly. It's natural, even if they drive us crazy when they're at home.'

'So you don't think we need tell Sebastien to hurry back to see Mamie?'

'It's entirely up to you, of course, and your son, but based on how she is tonight, I see no need for alarm. Elderly people fall over and break hips all the time.'

'Okay,' says Eric, 'thanks for your advice and your care. We'll leave Sebastien where he is in the meantime and we'll see you tomorrow.'

As they walk back to the car, Catherine says, 'I hope we're doing the right thing. You know how much Sebastien adores his grandmother. He'll never forgive us if anything happens to her and we don't tell him.'

'You heard what the nurse said.'

'I know I did, and I believe her. But I'm calling the campsite in the morning. Sebastien can decide for himself.'

***

CHAPTER 39

I always wake up before Thomas and the stupid Fat Controller now. Every morning. I open my eyes and remember. It feels like somebody kicks me hard in the belly every single time.

I used to sleep right up till Thomas whistled. Sometimes, if I was really tired, I didn't even hear the whistle and Mum would come in and sit on my bed. She'd stroke my hair or my cheek and say, 'Wake up, sleepyhead.' She always sounded in a good mood, as if she was really happy to see me. I think she used to hope, every single morning, that I would speak. There's a song called "This is the day". The other kids used to sing it at Sunday school, before Mum stopped taking me. I liked it because it was one with clapping in it, so I could join in. Mum used to sing it to me some mornings before I got up, but she'd change the words. 'This is the day when Charlie will speak, this is the day CLAP! this is the day CLAP!' Then she stopped. Can't remember exactly when but I think maybe one of the doctors told her it wasn't helping. Can't remember when she gave up trying to find ways to help me. Now they've just got used to having a boy who doesn't talk. Like it's normal.

One person still believes I can talk. Natalie. She's up to something. I can tell. Every time she sees me she asks me questions, just little ones that need a yes or a no. It's like she's playing that game with me where you try to trick the other person into shouting 'Yes!' or 'No!' Except this isn't a game. It never was, but now, just when I thought I could talk, when I was getting ready to try, things got much so much more serious.

The door opens and Mum rushes in.

'Come on, Charlie. Get up.' She doesn't sit on my bed. Just blasts about the room picking things up and putting things away. She picks up my clothes from yesterday.

'Oh yes, that's right,' she says, as if she's talking to herself, not me. 'Have you seen those new blue shorts? And the shirt that goes with them?'

Shake my head. The shirt's under the mattress now. Didn't know where else to put it. I stay in bed so Mum can't look for it. She doesn't know it's there, but I'm still scared she'll find it.

'Well, clothes don't just disappear, do they?' Why does she talk in that snippy way all the time? 'There's something else I've been meaning to ask you.'

I stick my head up, like the meerkats on the telly, and try to look really interested.

'Where's the throw that's supposed to be on the end of your bed?'

I make a puzzled face, as if I'm trying to remember what she's talking about.

'The red fleece one?' She touches the end of my bed. 'It's supposed to lie across here, to dress the bed, like those cushions you always throw into the corner.'

Dressing a bed, what a stupid idea.

She points at two fat cushions, one red with white dots and the other bright blue stripy. They're lying in the corner, where I throw them every night. How am I supposed to get into my bed if I don't? I hate cushions. Why can't Mum see that?

'These things cost money, Charlie.'

Oh no, not the money lecture again. I throw back the duvet and jump out of bed. It works. She stops talking. Good, she'll go away now.

'What's that mark on your side?' She comes over and lifts up my jammy jacket. I push it down again and step away from her. I clasp both hands over my private parts, like I used to do to show I needed the toilet.

'Do you need the toilet?' she says, as if I'm five years old again. Nod and head for the door.

I close the bathroom door and lock it behind me. That was close. I thought she was going to examine me. I pull the jammy top over my head – another thing that annoys Mum. I'm supposed to undo the buttons. Dad gets a row for it too. There's a great big shiny mirror all along one wall above the basin.

The bruises are fading, but not very fast. The one Mum spotted must have been from a hard kick. It's still a bit purply with yellow bits round about. What if she asks to see it? I'll pretend I'm in the shower and stay here till she goes downstairs. Then we'll be in a rush to get to school and maybe she'll forget.

I turn on the shower and duck out again fast before I get soaked. Let it run and stand by the door, waiting.

Mum thumps on the door, right by my ear and I nearly pee my jammies.

'Charlie! A shower? Seriously? We don't have time. Charlie? Do you hear me?'

She bangs again but this time I've got my hands over my ears. 'Charlie! Oh, for God's sake.'

She's on the stairs, clattering down. Even her feet sound cross with me.

Listen for the kitchen door. Expect it to bang. When it does I turn off the water and sneak back to my room. Get dressed double-quick, tucking my polo right into my school trousers so Mum can't yank it out and inspect my bruises. Thought about putting some of her make-up on them as a disguise, but what if she came in and found me? Using her posh stuff that costs a fortune. Her skin reacts to anything but Chanel, I heard her telling Joyce one day. Joyce sniffed, that way she does and said, 'I could put chip-pan oil on my face and it would think it was getting a treat.'

If Joyce cleans my room today she might find the shirt. Can't leave it there, even though it's a good place for hiding stuff. People even keep money under their mattress. Heard Dad saying that.

'Interest rates are so crap, we might as well stick our savings under the mattress.'

Mum said, 'What savings? We don't have any, remember?'

Think Dad was joking but Mum's sense of humour has kind of disappeared. She'll be up here looking for me in a minute, on the warpath. I stick my hand under the mattress and feel around for the shirt. Can't find it.

'Charlie! If you're not down here in ten seconds…Ten! Nine!'

I don't know what to do. She sounds so angry. Has she found the shirt?

'Eight! Seven!'

***

CHAPTER 40

France

Catherine steps through the bower of honeysuckle around Mamie's garden gate and pauses to inhale. The sweet aroma seems to hang in the air, like a mist of cologne. Avoiding the bees, already hard at work, their buzzing loud against the morning quiet, she bends to run her hand over a tall clump of lavender. The plant obliges her with a blast of the intense fragrance that Mamie loves so much. She's going to have a bumper crop this summer, plenty to keep the linen fresh over the winter. Soon it will be time for her to gather the flower heads and pack them into tiny muslin bags, capturing their summer scent. Catherine has always liked the old-fashioned way her mother-in-law places the embroidered sachets amongst the sheets and pillows in her linen cupboard. Sebastien says the smell of lavender reminds him of sleeping at Mamie's and claims he sleeps better there than at home in his own bed.

How on earth must he be sleeping these days, living amongst strangers in some kind of dormitory? Best not to think about it.

Catherine opens the front door and lets herself into the dark hall. She turns to lock the door, knowing Mamie never does, but Catherine's city-girl habits die hard.

'Eric? I'm back, honey. Put the kettle on, will you?'

Eric was supposed to be getting the rest of breakfast organised while she fetched the bread but he's nowhere to be seen. She goes to the foot of the stairs and calls again. Shrugging, she heads back into the kitchen, places the baguette on the table and turns to fill the kettle.

With the table set and the coffee brewing, she goes to the door and steps into the garden. 'Eric, can you fetch me down a jar of jam, please? I'm not climbing on any stools.'

She hears his footsteps on the gravel and waits for him to come along the path laughing, but when he appears his face is white and drawn.

'What's wrong? Has something happened?'

He holds his phone towards her, as if that answers her question. 'Please. Not Sebastien!'

He looks at her, his eyes full of sorrow and shakes his head.

'Mamie?'

Eric doesn't have to answer. She goes to him and takes him by the arm.

'Come inside and sit down, sweetheart. Tell me.'

'We should have stayed, Catherine. Been with her.' He hides his face in his hands and says something, his words muffled.

'Did they get her priest?'

'Not in time, apparently.'

'Does Paul know?'

'It was Paul who rang me. Hospital called him ten minutes ago.'

'Does he know what happened?'

'No. Don't think the doctors even know what happened. She just died.'

'In her sleep? Surely that's the way most people would wish to go. I would.'

'Without saying goodbye to any of us?'

Catherine wonders for a moment which would be worse: knowing you're breathing your last but seeing beloved faces around your bed or just slipping away peacefully, knowing nothing.

'Oh, I don't know, Eric. I'm just so, so sorry.' She goes to his side and pats his back, wishing he'd stand for a hug, or even raise his face so she can kiss his forehead. Show him she shares his sorrow. She loved Mamie and Sebastien adored her. Sebastien. He needs to know.

'What do you want to do? Should we go to the hospital?'

'Not much point.'

'Is Paul there now?' She hesitates, knowing it might hurt him, then asks, 'Was Paul with her?'

'Nobody was with her. Didn't you hear me? I told you, she was all alone.'

'But she wouldn't know, Eric. She was heavily sedated, her pain under control. The nurse said so.'

'Why didn't we stay, Catherine? Why did we leave her?'

She starts to remind him about the nurse's advice to go home and get a good night's sleep then changes her mind. That won't help. Eric is a man who likes to do the right thing. He also hates making a mistake and he'll consider this a big one, even though they were simply following professional advice.

'No one knew by the sound of things.'

'They're supposed to know. That's their job. How could that stupid nurse send us home, when my mother was knocking at death's door? More importantly, why didn't they get my mother a priest, any priest?'

'Eric, the last thing you need to worry about is your mother's immortal soul. I don't think I've ever met a more devout and truly good human being. I can't imagine she'd have any sins unconfessed, can you?'

'That's not the point. She would have wanted a priest there, and her family, of course. Instead we're wasting time in her kitchen worrying about getting jam off the shelf.'

Catherine knows anger is a common reaction to the death of a loved one. She also knows there is little she can do to ease Eric's pain, or the guilt he's feeling at the moment. This will all pass, in time. She places her lips gently on the top of his head and whispers, 'Sorry, darling. I'll go and tell Sebastien what's happened. He'll be so upset. I wish he wasn't so far away.'

'Well, he'll have to come home now. You'll get your wish.'

There's no point in talking to him. He doesn't mean to be unkind, she understands that. Give him ten minutes and he'll be looking for her, keen to apologise for his harsh tone.

Catherine closes the kitchen door quietly behind her and selects Brackenbrae from her list of contacts.

'Brackenbrae Holiday Park. May I wish you a very good morning, Pim speaking.'

As if she can't work that out for herself. 'Good morning. This is Catherine Lamar, Sebastien's mother. Sorry to bother you.'

'Nothing is a bother, Mrs Lamar, let me assure you. Would you wish to speak to Seb this morning?'

She bites back the reply that it might have been nice to speak to him on the last two occasions she's called, but what's the point, under the circumstances. 'Yes, please, I have some important news to share so this time it really is imperative that I speak to him. Can you help me with that, Pim?' Using his name might establish some sort of connection with this rather formal young man. Or it may have the opposite effect.

'I shall certainly do what I can for you, Mrs Lamar. Now, let me see. Seb should be in the playbarn, but he sometimes runs a little late. Oh hang on a moment, please. We are in luck.'

Catherine hears a clunk and assumes Pim has laid down the receiver. She waits, hears his voice calling, 'Seb! Seb, your mother's on the phone.'

There's a pause in which Catherine hears nothing then, 'Can you come and take her call, please?'

Why would Sebastien hesitate to come and speak to her?

'She has some important news to share.'

She hears a muttered, 'Fine,' and holds her breath.

'Here he is, Mrs Lamar. Have a pleasant day. There you go, Seb.'

'Sebastien?'

No answer. Is he still so angry he won't speak to her?

'Sebastien, how are you?'

He clears his throat. 'Okay.'

She waits for more then decides to push on. 'Well, my darling, I don't quite know how to tell you this, but I have some sad news for you. I'm afraid Mamie's died.'

A quiet, 'Oh.' Nothing else.

'We don't know yet what happened. She fell off a stool trying to reach a pot of jam, you know what she's like.'

Catherine expects him to say something and gives a small embarrassed laugh when he doesn't.

'Anyway, she lay all night till little Josiane, you know Josiane?'

'Yeah.'

His voice sounds gruff, with emotion no doubt. This must be awful for him to get such news over the phone. She longs to put her arms around him, to comfort her sad boy a little.

'Well, Josiane found her. Seems Mamie had lain there all night. Isn't that horrendous?'

He doesn't respond. She pictures him truggling to hold back tears, not wanting to cry in front of Pim.

'Dad and I rushed down to Carcassonne when we heard and went straight to the hospital, you know, that big new one they've built? She seemed fine. Settled for the night, sedated or medicated or whatever you call it when they attach people to one of those drip things. Anyway, the nurse was adamant she was in no pain and that we should go away and get a decent night's sleep ourselves. It had been a long and stressful day, so we went back to Mamie's. I thought of you when I smelled the lavender on the pillow. Remember how you always loved that smell?'

A grunt. Nothing more. Oh, her poor, poor boy.

'Sorry, son, I'm not making this very easy. Dad is being very hard on himself for leaving her bedside, but what were we to do when the nurse insisted Mamie would be alright? We were encouraged to believe she might have an operation today to fix her broken hip. At least poor Mamie won't have to go through all of that.' She's babbling but it's hard to keep up a one-sided conversation. Why doesn't he say anything? Because he's trying to come to terms with the devastating news she's just delivered on this lovely summer's morning.

'What's the weather like in Scotland?'

A quiet spluttering sound, like a sob, is all that comes by way of a response. It was a ridiculous thing to ask, of course. She should speak of practical things. Men are better at dealing with the practical than the emotional.

'Will you sort out your own way back? Best to come straight here, I think. Dad says there's a direct link from Scotland to Carcassonne, but not every day. Maybe you'd be best to fly to London first? I really don't know.' She runs out of words as the reality of the situation hits her. Here's her son, far away from home, being told he'll never see his beloved grandmother again and she's wittering on about flights without offering a single word of comfort to him.

'Sebastien, my darling, I am so, so sorry. I can't imagine how much it must hurt you to hear this news when you're so far from home. I wish I could hug you.'

Her words dry up as her tears start to flow.

'Sorry, son, will you be alright?'

'Yeah.' So gruff, so full of pain. She ought not to prolong this. Much though she hates to let him go, she must allow him to go off on his own and cry his eyes out, somewhere private.

'That's good. Take care of yourself and we'll see you soon. Love you, darling.'

A loud sniff. Poor thing.

'Bye, darling boy.'

***

CHAPTER 41

Scotland

Now what's he supposed to do?

He bangs his hand on the counter and turns to Pim. 'Fuck!'

'The news is very bad?'

'Mate, you have no idea. It could hardly be any worse.'

Pim crosses the office and gives him a pat on the shoulder, looking embarrassed. 'I am very sorry. I assure you I was not ear-dropping on your conversation with your mother, but I can tell you are upset.'

'Upset doesn't cover it.'

'Is it something you would like to speak about, perhaps? A trouble shared with a friend is a trouble divided into two equal parts. Isn't that what you say?'

'What? Yeah, something like that. Hey, listen, Pim, I'd be grateful if you don't mention this phone call to anyone. It's kinda private, you know? My mum wouldn't like the idea of people she's never met talking about our family.'

'I understand perfectly, and I shall be the very model of discretion, I assure you. It is part of my personality.'

'Good.'

'Seb, before you go?'

Gus sighs. What now?

'I am very sorry, whatever has happened.'

'Appreciate it, mate.'

Natalie is already busy when he opens the door to the playbarn. She's dragging a table across the floor, its legs screeching like a tortured cat.

'This is going to be a real pain in the arse,' she says. 'Stacking all this away every time there's a wedding then hauling it all back out again. I'm not sure they've thought this through properly. Still, it won't be my problem. Can you give me a hand with the chairs, please?'

'If the wedding business takes off they won't need a playbarn, or us. Have you thought about that?'

'They'll need us for this summer, surely?'

'You think so? Mrs Boss seems pretty determined to get started as soon as poss. I'm thinking I might take off. See if I can find another job for the rest of the summer, or longer. Not sure this is for me.'

'Jump before you're pushed, you mean? Why would you do that? Let's just ask the boss if he's planning on keeping us on. Weddings aren't the kind of thing folk book on a whim. Brides certainly don't book places that aren't even ready. The work hasn't started on the tower yet and that's to be Brackenbrae's USP, apparently.'

'Nah, maybe you're right.'

'You okay? You seem kind of down this morning. That's not like you.' She touches his arm.

He pulls away, not comfortable with touchy-feely stuff. 'How do you know what I'm like, Nat? You hardly know me.'

'I know you're a kind, caring guy with a great sense of humour and a soft spot for kids. Charlie loves you. I can tell.'

Gus gives a snort. 'Oh really? How can you tell that?'

'Just the way he looks at you, like he's fascinated or something. I don't know. It's just, this might sound daft, but I sense a kind of special bond between the two of you.'

'You're full of shit, Nat,' he says, shaking his head. If only she knew.

'That's another reason I don't want you to leave. I think, between the two of us, we can have Charlie talking before the summer holidays are over.'

'You really believe that's a possibility? The kid could talk anytime?'

'Well, maybe not anytime. But we've got almost six weeks to help him work up to it. He just needs to be encouraged, made to feel confident enough to try. Think what an achievement that would be, Seb. How empowered he'd be to face all the challenges of high school, if he can talk like all the other kids. You and I can make that happen.'

She sounds as passionate as the worst kind of Bible-basher. She's scarily committed to achieving her goal.

'Are you absolutely sure that would be the best thing for Charlie?'

She looks at him as if he's lost his mind. 'Am I sure? What kind of a crazy question is that? Of course, I'm sure. That kid's life will be a misery for the next four or five years if we don't help him. You don't know kids, but I do, and they can be the most evil, devious, cruel little shits when they find a victim.'

'Do you think Charlie will be a target for bullies? He seems quite robust to me.'

'Are you kidding me? He's a seriously sensitive wee boy. Why else would he have stopped talking in the first place?'

***

CHAPTER 42

Friday 29 June

Can't believe it's the summer holidays. Felt quite sad to leave school yesterday. For the last time. Think Miss Lawson was sorry to see us go. She was nearly crying and gave us all a hug. Some of the boys didn't want one but I did. I'm going to miss her. Mum bought Miss Lawson a present from me when she was up in Glasgow. A reed diffuser. I have no idea what that is but Mum said it was from a posh shop and Miss Lawson would be very pleased. Mum insisted I hand it over in a special white carrier bag with the name of the shop on the side. Jayden Jeffries gave her a packet of sweeties in an Aldi bag and Miss Lawson seemed just as pleased. Mum could have saved a lot of money.

Miss Lawson and Mrs Walker shook us all by the hand and said, 'Good luck' and then our names. Mrs Walker knows the name of every kid in the school. When Miss Lawson shook mine and said, 'Good luck, Charlie,' she bent down and whispered, 'Hope you find your voice, Charlie. You have great things to say. I'm sure of it.' Then she made her mouth into a funny shape, with her lips all tucked inside, and she nodded her head, over and over.

Now I don't know what I'm going to do with myself all day every day. It seems like a long time from June till August. About forty days. Surely I can learn to speak again in forty days, if I really want to, and I think I do. What's wrong with talking about normal stuff like chips and football players? I don't have to talk about the bad things that have happened. If I could speak, maybe I could sort things out with Seb. Stop him bullying me. Explain that he doesn't have to worry. His secret's safe with me. Then at the end of the summer holidays, he'll go away back to France and I'll never see him again. Nobody ever needs to know what happened that day. Yeah, that's a good plan. Why didn't I think of it before?

Before I say anything to him, I want to check some stuff on the Internet. I'll need to be sneaky and get into the office when that geek Pim isn't there. Maybe I can get in while he's in the café having his lunch break. Don't want him nosing around over my shoulder and telling Dad what I'm up to.

The kitchen seems full of people when I open the door, but it's just Dad, Mum and Joyce.

Mum pounces on me the minute I walk in.

'Charlie, did you ever find that blue shirt? Or the shorts I bought to go with it? They were from Next.'

'Ooh,' says Joyce, 'that must have cost a bob or two.'

What even is a bob? But thanks, Joyce, I don't need you making it any worse for me. I shrug and try to look as if I've no idea what Mum's talking about. Inside I'm thinking phew! I've been waiting for her to wave them in front of my face and say, 'Seriously, Charlie? A brand-new shirt? All covered in God knows what.'

That means the shirt must still be under the bed. I rise from the table, scattering Coco Pops everywhere and run out. Mum says, 'That boy!' Don't hear what else cos I'm taking the stairs two at a time. I lift the mattress and stick my head underneath so my shoulders keep it up and I can reach further in. My fingers feel around and there it is. Shoved right back. How did I manage that? Stand there for a minute with my head under the mattress while I try to decide what to do. The mattress is so heavy it feels like it's squashing my brain and I can't think. I grab the shirt and put the bed back the way it was. I'd like to find that red fleece but there's no way I'm going back into those gorse bushes, ever.

I open my desk drawer and stuff the shirt right in at the back. Then I pile up all my pens and colouring books and coloured pencils and a Tipp-Ex thing and an old pencil case from the drawer below, and a couple of comics. The drawer is so full I can hardly shut it. No one's going to find it there. Why would anyone look for a shirt in a desk?

The sun is pouring in my bedroom window and it's the summer holidays. Maybe things will work out alright after all. If I'm patient.

'What was all that about?' asks Mum, the minute I walk into the kitchen. I clutch my belly and make a face. Then smile to show her I'm okay.

Dad says, 'Right, I'm off out to clear some bracken.'

The smile drops off my face. I can feel it go.

'Want to come and help me, Charlie?'

No idea what to say. I should go with him and try to keep him away from the grave, but I can't go back out there. Even thinking about it makes me feel sick. My head seems to decide for me and gives a quick shake to Dad.

'No? You sure?'

Very sure. Nod to prove it.

'Okay.' Dad sounds a bit disappointed, but I can't help that.

'You still available to cover reception today, Viv?'

'Me? Why? What's happened to Pim?'

'He asked for the day off, remember?'

'On the first Saturday of the summer holidays? Please don't tell me you said yes.'

'His family are over from Holland. He's going to meet them in Glasgow.'

'Glasgow? Why didn't you get them to come here for a couple of nights?' She makes that tutting noise. 'Where were you when they were giving out the business brains, Richard?'

Why is she being nasty to him? He does his best. I want to tell her to shut up and stop being a bitch. Just as well I can't talk.

'I'm away to get started,' says Joyce. 'I'll be in the toilet block if anybody needs me.' She makes a face at me, as if to say, I'm outta here.

'Anyway, to answer your question, no, I'm not available today. I'm going to the big wedding fayre at the racecourse.'

'Today? I thought that was tomorrow?'

'Saturday's the best day apparently.'

'You might have told me.'

'Thought I did. Anyway, if we're going to be a success as a wedding venue, I need to make contacts in the business.'

'So you can check out the opposition?'

'Exactly, and who knows, maybe we'll be on the exhibitors' list at the next wedding fayre.' She seems excited and it's good to see her smile again. Dad must think the same. He goes and gives her a hug and a kiss.

'Okay, good luck. By the way, don't worry about reception. I'll put a sign on the door directing enquiries to the café. I should be back before the first check-ins arrive and if I'm not, Big Mark can give them a free drink and tell them to go ahead and use the pool.'

'Fine.'

'Sure you don't want to come with me, Charlie? I'll let you use the scythe?'

'Don't you dare,' says Mum. 'I prefer my boy with two feet, thank you very much.' She ruffles my hair as she passes. 'You be okay till Dad gets back?'

Nod.

'Good. I'm off to get ready. First rule of business – dress to impress.'

Will I be okay till Dad gets back? With Pim on a day off and reception closed? Will I? It's the chance I've been waiting for.

***

CHAPTER 43

Gus looks down at the airplane steps, sees his trainers and wonders if it was a mistake to wear shorts.

There's no one waiting to meet him, and he feels a huge wash of relief. Trouble is, he'll need to take a taxi now and he's short of cash. The plane ticket just about cleaned him out.

He gives the driver the address and sits back to watch the town go by. What's he going to say when he gets there? Hi, Mum, long time no see? Best to stick to a simple hello and say as little as possible till he sees how the land lies.

The taxi pulls up and the driver sticks his hand across the seat and demands a sum that seems ridiculous for such a short ride. Prices have gone up since he was last here. He hands over the last of his cash, hoping it's enough and climbs out.

Heads turn as he walks in. Because of how he's dressed?

'Son! You made it. Thank God for that.' Her thin arms go around him, and he smells her freshly washed hair as it brushes his cheek. It feels so good to be home, so good being hugged by someone who loves him. He never wants it to stop.

'Sorry about the gear,' he says when she pulls away to have a look at him.

'Don't worry about that. The only thing that matters is you're here. At last. Isn't that right?'

A man he doesn't recognise, but who looks vaguely familiar, shakes his hand then pulls him into a tight hug with lots of hard slaps on the back. Meant to be affectionate, he knows.

The man seems to have trouble speaking. 'Thanks for coming, son. Your mum was starting to panic but I told her you'd be here. I said you'd never miss your grandmother's funeral.'

Something about the man is troubling him, but Gus can't put his finger on what it is. When it dawns on him he blurts out, 'Your hair. It's the same colour as the dead guy's.'

'The dead guy's? What are you talking about, Sebastien?'

'Wait a minute,' says the woman. 'This isn't Sebastien. You're not my son.'

Gus sees the crowd of men in dark suits gathering, making their way towards him. He was crazy to think he could get away with this. 'Let's get this asshole out of here. Anyone who wears shorts to a funeral deserves to be taught a lesson.'

Gus throws a punch, a good one, connecting with bone. A woman screams and someone starts crying. He raises his fist again and someone grabs his arm, forces it up his back. He kicks out, swearing in a crazy mixture of English and French.

'Seb! Seb! Stop this noise.'

Gus flails wildly with his left arm, trying to punch the face above him.

'Stop! It's me, Pim. You're dreaming.'

Gus sits up, pushes Pim away and says, 'Dreaming. Yeah, dreaming, sorry.'

No more sleep. He lies awake till the first birds start to sing and dawn creeps into their room.

Guilty conscience will do that to a guy, he's heard. This is the first time in his life he's felt true remorse about anything. Sure, he's been disappointed in himself at times, especially when his temper has got the better of him. This black feeling that gets him the minute he wakes is something new. It stays with him all day long, following him around like a stray dog that won't go away no matter how many kicks it gets.

Eventually it's time to get up, shower and face the day. He rubs at his eyes as he crosses the courtyard wishing he didn't have to go to work. Ever since that phone call from the dead guy's mother, he's been having these crazy dreams.

Did she realise she was speaking to an impostor? Surely she'd recognise her own son's voice. A thousand times he has replayed their conversation in his head. Over and over again, trying to remember exactly what he said, if anything. Just a series of grunts and okays is all he remembers, surely not enough to make her suspicious.

But even if he got away with the phone call, say the woman was too upset to notice if his voice was deeper or higher or whatever, it's only a matter of time till the shit hits the fan. The guy's granny had just snuffed it and his mother expected him to go home. Right away. She made that obvious on the phone, talking about flights and all. An image of him walking down the stairs of a plane flashes into his mind, so real he tries to remember what he was wearing the last time he flew. Flashback to the dream. Great. As if flashbacks to the shooting aren't enough to torment him.

Funerals don't get arranged overnight. If the old dear has just croaked it, he'll have a couple of weeks' grace, surely, before Sebastien is expected back home. That should be long enough to make some sort of plan. If only he hadn't blown his first few weeks' wages, he might have enough for his air fare by now. But he had to buy his round, didn't he. Besides, it's a great laugh in the bar at night and about the only time he can forget what happened. After a few beers, even Pim can be quite funny and Big Mark is hilarious. The boss is on to a good thing. Pay your workers their wages then sit back while they spend them in your bar. Nice one.

Natalie puts her hands on her hips when he opens the door. 'At last. We thought you'd never put in an appearance this morning.'

'Don't start, Nat. I'm not in the mood this morning. Seriously.'

'Too long in the bar last night? I thought you looked like you were in for a session with Mark. That's why I left. I prefer a clear head, you need it for this job.'

'Nah, it's not that. I just didn't sleep, and when I did, I had this horrendous dream where I was about to get a kicking. Pim saved me.'

Natalie laughs. 'Pim? The hero? Was he wearing his pants over his tights, by any chance?'

Gus can't help laughing at the mental picture she's planted in his brain. No wonder Joyce calls her 'a wee tonic'. He's gonna miss this girl. Pity he's got to leave soon. They could have a good thing going if he stayed on.

As if she's reading his thoughts, Nat says, 'You know what you were saying the other day, about leaving early? You didn't mean it, did you?'

Gus rubs his hands through his hair. 'Know what, Nat? I've no idea what I'm gonna do and that's the truth.'

'Well, I hope you stick around. I think we make a good team. Speaking of which, Kidz Klub is about to get busy from now on and we need a programme. Will you take a look at this and see what you think of it?'

With a flourish, Natalie produces a beautifully printed list of activities for the following week. 'Don't worry if you don't agree with it. I can easily make changes.'

Gus points to Wednesday afternoon. 'What's this? Hiking with Seb. When did I agree to that?'

'You didn't, but apparently there's a big family coming in today with seven kids. I think it may be a blended family.'

'A what?'

'Quote, a blended family is formed when a couple moves in together, bringing children from previous relationships into one home, unquote. So, if Mum with three kids moves in with–'

'It's okay. I get it.'

'Well, they've asked the boss specifically if we will provide activities for the older children. It was a condition of their booking and they wanted two tipis for the full week.'

'So the boss said yes?'

'No, the boss said sorry because the tipis aren't available yet, not till he gets permission from the local council. He offered them two static caravans instead at a reduced price and some special activities for their kids. That's where you come in.' Natalie waves her hand like she's just performed a magic trick.

'Hiking? Where the hell am I supposed to go hiking, with kids in tow?'

'Well, here's my plan. The boss has agreed a special rate with the Farm Park. You know, on the main road? With the camel and everything?'

Gus lets his face do the talking.

'You have no idea what I'm talking about, do you?'

'You lost me at camel.'

Natalie giggles, and Gus thinks he could listen to that sound all day long.

'Well, it's a great hit with smaller kids. Apparently, it was Mrs Boss who had the idea we should start charging extra for some special activities. With our discounted rate at the Farm Park...' She circles her right hand in the air and waits for him to finish the sentence.

'Brackenbrae makes money?' He gives a nod of admiration. 'Gotta hand it to her. She's the one with the business brain.'

'Anyway, we'll all get dropped at the Farm Park. I'll spend the afternoon there with the wee ones, you'll take the teenagers for a hike and we'll meet back there for tea or ice creams, whatever.'

'Where precisely am I meant to go hiking? Along the main road to Dunure and back? Yeah, that'll be fun. If one of them doesn't die.' Shit! Why did he have to say that?

'Don't be daft. You will introduce them to the Ayrshire Coastal Path of course, one of Scotland's Great Trails.'

'Never heard of it.' Even as he says those words he's wondering. 'Ayrshire Coastal Path, that's ringing a bell. I've seen that somewhere.'

'On a sign, maybe?'

'Maybe.' A thought occurs to Gus that makes his stomach do a flip. 'It's not up here, is it, on the hill?'

'*Coastal* path? The clue's in the name.' Natalie points in the direction of the sea. 'Duh!'

'Thank God.'

'What?'

'Nothing, never mind. You're sure this coastal path is walkable with kids?'

'I've got no idea but the boss seems to think so.'

'Looks like I'm gonna find out.'

'We'll call you Sherpa Seb from now on.'

Gus doesn't ask what the hell she's talking about.

He's walking away when she calls him back. 'Speaking of Dunure, there's a cool wee pub down there. Serves great food too. I was wondering if you fancy going down some night?'

That's the last place Gus can go. Imagine if Farmer Boy and his mates were halfway through their pints when he walked in, the big rugby star from South Africa. But how does he say no to Natalie without making her suspicious?

'You asking me out on a date?'

As he hoped, Natalie blushes. 'Fuck off,' she says.

He does.

***

CHAPTER 44

Dad stops as he's going out the door. 'Last chance, Charlie. Want to come scything? Never mind Mum, she worries too much.'

A bit of me wants to go with him. I've been thinking a lot about the grave and what Seb said about animals digging up the dead guy. I'd quite like to check on him, make sure he's still buried, but I'm not going out on the hill again by myself. I've got something important I need to do.

Dad's holding the door open, waiting for me to make up my mind.

Shake my head. He looks so disappointed I feel sorry for him. I feel sorry for myself too. None of this horrible mess would have happened if I hadn't been determined to get Dad's attention and now he's asking me to go scything with him and I'm saying no.

'Sure?'

Nod.

'Okay, kid.' He turns away and I stare at the closed door.

I sit down at the table and pour a glass of orange juice, so close to the brim it nearly pours over and I can't lift it. Good job Mum's gone. I'm only allowed one small glass a day. It's bad for my teeth but good for my vitamin C. I lean over till my lips touch the glass and suck in the juice. It's the kind I like, the posh kind with bits in it, sweet and tangy at the same time and very orangey.

I try to drink it slowly to give Dad time to get his scythe and get away. I'd like to drink it fast and have another glass but then Mum will notice that the carton's nearly empty and I don't want to make her mad at me.

I put the milk and OJ in the fridge and the cereal in the larder. Bowl and spoon in the dishwasher then empty my glass and put it in too. He must be gone now.

Through into the hall and try the office door. Locked. Never thought of that. This door's always open to let Mum and Dad go back and forth from the house to the reception without having to go outside. I make a tutting noise then realise I sound just like Mum. That's not good. Maybe she's left her keys. That's my only chance. Can't get Mark to let me in. He'd be mega suspicious.

Yay, Mum's business keys are on the hook with the Minnie Mouse keyring she bought at Disneyland that time. I unlock the door, wait a moment to make sure no one's there, then sneak in and lock the door behind me.

There are three computers in here, so that more than one camper can get checked in at the same time. Dad says people don't like to wait in queues on their holidays and they shouldn't have to.

The reception is quite dark, apart from one wee window and the glass bit on the door. I can see Dad's note stuck to it. Over in the corner, light is coming from a screensaver. Dad must have been in early to boot it up the backside. He always says that because it used to make me smile.

It asks me for a password but it's okay. I know it. Dad once showed me how the system works, so I can help out if we ever get really, really busy.

Okay, I'm in. I blow a big sigh. Right. Now to find out some important stuff.

I type in: *when does bracken wither?* It's not that easy to find the answer without reading a whole lot of very serious stuff, about how much of a pest bracken can be. It takes over whole hillsides and nothing else can grow. No wonder Dad scythes it. Eventually I find what I'm after. October, and even then it doesn't wither away to nothing. That's true. I've seen it in the winter. The stems break as if they've got too big for their own good and tip over. It all turns brown and collapses and then the rain batters it into a mush. I suppose that just lies there till the new green shoots come up in the spring, like someone's planted a whole lot of pale-green violins.

So the gun won't be found unless someone actually trips over it.

Now I understand why Dad goes scything, to keep it under control. I thought he just wanted to keep the paths clear so that adders wouldn't come out and bite his campers. Or to keep the midgies away. What if he decides to cut the bit where the gun landed? I have to do something to stop him.

But first I need to check two more things. I type into the search box: *age of criminals in Scotland*. I'm hoping it will say sixteen because that's how old you need to be to vote. *Scotland's minimum age of criminal responsibility will be raised to twelve years, in line with UN standards, after the current minimum age of eight, the lowest in Europe, was labelled a "national embarrassment".* That was way back in 2016 so it must be the law now. What if I was only eleven when the hiker got shot? I read on till I find: *police would still have powers to investigate serious offences committed by children under twelve.* That means Seb is right. I'll be held responsible if anyone ever finds out what happened on the hill.

The last thing I need to find out is how to get blood stains out of clothes, so nobody knows I ever touched the dead guy. The results aren't good. I type in how to destroy blood evidence and find out that bleach would do it. Won't get Mum off my back though. Be better to put the shirt in the wash and hope she doesn't notice it. But I've seen her, sorting out the whites from the coloured things. Dad's always getting into trouble for putting his pants in the white section of their basket.

That reminds me, I've got to get out there, fast, before Dad finds that gun.

***

CHAPTER 45

Gus needs to talk to the boss about this crazy hiking idea. It's one thing keeping an eye on a bunch of little kids in the playbarn, where the biggest danger is getting scribbled on with a felt-tip pen, but being responsible for teenagers out on a coastal path? That's a whole different challenge and not one he signed up for.

Reception is shut. Of course, Pim managed to wangle a full day off, jammy git, just because his folks are here. Gus thinks he might pull the same stunt himself in a couple of weeks, take himself off out of here. It's getting a bit claustrophobic. He's scared to leave the campsite and go into Ayr with the others in case they end up in one of the pubs the dead guy has been in. The dead guy he's impersonating. He can't go to the pub in Dunure in case Kirsty or the farmer and his mates are there. That's another good reason for not venturing off the premises with a bunch of kids in tow. What if he bumps into one of the locals who recognise him?

Reception is closed but he finds Big Mark in the kitchen. He smiles when he sees Gus. 'How you doin?'

'Ok, bud. Just wondering if you've seen the boss?'

'He's out on the hillside, cutting bracken.'

'Shit!' The expletive is out before he can stop it. Why the hell would he be cutting bracken? The kid must have somehow told him about the gun.

'Problem?'

'Nah, just need to ask him something and I don't fancy traipsing about a hillside.'

'It's nice out there and the views are unbelievable. Will only take you ten minutes to find him. Follow the sign for Brown Carrick and you can't go wrong. Want a coffee before you go? I've just made one.'

The smell of freshly brewed coffee is tempting but Gus shakes his head.

Mark says, 'Suit yourself. No skin off my nose if you don't want a free coffee.'

Gus smiles to show he means no offence then hurries out and across the courtyard. Natalie hails him as he passes to show him a picture some kid has painted. Like he cares about that kind of crap.

As he passes reception a huge SUV pulls up and what looks like fifty kids of all ages jump out, the younger ones screaming with excitement.

A guy with long hair and a shaggy beard is stretching by the driver's door, as if he's just completed a long drive. When he notices Gus he says, 'Hi, can you tell me where we sign in?'

What the hell. It's like everyone is trying to stop him getting out onto that hillside.

Gus points to the café. 'Mark will sort you out.'

Before the man can ask anything else, Gus lopes off, jogging around the corner in the direction of the woods.

This is the first time he's been on this path. It cuts through a stand of trees and then leads into the gorse. His stomach gives a heave at the memory of the smell that used to remind him of innocent, nice things like the beach and suntan oil.

As he weaves his way through the bushes, trying not to gag on the heady scent, he wonders what he's going to say, or do, if he finds the boss with a gun in his hands. His own gun that he doesn't even know is missing, presumably. He speeds up in the hope of finding the boss before the boss finds the gun. Or worse, the grave.

God, he hadn't thought of that till now. Gus has thought once or twice of going out to make sure the body is still covered but he doesn't want to attract attention to himself or the burial site. Also, he's pretty sure he'd have heard about it by now if the body's been found.

This must be the way the kid came that morning and the way he went home. God knows how he must have felt trudging back, having seen a shooting, been forced to carry a corpse and then got a beating for his troubles. For the first time, Gus actually feels a little bit sorry for Charlie, who's not a bad kid.

As he comes out of the bushes he catches sight of the boss and by his side, his son. Gus's sympathy for the kid vanishes. Little bastard must be showing his dad after all.

Gus has to make a real effort to walk at a normal speed towards the two of them. He wants to run up and grab the kid by the scruff of his neck. As he watches, Charlie points down the hill, in exactly the direction the gun was thrown. What's made him so brave all of a sudden?

Gus tries very hard to keep his eyes downstream. Last thing he wants is to give himself away by glancing towards the grave.

The boss is first to see him coming. Gus watches the kid's face and tries to read his expression. He looks scared, but then he always looks scared when he sees Gus.

'Hi, Seb, what brings you out here?' He holds out a red blanket-type thing and waves it in the air. Water flies off the sodden material and sprays Gus.

'Sorry about that. I'm just asking Charlie if he knows why the cover off his bed should be lying out here in the gorse.'

The kid looks as if he hasn't a clue what his Dad's talking about. Gus can tell he's pretending. Time to bale in. 'I heard you were scything and thought maybe you could use a hand. Didn't realise this was one of your jobs.'

'One of the many.' The boss sighs, like it's all too much for him, and dumps the blanket on the ground. 'Bloody bracken would take over the entire hillside if we left it. That's where we got our name, of course, a brae being the Scottish word for hill.'

'Got much left to do?' Gus hopes the answer is no.

'No, not really. We're just about done for today, aren't we, Charlie?' The kid nods and looks as relieved as Gus feels.

'Do you have this whole hillside to cut?'

'Oh, for God's sake, no. I just aim to keep the bracken from encroaching on the footpath, that's all.'

Charlie nods again, as if he's hoping Gus will believe his dad.

'Great view from up here.' Gus turns on the spot, as if he's admiring a three hundred and sixty degree view, when in fact he's checking out the side of the stream, hoping the collapsed bank is still in place. He wonders briefly what the hell he'd do if he spotted an arm sticking out, or a foot. For a moment the scenario seems surreal, as if he's dreamed the whole thing, but a quick look at the kid's face reminds him it's all too real. He turns back to face the sea and points down to the coast. 'Actually, Boss, I was hoping to speak to you about this hike you have planned.'

'Not really a hike, Seb. Just something different to offer the older kids.'

'You know I don't have any training or qualifications in outward bound activities?'

The boss laughs. 'Not asking you to abseil off the Heads of Ayr, Seb. Don't be daft. Just a stroll for an hour or so, maybe a stop to eat some sandwiches. Whatever you think they'd like.'

Gus decides laughing is a good idea, as if he knows he's being a bit 'daft'. Seems the boss has his heart set on this walking lark.

'Well, I think the family has arrived. Want me to do a bit of scything while I'm out here?'

'Tell you what, I think that's a great idea. You and Charlie can stay and do a bit more and I'll head back and see the new arrivals are happy with their accommodation.'

'The guy looked a bit hippy-dippy to me.'

'Like the kind of man who fancied a yurt, perhaps?'

'I wouldn't know about that,' says Gus, 'never having heard of a yurt before I came here.'

The boss suddenly turns to face the stream. Gus is sure he hears the kid gasp. 'All of this area here will be for glamping. That's my dream.'

Desperate to take his attention away from the hillside, Gus touches his arm and points up the coast. 'Where is that?'

'In the far distance?'

Gus nods. 'Yeah, way over there.'

The boss points out a whole lot of places whose names mean nothing at all, but Gus smiles and makes noises and comments to show he's impressed.

'Right,' says his employer, 'I'd better go. Take care of my son. I want him back with two feet and ten toes, remember.'

Charlie takes a big stride towards his father, as if to say, take me with you.

Gus says, 'Will do. Okay, Charlie, can you show me how to handle this thing? I'm the one likely to lose toes, I think.'

He sees the boss hesitate for a moment and regrets his words. 'Joking, Boss,' he says with a laugh. 'I've handled a scythe before. No worries.'

'Remember to take that fleece home when you go, Charlie. Expect your mother to be unhappy.' He raises his eyebrows then turns away. They stand and watch him make his way along the path till he disappears into the gorse and Gus is sure he'll be out of earshot.

'Well, well, well. You had me going for a minute there, Charlie boy. Thought you were spilling your guts.'

Charlie shakes his head.

'Just as well. Can you imagine what sort of shit would rain down on your poor dad's head? This peaceful hillside that he loves so much would be swarming with cops. Not that Daddy dear would be here to see it, of course. He'd be locked up. Wonder if they do family rooms in Scottish jails? You'll certainly need someone looking out for you when they put you away.' Gus looks worried, as if Charlie's fate is the worst thing he can imagine.

'Now, while we're out here, why don't we take a little look to make sure our buried treasure has stayed buried, shall we?'

Charlie looks like he'll burst into tears at any moment. He backs away, shaking his head. Gus pounces and grabs the kid's arm, squeezing it tight enough to hurt. 'Don't say no to me. Unless you want more of what you got the last day? No? I thought not.'

He pulls Charlie with him and walks towards the stream, surprised to find the burial spot is much harder to identify than he imagined. The bank has collapsed on itself in several places, making their handiwork look like a natural part of the landscape. Still, just to make sure, he drags Charlie with him as he climbs the hill, checking, relieved when he can see nothing out of the ordinary. Again, he has that weird feeling of unreality, although he has relived the shooting and the burial many times in his sleep.

'Good,' he says on a loud outbreath. 'Looks like we're in the clear and we're going to stay that way, aren't we?'

Charlie nods.

'Still not speaking? That's also good.' He puts his lips close to the kid's ear and says, 'Don't think it hasn't occurred to me that you could write all this down, but you wouldn't do that, would you, Charlie?'

He feels the kid's head shaking from side to side and draws back so he can make eye contact.

'No, because we both know that would be a very bad idea. Apart from getting you and your dad sent to prison, you would ruin everything for your mummy and daddy. All of this. No glamping. No weddings. No business. No house. No cars. No nothing. Got that?'

Charlie nods and a single tear runs down his face. Gus feels tempted to wipe it away. He feels like shit, making this kid so miserable, but any show of kindness could mean disaster for both of them. He raises his hand to give him a slap, just to remind him what it feels like, but can't do it. Instead he says, 'Wipe your face. You're far too big to be crying like a baby.'

Gus lifts the scythe and puts it over his shoulder. The weight reminds him of the gun. 'What's with the blanket, by the way? Something to do with the gun?'

Charlie nods.

'Thought so. You'd better take it home then. Get it washed. Where do you think the gun is?'

Charlie points in a vague downhill direction.

'Do you think we should look for it?'

Charlie shakes his head.

'Won't that bracken stuff wither away in the winter?'

Another shake. The look on the kid's face is reassuring. He seems sure, as if he knows the gun will remain hidden.

'Okay, let's leave it there then. We'd better hope, for your sake, it never gets found.'

***

CHAPTER 46

France
Friday 20 July

Catherine drops, exhausted, onto a chair. 'Eric,' she shouts. When he appears in the doorway, she says, 'Remind me why I volunteered for this.'

Eric laughs. 'I did warn you.'

Catherine thought coming here to sort out Mamie's house would be good for her. Get her away from Paris for a few days and force her to think about someone other than Sebastien.

The funeral was awful. Right up till the very last minute before the service began she was convinced he'd come. She imagined him dashing into the little church, out of breath, embarrassed, whispering apologies. She could see him turning around to smile at his relatives, confident they'd forgive him anything, as usual, then becoming suddenly solemn and sad as he caught sight of Mamie's coffin. She'd looked forward to taking his hand in hers, giving it a reassuring squeeze, comforting her child as he grieved for his grandmother. She was sure their shared grief would be enough to mend the rift between them and all would be well.

But, of course, Sebastien didn't appear and all day she had to endure questions and make excuses, coping with her disappointment whilst trying to hide her hurt from Eric's family. At least Mamie didn't know her beloved grandson was missing from the ranks of mourners as they made their way from the church to the graveyard, moving at the pace of her oldest friend.

'Shall I make us a cold drink?' says Eric. 'Take it out to the garden? You look like you could use a break.'

'That sounds lovely. I thought this would be ideal therapy for me, working my way through Mamie's house. I expected it to be monotonous but just a question of sorting and organising things, making decisions about what to keep or discard. But, oh dear.' She spread her hands and looked around the room, once so tidy and now filled with packing cases, cardboard boxes and plastic bin bags.

'I know what you mean. Dealing with someone else's worldly goods is quite different from organising one's own belongings.'

'A lifetime of personal possessions. More than one lifetime. Your father's, your brother's.'

'I dare say some of this stuff goes even further back than that. Remember this was my grandparents' house.'

'There's just so much. It's overwhelming. I can see why people talk about downsizing. Remind me to throw out all of our old junk so Sebastien is never faced with a job like this.'

'You have to switch off the sentimental part of your brain. My brother's taken everything he wants.'

'That wasn't much help. A clock and a necklace of your mother's.'

'The kids took some stuff, to be fair. Now it's a question of how we dispose of what's left, I suppose. Should we save something for Sebastien, do you think?'

'No, I think Sebastien would be here himself if Mamie meant anything to him.'

'Come on, time for a break. Let's go get a cool drink.' Eric hauls her to her feet and gives her a hug.

Already this morning she's had two false starts. First the kitchen proved to be too big a job for her to tackle on her own and then she was forced to give up on a bureau full of papers because she kept coming across photographs of Sebastien. She found photos of her son as a tiny baby, indistinguishable from his cousins when they were newborns, recognisable only by his clothes or the arms cradling him. She came across snapshots of Sebastien as an adorable toddler, his strawberry-blond hair sparkling in the sun. There are even photographs she's never seen before – a teenage Sebastien smiling amidst a tumble of adoring little cousins, snapped during a stay at Mamie's on a summer's day. His hair darker but still glinting copper and gold. When she unearthed a picture taken earlier in the year, at the family Easter party, she had to sit down. Memories of the day flooded back to her, making her feel quite faint as she gazed at Sebastien, sitting between her and his father, an arm flung casually round each of their shoulders. All three of them beaming at the camera, untroubled and carefree. She found herself kissing the photo and then clutching it to her chest, hands folded over it like a peasant woman treasuring a family bible.

She shed a few tears, not sure whether they were for her missing son, for poor dead Mamie, or for herself. Then she dried her eyes and told herself to get on with the task she was here to do.

She doesn't tell Eric any of this, of course. She's trying very hard to convince him that she's coping.

'Sitting in this garden is like walking through the perfume department of Galeries Lafayette.'

'If you could bottle this fragrance you'd put Guerlain out of business. It's divine, isn't it? I could sit here all day, eyes closed, just breathing in the scent of roses, gardenia and honeysuckle.'

'Tempting though that sounds…' Eric drains his glass and gets to his feet.

'Can't we sit a little longer? Take a look at this.'

She hands him the old photo she found in the bureau, its corners brown and curling. 'I think it must have been taken here, in the garden. Look, there's the big plum tree.'

There are three little boys in the photo, dressed in identical outfits, probably the work of Mamie's clever hands.

Eric says, 'I've never seen this.'

'Do you remember it being taken?'

Eric shakes his head, staring at the photo. He points to the smallest boy and says, 'That's me. What age? Two, maybe.' He turns the photo over. Pencilled on the back, in Mamie's writing, it says: Auguste's eighth birthday. 'Auguste,' says Eric, in a whisper.

Mamie's 'lost boy', the one nobody ever talked about.

'What happened to him, Eric?'

'I'm not really sure. He went away when I was still quite young. Got sick or something.' Eric frowns, as if he's trying to dredge up a memory. 'I vaguely remember him dressed as an altar boy. I think I remember something about him going to be a priest, but I might be making that up. All I know is, Paul and I were told not to talk about him as it made our father sad.'

'Poor Mamie, that's awful. She told me recently she had lost a boy. That's how she put it.' Catherine wipes her eyes, wishing she'd never shown Eric the photo. 'I wonder what happened to him, why he got lost.'

Eric sighs. 'Well, we'll never find out now.' He reaches for her hand and she stands to hug him. As they hold each other close, she knows he's thinking of Sebastien too.

'I'm going to make a start on Mamie's linen collection.' She thinks it might be a safer option, less emotional.

Eric whistles in admiration. 'Good luck with that.'

Catherine hauls opens the middle drawer of the immense linen chest at the top of the stairs and the smell of the immaculately white bedlinen reminds her of Sebastien. When he was little he always used to ask, 'Why doesn't my bed at home smell of flowers?' She used to tell him it was Mamie's magic that made all the beds in her house smell of summertime. She raises a pillow cover to her face and rests her cheek on the cool cotton, worn smooth and soft by years of Mamie's laundering.

As Catherine lifts a pile of sheets from the drawer, a tiny bag of lavender drops to her feet. She lifts the little sachet and turns it over in her hands, admiring the intricately embroidered initials – a P for Paulette interlaced with a lavish L. She imagines Mamie as a young bride-to-be, preparing her trousseau and excitedly entwining the initials of her married name. Or perhaps she sat, heavily pregnant, amongst her lavender and stitched away the hours as she waited for the birth of her first son. This year's lavender will go unharvested; the little bags will never be refilled with a fresh batch of scented flowers. Another family tradition gone forever with Mamie's passing. Catherine sniffs the lavender, its scent now faded and stale, and pops the tiny sachet into her pocket.

She removes sheets and pillowcases, table covers and napkins and piles them into boxes, ready to go. There's a big demand for 'vintage' linen these days. A friend in Paris paid a small fortune recently for a bundle of old-stained table covers, which she then had professionally laundered to grace the tables at her daughter's château wedding. Perhaps Catherine should be selling these on the Internet rather than giving them to a charity for stray dogs.

Only one drawer to go. When she opens it, she doesn't find more sheets and table linen as she expected, but finds items wrapped in once-white tissue paper that has darkened and crisped with age. Feeling like a tomb raider, Catherine gently unwraps the first parcel and finds a bridal veil. In another, a coronet of orange blossom so dried that the petals drop as she lifts it. Another carefully wrapped bundle contains a christening gown and three tiny pairs of satin bootees, all hand-stitched. It's like a history lesson of the Lamar family, Mamie's family.

Catherine gently lifts out one last paper-wrapped item and is about to open it when she notices, right at the back of the drawer, a yellowed envelope, with Mamie's name and address. It carries an American stamp and is post-marked San Francisco, dated 1989. Inside is an order of service from a funeral mass, with a photo on the front that makes a shiver crawl up Catherine's spine. It could be a younger version of Eric, or an older version of Sebastien. Below the photo, it says 'Auguste Didieri Lamar 1955–1989'. A white card, edged in black, carries a handwritten message: 'Dear Mrs Lamar, I lost my beloved Auguste three weeks ago and do not know how I can go on without him. He made me promise long ago that I would let you know when this day came. He loved both you and me, right to the end.' It is signed, simply, Jonathon. Catherine knows what killed a lot of young men in California in the late eighties. Poor Auguste, he must have suffered terribly. She thinks of her own son, so precious, and wonders how Mamie kept going, with a secret like this hidden in her memory drawer.

The old lady's words come back to her, as if she's right here in the house.

'I can tell you this, if I had my time again, I would do things differently. I'd be quick to forgive and try hard to forget. Trouble was, Henri could never forgive and then it was too late. I waited too long. Please don't make the same mistake, Catherine.'

'Eric!' Her feet clatter on the wooden stairs as she hurtles down towards him.

'What is it? You look as if you've seen a ghost.'

She pushes past him. 'Get the car keys. We're going to Scotland. Right now.'

***

CHAPTER 47

Scotland

Natalie is laying out drawing paper in all the colours of the rainbow.

'Can you please get me the felt tips, Charlie?'

He nods and she waits, expecting more. He stretches his lips way back, exactly like she's told him and says, 'ee-ess.'

Nat squeals and high fives him. 'Did you hear that, Joyce? Say it again, Charlie.'

Joyce comes over, her mop dripping a trail across the playbarn floor and says, 'What?'

'Charlie just said a word. Didn't you?'

He nods. He's not saying it again. That was for Natalie only, to please her. He's not going to perform like a seal. Anyway, even if he could talk normally, he's not going to. In case he gets arrested. Better to say nothing.

Joyce looks right into his eyes. 'Did ye, son? That's pure brilliant, so it is.'

'Can you say it again for Joyce?' He can tell from Natalie's eyes how much she wants to help him. He thinks for a moment, stands with the two of them staring at him then shakes his head.

'No?' She looks disappointed but her voice is bright, as if she's trying not to show it. 'Okay, not to worry.'

The two of them walk away and Joyce whispers, 'Did he talk? Seriously?'

I want to shout, 'Hello! I'm still right here you know.'

Nat's hair swings from side to side. 'Change the subject,' she says.

'Oor Alex was talking about Seb again yesterday.'

'Oh yeah?'

'When he came to pick me up. He was waiting for me in the courtyard and Seb walks across. "Who's the big guy wi the tats?" he says. I'm like, "That's Seb. The French guy you met in the pub that night." He's like, "Well, he's bulked up since I saw him."'

'He does have a fine set of muscles, I must agree,' says Nat, turning to smile at me. 'What do you think, Charlie?'

Nod. I know all about his muscles.

'Oor Alex swears the guy he met in the pub didnae have tattoos.'

'Well, that's weird. Seb is covered in them.'

'You like tattoos?'

I hope she says no.

'In moderation.'

What does that mean?

'Know what you mean.'

Thanks, Joyce, not much help.

'To be honest, I'm not so keen on the one up the back of the head,' says Nat, 'but the kids seem to think it's cool. Do you, Charlie?'

I hate his tattoos. 'Funny that.'

'What is?'

'Oor Alex was adamant the guy in the pub didnae have any tats.'

'Must have been a different guy then. Did Alex have a few wee nips that night?'

Joyce laughs as if Nat just told a joke. 'Aye, same as every other night.'

'Unreliable witness, then. Isn't that what they say on the telly?'

'What colour would you say Seb's hair is?'

'Ooh, that's a hard one. Shaved head and all that.'

'Do you think he's bald?'

'No, that's just his style. Goes with the muscles and the tattoos, doesn't it? His stubble is pretty dark, so I'd say his hair is brown. Maybe even black. Who knows?'

'Not red then?'

Nat giggles. 'No, he's definitely not a redhead.'

Joyce raises her eyebrows and Nat giggles in a way that makes me feel weird, like when I hear a joke I don't understand.

'You can tell by his eyebrows,' says Nat, with a kind of 'so there' look. 'Anyway, why?'

'Alex was adamant the guy in the pub was called Seb and he had red hair. He called him a ginger.'

'Guess there was more than one Seb out on the piss in Ayr that night then.'

***

CHAPTER 48

I know he's away on a 'hike' with two kids from the Dutch family. Also know he's not happy about it. Heard him moaning to Natalie. 'Didn't sign up for this shit. What if one of them falls and breaks an ankle or has a heart attack or something. What am I supposed to do?'

Anyway, that's his problem. All I need to know is that he's going to be away this afternoon. Pim is on reception. Dad is out at Phase Five. Don't know where Mum is, but it certainly won't be in the 'boys' dorm' as Dad calls it. I've heard her talking about it with Joyce when she was complaining about the mess Seb and Pim were leaving.

'It's a pigsty. You should see it.'

'No, thank you,' said Mum. 'Wild horses couldn't drag me in there. Can only imagine what it smells like.'

I make sure no one sees me going into the old building at the back of the yard. Sneak past Natalie's room even though I know she's in the playbarn.

Careful as a bomb diffuser, I turn the handle and gently push the door. I hear someone groan as if he's in pain. Wait for a voice to say, 'Who's there?' Stand like a statue, waiting and waiting. Move the door a tiny bit more. It groans. A little laugh gets out, like at the cinema after a scary bit, when everybody laughs. Tiptoe through the doorway and push the big door closed, feeling daft when it groans a third time.

A deep breath in and then blow it out again, fast. It's stinking in here. I screw up my nose and cover my mouth while I try to work out what to do next. Need to let my eyes adjust. The curtains are closed, making everything dark red like blood. Wee slices of light have broken into the room.

When my eyesight gets back to normal, I spot two beds. How will I know whose is whose?

One looks tidy with the bed all sorted. Mum would like it.

The other one's got a rucksack dumped on top of it but most of the stuff that should be in it seems to be lying on the floor or draped over a chair. I go a bit closer and see boxers and socks, sandals and shorts and a wet towel hanging over the end of the bed. The smell's even worse over here, probably the socks. Recognise some T-shirts that Seb wears all the time.

No idea what I'm looking for. Or even why it seemed a good idea to come in here.

I lift the rucksack and take it nearer the window so I can see what's in it. Not much is the answer. Couple more T-shirts. I lift one out and then drop it, as if it burned my hand. I've seen it before. Seb was wearing it that day the hiker got shot. I shiver, as if someone blew cold air on me.

At the bottom of the rucksack is a poly bag, clear like the ones Mum puts sandwiches in. Inside is a passport. I throw it back into the rucksack and open the zipper on one of the outside pockets.

If someone came in right now and said, 'What are you doing?' of course I couldn't answer. Not because I don't talk but because inside my head, I don't know the answer.

Don't know what made me suspicious. Think it was when Joyce mentioned the tattoos. Then they started to discuss the colour of his hair. The hair he shaves off. Whether it was red. It was the word ginger that make me think, wait a minute. I've no idea what I'm hoping to find in Seb's bag, but I go ahead and unzip one of the pockets.

Pull out a wallet thing and open it. Bits of paper and stuff. An email from Dad with our logo at the top, offering Seb a job. A thick bundle of money in an elastic band, some euros and lots of our kind of money, sterling. Don't have time to count it but I flick over some of the corners and there must be hundreds of pounds. Wow! I've never seen so much money. Dad must pay them a lot. Should I steal it? That would be a good way to get my own back on Seb for hurting me. I picture his angry face, remember his rage that day, remember how scared I was that the beating would never stop. I put the money back, trying to make sure it goes in the same place I found it.

My fingers feel something else in the wallet, but there's nothing to be seen. I wonder if there's a secret compartment. I feel like a spy as I fiddle around, poking my finger in till it catches the edge of a notebook or something stuck behind the lining. Another passport. A green one this time. My stomach does a kind of flip over. How can one guy have two passports?

Republic of South Africa it says, in golden letters. République d'Afrique du Sud. That's French. Maybe that's why he speaks both. Flick through looking for the photo. There he is, Seb, on the inside of the back cover. Younger looking, but Seb.

Surname: WEBB

Given names: ANGUS JOHN

Read it again. Where's the Sebastien?

Throw the passport onto the bed and delve to the bottom of the rucksack. Slide open the plastic zip thing and tip out the passport. This one's burgundy, like mine, but French. My stomach feels all fizzy, like when I open presents and I'm nervous in case what's inside isn't what I was wanting.

Turn to the photo. Can't say I recognise the face. Just a young guy, ordinary looking. Check the names.

LAMAR

SEBASTIEN, LOUIS

Sit down on the bed, kind of collapse, really, like my legs went weak. Feel the wetness of the towel. Hear a voice outside, in the distance, a wee child shouting for her daddy.

Wish I'd never come in here. Wish I hadn't snooped. Curiosity killed the cat – that's a proverb. Miss Lawson says a proverb is a simple saying, often repeated because it expresses a truth. It means being nosy isn't good. Unless you're a detective, and I'm not.

A detective would be saying, 'Okay, this man is pretending to be the guy that he's just killed.'

Why would anyone do that?

Don't know the answer but I do know this passport is evidence. Bet the T-shirt on the floor is evidence too. Don't want to touch it but know I've got to check it. Using two fingers like a crab's claw, I catch a tiny bit of T-shirt in my pincers and hold it up. Too dark to see clearly but there are definitely stains and dirty marks on it.

Make up my mind really fast. Wrap the French passport up in the T-shirt. Not so bothered about touching it now. Just want to get out of here as quick as I can.

Put the other one, the green one, back where I found it. Have to make everything look like it was before I came in. Or I'm in deep trouble.

***

CHAPTER 49

'Seb? Can you come in here for one moment, please?'

Gus clicks his tongue against his teeth. What the hell does Pim want now?

He turns to his walking companions, the two Dutch boys. Nice kids actually, and no trouble. 'Thanks, dudes. Really enjoyed that.' Gus is surprised to find he means it.

'Me too,' says Jakob, the sixteen year old.

'Can we do it again? asks his younger brother. 'Maybe tomorrow?'

'Err, do you mind if we take a rain check on that one, guys? Think we've got a schedule to follow and that Natalie is a real slave driver. Don't be fooled by her cute smile.'

'Oh, okay.' The kid's face speaks his disappointment and Gus feels bad. They've clearly had a good time and being stuck in a place like this with your parents and younger siblings can't be much fun. 'Tell you what, why don't I see you at the pool later and maybe we can get some water volleyball going? I'm sure I saw a net somewhere.'

'We'll get our old man to play. That should be a laugh.'

Gus holds up his open palm and both boys slap it in a high five. 'Later,' he says and heads for reception.

'What is it, Pim?'

'No necessity for looking glum, Seb. I have a pleasant surprise for you.'

'Listen mate, I'm really not in the mood for games here. I'm just in off a hike with an hour to shower and grab some food before I go on duty at the pool. What do you want?'

Pim smiles like a moron. 'It's not what I want. It's what you want.'

Gus sighs loudly. It's that or hit the guy in the mouth.

Pim seems to pick up the vibe. 'No need for hostility, Seb. I have a parcel for you, that is all.'

A parcel? Who'd be sending him a parcel? His mother has missed his birthday for the last two years and, anyway, it's not till September. He takes the small package and mutters his thanks.

There's a handwritten label front and back. One says Sebastien Lamar and the campsite address. The other says from Catherine Lamar and a neatly written address in Paris. Shit. The dead guy's mother. Has to be.

'A gift from your mother, I suspect,' says Pim, beaming like a department store Santa. 'Might congratulations be in order? Or a celebratory drink in the bar later this evening?' He rubs his hands.

'Yeah, sure. If you're paying! Catch you later.' Gus smiles as the door marked reception swings closed behind him.

In the dorm the curtains are still shut. 'Can't see a thing in here,' he mutters, grabbing a handful of material and yanking it so hard the curtain comes off the railing.

With a bit more light he unwraps the parcel. Whatever it is, the sender has packaged it well, protecting the contents with bubble wrap and then foam. The last piece of wrapping peels away to reveal a white box whose logo Gus recognises right away. A brand new iPhone.

Taped to the underside of the box is a little handwritten note.

Afraid your old phone didn't survive its night amongst the cows.
What? Some sort of secret code?
Happy birthday, my darling. Rest of your presents when we see you. Call soon, please. 0633142677 (in case you can't remember without your phone!) Love you.

A nice new phone could be handy, but it makes life a bit tricky too. Clearly this woman will be expecting a call soon. He got away with grunts and okays when she called before, but he won't manage to fool her a second time.

He taps the box off his chin while he decides what to do. Sending a text might be the answer, but first he needs to think carefully what he wants to say and how to say it. A job for later.

He sticks the packaging in the waste bin, grimacing at the rubbish that's already in there, mostly Pim's, and drops the phone box into the rucksack. He adds the coastal path guidebook and mutters, 'Good choice, Granny.' The boss was well impressed this morning when he introduced Gus to the two boys and their dad, and, with the book, the path was easy to find.

Even though he knows exactly how much he's got saved, Gus takes out his cash and counts it. Still not enough. He rubs his hand over his chin and cheeks, back and forward, back and forward. This woman's bound to get suspicious when her son doesn't come home for his granny's funeral and shit's gonna hit the fan, big time. He's either got to get out of here before that happens or play for time till he can make enough money to cover his flight.

***

CHAPTER 50

'You're wrong, Catherine. I *do* understand, perfectly well, why you want to go right now.'

'No, you don't. Otherwise we'd be there already.'

'Look, darling. It made no sense to go when you asked. We could have flown past each other, the two of us on one plane and Sebastien on another, on his way home.' He moves his arms through the air, as if to help her visualise.

'Except he wasn't on his way home, was he?'

'We know that now. Anyway, a few more days won't make any difference. The funeral is over. Sebastien has missed it. There's nothing we can do to change that.'

'I've been thinking it may be my fault he didn't come in time. I assumed he'd want to be here, so I didn't make it sound urgent enough. This is the first death in the family since Sebastien was a child. He doesn't know about these things, how quickly they're arranged.'

'Oh for goodness' sake, Catherine, he's an adult. Everyone knows there's a six-day limit. It's the law.'

'Why *would* Sebastien know that? He's never heard it talked about as far as I know.'

'Surely his employer would tell him to hurry home?'

'I've been doing some research online. There's no six-day limit in England.'

'Sebastien's in Scotland.'

'I know that,' she snaps, 'it was just a slip. Anyway, same thing. It can take weeks for a funeral there.'

Eric looks genuinely shocked. 'That can't be true.'

'It is. After Christmas, some families had to wait three or even four weeks. What if the people Sebastien is working for have told him there's no rush?'

'I should think that's unlikely, but you have a point. I assume you've phoned him to ask where the hell he is?'

Catherine nods.

'And?'

'It went to voicemail. He hasn't called back yet.'

'Probably because he hasn't got the parcel yet. Did you leave a message?'

'I sent him a note with it, asking him to call me as soon as possible.'

'Well, I suggest we get on with the house. There's not that much left to do. You've been amazing. I promise you, the moment we're finished, we'll head for Scotland. If we hear from him before then, all the better.'

'What if we don't?'

***

CHAPTER 51

Scotland
Thursday 26 July

I hate my life.

Hate living here. Everyone says, 'You're lucky, Charlie. Wish I lived on a campsite. You've got your own swimming pool and your own café.'

They think I just go and help myself to ice cream and Cola whenever I like. Jayden Jeffries even said, 'Can you, like, just go and steal vodka if there's, like, nobody watching?'

It's even more rubbish in the summer holidays. Never see my friends. Dad's too busy. Mum's 'run off my feet', whatever that's supposed to mean. Seems to me she's always getting dressed up and swanning off to 'meetings'. Hope they're not all with that sleazy-looking guy in the flash car.

Got this red bit on my arm where I keep scratching. Not because it's itchy or got a rash. More like it's a habit now. Mum hasn't even noticed it. Sometimes I think she doesn't care. She hardly ever gives me hugs. Not like she used to when I was wee.

Natalie used to hug me too but she doesn't any more. I heard her telling Joyce one day that teachers aren't allowed to hug pupils.

'Whit?' Joyce said. 'That's shite.' I love Joyce. She's the only one that treats me the same, still gives me a squeeze sometimes. Don't see why Nat can't hug me. She's not even a proper teacher yet and, anyway, it's not as if I'm her pupil. Although you'd think I was, the way she's always trying to get me to talk. Funny really. She's desperate for me to talk and there's Seb, or whatever his real name is, desperate for me to keep quiet. It would be funny if it wasn't so sad.

Kidz Klub is a waste of space. Rubbish activities, full of babies and he's there all the time. Everywhere I go, he's there. In the café, in the playbarn, at the pool. Watching me. As if he's trying to work out what I'm going to do.

Every day I wake up and wonder when he'll notice his T-shirt's missing. Will that make him check for the dead guy's passport? He's bound to know it's me. Who else would take it?

Kidz Klub finishes in the middle of August. That's just a few weeks. Then he'll be gone. All I have to do is keep out of his way till then. Except there's one thing I need to do first. Maybe it's crazy, but I'm still going to do it.

Dad deliberately built the pool where it would get shelter from the wind. It still causes arguments. Mum says campers would prefer to sit on their loungers and admire the sea view. Dad says the wind would blow them and their loungers to Ailsa Craig.

Can hear his voice before I get anywhere near the pool. Calling out a score.

'Dad and Jakob's team, nine. Lucas and Seb's team, ten. Game point, boys.'

I sneak up to the corner and stand behind the big bush that grows there. Dad planted it as a windbreaker. Peek through the leaves so I can see the players, but they can't see me. He's in the water, taking part. His back's to me and he's about to serve. He holds the ball high. His big muscly arms are wet and shiny. His coloured tattoos sparkle like jewels in the sun. It goes quiet as if everyone is waiting to see who'll win.

I've been practising this over and over, but I don't know if I can do it. I take a big deep breath, push out my lips and, just as he's about to serve, I shout, as loud as I can, 'Webb!'

He turns his head towards the sound and the ball goes straight into the net. The other team cheer and jump about, high fiving. He stands and stares in my direction but I know he can't see me behind the bush. I also know he definitely heard me. Shouting his real name. That's proof.

His teammate slaps him on the back. 'Let's do this, Seb.'

That's when I realise all my effort was a waste of time.

Webb sounds just like Seb.

***

CHAPTER 52

It's time he was headed home to South Africa. He's starting to lose it. The guilt's getting to him. Driving him mad.

Today at the pool, right in the middle of a game, at match point for fuck's sake, he heard someone shout, 'Webb'. He could swear he heard it and yet, when he looked round, there was nobody in sight.

He accused one of the kids he was playing with. Said, 'You put me off.' Told him, 'Don't shout, "Seb!" when I'm serving.' They stared at him as if he *was* mad.

'I didn't,' said the boy.

'What did you shout then?'

He looked so hurt his dad chipped in. 'Lucas didn't shout anything. He knows how to play by the rules.'

Cost him the game and a round of cokes for the winners. But that's the least of it.

If the kid didn't shout, then who did? Who could possibly know his name's Webb? He must be mistaken, and yet...

Annoyed at himself for feeling so neurotic, he reaches under the bed and pulls out his rucksack. Finds the travel wallet and pokes his finger into the rip in the lining. Lets out a relieved sigh. The passport's still there, safe and sound. Of course it is. He imagined the whole thing.

Without stopping to wonder why, he roots around in the bottom of the bag. He relaxes a little when his fingers touch the plastic bag, but when he takes a hold of it, he realises it's empty. He catches the rucksack by its bottom corners and upends it, holding it high over the bed and shaking hard. The iPhone box bounces on the bed and hits the floor. A T-shirt drops out followed by one sock and the sandwich bag, minus its contents. A final scrap of paper flutters to a standstill and some dust motes catch the light, swirling above his bed.

Gus sits and the bed complains at the sudden weight. 'Shit,' he whispers, putting both hands to his head.

Though he knows the passport's gone, he checks again, lifting the items one by one from the bed and dropping them. Something else is wrong here. He shakes his head, annoyed that he can't think what it is. Then it comes to him, swift as a kick in the balls and just as much of a sickener. The T-shirt with blood on it. It's been taken too.

The little bastard. Got to be him. Who else could it be? Pim wouldn't touch his stuff. Okay, he's a boring arsehole, but he's harmless and unless. Gus has lost all judgement of character, Pim's a straight-up honest guy. He'd bet on it.

The only other person who ever comes in here is Joyce and he didn't have her marked down for a thief either.

'Fuck!' His money. Has it gone too? He rummages through the stuff on the bed, his panic growing when he can't find the travel wallet that he had in his hands only moments ago. He lifts the rucksack and throws it at the far wall. Then he hits the floor as if he's been told to give a coach ten press-ups and peers under the bed. Spots the wallet. Collapses onto his belly, all the air escaping from his lungs as he flops, relieved. He lies there for a second then grabs the wallet and rolls over on his back to check. The money's there. Thank fuck for that.

Should he count it? What's the point? A thief would have taken the lot, especially the iPhone. No thief could resist that. Poor little Joyce. Wrong of him to suspect her, even for a moment. He *is* losing the plot.

That leaves a prime suspect. The little shit's got some nerve. What the hell made him come in here and start sniffing around, after all these weeks? He must have known what would happen to him if he got caught, and what will happen to him if he really has taken anything.

If Charlie's got the passport, then Charlie knows Gus isn't who he says he is. He also knows the identity of the dead guy on the hill. Plus, he's got evidence now to link Gus to the body – a T-shirt to prove he was there.

Gus batters his forehead with his fist. Why did he keep the T-shirt all this time? Why didn't he wash it, or burn it, or whatever? Get rid of it. Passport too. He was stupid to keep that, looking back. But he'd so little time and none of this crap was planned. He just reacted to situations as they happened. What else was he meant to do?

Anyway, it's time now for some planning. Bit late, but still, damage limitation at the very least. Starting with Charlie and frightening the shit out of him.

***

CHAPTER 53

Friday 27 July

I open the back door and feel the warm air on my face. Nice day, I think, then pow!

He must have been waiting for me. Had it planned. Knew Mum and Dad had a meeting in town. Knew Joyce had gone to start on the toilets. Knew Natalie was in the playbarn. Knew I was going at nine o'clock to help her. Probably even set that up.

The perfect trap. Set it and wait, like a spider.

He slams into me, using his weight like a wrestler to force me back inside.

His hand's round my throat with his thumb pressing hard on one side, like he's going to throttle me to death. Pushes me against the wall and lifts me by my chin till my legs are dangling. I kick out and he leans into me, so close I smell his body spray. He traps my legs so I can't kick.

I punch at his shoulders, try to get his face but he's too big, too strong, too old for me. I stop struggling, like a fly wrapped up in spider's web.

He says, 'Morning, Charlie,' nicely, as if he's just met me crossing the courtyard. He even smiles.

'You know, all the time I've lived here, I've never been inside your house. Looks lovely.'

Even if I want to nod, I can't move my head.

'Big house too. Lots of good places to hide stuff, I bet?'

Try to make my eyes stay still and not show any reaction. Want to swallow. My mouth is filling up with saliva, like at the dentist.

'Bet you've got your own bedroom, eh? That must be nice.'

I smile a little bit and feel some spit dribbling down my chin.

'That's where we'll start then.' He lets go of my neck and I drop to the floor and stagger a bit. He catches my arms to keep me from falling over. 'Steady,' he says.

I stand there rubbing at my neck trying to work out what to do. Looking around the kitchen for a weapon I could use.

'Lead the way,' he says.

I have two choices: hit him with a frying pan or do as he says.

I lead the way. Out into the hall and up the stairs. Number six from the top creaks twice. Quietly for me and loudly for him. Stop outside my room. He nods at the door, telling me to go in, and shuts it behind him. I'm trapped again.

He looks around, as if he's thinking about buying our house.

'Very nice,' he says. He points to my bed. 'Is that the same red fleece you lost on the hill? It's come up nicely, hasn't it?'

I know how a fly feels as it waits for the spider to eat it.

He takes a step closer and leans in, watching my face. 'You took something that belongs to me, I believe.'

Shake my head slowly, keeping my eyes on his. If you look away they know you're lying. Jonny McCreadie told me that and his big brother's in the army.

'Okay, let me put it another way. You took something I had that belongs to someone else.'

Try to stare at him but my eyes keep looking at the window then back to his face then at the window.

'Thought so,' he says, as if I'm admitting to stealing his stuff. 'Okay, then. This is quite simple, Charlie. You know what I'm looking for. Hand it back to me, right now, and you can go and help Natalie. Oh, I've told her we'll both be a little late, by the way.'

I don't move.

'No?' he says. 'Alright. There's another way. We can look together, but that will involve me trashing your lovely room, cos I don't have much time, you see.'

He rips the fleece off my bed, then the cushions and the pillow. I try not to watch as he throws them and the duvet across the room and tears the sheet off. I grab at his arm, feel the muscles and realise how much damage he can do. To my house and to me.

'Ah, you want to help after all?' He laughs a pretend laugh, kind of nervous. Something about it tells me I'm not the only frightened one.

He heaves the mattress up like it weighs nothing. Then raises the whole bed, checks underneath then dumps it down with a bang.

He spots my desk and opens the top drawern. Pens and coloured pencils fly everywhere. He grabs a Tipp-Ex and throws it at me. I cringe and cover my head with my hands. He unzips my old pencil case and checks inside as if anyone would be stupid enough to try to hide a shirt in a thing like that. A colouring book skims past my face like a Frisbee and a couple of comics flutter to the carpet. He mutters the F-word and snatches at the handle of the second drawer. It pulls right out and lands at his feet. He kicks my stuff up in the air as if it's rubbish then stands like a mad bull waiting to charge. He rummages through all the clothes in my chest of drawers, panting as if he's in a race. His shaved head is all shiny and wet. I'm sweating too.

'Get me a glass of water, Charlie.'

Can't leave him alone for long in case he goes and looks in Mum's room. I'd never get it back the way she likes it. She'd know if somebody has been in there.

'Move!'

I run to the bathroom and fill the fancy glass my toothbrush sits in. Sure it tastes yucky but he doesn't seem bothered. He drinks the lot and puts the glass down, his eyes fixed on something. The wardrobe.

He edges it out from the wall. Even for him it's too heavy to move far. He peers in behind it.

'Aha!' he says, and tries to shove his arm into the space. It's too muscly.

He looks at me, with a big false smile on his face. 'Nice try, Charlie, but no cigar, I'm afraid, mate.' The smile's gone.

'Get over here. Now stick your skinny little arm in there and get that out for me.'

Push my arm into the space, right up to my shoulder till my fingers touch the sheet of paper that's stuck to the back of the wardrobe. Think about leaving it there but I know he'll get it if I don't.

Hand him the paper and start sorting my bed. Don't want to watch him reading it.

'A guarantee. Shit!' He throws it away like a piece of rubbish. What did he think? I'd write a confession and hide it there.

He doesn't look happy. I run for the door but he catches me by my sweatshirt. I give up right away so he lets go.

'Charlie, it's like this. I'm not going to be here much longer. I know you've got the passport and my T-shirt. You think they link me to the guy on the hill.'

Funny how he calls him 'the guy on the hill' as if he's out there taking photos or enjoying a picnic. Not lying dead in a homemade grave. Shot and buried in half an hour. By us.

'Now, surely you can understand why I feel a tad uncomfortable knowing you've got those things? How do I know you're not going to take them to the cops the minute my back's turned?' He scratches the top of his head as if he's trying to solve a puzzle. I know it's all an act.

'Oh yes, now I remember. It's because you can't take them to the cops without them finding the gun and we know whose fingerprints are on the gun, don't we, Charlie?'

Nod.

'Maybe you think they'll be washed off by now?'

He's been reading my mind again.

'Well, let me tell you, I've been checking, and they won't. The oils from your grubby little paws will be on that gun for a long, long time.'

Know he's right. I checked it too.

'Something else I learned is that they can tell if a gun's been fired. Anyway, we've talked about all this. You already know what happens if the gun gets found.'

Right again. But I still think it makes sense for me to have some evidence that proves he was there.

'You probably think that stuff you stole from my room is some kind of evidence?'

How does he do that?

'Well, it proves nothing. You can't prove I took that passport and the blood on the T-shirt means nothing. So I got some guy's blood on me? Big deal. I can say I had a fight with him the night before, in Ayr, when we were both drunk. Doesn't make me a murderer, does it?'

He's right.

'But your clothes? Now that's a different matter. Why would a boy like you have a dead man's blood all over him? Why would your fingerprints be on the gun that killed him? Don't need to be Sherlock Holmes to work that one out, eh, my dear Watson?'

He puts his arm round my shoulder, as if he's my pal.

'Here's what I think you should do, Charlie. Because I think you need some friendly advice. I think you should get rid of all the "evidence" you've got.'

He makes his fingers draw little curls in the air when he says 'evidence'.

'Destroy it, for good. You know how to do that? The only way to do it?'

Shake my head, even though I do know because I've been doing some research of my own.

'You burn it. That's the only way. You can't wash out blood. You have to burn the whole thing. So, here's what I suggest. You take yourself off somewhere that no one will see you and you light a fire, just a little one, you don't want to attract attention, and you burn your shorts and shirt and you burn my tee and then when you've got a nice little blaze going, you tear up that old passport you found and you feed it into the flames one page at a time.'

He makes it sound like fun.

'Might even be fun, if you like fires. I do, but you won't give me the stuff to burn, will you?'

No, I won't.

'Thought not. Well, I'll just have to trust *you* to do it, won't I?'

Nod, really hard, to show I mean it.

'Because you know it's the best thing for both of us, don't you?'

I close my eyes.

'Don't you, Charlie?'

***

CHAPTER 54

'Charlie not here, Nat?'

'Not yet.'

'Thought he was supposed to be helping us?'

'I thought that too. Want to give me a hand boxing up this paper?'

'Sure thing. Listen, before he comes in, I just want to say, I think you've done a brilliant job with Charlie.'

Nat looks at him and smiles. 'Oh, thanks, Seb. That's really nice of you to say so. But I can't take all the credit. You've been helping him too.'

If only she knew. 'No, the credit's all yours.'

'Rubbish, you've built a great relationship with Charlie. That's why he's talking, I'm sure. He trusts us. He won't talk in front of Joyce, you know.'

Interesting. 'Won't he? I'm surprised. Thought he likes Joyce.'

'He does, but maybe he just doesn't feel as comfortable with older people as he does with us. I think he relates better to younger people. His mum tells me he loved Miss Lawson, his P7 teacher and she's really young.'

Shit. 'Did he talk to her?'

'Oh no, he won't talk in that school. His behaviour is too patterned there, he's comfortable, everyone accepts him as he is. But what a difference it will make to his life when he goes to high school. I think he's terrified, you know.'

'Yeah, I can tell he's afraid of something. But listen, this speech thing, I don't want to burst your bubble but he doesn't say a whole helluva lot to me. Does he *really* speak to you? Like, normal talking?'

She blushes and Gus panics for a second, wondering what the kid might have told her.

'Well, obviously I can't take all the credit, you're deeply involved with Charlie too.'

Get on with it, he wants to scream, desperate to know what the boy's been saying, or more crucial, what he's capable of saying.

'Not sure how to tell you this.'

'Come on, put me out of my misery.'

'Okay, to be completely honest, he's making sounds.'

Gus laughs and regrets it. 'Sorry to laugh, Nat. But you made it sound like Charlie's reciting Shakespeare and now you tell me he's just making noises?'

'Not noises. Sounds.'

'There's a difference?'

She's getting pissed off. He can tell. Time for some sweet talk. He gives her his best smile. 'I'm forgetting you know about this stuff. You're gonna make a brilliant teacher. You care so much, don't you?'

'I do care. How could you not?'

Don't answer that one.

'Listen, Nat, I can't tell you how much I want Charlie to speak again. For your sake, as well as his.'

'I know you do. I'm sorry if I made it sound better than it is. But he has said one or two words. That's a start, isn't it?' She clasps her hands and lifts them to cover her mouth. She reminds Gus of a Disney princess. 'Oh, Seb,' she says, 'I'm *very* optimistic.'

'Well, that's great. You should be. You've worked really hard with him.'

'You have too.'

Gus shrugs. 'What words have you actually heard him say?'

She blushes again but this time it doesn't spook him. No wonder she's embarrassed, claiming the kid's 'talking'. What a load of bullshit.

'He says "yes".'

'What else does he say?' Gus realises, a beat too late, that this isn't the right reaction. 'Does he?' he says, trying to sound amazed and impressed.

'Isn't that amazing? Are you impressed?'

'I am. S isn't the easiest letter to say, is it?' A picture of Charlie comes into his mind, that day when he tried to force the kid to say sorry. It was like his tongue was paralysed and he couldn't get the word out.

'No, the s sound is a difficult one. I got three million results on the web when I went looking for advice. Some kids don't master it till age seven, and some of them never.'

'But Charlie's got it? Well done, you.'

'More like well done, Charlie. You know what this means, don't you?'

'You tell me.'

'It means that he can say anything he wants, if he wants.'

'If. Is that important?'

'So important. Charlie chose not to speak, all those years ago, for whatever reason. It's not that he can't, it's that he won't. He's just proved it. All he needs now is encouragement and there'll be no shutting him up.'

***

CHAPTER 55

Friday 3 August

'Good morning, Brackenbrae Holiday Park. This is Pim speaking and I am at your service.'

Catherine wonders, while she waits for him to finish his spiel, how on earth Sebastien can stand working with this idiot.

'How may I help you on this lovely day?'

She smiles as she imagines Sebastien telling them all about Pim. He does very funny impersonations and Pim sounds like an ideal candidate for ridicule.

'Good morning. This is Catherine Lamar.'

'Ah, Seb's mother. How are you?'

The young man has remembered her. Catherine feels guilty for thinking mean thoughts of him.

'I'm well, thank you, Pim. Just a little frustrated by my son. I don't suppose you deal with the mail as part of your job, do you?'

'Indeed I do. In fact, I am somewhat of a Johnny-All-Jobs.'

'A Jack of all trades?'

'Yes, that too. Do you have a specific reason for asking about the mail? If it is appropriate for me to answer your enquiry, I certainly shall endeavour to help you.'

'Thank you. I sent Sebastien a new phone as a birthday gift. Do you know if he got it?'

'Oh, I am so sorry.'

'That it didn't come?'

'No. That it was Seb's birthday and he did not mention it. I would have enjoyed the pleasure of buying him a pint of beer.'

It's strange that Sebastien hasn't told anyone about his birthday. He has always enjoyed his birthday. As a little boy he thought the special day was his alone and had been quite put out to learn he wasn't the only one ever born on 9 June.

'Did the parcel arrive?'

'Certainly, a parcel came for Seb and, if my memory serves me correctly, the dimensions were similar to those of a mobile phone box. I hope that information is helpful to you?'

'Yes, thank you. I wonder, could you please render me another small service?' Why is she speaking like Pim? His verbosity must be infectious. 'Can you ask him to use his new phone to call me, please? Tell him his mother's getting frantic.'

'Frenetic?'

'Either one will do, as long as he gets the message. Thank you.' She hangs up and scowls at Eric hovering in the bedroom doorway, knotting his tie.

'Shouldn't you be at work by now?'

'Meeting clients at their hotel, Le Bristol.'

'Very nice.'

'So he got the phone? Why isn't the little bugger calling us? Oh, don't cry, darling. He'll get round to it. Typical boy.'

'That's what my friends were saying. Boys never keep in touch. Girls, yes. Marie-Claude's daughter calls her every day. That must be nice. Then again, Pauline says her son only gets in touch when he needs money. They say I shouldn't worry, and that Sebastien is simply too busy working and having fun to think about his old mum. The consensus is that I need to chill out and get used to it before he disappears to university.'

Eric tilts his head and raises his eyebrows.

'I'll try, all right?'

***

CHAPTER 56

The phone's been charging all night and now it's decision time.

Seb's mother's 'frenetic', according to Pim, whatever the hell that means. Doesn't sound good. He doesn't want her doing something that blows his cover. Not when he's got this close. The ticket's bought and he's good to go. One last wage packet to give him some spending money for the journey, a few goodbyes and he's outta here.

The boss would like him to stay on, help him close down at the end of the season. He even offered some labouring work on Phase Five. The council have given him the thumbs up to go ahead with his glampsite. The boss has explained how he's hoping to have the yurts erected in time for Christmas. He expects to be fully booked and says people will flock to Brackenbrae to bring in the new year. He was desperate to show off his plans, but Gus gave them a body swerve. The boss and his crazy plans are of no interest. This time next week they'll be nothing but a memory. One he'll be trying his hardest to forget.

Full charge. Full signal for once. No excuse. He has to make contact. By text, so he doesn't have to risk speaking again.

Reading from the slip of paper she'd stuck to the back of the phone, Gus keys in the woman's number then starts to type his message.

Hi Mum
Now what?

Hope u r well

No, better make that both well. Oops, and don't forget the dead granny. What was it they called her again? Mamie.

So sorry about Mamie I loved

The word disappears, replaced by a heart. He decides to leave it. The dead guy looked like he'd be a fan of emojis.

her very much Sorry I had to stay here and work

High season

Be in touch

Luv Seb

He adds a smiley face with sunglasses and a rainbow. He reads it aloud, nods approvingly and hits the blue send arrow.

Right, that's it done. Should put the mother's mind at rest long enough to let him get away. After that, well, he's got his story sorted.

As long as he makes sure Charlie doesn't decide to tell a story of his own, all will be hunky-dory.

***

CHAPTER 57

France

'Eric! Eric!'

'I'm in the shower.'

'Well, hurry up!'

Catherine clutches her phone to her chest, closes her eyes and whispers, 'Thank you, God.'

She sits on the bed and waits for Eric. He comes into the bedroom with a towel wrapped round his waist and another draped round his neck. He lifts one end and rubs at his hair. 'What's the rush?'

She holds out her phone.

'Sebastien? Did he ring?'

'A text.'

'That's great.' He looks at her and says, 'Isn't it?'

She gives him a smile, knowing he wants her to be happy. 'Of course it is.'

'What does he say?'

'Mmm, not much, actually. Here, read it.'

Eric reads the little message. She watches for a reaction but he simply hands the phone over, saying, 'Short and to the point. You disappointed?'

'A little bit, perhaps.'

'At least we know he's okay.' Eric starts to get dressed, his back to her.

'Do we?'

He turns to face her, adjusting the waistband of his pants. 'Oh, Catherine, not this again, please.' He sits on the end of the bed to pull on his socks. The mattress moves under his weight and she leans on her hand to keep steady. If only her emotions were so easy to control. She bites down on her lip.

'What's the matter, darling? You've been waiting weeks to hear from him. Now you have and you're still not happy. I don't understand what's going on.' He gently taps three times on the side of her head. She'd like to laugh but it's impossible.

'I've just got a feeling something's not right.'

She hears the sigh before he speaks. 'A feeling?'

'Yes. No. Well, more than a feeling. A suspicion.'

This time he makes no effort to muffle his sigh. 'Oh, Catherine. This has to stop. He's a young man now. Ready to leave home and you have to accept that fact, even if you don't like it. He's found himself a job, made his way there and working hard. You should be proud, not suspicious.'

That hurts. 'I *am* proud,' she says. 'It's just that…'

'What?'

'There's something about that message. Didn't you notice it yourself? Hi Mum? Luv Seb? Eric, when did Sebastien ever call me "Mum"? He knows I hate it.'

'He was joking. Oh, for goodness' sake, Catherine. You need to relax.'

'*Luv* Seb? L, U, V?'

'It's the way young people communicate, Catherine. There's nothing sinister about it. Didn't you tell me he's calling himself Seb this summer? I actually rather like it. Seb.'

Eric repeats their son's name as if he's trying it out. The way they used to when they were trying to choose baby names before he was born. Sebastien Louis Lamar. Sebastien from his family and Louis from hers. Her paternal grandfather. They were never able to agree on names for a girl, but boys names were easy to choose. Just as well she had a little boy.

Catherine's mind fills with images of Sebastien as a cute toddler. Always smiling, as if he knew life would be easier if he charmed everyone who spoke to him.

'What about the rest of it? All those silly little pictures.'

'Emojis.'

'Pardon?'

'Emojis. That's what those little hearts and smiley faces are called.'

'How on earth do you know that?'

'My secretary uses them all the time. Everyone does.'

'I don't. I wouldn't know how to make a smiley face, especially one with sunglasses. Look.'

She holds out her phone. He peers at the text message. 'I rather like the little rainbow. That's quite jolly, and he does say how much he loved Mamie.'

'With a little pink heart? I thought you'd be angry at the dismissive way he explains missing her funeral.'

'All water under the bridge now, Catherine. Mamie would never have borne a grudge against her beloved Sebastien, so what's the point in my continuing to be cross with him?'

'I suppose you're right. She'd have forgiven him anything.'

'You still haven't explained why this text bothers you so much?'

She hands him the phone and says, 'Read it again and tell me what's missing.'

He does, shaking his head and handing back her phone. 'Sorry, I don't know what you're getting at. Unless it's the rest of the words "you are"? I know how much you hate those abbreviations.'

'That's my point. Sebastien knows that too.'

'To be fair, he only does it once.'

'Anyway, that's not the right answer.'

'Catherine, I'm barely dressed, it's not even breakfast time and I feel like I've been interrogated. Just tell me what you're getting at.'

'Punctuation.'

'You've lost me. I need a coffee.'

She follows him to the kitchen but when she tries to speak, he waves his hand by the side of his head, as if to say, I'm no longer listening.

'I don't think Sebastien sent this text.'

'What?'

'I don't think–'

'I heard you, Catherine. I have no idea what you're talking about, that's my problem. Who else, other than Sebastien, would send us a text from Sebastien's phone?'

'Someone who's stolen it?'

'Why would a thief do that?'

'To pretend he's Sebastien.'

Eric's coffee cup hovers in mid-air, halfway to his mouth. 'Catherine, have you any idea how mad that makes you sound? I'm not even going to answer it. I'm going to finish my coffee, grab my briefcase and go to work. As for you.' He stops and points at her. 'You need to get out and do something to distract yourself before you go completely bonkers.'

The funny word makes them both smile. 'Maybe you're right. I'll call Isabelle and see if she's free for lunch.'

'Great idea. Go to Le Canard Bleu. Have some Champagne. Giggle and be silly for a bit.'

'Can we talk about this later?'

'No, Catherine. We *cannot* talk about this later. Yesterday you were frantic because you hadn't heard from your son for weeks. Now he's been in touch and you're complaining about his lack of punctuation.'

Hearing the words from Eric's lips makes her feel foolish.

'You're right. We won't talk about it any more. I promise.'

She doesn't promise to stop thinking about it, however, and when Eric leaves for the office, she goes online. Looking for flights to Scotland.

***

CHAPTER 58

Scotland
Friday 10 August

When I was little, I used to say a prayer with Mum. Every night, before I went to sleep. Then when I got bigger, Mum would tuck me in and give me a kiss. She'd always ask if I'd said my prayers. I'd nod, even though I didn't really say them any more. It was stupid. 'If I should die before I wake, I pray the lord my soul to take.'

What does that even mean? I know some people, the good ones, go to heaven when they die. That must mean the lord takes their soul. I like the idea of some nice, kind man, or an angel even, coming to take Robbie's mum and his baby brother to heaven.

But what about the bad guys? Where do they go if the lord doesn't take them? Did the lord take Robbie's soul?

What about the dead hiker on the hillside? He looked nice. Does the lord know he's out there? Will someone come and take his soul? I hope so, but I don't pray for it.

Every night now, instead of saying prayers, I say something else. My sounds and my words. Very quietly, so Mum and Dad don't hear me, I practise.

Starting with noises like ah, eh, ee, oo, saying them a few times each. Natalie calls them warm-ups. She says it's just like a runner warming up his muscles by doing stretches. 'These are stretches for your voice.' That's what she said. 'They'll make it easier for you to say words and then whole sentences when you're ready.'

Then I go on to the harder ones like ssss and say them a few times.

'Seb, Seb, Seb.' Then it's time for the p sound. 'Piss, piss, piss.' That one makes me smile. Mum can't stand it. If Dad's complaining about the rain, he sometimes says, 'Oh no, look at that. Supposed to be sunny and it's pissing down.' Mum wrinkles up her nose to show she doesn't like him to say pissing.

'Piss off.' That's what Jayden Jeffries says, although sometimes it's the F-word. Mum would kill me if I ever said that, so there's no point in even trying it.

Imagine Mum's face if I said, 'Piss off!' to her.

Should say it to Seb. Next time he's threatening me. Just look him in the eyes and say, 'Piss off, Seb.' That would show him.

I know I won't. Too scared. That's one reason. The other one is, I don't want him to find out about the talking. What if he decides he can't go away and leave me to tell anyone what happened that day. Already know he's worried that I'll write it all down and show it to someone. Bet he thought that's what was stuck to the back of my wardrobe. As if.

Nearly wrote it all down in 'The Long Weekend' essay, but after a few sentences I decided to rub it all out. Didn't want to get 'referred'. That's what happened to Jonny McCreadie because he has 'issues'.

After that I knew it wasn't the kind of thing you write down on paper. At least, not yet.

Footsteps on the stairs. Mum's. Sixth one creaks.

'Rise and shine, Charlie!' She opens the blind and I bury under the covers like a mole. The duvet smells of that flowery stuff Mum puts in. She pulls it off me. Not fair. 'Come on, time you were up. Busy day. School uniform shopping.'

Hate shopping. Takes ages and there's something important I have to do today. Shake my head.

'Don't say no to me, Charlie. Traipsing round shops looking at black school trousers isn't my idea of fun either, but it's got to be done. Today. It's only a week till the schools go back. Everything's probably sold out already. We should have seen to this weeks ago but I don't know where I was supposed to find the time. So get up, please. Now.'

I know that voice. I slide over, as slow as a slug, to the edge of the bed and put my feet on the floor.

Mum lifts the red fleece. 'How many times do I have to tell you not to throw this on the floor?' She folds it and lays it on my desk. 'What's to stop you doing this at night instead of heaving it into a corner? Oh, and by the way, under no circumstances are you to take anything out of this house without asking me. A brand new fleece dumped out there in the bracken to rot like a rag?' She shivers as if I've committed a terrible crime.

I reach for yesterday's clothes, but she snatches them from me and dumps them in the dirty basket. 'No, you don't. Clean clothes and a shower first.'

The door shuts behind Mum and I whisper, 'Piss off.'

***

CHAPTER 59

'Nat, any idea where Charlie might be? I want to say goodbye.'

'I think he's going into town.'

'Oh, is he? That's good. I'm glad he's got mates. He's a nice kid.'

'He is, but I don't think he's off for a fun day with his pals. The boss mentioned Charlie's in a right mood and his mum had a strop because she wants to go and get his school uniform sorted and he doesn't.'

'Can't say I blame him for that. But she's strong medicine, Mrs Boss.'

Nat rolls her eyes. 'You can say that again.'

'She's strong med– Oi! That hurt!' He rubs his upper arm.

'You deserved it. Anyway, I'm going to miss beating you up. Have to make the most of it while I've got the chance.'

'Yep, not for much longer.'

'When's your flight?'

'Leaving here about four.' Best not to be specific.

'Looking forward to going home?'

'Eventually.'

'Will we keep in touch?'

'Sure. You've got my number. Come on, one last hug. In case I don't get the chance later.' Gus pulls her into his arms and squeezes tight. When he lets her go, she's got tears in her eyes.

'Thanks for a great summer, Seb,' she says.

'Hey, what's with the tears?' In the fake Scottish accent that always makes Joyce and Nat laugh, he says, 'This isn't goodbye, it's just cheerio.' He rolls the, like they taught him weeks ago. 'Be sure to tell wee Joyce I'll never forget her, will you?' She nods. 'Now give me a smile.'

When she does, he says, 'That's my girl. Okay, I'd better run, see if I can catch Charlie and his mum. I've got fond of that kid.' Might as well play the game till the last minute. 'Tell him to make sure he remembers me, will you?'

'I'll do that. Now get lost. I've got work to do. Typical of you to skive off before it's done.'

'Sorry, my grandmother died recently, remember? My family needs me.'

Natalie's face shows her embarrassment. Exactly the reaction he was looking for. He wants her to remember the reason he's leaving but not feel like asking too many more questions.

A final hug and he's out of that playbarn at last.

He's already said bye to Pim who, as usual, was making his bed with the precision of an army recruit.

Gus offered his hand but Pim ignored the handshake and grabbed him in a hug that felt a bit too close for comfort. He whacked his skinny back and pushed Pim away. 'Bye then, buddy.'

'I consider myself extremely fortunate to have had such wonderful colleagues with whom to work. You will remain in my heart for a long time to come.'

Sounded like the guy had written a farewell speech.

'Ditto, mate. But, taxi…' Gus waved his hand in the direction of the gate.

'Yes, sorry. Of course, you must go. Shall I come and wave goodbye?'

'No way. Don't like goodbyes, me. You might see me cry. Think what that would do for my tough guy reputation.'

Pim's laughter had followed him out the door. Could have had a worse roommate.

As he crosses the courtyard the café door opens. Big Mark shouts, 'Safe journey, pal. Come back and see us.'

'Might just do that.' He waves a salute.

'Got time for one last beer before you go?'

Gus checks his watch. 'Sure, why not.'

Mark opens two beers but disappears back into the kitchen with his half-full bottle. Left alone, Gus looks around, impressed as ever with the imagination that can turn an old cowshed into a restaurant. Maybe this wedding business isn't such a mad idea after all. If anyone can do it, the boss and his wife can. Will change the place though. Not that he cares. He'll never be back, that's for sure.

Gus drains his bottle and puts it on the bar. 'Bye, Mark, thanks.'

No answer. Everyone is moving on already. By tomorrow it will be as if he was never here. Apart from the body buried on the hillside. Gus wishes suddenly he could see the kid before he goes. Just to make sure.

He hesitates outside the owners' house, wondering how rude it would be to knock on the door. This part of the site is out of bounds for campers and staff, but hell, what they gonna do? Sack him?'

The doorbell chimes like a cathedral and he waits, hoping Charlie will answer.

The door opens. 'Yes?' says his employer.

'Hi, Boss. Only me.'

Her frown changes to a smile and her tone melts from icy to lukewarm. 'Oh, it's you, Seb. What can I do for you?'

'I know you're in a rush, but I didn't want to leave without saying goodbye.'

'That was nice of you. Thanks. Well, goodbye, and good luck.'

The door starts to close. Gus touches it with his hand, just enough to slow its movement. 'Is Charlie there?'

'Yes, but he's in a foul mood. Teenage hormones!'

'Can I see him for a minute?'

'I suppose so. Charlie!'

No wonder the kid's moody if she bawls like that all the time.

'Bye then,' he says, hoping she'll take the hint and leave him alone with the kid. 'Thanks so much for everything. It's been great.'

She disappears inside. He hears her say, 'Seb's at the door. For you.' There's a silence and he imagines the look on the boy's face. 'Go and shake his hand or something. Be polite and hurry up, please.'

Charlie comes to the door but stays well inside the hallway. As usual, Gus is surprised by how small and slight he is. The kid's eyes are wary, full of mistrust. Maybe he's been telling himself he'll never see Gus again and now here he is, right on the doorstep.

'Hey, Charlie. Just came to say goodbye.' He gestures to the kid to come out and close the door. Charlie obliges but leaves the door only half shut.

Gus keeps it light and friendly, but loud, in case Mrs Boss is listening. 'It's been a great summer. I've had a blast. All those things we did together. I'm never gonna forget them. Bet you're the same?'

Charlie nods.

Gus leans towards the door and Charlie flinches.

'Chill, Charlie. I was only going to close the door, to stop the draught annoying your mum. You do the honours.'

Keeping his eyes fixed on Gus, Charlie reaches for the handle and the door clicks shut.

'Thought I'd swing by before I go pick up my rucksack and head on out of here. Just to make sure, one last time, that we're on the same page. Know what I mean?'

Charlie continues to stare.

'See, a little bird tells me you can talk now.'

The shock shows in the kid's face.

'So it's true? That's very impressive.' Gus gives a slow, muted hand clap. 'Bet you're not so scared of going to high school now you'll no longer be a freak, eh?'

Charlie looks as if he'd like to kill him, and he can't blame the kid. But this is no time for Mr Nice Guy. 'Anyway, Charlie. I'd like to give you a little test before I go. Don't look so worried, it's easy and it won't take a moment. I know your mum's in a rush.'

Charlie breaks eye contact for the first time. He looks at his feet as if they're suddenly the most interesting thing in the world.

'I want you to promise me, out loud, that you'll keep our secret. That's okay, isn't it?'

The boy's head moves up and down, ever so slightly, but enough to show his agreement.

'So, repeat after me. Cross my heart…'

Charlie's head shoots up and he looks into Gus's eyes as if he can't believe what he's hearing. 'What's the problem, Charlie? I'm sure you know that saying, cross my heart and hope to die. Kids say it all the time. Now I want you to say it to me, that's all. But say it so I know you mean it.'

He watches Charlie come to a decision, as clearly as if he can see inside the boy's brain. He's deciding on the quickest way to get rid of him, for good. 'Right decision, Charlie. You say the words and I'm out of here. But don't take too long. My taxi will be here any minute. Come on, cross my heart…' He waits, waggling his fingers to hurry the kid up, not really believing he'll speak but wanting to find out one way or another before he goes.

Charlie takes a big deep breath, like a singer about to launch into a song. 'Cross my heart,' he says. Shit, Natalie was right. He can talk. Okay, his voice is a bit wavery and uncertain, but that's to be expected after so many years of silence. Gus waggles his fingers again and raises his eyebrows.

Another huge intake of breath. 'Cross my heart and hope... *you* die!'

***

CHAPTER 60

Why did I have to say *that*? Should have said nothing. Left him wondering if I really can talk. Or if I had to speak, I could have said what he wanted. What harm would that have done?

Instead I said *that* and ran away and hid. Like a wee stupid kid. Bet he's raging.

Mum's mad at me too. First because I disappeared when she was ready to go and then because I refused to go into town with her. I just stood with my arms crossed and my head down till she gave up and went away, muttering, 'Well don't blame me if you don't like what I buy.'

How could I go shopping with her? Even if I didn't have all this other stuff going on, imagine if the other boys saw me. Why can't she just give me money and let me go in on the bus and get my own stuff? Or buy it off the Internet.

Dad came in for coffee in the middle of it. He just shrugged his shoulders and said, 'Up to you, Charlie.' When Mum wasn't looking, he whispered, 'Sometimes it's better to just do what she wants. Makes life easier.' Mum caught him winking at me and another row started. Then she raced off in the car.

Glad she's gone. There's no chance of her finding what I've done to her precious cushions. I unzip the spotty one and pull out my shirt and shorts. I zip it closed then bash it a few times with my fist till it looks the right shape. The blue stripy one's been guarding the T-shirt and passport. I puff the cushion up and sit them both on the bed the way Mum likes them. From tomorrow I can go back to leaving them lying in the corner now they've got nothing to hide.

I stuff everything into a carrier bag and head for the tower. I push open the old rickety door and dump all the stuff on the floor. Wish they'd left the tower the way it was. When the builders come back from holiday they'll put the new fancy door on and I won't even be able to get back in here.

No time to think about that stuff. Got to get this done before Mum comes back.

I kneel on the dirt floor and make a little pile of clothes. First his T-shirt, then my shorts and finally, on the top, the checked shirt Mum bought to match. She'd have a fit if she could see me setting fire to brand new things from Next. I break off bits of firelighter and stick them in amongst the clothes. Don't like the smell on my hands. Pinched them and a bottle of lighter stuff from the shed where Dad keeps the barbecue. He'll never notice it's missing because we never have a barbecue these days, even when it's nice weather. Mum says barbecues give you cancer but that's just her excuse for never having one. Mackenzie McMullen's always going on about having barbecues with all their neighbours and everybody getting drunk and lying down for a sleep and getting sunburnt.

I've got a box of matches someone left by the campsite barbecue ages ago. Kept them here with my other private stuff but that's all been moved now, to let the builders in.

The builders have been here for weeks already but there's not much difference that I can see. I'd like to climb up and take a last look out my spyholes, but the builders threw away my ladder and took theirs away with their tools. As if we'd steal them. Mum's plans are for a spiral staircase up the middle but that's not here yet. Apart from the woody smell of some bits of new timber, the old tower feels just the same. Bare walls made of rough stone with some chunks jutting out further than the others. Dad says that's where the old stairs used to be. Don't think I'll risk it. Don't fancy a broken leg for starting at my new school.

Okay, time to do this. Wish I'd brought some newspaper to get the fire burning, but the firelighters should do the trick. If they light charcoal they'll light a few clothes, easy-peasy.

I take a match out of the box and close it again, to be safe.
Draw it along the side of the box. Once, twice, nothing happens.
On the third go, all the pink stuff comes off the end and I'm left
with a tiny stick. Open the box, shut it again and have another go.
Same thing. This is crap. How can I light a fire with no matches?
Bet they were sitting out in the rain. Should have pinched that
fancy thing Mum uses to light her candles. One more try then I'm
going to get it. I choose one from the bottom of the box and it
sparks and lights first time. I like the smell. I hold it to some bits
of firelighter and start some white flames. Then the match burns
my fingers and I drop it. Suck my fingers for a moment then take a
bundle of matches from the box and hold them to the flames. The
matches flare suddenly, and I throw them on the clothes. Some
touch the lumps of white stuff and set them alight. Others just
drop and go out. I do the same till all the firelighters are burning
then sit back and wait.

The flames start to die down before all the clothes are burned.
This is no good. I've got to keep the fire going till everything burns
away to nothing. I'm destroying evidence and that only works if
you destroy it all, completely. Can't leave half-burned rags. How
suspicious will that look?

Don't know what to do. There are bits of wood leaning against
the wall. They'd make a great fire but they're too big for me to
break and I've nothing to cut them up with.

Oh yes, the lighter stuff, fluid or gel or whatever it is. Dad just
squirts it over the charcoal and it lights like magic.

I undo the cap and pour a little on the sleeve of the shirt near
the firelighter. It catches and burns. Perfect. I stand up, hold the
bottle in both hands and squeeze hard. The liquid skooshes out
and covers the fire and a bit of the floor. For a second I think I've
put the fire out. Then a ball of flames inflates like a huge balloon
and I know I've made a bad mistake. The heat balloon bursts and I
smell burning on my face. I step back and watch as the fire spreads
to the wood. It catches, and flames climb like some crazy plants,
up and up. Smoke catches in the back of my throat and my eyes

sting. I cover my nose with my hand and try to breathe through my fingers, but it feels like my nostrils are burning. I need to get out of here. I can see the door but I can't get to it without stepping through the fire.

This is what I did to Robbie and his mum and their little baby. Everybody said they were all asleep, the firemen found them in their beds, that they inhaled stuff from the burning furniture and they didn't know what was happening.

But I know what's happening to me. And I deserve it. Because I've said it again. So I'm going to die in a fire, just like them. I sit down and wait. Then I think of Mum and Dad.

'Dad!' My voice is too quiet. It's not been used enough.

'Dad! Help!' The smoke gets down my throat. I cough then choke as if I'm going to be sick.

It's no good. He'll never hear me.

***

CHAPTER 61

Gus is almost at the gate when he hears someone shouting his name. The one he thought he'd never hear again. He signals to the taxi driver to let him know he's coming then turns, expecting to see Natalie, waving him off. The courtyard is deserted. He feels a spike of disappointment. It was good being popular. Still, he'll be glad to get away. Sure, there have been fun moments, most of them with Nat, but too many sleepless nights. Too much angst. Side-effects of the steroids or maybe coming off them too suddenly. Back on them when he gets home. He's losing muscle mass by the day. No team will take him on unless he beefs up again and fast.

There it is again. He stops walking and listens.

'Seb! Help!'

He drops his rucksack. Is that little bastard having one last go at winding him up? No, wait a minute. The kid's gone off with his mother.

The taxi driver winds down his window. 'Any chance you gettin in, pal? I've other hires on.'

'Yeah. Hang on a minute, buddy. Got to check something first. I'll be right with you.

As he walks back towards the courtyard he sees the smoke. Coming from the tower. Leaking through the tiny windows and rising, dirty against the sky. Gus breaks into a run.

Without thinking, he leans his weight against the old door and shoves. It moves but doesn't open. Something's blocking it. He hopes it's not the kid's body. Smokes seeps out from underneath and round the edges. He steps back and prepares to shoulder charge. As if he were attempting to take out an opponent with the illegal move, Gus rams the door and feels it give. He stumbles into flames and smoke, seeing nothing and no one. Has Charlie tricked him into an ambush? Making his own wish come true, like a curse.

'I'm up here.'

He follows the sound and sees the kid, perched on the stone platform. For a second, he tells himself to walk away. This is the perfect solution. Mute kids can talk but dead ones can't. He should get out of here, save himself, go jump in that taxi and don't look back. He owes this kid nothing. In fact, meeting this kid was the worst thing that ever happened.

'Help me, please.'

Don't do it. Help yourself. Run, get away while you still can.

'Jump!'

'What?'

'Jump, you little bastard.' Gus holds out his arms.

'I can't.'

'You can. I'll catch you. Now, jump!'

The kid's sobbing. No wonder he's terrified. Gus feels more afraid than he's ever been in his life. This is a danger more immediate than a murder charge. 'Trust me. Please, Charlie, jump.'

'No.'

'We'll both burn to death. Is that what you want? More people dying in a fire because of you? I'll count to three and you'd better jump on three. Ready? One, two, three.'

The kid lands on him like a load of cement. Gus buckles under the sudden weight and they both collapse on the ground. The kid is first on his feet. Gus shouts at him, 'Run, Charlie! Get out.'

Charlie doesn't move. He reaches for Gus's hand and helps him to his feet then pulls on his arm and the two of them burst into the clear, fresh air.

'What the hell's going on?' The boss gathers his son into his arms. 'Charlie! What happened?'

'A bit of fun gone wrong, Boss. He's been messing about with matches. I should have told you – I noticed the last time I was in there.'

'Yes, you should have told me. This is your fault. Your negligence caused this.'

'What? I just saved the kid's life.'

The boss ignores him, peering into Charlie's face to see if he's okay, then hugging him again.

Big Mark appears, and a few campers. 'Shit, Boss. I just heard the commotion. Anything I can do?'

'Thanks, Mark. Charlie was in a fire but I think he's okay.'

'You should call an ambulance. Get him checked over. You too, mate. You okay?' Mark clasps Gus's shoulder. 'Come and get a beer. You're a hero.'

'Thanks, but I'm heading off. Got a plane to catch, remember. If my taxi's still there.'

'Seb!' Natalie runs up, hugs him. 'What happened?'

'Charlie set a fire in the tower. It got out of hand. I saw the smoke in time and he got out. No big deal.'

'Oh my God! Are you hurt? Charlie, are you okay? Boss, what can I do?'

'Take Charlie into the house while I call his mum, and an ambulance.'

Ambulance. That likely means the police. 'Guys, I've got to go. That plane won't wait for me.'

No one answers. The boss is on the phone. Nat is focused on Charlie, walking him to the house, telling him not to worry.

Gus shouts, 'Charlie!'

When the kid turns around Gus says, 'In future, be careful what you wish for, bud.'

***

CHAPTER 62

Saturday 11 August

'Charlie, are you awake?' Mum's voice is gentle, like it always used to be. Maybe I'm dreaming.

'Can you open your eyes for me, sweetheart?' Yep, must be a dream.

I open them and she's there, sitting on my bed, looking at me with her face all soft and loving.

'Morning, my sweet boy,' she says. 'How do you feel?'

Nod and smile to let her know I'm fine.

'Dad and I have been so worried about you. I still can't believe you've been in a fire.' She puts her hand to her throat. 'It must have been awful.'

Actually, it wasn't so awful. Once we got out of the smoke and smelt fresh air. The paramedics came racing into the courtyard with their blue light and siren going and everything. They took me into their van and put a mask on my face and made me breathe oxygen for a while. They attached wires to me and printed out wee skinny bits of paper and studied them. They kept asking over and over if I felt okay. I nodded every time. I did feel okay, just a bit shocked.

'He doesn't speak,' said Dad.

Decided to leave it that way. Look what happened when I finally did speak. The curse came back.

'Looks like you're one lucky young man,' said the lady paramedic, who reminded me a bit of Lara Croft in her green jumpsuit thing. 'You're going to look a bit weird for a while with no eyebrows, but they'll grow back. But you could have died, you know that, don't you? The guy who saved your life, he could have died too.'

Just like I hoped for. The terrible thing is, when I said it, I hoped he *would* die.

Mum arrived and started to cry, as if she couldn't stop. Last night she kept hugging me for no reason. It was nice for a while but then it got too much. I still let her do it, though.

So far nobody has shouted at me for starting the fire, but it's bound to happen. The minute they stop feeling sorry for me.

Last night I listened from the stairs.

'Why do you think he did it?'

'He's a boy,' said Dad. 'Boys like to play with fire. I know I did at his age.'

'But I thought he knew better. I thought we'd taught him better. He could have died. Seb too.'

'I know that.'

'Do you think it was a cry for help?'

'A what?'

'A cry for help, you know, when people do something crazy, like attempted suicide and all they want is for someone to pay attention.'

At last. Why did it have to take them so long? Why couldn't they have worked it out for themselves, before I took the gun?

'Why would Charlie do something like that? We pay him attention.'

'Do we?'

There was silence and I imagined them both thinking about me and remembering all the 'not now' and 'I'm busy' and ' maybe later'. Mum realising she'd stopped hugging me and speaking kindly. Dad realising how long it's been since he kicked a ball with me.

'I feel so ashamed, Viv.'

Hooray. Now Dad's going to tell her how bad he feels about not spending any time with me this summer.

'That poor guy's a hero and I told him the fire was his fault.'

'You were in shock.'

'That's no excuse. I blamed him for not telling me my son's been playing with fire. As if that was his responsibility, not mine. Then I let him leave without even thanking him for saving our child's life. We should have given him every penny we had, recognised his bravery and rewarded it.'

'He wouldn't have taken our money.'

'That's not the point, Viv. I didn't even offer him my hand. After he risked his life. We owe him. Big time.'

Risked his life. Hadn't thought about it like that. Dad's not the only one who owes him.

'Charlie,' says Mum. 'You sure you're ok? You looked like you'd drifted off there for a minute. Should we pop up to the hospital, do you think? Do you feel sick, from the smoke?'

I feel perfectly fine. It's nice to be fussed over though.

'Dad and I took turns to look in on you through the night. It was like having a baby again. You were sound asleep, every time. Would you like breakfast in bed, as a little treat?'

Not sure what to do. Want to get up. But if they see I'm okay, I'll get into trouble for the fire and they'll go back to how it was before.

'Listen, sweetheart,' says Mum, 'Dad and I have been talking.'

Here it comes.

'We want you to know that we're sorry. Both of us. But you shouldn't have set fire to the tower.'

So that's what they think I was up to. Oh well, it's much better than the truth. Shake my head so Mum knows I'm sorry about the fire. Because I am. But I had no choice.

'We know that was your special place and I stole it for the wedding business without even asking you. That wasn't fair. A boy needs a den. A man cave. So, here's what we're going to do. Dad's going to build you a cabin of your own, where you can 'hang out with your homies'.'

She says the last bit in a kind of gangster accent, trying to sound cool, but it doesn't work. Like the idea, though, and nod a lot to show her.

'But first, you need to earn it, by being brave at the big school and doing your best.'

Knew there would be a catch. Keep nodding though. My plan was to speak to them and tell them not to worry, I'll be okay at the Academy, but don't think that's going to happen now.

'Now, what about breakfast?'

I throw back my duvet to show her I'm getting up.

'Good boy!' She hugs me tight and says I still smell a bit smoky. 'I didn't get the chance to buy your school clothes yesterday, with all the drama. Don't suppose you want to come shopping with me?'

Pushing your luck, Mum.

'Didn't think so. Well, I've got to go to town for a meeting, but Dad says he'll stay close to the house and keep an eye on you. Is that okay?

It's perfect.

The two of them hover around me while I eat my cereal, checking if I want more OJ or would I like some toast, maybe a boiled egg? This must be what it feels like to be the Queen. Mum hugs me three times then twice more when she comes back downstairs, dressed and smelling perfumey. Wonder if she's meeting that guy again, the one with the flash car, and why Dad's not suspicious.

She picks up her huge handbag. 'Now, you sure you'll be ok, Charlie? I can cancel my meeting if you'd rather I stayed here? We could curl up on the sofa with a movie and popcorn.'

And get hugged to death? I don't think so.

'Maybe we could get Natalie to babysit?'

Babysit? She can't be serious.

'Off you go, Viv. You don't want to be late. Have you got all the paperwork you need? Maybe this is the day he'll sign. Charlie will be okay here with me, won't you, kid?' He ruffles my hair like he used to. It annoyed me before. Quite like it now, and his smile. 'You can have a day with the Xbox.'

'But don't you want to be out at Phase Five today?' says Mum.

'I can go later. Don't imagine it will be very exciting, what's happening today. You go ahead. We'll be grand. Joyce will be dotting about, and I'll be around here somewhere if Charlie needs me.'

Awesome. They don't usually let me play Xbox during the day, unless it's raining. Even then, they ration it. 'Time's up, Charlie,' they say. No matter how many sad, disappointed or angry faces I make, it gets switched off, every time.

Dad switches on the Xbox and brings me a can of cola. He watches me play for a little while, as if he's scared to leave me. Finally, he gets up and goes. I'm just about to complete a level I've never got to before when the doorbell rings. Not going to answer. Need to concentrate.

It rings again. I should go, in case Dad finds out.

The third time it rings, my concentration is wasted and I get wiped out. Might as well open the door now.

It's a lady and a man. With suits on. Before they even speak, I know they must be the police.

***

CHAPTER 63

The look on the boy's face is far from welcoming. Catherine was right. They shouldn't have invaded the owners' privacy. Pim at reception said as much, just in too many words, but Eric is determined to speak to someone as soon as possible, having come all this way.

'Hello, is your father at home?'

The boy stares, as if he doesn't understand.

'Your dad, he means your dad. Is he in?'

Eric gives her a look. He knows her English is better than his, but he doesn't like being corrected.

Still no reaction from the child. He's small, probably ten or eleven, and simple, judging by his lack of reaction.

Catherine bends at the knees till her eyes are level with the child's. 'My name is Catherine.' The boy's eyes have a wild look in them, as if he's terrified of her. 'There's no need to be afraid. What is your name?'

The boy's lack of response is quite unnerving. She straightens and smooths her skirt with both hands.

'This is pointless, Eric. We should wait in the café, bar, whatever it is, until the owner comes. Pim said he'd find him. It's obvious this child can't help us.'

A voice booms from behind the door. 'Charlie! Don't just stand there. Let the folk in.'

A man steps into the doorway and holds out his hand. 'Hi, I'm Richard. Please, come in.'

As he leads the way down the hall, the boy slinks up the stairs and sits at the top. She smiles at him, but his face remains unreadable.

'Can I get you a tea, coffee?'

'Thank you, that's very kind but we don't want to take up too much of your time.'

'I understand you're looking for Seb? Did Pim tell you?'

'Tell us?'

'Seb's a hero. An absolute legend, as young people would say.'

Clearly Sebastien has done well this summer. Catherine enjoys a moment of pride and can't resist wanting to hear more. 'A hero?'

'Yes, he saved my son from a fire.' The man covers his mouth and blinks several times.

'The little boy who answered the door?' Poor child. No wonder he looked so shocked.

'Yes, Charlie, our only child. God knows what would have happened if Seb hadn't turned back.'

'Back from where?' asks Eric.

'He was leaving. Literally about to get into a taxi when he saw the smoke, ran back, broke down the door of that old tower in the courtyard, and saved our Charlie's life.'

'Oh, my good God,' says Catherine, imagining what might have happened to her only son.

'Yes,' says the man, as if he knows where her mind's going, 'he put his own life at risk. No two ways about it.'

Catherine touches the back of a chair.

'Sorry, sit, please. Sorry, I should have said. Can I get you a glass of water?'

She shakes her head. Only one thing matters to her. 'Sebastien's here? Thank the lord.' Her shoulders drop as she breathes out a deep sigh.

The man's face tells her she's got it wrong.

'No, he's not, I'm afraid, and to my shame, I let him go without thanking him properly. I was so taken up with Charlie and the paramedics were here and there was just too much going on.' He stops and shakes his head. 'That's no excuse. I'm sorry. Please let me give you something, a reward to pass to Seb, with our thanks.'

Eric says, 'Absolutely not. I won't hear of it.'

Catherine gets to her feet and takes her husband by the arm. 'We have to go, Eric. Sebastien will be home by now. With no one there to welcome him. We need to make sure he's okay.' She turns to the man. 'Did *you* make sure he was fine before you let him leave? What if he looked okay but then he collapsed? He could be anywhere, lying ill, or…' She covers her face with her hands, feels them shaking. Eric touches her shoulder, trying to reassure and calm her.

She feels a light touch on her other shoulder and opens her eyes. 'Please don't worry. Seb was thoroughly checked by the paramedics. Given oxygen.'

'Oxygen!'

'Just as a precaution. While they ran a whole battery of tests – heart, blood oxygen level, you name it. Both he and Charlie got the all clear. Otherwise, we wouldn't have let him go, I promise you. He'll be right as rain. I don't think you need to worry about getting home in time to arrange a hero's welcome. I'm sure Seb said something about doing some more travelling.'

'So he didn't fly to Paris?'

'You know, I couldn't tell you. Hang on, maybe Charlie knows.'

He calls the boy's name and the child appears, reluctantly it seems, and stands near the door.

'Charlie, this is Seb's mum and dad. They've come on a surprise visit and they've missed him! Can you believe that?'

The boy looks at Eric, then Catherine. She could swear he looks afraid. Horrified is the word that comes to her mind.

'Just wondering, son, do you know if Seb was flying straight to Paris?'

The boy shakes his head.

'Is that no, as in you don't know?'

The boy nods.

'You don't know? Yes, he was a bit vague about his arrangements, wasn't he?'

More nodding from the boy.

'Charlie doesn't speak,' says the man, with no further explanation.

Catherine smiles at the child but gets nothing in return. In her head she says a prayer of thanks that her son is normal, if a bit inconsiderate.

'Well,' says Eric, 'we won't take up any more of your time. Catherine has Sebastien's number. We'll give him a call later and find out when he'll be home, so we can get the fatted calf ready. Thank you for your help.'

'I'm the one who's grateful to you for raising such a superb young man. You can be very proud of him. I hope all the drama didn't make him miss his plane. Please, let me give you some money, in case he had to pay for another flight.'

Catherine acknowledges the kind words with a smile and shakes her head. Drenched in disappointment, she cannot trust herself to speak.

Eric says, 'Wouldn't it be ironic if Sebastien was sitting stranded in departures at Glasgow Airport last night when we walked through arrivals?'

Catherine knows he's trying to cheer her up. She owes it to him to play along and laughs, as if any of this was funny.

Just as he's showing them to the door, a mobile rings in the man's pocket. He checks the screen, frowns and says, 'Sorry, I need to take this. Can you see yourselves out?'

As if they're already forgotten, he turns away, listening, then shouts into the phone, 'Christ, no! Don't touch anything. I'll be right there.'

***

CHAPTER 64

We were on the news tonight. Well, not us. Brackenbrae. The hillside, with the digger sitting there by the side of a white tent. Dad said when he imagined Phase Five, that's not the kind of tent he had in mind. Mum and Dad are worried.

'Nobody has their wedding where a body's been found. It's a nightmare. Who brings their kids to a place like this for a holiday? We're ruined, Richard. It's so unfair. Just when Alan had agreed to invest so much money in us. His lawyers won't let him sign the papers now.'

She seems more worried about the business than the guy in the grave or the poor digger driver who dug him up when he was trying to divert the burn. Dad says he was shaking like a leaf and vomiting everywhere.

'Mystery man found at holiday park.' That was the headline. Mum and Dad didn't want me to watch but I refused to go upstairs.

'How did the media find out so fast?' asked Mum.

'Oh, Viv, the hillside's swarming with cops and you can see that crime scene tent from the main road.'

It was weird watching a man with a microphone standing outside our gates talking to a camera. 'We understand that, in the course of some preparatory land work for an extension to this popular holiday camp, the body of a man was uncovered earlier today. He had been buried under a landslide of the river bank. His identity has not been revealed and we understand his next of kin have yet to be informed. The man is believed to be white, in his late teens or early twenties and possibly a hiker or hill-walker. Police say the death is being treated as suspicious and a major investigation is underway. This is James Mitchell, reporting for BBC Scotland from the Carrick Hills, near Ayr.'

The police spent a lot of time talking to Dad. They interviewed Pim and Natalie, Joyce and Mark, Mum too, of course, and a few holidaymakers. The place was in what Dad called 'lock-down' – no one was allowed out and no one could come in. There's a police car parked at the entrance and blue and white plastic tape everywhere. Dad says the hillside looks eerie tonight, with floodlights up everywhere and shadowy figures inside the tent.

The guy who killed the hiker got away just in time. I'm glad the real Seb's mum and dad left before Dad found out what that phone call was about.

The house phone rings and I hurry to the stairs to listen. Dad speaks into the phone, too quietly for me to hear, then hangs up and shouts, 'Viv. You are never going to believe this. I've to go to the police station.'

'What, tonight?'

'Yes, and they told me to take all paperwork relating to my guns.'

Guns! That must mean they've found it and traced it to Dad already. Oh, shit, shit, shit.

I run and jump into bed, stick my head under the pillow but I can't switch off my brain.

It's late when I hear a car pull into the courtyard. Jump up and look out, hoping it's Dad.

From the top of the stairs I can see light round the living room door. Mum's still up. She shoots into the hall as Dad comes in the front door. Hope they don't look up.

'Oh, thank God,' she says, hugging Dad. 'I thought they'd arrested you.'

'Don't be silly, they can't arrest me. I've not done anything wrong. But it *is* my gun they found, no doubt about it. With one set of fingerprints. Not mine.'

'Then whose?'

'Well that's what the police will have to find out. They're coming tomorrow morning to fingerprint everyone who works or lives here.'

'Lives here? You don't mean…?' She points towards the stairs and Dad looks right at me. 'Charlie,' he says. 'Go back to bed, son. It's alright. There's nothing to worry about. Off you go, we'll see you in the morning.'

What's the point in sending me to bed? It's not as if I'm ever going to get to sleep now.

***

CHAPTER 65

France
Sunday 12 August

'Maybe we should have stayed and enjoyed Scotland, Eric,' she says at breakfast. He rolls his eyes and says nothing.

She was the one who insisted they cut their trip short.

Eric had wanted to stick to their plans. A night or two in Ayrshire then a few days in Edinburgh to take in some of the famous festival. 'This is a beautiful part of the world,' he said as they drove out of the campsite and down the hill. 'It's a shame to miss it. Look at that view. I wonder if that's Ireland you can see in the distance, look, just there. Can you see?'

'I don't care about the view,' she said. 'I want to go home. Now, please. I'm sure we can change our flights and what if Sebastien's at the airport when we get there? We could surprise him and fly back together. Wouldn't that be a wonderful end to his summer? Maybe we could even treat him to first class as a reward for being such a hero.'

'More coffee, darling?' she says, lifting the cafetière.

Eric nods, mouth full of croissant.

'Can you believe our son rescued that little boy from a fire?'

'Yes, that's quite something, isn't it? I'm convinced his parents were making it out to be so much more dramatic than it really was. The boy looked fine to me.'

'I thought he looked distinctly odd, but maybe he was traumatised. Oh God, I hope Sebastien's alright. Smoke inhalation can be life-threatening, you know.'

'I'm sure he is. By the way, I was right all along. Spending the summer away from home has made a man of him.'

'When do you think he'll be home?'

A shrug of Eric's shoulders tells her two things. One, he doesn't know and two, he doesn't want to talk about it, again.

She'd been so sure on the way to Glasgow Airport that Sebastien would be sitting there in departures looking fed up. She'd been imagining the way his face would light up when he spotted them. The airport was busy, the bars full of holiday-makers getting into the spirit. Despite looking everywhere, right until the moment their flight was called, she could not see him. Once they were in the air, she waited till the seatbelt sign went off and then walked up and down the plane, checking every passenger, like a steward before landing. She even waited outside the toilet, in case Sebastien was in there, then went back to her seat, so dejected that Eric got cross with her and told her to sit down and stop being so foolish.

'I was certain Sebastien would be here waiting for us. This place feels even emptier than it did before we left.'

Eric swallows a mouthful of coffee and says, 'That's nonsense.'

'I wonder why he's not answering his phone?'

'Hope he hasn't lost it again, the idiot.' Eric's smile is half-hearted, and she can't tell if he's joking.

'Excuse me, our son's *not* an idiot. He's a *hero*, if you don't mind.' Her jokey tone works and Eric smiles, properly this time.

'I'm going to send him another text. Each time I phone it goes to voicemail and I don't want to leave another message – I've run out of things to say.'

'Have you tried the two hardest words?'

'If you mean have I said I'm sorry, the answer's yes. I've said it so many times in so many ways, *and* I've told him how much we love him, just in case he's forgotten.'

'Have you asked him to please come home soon because you're driving his father crazy? That might work.'

***

CHAPTER 66

Supposed to be eating my Coco Pops, to please Mum, but I'm not hungry. Dad comes in and throws a pile of newspapers on the table.

'Fame at last,' he says, spitting out the words like there's dirt on his tongue. 'Whoever said there's no such thing as bad publicity is a total arsehole.'

'Language, please.' Mum points at me.

'I'm watching my language, believe me.' He kind of collapses on the chair beside me, leans on the table and covers his face. 'Oh, Viv,' he says, so sadly that I think he's crying. 'Read them. No, don't. It will upset you.' He looks up and gathers the papers into his lap. 'I couldn't face going to the wee shop. I drove to Alloway, so no one would know me. Folk were talking about it. Somebody said it was drugs related. One guy I've never seen in my life actually says, wait for it, "I know the owners and between you and me, they think it was a revenge killing." A revenge killing? Jesus! It's Ayr, not the bloody Bronx.'

'Oh, Richard, you know what folk are like. If they don't know the facts, they make something up.'

'Wait till you hear this.' He flicks through the papers. '*The Herald* is ok. Not saying much.'

'Cos there's not much to say, that's why.' Mum comes and looks over his shoulder, touches a headline and reads it out. 'Murder mystery at idyllic holiday camp. That's okay. Idyllic is good.'

'Yeah, but look at this crap.' Dad flicks the top of one of the smaller papers so hard it tears the front page. He points to the huge letters of the headlines and reads them out. 'Brackenbrae

— more like Pack 'n' Pray! Thinking of holidaying here? Better *pack* your bullet-proof vest and *pray* you don't get caught up in a shoot-out. "I thought we were coming to the beautiful west of Scotland not the Wild West," says Jason Morton, 37, from Leeds, who claims he heard gunshots.'

'How did they get those photos?'

'Long lens. The paparazzi can be miles away nowadays and still get pictures.'

She points to someone in a white hooded suit holding something up. 'That could be anything he's lifting out of the bracken. A stick, anything.'

I try to get a better look at the photo. Dad pulls the newspaper away but I get enough time to see. It's the gun he's holding up. Got to be.

'You might as well tell him, Richard. He probably heard us talking last night.'

'The police were searching the hillside for clues, Charlie, and they found a shotgun.'

'Tell him the rest. He's going to find out anyway.'

Dad blows out air. His top lip vibrates. 'Okay, they found one of my guns.'

'Ask him.'

'Charlie, this is a daft question, because you don't even know where I keep the keys to the gun cabinet, but...' he hesitates, as if he doesn't want to ask me.

'Did you take Dad's gun, Charlie?' says Mum. 'That's what we need to know.'

I stare at her. Keep my head steady so it doesn't give me away.

'No wonder he looks shocked.' Dad turns to me and takes my hand, 'Sorry, son. We've got to ask.'

I'm still wondering how to respond when the doorbell chimes. Miss Lawson sometimes says, 'Saved by the bell,' if somebody's in trouble just before home time. That's what I'm thinking about as Mum goes to answer the door.

She comes back with a man and a woman and kind of shows them into the room, like they're important visitors. They say hello and introduce themselves. Dad holds up a mug and says, 'Coffee?'

They say they're here for a 'wee chat' with me and to get some fingerprints. When she hears this, Mum goes ballistic, asking what business they have with me and how could I possibly have anything to do with what happened.

The man interrupts her. 'You do understand we're being as accommodating as possible here? This is not standard practice. We're only coming to you because of your son's, erm, handicap.'

'Charlie's not handicapped,' says Mum in her snippy voice. 'He just doesn't speak.' Wish she would shut up. It sounds like Dad's arranged for me to be interviewed here, but if she's not careful, I'll get taken to the police station. Imagine that in the paper.

'He *doesn't* speak?' The policeman looks at Dad. 'We were led to believe your son *can't* speak. There's quite a difference.'

Mum says, 'Charlie hasn't said a word for five years. His school will certify to that, if you want.'

Snapping at them won't help.

'Viv,' says Dad, 'this isn't helpful. Come on, let's leave these good folks to do their job.'

'What? I'm not leaving my son alone with two policemen, sorry, police-people, whatever you call them.' She waves a dismissive hand towards the inspector and his female colleague. 'He's only twelve, for God's sake.'

'In Scotland that makes him old enough to be legally prosecuted if he commits a crime.'

This is news to Mum. I can tell by her face.

'Therefore, it's quite appropriate for Charlie to be interviewed, informally, on his own. So, if you wouldn't mind?' He gets up and holds the kitchen door open.

'I do mind, actually,' says Mum. 'Do you want Dad or me to stay with you, Charlie?'

Think for a minute then shake my head. Don't want to look as if I'm scared of the police. That will just make them suspicious.

Mum sniffs.

'Come on, Viv. He's in good hands. Let's go. We'll be right here, Charlie, just outside the door.'

'Right, Charlie,' says the policeman, once they've gone. 'Just a few wee questions for you. No need to be frightened. My colleague, DS, that means Detective Sergeant, McManus will ask you and you can nod or shake your head.

The policewoman smiles at me and I can tell she's trying to get me to relax so I'll say something that incriminates me. I've seen Taggart on TV.

'Charlie, you're twelve years old, is that right?

Nod.

She beams at me as if I've answered the winning question on Mastermind or something. 'You're quite happy to speak to us today?'

Nod again. She asks a lot of that kind of stuff and I just keep nodding. I'm beginning to wonder if she'll ever ask me anything interesting when she says, 'Did you know we found a gun, belonging to your dad, which was lying hidden in the bracken?'

I pretend I didn't know by trying to look surprised.

'Did you hide the gun there, Charlie?'

That one's easy. I didn't.

'Okay. Do you know who did hide the gun?'

Shake my head.

'The gun had been fired, Charlie. Did you know that?'

Know that? It nearly blew my ears off.

The other cop, the man, sits down beside me and leans in close. His breath smells of coffee and I sit back in my chair to get away from it. 'This isn't really helping us much, Charlie, and see, we could do with some help, to tell you the truth. We've got a dead body, a nice young man, by the looks of it. Not doing anybody any harm as far as we know and now, not only is he dead, but he looks as if's been shot. We've also got a gun. A gun which has been recently fired. That gun belongs to your dad and it's got some fingerprints on it. Can you see where I'm going with this?'

He's going to say he's arresting Dad.

'Right, young man, you're absolutely sure you don't know anything?'

Nod. I know everything, but even if I could tell him that, I wouldn't.

He opens the door to let Mum and Dad in. Dad flaps the newspaper in the air. 'Have you seen this?' he asks the detectives, then reads from the front page. 'Sources say he was shot once in the head. Was it a drug deal gone sour? Or just a stupid prank gone wrong?' He throws the paper down as if it disgusts him.

'Ach, you don't want to worry about that. Wrapping for tomorrow's fish supper we used to say, but now it's all polystyrene containers. Makes the batter soggy.' He turns to the woman and laughs.

'Can you tell me how they get their information and why they're allowed to publish this stuff?'

'Believe me, sir, it pains me as much as it does you.'

'I somehow doubt that.'

If they were going to arrest Dad they'd be telling him not to be cheeky and putting handcuffs on him. Instead, they just say, 'Right, let's get these fingerprints sorted out. You too, please, madam.'

Mum goes ballistic again.

***

CHAPTER 67

South Africa
Wednesday 15 August

Gus knows he's being watched. He can feel their eyes on him and each time he looks over he catches one of them staring. The others are trying to look cool and casual. Not very subtle.

He sneaks another look and sure enough, he's under scrutiny. This time by the short one with the blonde hair.

Undercover cops? Not under much cover in those tops, that's for sure. Nah, he's being paranoid. Nothing's going to happen to him now. He's home and dry. Picking up his life as if he's never been away. Pity it's still a bit chilly for the beach but hey, winter's over and the hot days will be here again soon enough. Anyway, the sky is clear and the ocean's blue – a bit different from the steely grey water and leaden skies he left behind in Ayrshire.

When he makes eye contact with Blondie, she blushes and giggles. He leans back on his arms to show off his shoulders and biceps in his tight white T-shirt. Blondie giggles even louder and her two friends turn to stare at him. Quite openly this time. It's clear they fancy him.

He reaches into his jeans pocket and pulls out his phone. Another missed call. Same number and another voicemail. He listens for a moment to the pleading and apologising on the other end then presses three to delete.

There's a text from her too. *Sebastien. We know you want to travel but please, can you come home soon? We miss you.*

He gave up replying a while ago, before he left Scotland. Might be time to block all contact from the woman. He should probably have got rid of the phone, but it's an iPhone 8, all glass.

'Nice phone.'

Exactly. He takes his time putting the phone away before he looks up. 'Hey, gorgeous girls! Come over here where I can see you better,' he says, pushing his Ray-Bans up onto his forehead.

Timid as kittens, they sidle across and stand in an admiring circle around him. They look a lot younger close up. Jail bait, his Dad used to say.

'Haven't seen you at the beach before.'

'No, we're supposed to be at school,' says the blonde.

'Shut up, Lizelle!'

So he was right. Pity.

He flirts a little, just to make them feel good. Then, because he's a bit too tempted by the curvy brunette, who doesn't look like any girl he ever went to school with, he stands up. 'Bye, babes,' he says. 'See you around.' He jogs off down to the water's edge. When he turns to see if they're watching, he gives a little wave and keeps running.

He picks up a pebble and throws it, watching it skim across the surface then disappear into a wave. Things aren't as bad as he feared. He's got it all sorted. Place at college arranged, back on the steroids, back on the team, and a different girl every night, if he wants one. Yeah, life will be good. He's gonna be okay.

His journey back to South Africa was easy. He was overjoyed to make it into the air without being arrested. He had a few drinks on the plane to celebrate, but was careful to have no more than a few. He didn't want to risk drawing attention to himself when the plane landed. He saw that as the final hurdle – getting past immigration and customs. He didn't want anything to stop him getting home.

There was one scary moment when a grim-faced, female official stepped in front of him in the queue at immigration and held out her arm. 'This way, sir,' she said. He started to panic till he realised everyone behind him was changing queues too. Safely through to the other side, he walked away a few steps then punched a victorious fist at the sky. He'd made it. He was home.

Now it's as if he's never been away.

Well, apart from the nightmares. He thought they'd stop once he got away from that place, but he had one again last night. It's always the same. He's walking through those yellow, coconut-smelling bushes. It's a beautiful day and he feels happy. Suddenly, right at his feet, a rotting corpse rears up out of a makeshift grave. He wakes up, lashing sweat and panting like he's just sprinted the length of a rugby pitch.

In the daytime, out here at the beach, it all seems too bizarre to be true, as surreal as if it never happened. Maybe it never did.

***

CHAPTER 68

Scotland
Thursday 16 August

Mum says I've to get some sleep. But how can I? I sneak to the top stair and listen.

Been picking up wee bits through the day, but mostly Mum and Dad try not to discuss it in front of me. Dad doesn't buy the newspaper any more, and we're not important enough to be on the telly.

Dad says, 'It's my gun, Viv. There's no denying it. Doesn't matter if I haven't clapped eyes on it for months. My gun.'

'I know, but with Charlie's fingerprints on it.' Mum's crying, I think.

'Yes, but surely there must be a few traces of mine?'

'What are you saying?'

'I'm saying I've come to a decision. I'm going to confess and say it was me.'

'You can't do that. You'll go to jail.' Mum's definitely crying.

'So will Charlie.'

'But he's a child.'

'Yes, a good child.'

'However, that gun got out there and whatever happened, we know Charlie didn't kill that young man.'

'I wish the police could find out who he is. Then at least, they might work out a reason for what happened.'

'One that puts you and Charlie in the clear and puts his parents out of their misery. Surely they must be dead too, or they'd have come forward to claim him. Can you imagine if it were

Charlie buried out there and we'd no idea where he was or what had happened to him? Oh, please don't let them take him away, Richard. I'd die if he got sent to one of those terrible residential centres with a crowd of criminals.'

'Shh, don't cry, Viv. It'll be okay.'

'How will it be okay? They'll blame Charlie and take him away or they'll send you to prison. Maybe both. Why did this have to happen?'

That's what I keep thinking. How come the bad guy gets away with it? I know he saved my life and all, and I know he says he'll come back and get me if I don't stay quiet, but that was before the digger disturbed the body. He thought we'd never get found out but he was wrong. Now Dad's going to take the blame for something he never did. That's not fair. It's time I stopped being such a coward.

I run to my room and put my hand under the mattress. Before I can change my mind, I run down the stairs, shouting, 'Wait. *I* know who he is.'

When I burst into the kitchen Dad jumps to his feet and Mum gives a wee scream.

'Who's doing all the shouting?'

'Me.'

'My God,' says Mum, all breathless. 'Charlie, you spoke.'

I nod and hold out the passport to Dad.

Mum grabs me in a hug. I push her away and watch Dad's face. He says, 'I don't understand.'

'Look at the name.'

'Sebastien Lamar? I don't get it. I don't understand why you've got Seb's passport?'

'Richard, Charlie's speaking. Oh my God.'

'Look at the photo.'

'You can speak, son,' says Mum.

Smile at her, so she'll stop saying I can speak. 'Yes, Mum, I can.'

She bursts into tears and wails, 'You called me Mum.'

'I think we all need to sit down,' says Dad, putting the passport on the coffee table, 'and I need a brandy.'

I tell them I took the passport out of the dead guy's pocket so he couldn't be identified. Before I buried him, accidentally, when the river bank collapsed under my feet and covered him. After I threw away the gun. To hide it because it was a murder weapon, even though I didn't mean to shoot him. It was an accident. Tell them I thought the bracken would hide it, even when it all withered down. I thought the rain would wash away my fingerprints. Tell them I'm sorry for taking the gun. But I only did it to get them to pay me some attention.

Mum tries to cuddle me but I don't want to be hugged. If she'd hugged me more instead of worrying about her stupid house and her stupid campsite and her stupid weddings, none of this would have happened. But I don't say any of that.

Even though my voice is wobbly, I tell them, 'You were always too busy, both of you. I'd follow you, Dad, carrying my ball, hoping you might give me a kickabout, but you'd not notice me or you'd see me and say, "Sorry, Charlie. Not right now." You were always going shopping for stuff, Mum, or having important meetings, and then you both got so worried about the business and you always seemed angry at each other and I was scared you were going to get a divorce and it was as if I was invisible because I didn't speak.'

'But now you do,' says Dad, in a quiet, calm voice.

It's as if, now I've remembered how to talk, I can't stop. I tell them I knew how to get into the gun safe because I was watching the day the firearms officer came to check Dad was following the rules. I explained that I thought Dad would either be pleased with me for shooting some rabbits or he'd be mad at me for taking the gun, but at least he wouldn't ignore me any more.

This seems to make Mum cry even louder and she spills her brandy, all over one of her fancy cushions, but she doesn't look bothered. She just goes, 'Oh, Charlie...' with a big wail at the end.

'Son,' says Dad, touching me on the arm, 'can you tell us why you stopped talking? When you were small?'

'Because of the curse,' I say, and then I start crying and I'm so angry at myself for being a big baby. This time, when Mum hugs me, I let her and it feels wonderful. I tell them about Robbie and how he made me touch him.

'He what?' says Dad, his eyes wider than I've ever seen them. 'Jesus Christ. Did he do anything else?'

Not sure what he means, but I shake my head.

'He didn't …' Dad goes quiet, as if he's not sure what to say.

'Richard,' snaps Mum. 'Stop this. There's no point.' She kind of cradles my face in her hand and makes me look at her. 'Charlie, did Robbie hurt you? In any way?'

'No,' I say, wishing we didn't have to talk about this.

'Son, why didn't you just tell us?'

'I didn't want to, I felt dirty. And I was scared you'd be angry with me. I knew I should tell you and I was going to. Then the next morning, you told me that Robbie and his mum and the wee baby had died in the fire and I believed it was all my fault because of the curse.'

'Oh, son,' says Dad. 'We wouldn't have been angry at you.'

Mum gives a kind of laugh through her tears. 'Charlie, darling, there's no such thing as a curse.'

'There is. I said it to Robbie the day before the fire. Then I said it again to that Seb guy and we both nearly got burned to death.'

'What did you say, son?'

I don't want to say the words out loud. What if saying them to Mum and Dad puts the curse on them and they die too? I shake my head. 'Can't tell you. It's a curse and I'm never going to say it to anyone ever again.'

Mum and Dad give each other a look. I can tell they think I'm crazy.

'Listen to me, Charlie,' says Dad. 'What happened to Robbie's family was tragic, but it was an accident. A terrible accident that had nothing to do with you.'

'But I caused the fire.'

Their eyebrows come down over their eyes. I can tell they're thinking about me 'messing about with matches'. Mum turns her head to the side when she says, 'How could you have started the fire, Charlie? It was the middle of the night.'

'Don't even go there, Viv. It was an electrical fault. That was the official finding.'

***

CHAPTER 69

France
Friday 17 August

Catherine is grinding coffee for breakfast when the phone rings. She stops the machine and shouts, 'Eric, can you get that please?'

Coffee forgotten, she strains to listen, just in case it's their son on the line. Something in Eric's tone troubles her and she bites at her lower lip as she walks into the hall.

'Is it Sebastien?'

Eric puts his finger on the mute button. 'It's someone from Police Scotland but I think they might know where Sebastien is.'

Catherine clamps her crossed fingers to her lips and resists the urge to bounce like an excited child. Eric puts his hand on her shoulder, as if to keep her grounded. She touches her head to his so she can hear the voice on the other end.

'Mr Lamar, we may have found your son.'

Catherine's hopes take off like a rocket. 'They've found him? Oh, thank *God*.'

'My wife is listening in,' says Eric, 'I hope that's alright?'

'Of course, sir, it's appropriate that you both hear what I have to say.'

There's a pause and Catherine thinks she can hear the man on the other end taking a deep breath.

'Mr and Mrs Lamar, do you think it would be possible for you to come to Scotland, please?'

'When?'

'Ideally, in the next few days.'

'Well, of course, if you think it's necessary, but I'm not sure I understand why you're asking.'

'We may need you to make a formal identification for us.'

'Why can't Sebastien identify himself? Don't tell me the daft little bugger has gone and lost his passport now?'

'Sir, I'm most terribly sorry, but the young man we believe to be your son may have been shot.'

'Oh, my good lord. Is he badly hurt?' asks Eric. 'How serious is it? Can he be moved to Paris?' Catherine, knowing suddenly, touches his arm to tell him to stop talking. The silence at the other end of the line is ominous.

'Sir, we cannot be certain this young man is your son until he has been formally identified.'

'For God's sake, man. Out with it!' Eric doesn't often shout at people, but Catherine understands his frustration. Her heart beats at twice its normal speed. She knows this is the moment she's been dreading since Sebastien left.

'Perhaps you and your wife would prefer to sit down?'

Eric looks at her and she shakes her head. 'We're fine,' he says, his voice sombre.

'I'm sorry to tell you that a young man has died. His body has been found on the grounds of Brackenbrae campsite near Ayr.'

Eric interrupts, shaking his head and shouting, 'Hang on a minute, hang on there. What makes you think this is Sebastien? You can't phone me up and tell me it's my son. You don't know my son. This body you've found could be anybody.'

'You're quite correct, Mr Lamar. We're unable to say for certain, at this time, that the young man we've found is your son. It would help us with our investigation if you could come and make a formal identification, positive or otherwise.'

Catherine gently takes the phone from Eric's hand. 'We will make arrangements to be with you as soon as possible,' she says. Her voice is calm and controlled, as if she has been expecting this call and preparing herself for it. 'Where is our son?' she asks. Eric, crumpled by her side, seems unable to speak.

'The Procurator Fiscal has instructed a post-mortem examination. The body has been taken by CID to the mortuary at Queen Elizabeth University Hospital in Glasgow, but the post-mortem cannot take place until a formal identification has been carried out. In this case, by two people, because of the circumstances.'

'What circumstances?'

'We call it a suspicious death, Mrs Lamar. I regret to tell you that your son may have been the victim of a murder. I am most terribly sorry.'

A few lifetimes pass in silence. A siren screams up from the street and Catherine feels her legs weaken under her, as if her body has become too heavy for them to bear. Eric helps her sit and squats, holding her hand, his eyes full of fear.

'We'll be there tomorrow, at the latest,' he says. 'Tell them we'll leave right away and get on the first available flight.'

'Do you know someone who could drive you to the airport?'

'Don't worry about that,' says Catherine. 'Just tell us where to come and we'll be there, as soon as we can.'

Her hand shaking, she writes down an address in Glasgow and a phone number and hangs up the phone. Eric sits, half-collapsed on the floor, looking as if all his strength has deserted him.

Catherine takes command. The sooner they get there, the sooner she'll see her boy and whatever's happened, that's all that matters right now. 'Come on, Eric,' she says quietly. 'Let's go and do what we have to do.'

He looks up at her, his face as aged as his father's in the days before he died.

***

CHAPTER 70

South Africa
Thursday 30 August

Gus can't sleep.

A gentle voice asks, 'Are you still awake, Gus?'

'Yes, I'm awake.'

'Do you need a little medication to help you sleep?'

They know he suffers from sleeplessness and nightmares. They don't know the reason why.

He shakes his head. It's tempting, but he needs to prove he can do this on his own. Medication makes no difference anyway. Even with the pills he gets, at best, an hour of sleep. Some nights he gets none at all.

'No, thank you,' he says, 'I'm doing okay.' He hears his door close, the tiny click barely audible. He listens as the almost silent footsteps go padding off down the corridor.

Many nights he's been too exhausted to fight sleep. That's when the guy in the grave comes back to haunt him. Gus rolls over, punches his pillow and buries his face in it.

A hundred times a day he wishes he could rewind his life. If only he'd walked on past the kid that day, not got involved. Or maybe if he'd called the police, told them it was all a horrible accident. Charlie would have backed him up. He might even have spoken sooner and been a witness in court. But oh no, Gus had to try to outsmart everyone, burying the body and pretending to be the guy he killed. How could any of that ever have seemed like a good idea?

The shrinks in this place have advised him to focus on happy memories. Soon, he hopes, he'll be so good at it, he'll be able to put all this behind him. Once he gets out, he'll be ace. He's planning to stay chilled, and off the steroids. Thinking nice, happy thoughts, like the ones he had when he got off the plane and his feet touched his homeland for the first time in a year.

He thought it was going to be easy, that he'd got away with it, but then the nightmares started up. His sleep became more and more disturbed. It was hard to concentrate in the daytime, so he'd started to take high caffeine drinks and then pills, telling himself everybody took them. He packed in his college course and that didn't help, only gave him more time to dwell on things. Pretty soon he was no fun to be with, unless he was drunk. His friends began to avoid him and only the desperate girls paid him any attention.

A toilet flushes somewhere in the building, pipes gurgling for a minute then subsiding into silence.

Then came the day on the rugby field when a player with red hair rose out of the scrum right in front of him. Gus went berserk, seeing only the demons that tormented him day and night. It took the combined might of his teammates to drag him off and restrain him, but he'd managed to hurt the poor guy by then. Badly hurt him.

It was the solicitor who suggested a way out.

'Gus, it's a long shot but I might be able to get you off.'

'You serious, man?'

'Yes, but you'll need to volunteer to undergo psychiatric treatment.'

'No way! You suggesting I'm a nutter?'

'I know you're not, but we agree you have serious anger issues, your 'red mist'. As that poor bugger found out to his cost. My God, you say he didn't even do anything to provoke you. Take my advice and, if you're lucky, you *might* avoid a prison sentence.'

So, Gus agreed to be admitted to Sunnyvale, a branch of the state mental hospital. He was happy to cooperate, terrified of going to jail and having to survive among real hard men. His physique, which he's always seen as an advantage, would attract all the wrong types, for all the wrong reasons.

Spending a couple of months in this place, surrounded by real nutcases, is nothing. A small price to pay if it keeps him out of jail. All he has to do is remain calm, keep his temper and be a good boy. Take the classes, deal with his issues and prove he's learning to manage that anger. The doc has told him how pleased he is with his progress, several times. He's an exemplary patient, apparently, almost ready to leave.

Somewhere far off in the night, a powerful motorbike roars up through the gears, increasing speed and fading into the distance. He feels sick with longing for the open road, for his precious Harley, locked up in a mate's garage.

Soon he'll be out of here and he can put all this behind him and pick up the pieces of his life. The first thing he intends to do is take that bike of his for a run up the coast road. He imagines racing along the highway, the wind in his hair and the sun on his back. The shrinks are right, those good thoughts work, he thinks, as he relaxes for the first time in days and feels himself drifting off to sleep.

***

CHAPTER 71

France

Catherine stirs and turns over onto her back, disturbed by a persistent ringing that sounds remarkably like their doorbell. She knows she ought to get up and answer it but can't summon enough energy to get out of bed. Perhaps Eric has forgotten his key? She glances at the clock beside her bed; 11am. So, not Eric then. The postman? No, ridiculous. He would, of course, leave any mail in their box in the foyer.

The ringing goes on and on. She covers her ears with her hands but the racket continues, becoming louder and more difficult to ignore. She pulls the covers up over her head and tries to block it out. There is no one in the world that she wants to see, so whoever is at the door can go to hell.

The ringing continues. She grabs her pillow and presses it to her face, clamping it over her ears.

After only a few seconds, she pushes it away. She can't breathe and worse, even through a pillow, she can still hear the damned ringing. The din is impossible to shut out and whoever is at the door seems determined to get an answer.

With huge reluctance, she drags herself out of bed, every one of her limbs weary and weighing a ton. Throwing on a robe, she opens her bedroom door and trudges into the hall. As she passes the mirror she catches sight of herself and stops in her tracks. She hasn't seen her reflection since the day of Sebastien's funeral. She simply doesn't care how she looks any more. Nevertheless, she's shocked to see the spectral face looking out of the mirror. Her skin is pale and blotchy, her eyes are sunk deep into their sockets, with dark, purple shadows underneath. Her hair, always her crowning glory, is an unkempt, unstyled mess, grey at the temples. It hangs in a tangle to her shoulders, which are as skinny as a coat hanger, her dressing gown hanging off one side. Catherine has never seen herself look like this. Neither, she thinks with a tiny touch of regret, has Eric.

The ringing shows no signs of stopping. Better answer it, she tells herself. As she walks towards the door she can see, through the opaque glass, a tall figure.

She pulls the robe tight round her body and wonders whether it's wise to open the door. Normally, no one should be able to come to this door without keying their code into the external security entrance.

Whoever the visitor is, he's still ringing the accursed bell. She has to get it to stop. She opens the door and takes a step backwards, steadying herself against the doorframe. It can't be.

'Hey, Mum,' he says, and flips his hair off his face.

'Sebastien,' she whispers. 'My precious boy.'

'Sorry, Mum, forgot my key. You okay?'

He brushes past her, into the hall, where he shrugs off his jacket and slips his feet out of his trainers.

'Right,' he says, opening his arms wide, 'how about a hug?'

She hesitates for no more than a heartbeat, then throws her arms around him. He hugs her tight, just like he used to.

'I've missed my mum's hugs,' he says, holding on to her.

She can feel his chin touch the top of her head. She breathes in the smell of him. 'So have I, darling boy, you've no idea.' She eases away from him and gazes at his face. He looks wonderful. His eyes are sparkling, full of fun, his skin is glowing with health and his hair is shiny. He seems to have filled out, turned from a boy into a fine, handsome young man. She feels proud that he is her son, proud that she brought him into the world.

He looks into her eyes, smiles at her and says, 'Love you, Mum.'

'I love you too, son.' She smiles back, then hugs him tightly to her. She becomes aware that the ringing that woke her still hasn't stopped. It must be the phone. 'Let me just answer that, will you?'

'Sure.'

She lets go of him, moves away and picks up the receiver. 'Hello?' she says, then again, 'Hello? That's odd, they've rung off.' She turns back to her son, smiling.

The front door is closed. There are no trainers on the floor, no jacket on the peg.

There's no Sebastien and yet she senses him, still with her. She can feel his arms around her and hear his voice: 'Love you, Mum.'

She puts the phone back in its dock, then raises her head and looks at her reflection. The hair and face are as unenhanced as before, but she appears transformed.

'What happened there?' she asks the woman in the mirror.

'I have no idea,' Catherine's reflection replies with a smile, 'but it felt good.'

***

CHAPTER 72

Scotland
Tuesday 25 September

'Charlie! Can you come down?'

'I'm doing my homework.'

'There's someone here to see you.'

I hear giggling in the hall and Mum whispering, 'Shh, here he comes.'

'Surprise!'

'Natalie?'

'OMG, what a lovely deep voice. Say "Natalie" again, go on, please, Charlie.'

At first I shake my head, but they look disappointed so I say, 'Natalie,' but this time it comes out high and squeaky and they laugh. Hate it when my voice does that, but I laugh too.

Mum kind of shoves us through to the kitchen and starts to make tea. 'It's so good to see you, Natalie,' she says. 'You look great. Teaching obviously agrees with you.'

'I love it. Especially inset days like today – no kids.' She giggles, just like I remember from before.

'That's why I'm here. I was at Charlie's primary school at a sharing good practice course and I thought I'd swing by and surprise you. I met Miss Lawson, Charlie. She was telling me she hears great things about you from the Academy.'

Can feel myself blushing.

Mum says, 'He's amazing. We had a meeting with his year head last week and got a wonderful report. Doing well in all his subjects. Settling in easily, despite the difficulties, and adapting to secondary school life. Making friends. "He's a sociable, likeable, clever, well-behaved lad." Those are the very words the teacher used.'

'Stop, Mum.'

'I'm proud of you. Especially after all you came through.'

'Well done, Charlie. I'm proud of you too. That wasn't the ideal start to high school. But it sounds as if you're doing okay?'

Nod. Sometimes I still do. Just because I *can* talk, doesn't mean I always have to. Girls talk too much, I've decided. I eat a biscuit and sit listening to Mum and Nat.

'So, eventually the police told us they were sure Charlie was covering up for someone. That's when it all came out.'

'He seemed such a nice guy, didn't he?'

'He was charming,' says Mum.

'Not to me, he wasn't.'

'I know, sweetheart, he terrified you. We know that now.'

'And we all thought he was a hero, the day he left,' says Nat. 'The day of the fire. Explains why he was in such a rush to get away, doesn't it?'

Mum nods, agreeing. She's said the same thing, quite a few times.

'What about the business?' says Nat. 'If it's okay to ask?'

'We've no idea, to be honest. The insurance will cover the damage to the tower and the payout will help meet the refurbishment costs, if we go ahead. Not sure this is any bride's idea of a perfect setting for a wedding now.'

'It's still a very beautiful place.' Nat waves an arm in the direction of the sea. 'That view hasn't changed. It takes my breath away, every time.'

'We're going to wait and see. Ironically, on the day of the fire in the tower, an old friend of mine had finally agreed to invest in Brackenbrae. I thought all our worries were over and then I got the phone call. From there, all hell broke loose.'

Nat touches Mum's hand. 'But you've come through it, haven't you?'

'So far, yes, and *I've* still got my boy, which is more than can be said for poor Sebastien's mum. God only knows how she'll cope, but thank goodness she sent that phone.'

'Sorry?'

'Seb, the real Seb, lost his iPhone on the way here so his mum sent him a new one, which the other guy kept for himself. Poor woman was phoning and sending texts.'

'Thinking it was her son on the other end?'

'Yes, and getting increasingly worried when she got no response. But that phone is the vital link, the only link, to the guy we thought was Seb. He turned out to be the real mystery man. The police don't tell us much, but we know they're tracing the phone.'

'But Charlie's in the clear?'

'Of course he is. He did nothing wrong.'

'Apart from taking the gun, Mum. If I hadn't done that, none of the rest would have happened.'

'Charlie, we've talked about this. That was a stupid thing to do, we all agree, but we know why you did it and it's not a criminal offence, is it?'

As if she wants to brighten the atmosphere, Nat says, 'What about all these friends you're making, Charlie. Are they cool?'

Nod.

'Come on, then, tell me. Remember you used to talk about Jayden Jeffries and Mackenzie what's-her-name?'

'Mackenzie McMullen. They weren't really my friends.'

'I know that. They were classmates.'

'I never see them now.'

'Well, that's the great thing about 'big school', you meet a lot more people. Listen, have you got a nickname?'

Nod then laugh. 'Yeah.'

'Have you?' says Mum. 'You didn't tell us that.'

'Only the coolest kids have a nickname,' says Nat. 'Do you like yours?'

I do kind of like it, even though I probably shouldn't. I was worried that folk would hear about the not-talking thing and make a fool of me, but the guys I'm friendly with just laughed. Then Ian said it and it stuck.

'Can we ask what it is?' asks Nat.

I nod and laugh again.

'It's Noddy.'

***

CHAPTER 73

Birds are singing in the hospital garden and from his window Gus can see mountains against a deep blue sky. A smudge of high cloud drifts past the sun. It's a beautiful spring day, perfect weather to be set free.

Soon he'll be out there, racing along the highway, a beast of a bike roaring between his legs. His hand goes to his crotch as he imagines the delights that await him when he hits the beach. He's in top shape physically, probably the best of his life, and all without the aid of drugs. Just hours and hours in the gym, encouraged by a doctor who takes the 'healthy mind in healthy body' approach. A few days in the sun will bring his colour back and he'll have to fight the babes off.

The weeks have been long in Sunnyvale, but true to his word, he's been a model patient, keen and willing to learn how to manage his anger. He has listened and made notes, read all the suggested books and done everything right. His doctor, well, psychiatrist really, has been impressed, making very encouraging noises at his last assessment meeting. Gus is sure everyone knows he was never crazy, just a big guy with a temper to match. He's a reformed character now. He knows how to control that temper of his and he's safe to return to society. Of course, they couldn't let him out right away. He had to be seen to be undergoing some kind of 'punishment' for beating up that guy on the rugby pitch. That's okay, he's cool with that. Fair enough. He's done the crime and now he's done the time. Soon he'll be free to go and get on with his life – an upstanding citizen of South Africa.

While he waits to be called to Doctor van Beek's office, he tidies his few belongings. He's already decided to leave almost everything behind, a sign of the new start he plans to make.

'Doctor van Beek is ready to see you now, Gus. Please go through.'

The door to the doc's office is open. Gus is about to pin a bright smile on his face and step inside when he spots two policemen sitting behind the desk. His face freezes into a frown. He stops on the threshold and they look towards him. Hairs rise on the back of his neck. He's certain the cops can see the guilt on his face. He rearranges his features into a smile and steps forward, trying to look confident. Best to brazen this out and deny everything. That little bastard, Charlie, must have spilled the beans. After all this time.

His doctor is the first to speak, inviting him to sit and offering him a drink of water. The psychiatrist starts explaining to the cops that Gus has been making great progress, learning to deal with issues that stem from a childhood with an abusive father and a negligent mother, exaggerated by steroid abuse and blah blah blah.

Gus has heard this psychobabble so often he could recite it off by heart. There's no need to listen to it all over again. Instead he concentrates on the two policemen facing him. The first one has a tight little mouth sandwiched between a thin line of moustache and a goatee beard, trimmed with precision into a tiny triangle. Both moustache and beard look like they've been drawn in black marker pen. His eyes are like holes poked with a stick, so deep Gus can't read their expression. The other cop looks straight off the farm, his acne face is as round and red as a pizza. A topping of bright orange hair does nothing to make Gus warm to him.

The doc has stopped talking. It's clear Gus is expected to respond in some way. He feels like he's back in junior school. The teacher would interrupt his daydreaming with a question and he'd have no idea what she was talking about. He remembers how stupid that made him feel, how angry. He reminds himself that his anger is a thing of the past.

Doctor van Beek says, in his gentle, cajoling voice, 'The officers think you might be able to help them with an enquiry, Gus, and they'd like to ask you one or two questions. Fine with that?'

Gus wonders if he can say no, but he smiles and says, 'No problem.'

Moustache Man starts to explain that they're here at the request of police colleagues in Scotland, in connection with a body that's been found on a campsite where Gus is believed to have spent several weeks working.

Gus stops paying attention. But no daydreaming this time. He turns his mind to his options. He's vaguely aware of the cop's voice, droning on about pathologist's findings, but doesn't waste time listening to details. He hears only bits of medical gobbledygook that mean nothing to him. He picks up random words like head wound, instantaneous death, enough to tell him he's in deep shit. When he hears the cop say 'buried on the hillside' he glances at van Beek, whose eyebrows have disappeared under his hair.

Even half-listening, Gus hears enough to know that this is looking seriously bad. He starts to shake his head. He absolutely will *not* go to jail. Anything but that. He sees a way and decides to take it.

With a mad roar, he lunges forward and grabs the edge of the desk. He hurls it over on top of the two policemen. Their chairs topple backwards, trapping them underneath the desk. Doctor van Beek reaches for his emergency button, but before he can press it, Gus gets him by the throat and squeezes. The doctor's eyes start to bulge and his tongue pokes out, red and pointy. The cops scramble to their feet and Pizza Face moves forward. Gus thrusts the doctor at him with such force that the two men fall. Their momentum knocks down the third and they lie there, legs tangled like the Keystone Cops. Gus rampages around the room, bellowing and storming like a speared bull. He sweeps folders and notes to the floor, lifts his chair and hurls it through the window, all the time screaming, 'He deserved to die. He was a stupid, fuckin arsehole, running up at me out of nowhere. Right into the sights of the gun. It wasn't my fault. How the fuck was I supposed to know he was there?'

Out of the corner of his eye he sees the senior cop approaching and gets ready to take him down. When he notices the outstretched arm, he changes his mind. The cop bawls, 'Pepper spray!'

As if he's run out of steam, Gus stops and stands panting in the corner, chest heaving and hands raised in surrender. He doesn't want a face full of that shit. Anyway, he's done enough to convince them he's insane. Just to make sure, he cowers like a cornered animal, whimpering as if all the fight has gone out of him. Doctor van Beek tentatively reaches again for the button that will summon help.

It takes only a moment for two burly back-up guys to burst into the room and grab him. He puts up little resistance. If he struggles too much he'll be given a tranquilising shot. He can't let that happen. He must stay in control and stick to his plan. Allowing his body to sag between his two minders, he looks his doctor straight in the eye and says quietly, between gasps of air, 'I'm glad I shot him. Stupid people have no place in this world. I'd kill them all if I could.'

A spooky silence falls on the room. Gus can smell sweat from an armpit, maybe his own, and wrinkles his nose in disgust.

'Let him go,' says van Beek, 'and help me right the desk and chairs please.'

Gus can tell the men are reluctant to release him, but Moustache Man is still on guard, brandishing his can of pepper spray. He looks as if he'd like nothing better than an excuse to blast him with it. The two gorillas follow orders and leave Gus standing there while they move the furniture. The psychiatrist calmly gathers papers and folders into rough piles, as if he were tidying his room instead of clearing up after a brawl. 'Thanks, chaps, you can go now.'

The orderlies look at one another. 'Doctor, are you sure you don't want us to take the patient to his room?'

'No thanks. That will be all for now. I'll call if I need you.' Addressing Gus, he says, 'Let's take a seat and talk about this.' He smiles, as if this were a normal meeting.

Pizza Face steps close to his boss and mutters, 'The doctor's as mad as the loonies in this place. Can we go?'

'We'll go when we've done our job and not before,' says the superior officer, with an apologetic look at Gus's doctor. 'Now sit down and shut up.' Both cops sit, never taking their eyes off Gus, as if he might explode at any minute. Gus notices the pepper spray has not been put away.

Doctor van Beek rubs at his neck, coughs and says, 'Gus, it's important you understand that these officers aren't here to arrest you for murder. I'm not convinced you understood everything they said. You didn't shoot the young man.'

This is a trick. They're trying to trip him up, find out if he's really mad or simply pretending. He's far too clever to fall for that. 'Oh, I shot him okay.' He holds an imaginary gun and takes aim, one eye closed. 'Pow!' He mimes the recoil, remembering how it felt and hearing again the deafening noise of the shot. 'I got him right between the eyes. Clean kill. Like a sniper.'

'You're wrong, Gus. There was a post-mortem.' Van Beek flicks through a file of papers and holds one up. 'I have a copy here. It shows the young man died of a heart condition, not a gunshot wound.'

'Bullshit. A heart condition? What even is that? You saying he had a heart attack?'

'Something like that, yes.'

Gus forces out a laugh, making it sound as maniacal as possible. 'Cut the crap, Doc. Do you really think I'm stupid enough to swallow that? I *saw* the damage I did.' Gus gets to his feet. The two cops react but the doctor signals for them to remain seated. Gus adopts the stance of a marksman taking a rifle shot. 'Bullseye!' he crows. 'Never fired a gun in my life but I was still too good to miss the target.'

His doctor's voice sounds sad when he speaks, as if he feels genuine sorrow for Gus. 'We'll have plenty of time to talk about this in the months and years ahead, Gus, but I think it's important that you listen to what the police have to say. One thing is clear: whatever you may think, you are *not* guilty of murder, and you need to understand that. It may help you to heal. Now, I want you to pay attention and cooperate fully. Can you do that?'

The doctor inclines his head towards Moustache Man, who is opening a notebook, pen at the ready. 'Where were you, Angus Webb, on Monday 28 May this year?'

'On holiday in the Bahamas.' Gus chortles, as if he's said something hilarious.

'Did you, in the company of a minor, bury the body of Sebastien Lamar?'

Gus leans back in his chair and scratches his groin, hoping it looks as insolent as he intends. He remembers from a movie he saw one time that real crazies show no remorse. 'So what if I did?'

After a few more questions the cop gives up. The corners of his mouth droop, the moustache following. 'Thanks, Doctor, it looks like we're done here.'

As they rise to leave, Gus says, 'Can I ask one thing? Are you saying that guy's death was nothing to do with me?'

The policeman nods.

'But he had a head wound.' He places his finger in the centre of his forehead. 'Right there. I saw it. Like a hole. Blood all over his face and clothes. He'd been shot. It was obvious.'

'According to the pathologist's report, there was no gunshot wound anywhere on the body. Sadly, the young man died of some kind of congenital heart failure. Ticking time bomb, could have happened anywhere. Some would say he was fated to die that morning on that hillside.' He pauses, giving Gus time to take it all in. 'You're obviously not the ace marksman you thought you were.' His voice reeks of sarcasm.

'Wait a minute.' Gus sits up straight. 'That means I'm innocent, right?' He bares his teeth in a cocky smile and turns to the doctor. 'You heard that. I'm an innocent man. You just said two minutes ago, I've sorted out my anger issues, made great progress. So I can go, yeah?'

'I'm afraid it's not as simple as that, Gus. I'm sorry.'

'Oh, I get it.' Gus nods to show he understands the situation. 'You think I still need help after the way I kicked off in here, is that it?' He laughs. 'Don't worry about that, Doc. I'll let you into a secret. That was all an act, put on for the cops' benefit, when I thought they were here to arrest me.' He can't resist a gloating look at the cops as he says, 'Why go to jail, when I could stay in here?'

Turning his attention back to his doctor, Gus says, in his perfect-patient voice, 'I'm sound, Doctor, you know that. If you want to keep me here for a few more sessions of anger management, that's cool. I'll just have to put my plans on hold for a bit. As long as you let me out in time to catch a few sunny days. Got a big Harley waiting to take me to the beach.'

'Gus, I think it might be a good idea if you were to stay with us for the foreseeable future. We'll move you over to the secure block and the doctors there will find the best treatment for you.'

'Why? There's nothing wrong with me. This whole thing's an act. I've been acting since the day I walked in here. I thought you knew that.'

'I hope you'll be fit for discharge one day, but I don't think you should count on riding that motorbike any time soon.'

'But I'm innocent. You heard him.' He points to the policeman.

'Innocent?' says Moustache Man. 'Oh, that's what you think. You didn't shoot the victim, no, that's right. However…' He holds up his left hand and touches his thumb, ready to count. 'One, you failed to report a serious incident. Two, you tried to cover up what you believed was a murder by burying the poor lad. Three, you forced a child to collaborate with you. Four, you stole the victim's belongings, including his passport. Five, you used his identity to obtain work under false pretences. Then, of course, you left the country, attempting to pervert the course of justice.'

The policeman rubs his hands together as if he's looking forward to a treat. He leans in so close, each individual hair in his goatee is visible. He pinches Gus's cheek and wobbles it, as if he were talking to a naughty schoolboy. 'Know what, sunshine? I'd sell that motorbike, if I were you. And if you ever do get out of here,' he says, 'don't bother calling a taxi. We'll have a nice, shiny police car waiting to pick you up.'

THE END

Author's note and Acknowledgements

One character in this book *is* based on a real person, although I never met him. In the summer of 2010, a young man left a book on a French campsite, which I found. There was a letter inside and an envelope of money. I was intrigued! Had I not found that book, I would not have written this story or any other. Whoever you are and wherever you are, 'Sebastien', I hope you're safe and happy.

I know nothing of guns or the laws that govern their ownership. Thank you, David Hastings, for sharing your expertise. Any gun-related mistakes that may remain are mine.

Thanks are due to Stef Young for advice on matters medical and post-mortem and to the mortuary staff at QEUH, Glasgow.

My gratitude, as usual, to all at Bloodhound Books and to bloggers, librarians and bookshop staff for your support. Gentlemen of the press have also been kind to me.

I am very grateful to all my readers, but particularly thankful to those who read my early drafts and give me honest feedback. Margo McAllister, Lynda Pryde, Stef Young and Winnie Goodwin have all been with me from the start of this story, way back when it was set on a French campsite and called One Silent Voice. Thanks, Winnie, for your insightful comments on this, the re-written version.

And then, of course, there's Grant… where words fail me.

Lightning Source UK Ltd.
Milton Keynes UK
UKHW042335301118
333243UK00001B/58/P